Sinful

SUSAN JOHNSON

Sinful

LOVESWEPT®

DOUBLEDAY

New York   London   Toronto   Sydney   Auckland

fiction

Loveswept®
PUBLISHED BY DOUBLEDAY
a division of Bantam Doubleday Dell Publishing Group, Inc.
666 Fifth Avenue, New York, New York 10103

DOUBLEDAY and the portrayal of an anchor with a dolphin
and the word LOVESWEPT and the portrayal of the wave device
are trademarks of Doubleday, a division of
Bantam Doubleday Dell Publishing Group, Inc.
All of the characters in this book are fictitious,
and any resemblance to actual persons, living or
dead, is purely coincidental.

Book design by Patrice Fodero

Library of Congress Cataloging-in-Publication Data

Johnson, Susan, 1939–
Sinful / Susan Johnson.—1st ed.
p.   cm.
"Loveswept."
I. Title.
PS3560.O386458S5   1992
813'.54—dc20   91–41099
CIP

ISBN 0-385-42467-1
Copyright © 1992 by Susan Johnson
All Rights Reserved
Printed in the United States of America
August 1992
1 3 5 7 9 10 8 6 4 2
First Edition

Chapter 1

London, March 1787

Sinjin was almost finished dressing, his movements swift as he tied the fine cambric of his neckcloth with deft efficiency. The pungent scent of lovemaking permeated the over-heated, scented chamber, overlaying the signature lilac fragrance of the Duchess of Buchan.

Lying nude in the shambles of the bed, the Duchess briefly considered taking offense at her lover's abrupt departure and casual indifference. Only a moment of contemplation was necessary for her to decide against such foolishness. Not only would her anger be wasted on London's most profligate rogue, but Sinjin was the most beautiful man she'd ever seen: tall, lean, muscled and dark as sin, his sunny sky blue eyes offering seduction boldly with teasing, hot-blooded effrontery. And if classic physical perfection weren't enough . . . in terms of amorous expertise, he was sheer perfection. No one could make her feel the way Sinjin did or bring her to orgasm with such intensity.

Sighing, she half-turned on the bed so her reclining pose would be more provocative and said, "When will you be back?"

Interrupting his search for his coat—hastily discarded somewhere between the doorway and the bed in carnal urgency several hours ago—Sinjin took in the Duchess's lush, opulent pose, the extravagant fullness of her breasts, the supple curve of her hips. He recalled briefly how Cassandra could nibble on him with such attention to detail and, instead of lying, said, "In five days."

"Come and see me."

Sinjin St. John, Duke of Seth, Marquess of Fowler, Earl of Barton, Viscount Carvernon, normally was settled in at Newmarket for the entire race season, his passion for horseflesh, everyone knew, surpassing even his acute interest in female flesh. But he was making a swift trip into London five days hence to pick up an Irish filly being sent over from his cousin's holdings in Waterford. Pausing for a small moment at Cassandra's soft entreaty, he suddenly smiled, his starkly modeled features transposing instantly into a boyish charm.

"I'd love to . . . but I won't be able to stay long."

"How long?"

"An hour."

Cassandra was the Duke of Buchan's second wife, an ornament acquired after his first wife conveniently died before he was entirely too old to fully appreciate a woman of Cassandra's voluptuous beauty.

"*How* long?" she softly repeated, languorously twisting her supple body in such an ingenuously erotic way that Sinjin began immediately reconsidering.

"Longer than an hour," he answered with a rakish grin.

With Buchan very close to seventy, Sinjin wondered how the old Duke was able to withstand the sheer physical demands of his wife's passionate temperament. Someday, no doubt, Buchan wouldn't. And then Cassandra would be a very wealthy and *young* Dowager Duchess.

"You won't forget . . ." she murmured, sliding a finger into the damp cleft between her legs.

Sinjin took a small breath, glanced at the porcelain clock on the mantel and debated the importance of his arriving at Newmarket on time for the briefest of moments before exhaling and reaching down for his burgundy coat. The first race tomorrow had his bay up against Stanhope's grey from Ireland, and even Cassandra's adventuresome acrobatics in bed lost out to the excitement of that match.

Shrugging into his coat, he said, as if in explanation of his transient internal struggle, "My bay's running against Stanhope's much touted champion tomorrow."

"Good luck then," she softly whispered, the rhythm of her finger evident in the sultry hush of her voice. "Don't forget me."

Not likely, he thought, her erotic image triggering enormous reflexive responses in his tall, powerful body. And if Sinjin St. John hadn't been such a passionate devotee of the turf and a man of such iron will, Cassandra would have had a superior instrument of arousal at her disposal.

Chapter 2

"Take care of Archer's whip," Sinjin warned his jockey, unbuckling the closures on the woolen horse blanket that protected his thoroughbred from the cutting March winds. "He'll try to strike you and Romulus." Stroking the muscular neck of his prize-winning racer, he murmured softly to the huge horse, his deep low voice soothing, familiar to the sleek bay who turned his head to nuzzle gently at Sinjin's neck. "Stay clear of him, mate," Sinjin whispered, "so he doesn't savage you."

"The field's small, so you'll have room to maneuver," Sinjin went on, turning to his jockey, who was shortening the stirrups another fraction. "Romulus looked prime on his warm-up this morning." Sinjin grinned. "All you'll have to do is sit there."

"Don't I always with this flashy beast? He hates the cold, though. I hope they get under way soon." So saying, Fordham took a leg up from a groom, settled into the saddle and, glancing down at his employer, added, "You've got me bet now?"

"It's with mine at Randall's. We'll both be richer men at the end of Rowley Mile." Sliding his finger under the bridle leather, Sinjin checked to see that the bit was lightly set. Romulus disliked a heavy hand. He was the kind of horse who ran for the sheer pleasure of running and scarcely needed a jockey. "Bring it on home, now," Sinjin softly said, giving a last gentle pat to Romulus, then stepping back so Fordham could move through the small host of grooms toward the starting post. He paused for a prideful moment, surveying his prize-winning horse.

A short time later, Sinjin stood on the balcony of his viewing stand, Newmarket's Rowley Mile spread out before him, the open expanse of green downs rolling beyond to the horizon, a brilliant sun appropriately glorifying the beauty of the scene. As he gazed out over the course on the first day of the spring meet—the beginning of the race season—a familiar excitement gripped him. He loved the sight and smell and sound of Newmarket, the beauty of the horses, the bustle of the spectators, the provocative lure of betting, the overpowering thrill of winning.

Since buying his first racer at sixteen, he'd been committed to developing the best racing stable in England—in the world, grumbled those disgruntled bidders unable to match the prices the Duke of Seth was willing to pay for prime bloodstock. After coming into his majority and gaining access to his own funds, he'd won most of the important races of the last decade and, perhaps more important, held the record for winning the most prize money.

His love of racing had been encouraged by his mother, whose Irish family were breeders of champion racers and hunters. She'd taught Sinjin to ride at age two and always took him with her in her carriage to watch the races at Newmarket. Born with the blood of Irish horsemen in his veins, he'd grown up amidst the flurry and bustle of the race course.

His red brick viewing stand stood at the crest of Abingdon Hill, close to the finish line, its balustraded flat roof and balcony thronged with guests. Vintage champagne and a sumptuous buffet attested to the Duke of Seth's reputation for hospitality, but Sinjin and his friend, Nicholas Rose,[1] stood slightly apart from the festive camaraderie, their attention focused on the horses at the starting post.

The two dark-haired men were remarkably similar in height and muscular build, their long hair tied at the nape of their necks with identical black silk ribbon, their aquiline features tracing descent from a classical ideal. Only their coloring differed. Although Sinjin was tanned from an outdoor life, he was several degrees lighter than his Seneca companion, while his startling blue eyes would never be mistaken for those of a red Indian.

Sinjin St. John had notable eyes, beautiful eyes—too beautiful, many said . . . for a man. They were a genetic gift from his mother, who as The Matchless One had caused a sensation when she'd come to London. The dazzling Miss Bourke had taken the Ton by storm, disconcerting all the hopeful plans of mamas with marriageable daughters. The fair-haired beauty from Waterford had had her choice of all the noble lords.

"We're going to win everything this year," Sinjin cheerfully noted, racing his passion and content. His smile was boyish, open, the brilliant blue of his eyes alight with pleasure.

"You always do." His friend and factor's voice reflected the calmness of his disposition.

The two men differed in temperament as well. Sinjin exuded a powerful vitality, as though the startling sapphire of his eyes reflected an inner combustible heat. Women saw other things in his eyes—a tempestuous sensuality or teasing delight or hot-blooded passion.

But never calmness.

"How much did you wager?" Sinjin's voice was business-like, crisp. Betting on his horses was an art and a methodology. And a profitable enterprise.

"A few ponies."

"Go higher. I'll cover you." His swift calculations were almost evident in his concise diction. "You heard Olim this morning. Romulus is in top form." Sinjin's trainer had bet a hundred pounds on this race, indication of his confidence in the horse.

"With the quality of your racing stable, I make an extremely favorable profit without going higher." Nicholas believed in moderation in betting. His plans to return to his tribe required a great deal of money, and he chose not to take chances.

Sinjin negligently shrugged. "Suit yourself." Moderation was a concept outside his purview, in betting or otherwise.

"Soon I'll have enough to set myself up like a lord in the wilderness," Nicholas noted, his tone facetious.

"I've more than enough for both of us, dammit, Seneca, and you know it," Sinjin grumbled, using the familiar nickname by which Nicholas was known. He'd offered his friend carte blanche years ago with his fortune. This argument was of long standing.

Nicholas Rose had come back with Sinjin after the losing campaigns of the Army of the North in the colonial war in America, bereft of family after the massacre of his longhouse village by revolutionary troops. Sinjin understood him like a brother. He also understood his scruples, although he didn't personally believe in scruples.

"Archer was a last-minute change for Stanhope," Nicholas remarked, curtailing a fruitless discussion.

"No doubt with ulterior motives," Sinjin murmured. "I only

hope Fordham can stay clear of Archer's notorious whip," Sinjin went on, as though neither had mentioned America. Leaning forward on the balcony rail, Sinjin sought a better view of the starting line. Fordham and Archer were both winning jockeys, but complete opposites in style. Archer believed in physical riding, while Fordham preferred distracting his mount as little as possible. And Archer had won a number of his races with questionable tactics.

The gusty breeze tugged at Sinjin's hair as he leaned out past the protection of the porch. It loosened unruly curls from the ribbon at his neck and ruffled the leather fringe on his beaded jacket. He often wore an exotic Seneca jacket, the ornate beauty of the beadwork pleasing to him; he also found the supple leather eminently suitable as working attire at the race track. His hybrid ensemble of fringed jacket, doeskin breeches, exquisitely polished Hessians, snow white shirt and neckcloth set him apart from his aristocratic friends. But then, he was unconcerned with conforming, nor had anyone ever considered him conformable. Among his titled peers, he was, however, not only well liked, but a roguish role-model for many of his class, and a source of envy to those less adventuresome. While he loved England, Sinjin had traveled the globe; there was a world beyond the confines of Brookes, Whites and Boodles. Beyond the season of the Ton. Beyond, particularly, the restricting duties of his title.

"Damn him. Archer jumped the flag." Sinjin's gaze narrowed against the sun, contemplating the disposition of Fordham and Romulus in the muddle of mounts.

There had been a false start, and the horses were massed now in complicated confusion, the air thick with stable rhetoric. When the entanglement unraveled itself moments later, a curved line spread over the course; the center surged forward, offering, for a fraction of a second, a well-dressed front.

The red flag dropped, and with a flurry of colored silks, the eight sprinters were off. Not a large field for the principal two-year-old race of the year, but many owners who would have started preferred keeping their horses at home with Seth or Stanhope sure to win.

Sinjin's bay colt, Romulus, was quick out of the slips for a big one and for the first fifty yards held a decided lead. Then Fordham steadied him and Stanhope's grey rushed to the front, forcing a record-setting pace. Three other racers pulled nearly level with the two horses in the lead, while the Earl of Sutherland's horse was wide on the right. The other two horses were in difficulties already.

Descending the Abingdon Mile hill, to the consternation of Romulus's backers, he faltered and lost his pace. Fordham seemed to call on him without success, and six to four on the field went begging at the betting ring. As the field approached the bottom of the dip, Romulus began to pick up speed. But there *was* something wrong with his shoulders. Fordham appeared to give the mighty bay a startlingly savage shake.

"One hundred to two against Romulus!" shrieked one of the bookmakers. Sinjin, who had seen Romulus at his morning run, complacently took the new odds. Raking glances swiveled up from the crowd on the ground. At those impossible percentages, the young Duke of Seth could lose a fortune if Romulus didn't win.

"Fordham's waiting for the hill," Nicholas said.

"And he hasn't asked Romulus for speed yet," Sinjin quietly replied. "It's going to be close, though." His voice trailed off softly at the end, his blue eyes trained on his bay and Stanhope's grey three lengths ahead. Stanhope's jockey was whipping his mount, urging it to more speed. Fordham hadn't touched his whip, but he was hunched low over Romulus's neck, talking to him, the reins almost slack. Sinjin found himself holding his breath, waiting for the customary response from the young colt, waiting for the huge bay he'd helped train to recognize the critical need in Fordham's voice.

There. Finally. Sinjin exhaled in satisfaction. Romulus's stride had widened, the muscles that drove his long, beautifully formed legs rippling in awesome power beneath his glistening coat. His ears were slightly laid back, his strong legs tackling the ascent effortlessly. Gaining on his adversary, Romulus flew uphill as though he were on the flat, coming abreast of Stanhope's grey to the roar of the crowd. The two horses were locked together for a few moments on the strenuous uphill finish—too close for comfort, Sinjin thought, too close to Archer's reach—and then Romulus broke away as if the two horses weren't sprinting for the finish at a record-breaking pace. And he left the Irish grey behind in a burst of speed.

"He's got it," Sinjin breathed on a soft sigh. "What a beauty . . ."

"A thousand guinea prize and Stanhope's enmity," Nicholas Rose noted with a cheerful grin as Romulus swept past the finish post six lengths in the lead.

"Fifty thousand guineas," Sinjin corrected, adding his winning wagers to the prize money, "and Stanhope's enmity has nothing to do with horse racing."

"A woman then," the tall Seneca remarked, the second constant in Sinjin's life an obvious choice.

"A long-ago bet over Mrs. Robinson; Stanhope's a poor loser."

Even a Seneca from the American colonies knew of the notorious and beautiful Mrs. Robinson, although she had curtailed her availability for love of Colonel Tarleton years ago. And *all* of the Ton knew of the five thousand guinea wager written in Brookes' betting book at the time, between Sinjin and Stanhope, over who could first waylay the fair Perdita and lure her from her friendship with the Prince of Wales. In a drunken temper, Stanhope, it was said, accosted Sinjin the next morning as the young Duke of Seth was leaving the lady's dwelling on Berkeley Square. And when Sinjin had refused his challenge because Stanhope's inebriated condition made a duel tantamount to murder, Stanhope had further reason—when he sobered—to be humiliated.

With a wide grin, Sinjin acknowledged the cheers and congratulations of his guests as he moved swiftly through the crowded viewing stand to the stairway. Taking the steps in a leaping descent, he made his way through a continuing barrage of congratulatory greetings. Nodding and smiling, shaking hands, accepting the familiar accolades with his customary modesty, he strode across the green downs.

Twenty feet away Romulus caught his scent and whinnied. Ignoring the officials and Lord Bunbury, who stood with the winning King's Plate, Sinjin first offered his hand to Fordham with praise for his superb riding and then, slipping his fingers into his jacket pocket, extracted sugar lumps for Romulus.

"Well done, my beauty," he murmured, extending the sugar lumps on his open palm. He stroked the dark bay down the length of his fine nose. "You left the field behind."

Like the legendary Eclipse, Romulus won all his races in the same manner: Romulus first, the rest nowhere.[2]

The remainder of the day went swiftly. In the afternoon of racing, Sinjin's horses took all the firsts. Sinjin actively participated in the racing, doing groom's duty with a casual disregard for his consequence, helping tack up, giving instructions to the jockeys, rubbing down the mounts after their races, playing nursemaid at the end of the meet to his black racer, who had injured his foreleg in the last furlong of the day. At first there was concern the leg might be fractured, but after hours of heated poultices, the sleek grandson of Herod was moving more comfortably on the injured leg.

Leaving two grooms and a stable lad with the black in his paddock, Sinjin took his leave. The sun had recently set; the twilight air was cool, the wind diminished now as if readying itself for the night's slumber.

Sinjin's fatigue was minutely visible in his languid swinging gait, in the lazy downward drift of his dark lashes. He'd been up at dawn to ride out with his jockeys when they took his racers for their morning warm-up on the downs. The afternoon had passed at a frantic pace—exhilarating and victorious, but draining. And with his house filled with friends and a bevy of women brought up from London to entertain them all, he'd only slept a few hours last night.

On the perimeter of the course, at the edge of small copse near the far paddocks, his carriage waited, his driver dozing at the reins. Approaching the rig, he reached up and, grasping his driver's ankle, gave his leg a shake. "Home, Jed, finally," he said with a smile as the young, gangly, brown-haired man came awake with a groggy mumbled response. "Go slowly. I'm tired."

Chapter 3

His fingers still gripped the handle of the carriage door when he first noticed the figure inside.

"They say you'll . . . fuck anything in skirts." The woman's soft voice came from the shadowed interior.

Intrigued, he smiled faintly, put a booted foot on the wrought iron step and, balancing for a moment with the vehicle dipping under his weight, entered his luxurious black lacquered coach. Pulling the door shut behind him, Sinjin settled into the soft cushions of the seat opposite the woman just as the carriage began moving.

He didn't, of course. Fornicate indiscriminately. He had a very selective eye. But he was aware of his reputation as a libertine, as he was equally aware, with his vision becoming accustomed to the diminished light inside the carriage, that the young lady across from him was very young and very beautiful.

"And so?" he quietly said in response to her provocative, unusual greeting, the beaded decoration of his jacket catching the light in twinkling display.

"I want you to fuck me." Surely that would be plain enough for the Duke of Seth, who was said to bed women in casual and conspicuous quantity.

He hadn't been offered an invitation in those exact words before, because the ladies he dallied with were generally more refined. Or perhaps simply more polite, he considered, recalling numerous non-aristocratic females who'd shared his bed.

"Your invitation charms me, of course," he said, his voice amused. "But I'm late for a party I'm hosting at my racing box." Sinjin smiled his celebrated smile in courteous apology.

"It won't take long."

His brilliant azure eyes narrowed faintly in added curiosity, taking in the golden-haired young woman sitting bolt upright with her hands clenched together in her lap. This was obviously not a female desperately pining for his company.

But desperate she appeared to be, he thought, his gaze resting for a brief appreciative moment on her well-developed bosom. If he hadn't been so late, *and* if he didn't already have a houseful of cyprians waiting to entertain him and his friends, he might have considered her blunt proposition.

She was, after all, very lush in a dewy, opulent way, despite her ramrod-stiff spine. And his reputation as a libertine did have a decided basis in fact. Her full pouty mouth and enormous dark eyes particularly enticed him. She reminded him spectacularly of Romney's best portraits—sensual somehow in spite of her ingenue youth.

"I'm sorry, my dear, to have to decline." Even as he spoke, a small, less practical voice inside his brain was taking issue with his refusal.

"You can't!"

The woman's blurted words seemed to hang suspended for a crystalline moment in the shaded small distance separating them.

There, his small voice said with equal insistence. You see?

But he was dead sober and touched with weariness, too, after the long day with his horses and jockeys and grooms, after five races . . . after the past two hours in which he'd helped his racing crew keep heated poultices on his black's damaged right fetlock. Spring Fellow had come in limping after finishing his race with the gutsy courage so much a part of his nature. Their initial fear that his leg was fractured had only been put to rest after the past hours of treatment.

"Do I know you?" he asked, thoughtfully rubbing the dark stubble beginning to shadow his lean cheek. What was impelling her insistence?

"We haven't been formally introduced, although I know of you." The Saint—an ironic pet name, considering Sinjin's propensity for sin—was notorious throughout England, which was why Chelsea had selected him to deflower her. He was by repute the leading womanizer in the Ton—outclassing even Prinny's outrageous record. He was also conveniently at hand here at Newmarket.

"My name is Chelsea Amity Fergusson."

"Duncan's sister?" Sinjin's heavy dark brows rose fractionally. A proper young lady was propositioning him. Or was she . . . proper, that is? The brilliant blue of his eyes narrowed into a glinting scrutiny. At twenty-eight, he'd escaped the marriage trap numerous times . . . and a natural suspicion was now permanently ingrained in his psyche.

"Yes. He doesn't know."

I should think not, Sinjin reflected, knowing what Duncan would do to them both if he did. She seemed ingenuously sincere. And genuine. "You should be home," he gruffly charged, shifting lower in his lazy sprawl, his long black hair pulling out in loose disarray from the silk ribbon at his neck as his head slid over the blood red velvet upholstery.

But his small voice reminded him perversely that he hadn't said more expressly, "Go home."

"You probably want to know why." She spoke matter-of-factly, as though she were discussing the state of the roads, her eyes—a deep exotic purple, he noted now that his vision had adjusted to the dim light—very direct, like her voice.

No was his first reaction, swift and masculine. If she *were* Duncan's sister. No, he didn't want to know—regardless that she was exquisite. His experienced eye had taken note in the intervening minutes of the exact measure of her beauty: splendid, extravagant breasts; a diminutive waist; the obvious attractive length of her legs under the plain brown serge of her riding habit; the frothy beauty of her untamed burnished gold hair, only partially restrained by her small shako; and a luscious cherry red mouth made to be kissed.

"Tell me," he said, better judgment arbitrarily jettisoned as it was so often in his life, feeling less tired suddenly with the vivid softness of Miss Fergusson's mouth the focus of his attention.

"They're intent on marrying me off to Bishop Hatfield—who's a blackguard disgrace to the church even if it's the godless Church of England—to cover their horse-racing bets." She spoke in a rush of words this time, obviously perturbed. "My father and brothers, mostly my father," she added in clarification since the Duke's face had taken on a sudden intent look. "And he'll never marry me, the prissy stick, if I'm not a virgin. Pious bastard." The last two words exploded into the confines of the carriage with paradoxical invective.

Gazing at the delicious young beauty seated across from him, her lavish bosom still rising and falling in captivating agitation, Sinjin rather thought Bishop Hatfield would marry her under any conditions.

She was dazzling.

And George Prine, third Viscount Rutledge, Bishop of Hatfield, was a lecher of the worst kind—a Machiavellian, depraved one.

"Where the hell did George see you?"

"At the house we rented."

What he meant was, why haven't I?

"The reptile came over to look at a hunter we had for sale."

"You're not out yet." That must be the reason he hadn't met her before. An enchantress like Miss Fergusson wouldn't go unnoticed.

"Not for another year."

Good God, she was seventeen. Not that her age was an enormous stumbling block; the country girls and servant lasses he tumbled were probably not much older.

"Please take my virginity," she softly pleaded. "I'd be so very grateful."

When one looked like her, Sinjin thought, one need not implore. He could already feel himself beginning to rise to the occasion, the soft doeskin of his breeches stretching to accommodate his arousal.

While gossip had rated the Duke of Seth not only hot-blooded and disreputable, but the most bonny of men, hearsay hadn't fully prepared Chelsea for his stark, utter beauty. And licentious rumor had failed to note the magnetic splendor of his eyes, the awesome power of his tall, muscled form, the peculiar grace of his slender fine-boned hands—a horseman's hands. Nor had it mentioned, other than citing him as handsome, the divine perfection of his features: dark arched brows shadowing those seductive eyes; cheekbones modeled by the hand of God; a straight fine nose, mildly disdainful, as now—what was he thinking?—and a gently curved mouth she found herself wanting to touch to see if it was cool or warm. What would it taste of? she wondered, smiling.

When she smiled like that, open and warm and unconstrained, Sinjin mused, she lured one like the sirens of old.

"Duncan's a friend," he said as if the words were buffer to his feelings, her perfume insinuating itself as further invitation into his nostrils. Attar of roses unadulterated by any secondary fragrances seemed to suit her: heady, sweet, frankly sensual.

"He'll never know. With your experience, it can't possibly take long. Here, I'll help." She began unbuttoning the braid frogs on the jacket of her habit.

"No!" Reaching across the carriage, he stopped her fingers from their task, his action bringing him uncomfortably close to the luminous, disturbingly lovely purple of her eyes.

"Aren't I attractive enough?" she murmured. "You prefer dark-haired women like the Duchess Buchan?"

Good God, the entire nation must know his amorous activities if this young girl from the north spoke of Cassandra with such casualness. And no, he wished to say in answer to her artless question, I prefer luscious rosy-cheeked country maids like you who look sweet enough to eat. But he said instead, "You're enchanting, my dear Miss Fergusson. But entirely too young." There, that was well bred and virtuous. Letting his hand drop away from her, he leaned back again in his seat, struggling to maintain his emotional distance as well.

"I'm seventeen and three quarters, older than my mother was when she married," Chelsea protested, rebuffing Sinjin's attempt at gallantry.

The word "married" was sufficient to instantly check any unchaste impulses the Duke of Seth may have harbored. "I'll take you home," he gruffly said, his libido damped by the disquieting word. "Where are you staying?"

"At the Priory Cottage on the Duke of Sutherland's estate, but I'm not leaving." And so saying, she threw herself at him, bowling him over with the surprise of her attack, landing atop his sprawled body with soft delicious impact, pinning him beneath her on the carriage seat.

He could, of course, lift her away effortlessly, but Sinjin lay for a moment, enjoying the sensation of her delectable body pressed intimately to his, vividly sensitive to the scented silk of her hair brushing his face, susceptibly aware how very close her mouth was, wondering selfishly, a second later, how much he valued Duncan's friendship.

It was the devil's own dilemma.

Chelsea kissed him then, a light, untutored butterfly of a kiss. But breathy too and inquisitive, he sensed, just before his perceptive conscience reminded him he could gratify his carnal urges with any of the dozen women waiting for him at his hunting box. Chelsea

Fergusson's offered virtue, tempting as it was, might come at a pro- hibitively high price.

But his body responded on cue to the female body pressed to his —a fact immediately evident to the young lady advancing her suit.

"There, you see, you don't mean no when you say it," she whis- pered, her breath warm on his lips. And flushed with success, she impetuously tested the power of her attraction by moving her hips against his arousal.

His libido as impetuously reacted.

"I promise I won't cry out no matter how it hurts, no matter what you do. I won't, really . . ."

His erection, perversely impressionable to such lewd carnal sug- gestion, increased sizably. But when her small hand moved down- ward past the tangled fringe of his jacket to the waistband of his breeches, he stopped it firmly.

"No," he breathed on a suffocated exhalation of air, his fingers curled over her hand. He sensed imminent disaster in this innocent young miss, and terrifying images of marriage curtailed even the urgency of his sexual hunger. "No, no . . ."—a deep fortifying breath—"no."

Deliberately pushing her away, he sat up and, lifting her in his arms, deposited Chelsea Amity Fergusson—a maiden of extravagant sexual allure—back on the opposite seat where she belonged.

"Find someone else to rupture your maidenhead and keep George Prine at bay," he tersely ordered. "I'm not interested." Heated anger infused his voice, a reaction to the curtailment of his violent desire.

"I'm sorry," Chelsea whispered, tears beginning to well up in the purple radiance of her eyes. "It wasn't fair to you . . ." She was sitting upright again, like a young child reprimanded for untoward behavior, twin paths of tears beginning a flickering journey down her flushed cheeks.

"Oh Lord . . . don't cry," Sinjin murmured, uncomfortable and strangely discomposed himself. For a man of normally facile repartee, he was momentarily nonplussed. Perhaps her spirited inno- cence touched his sensibilities. Perhaps, more likely, he was touched by the exquisite display of poignant female beauty.

Reaching for his handkerchief, he drew it out and, stretching across the small distance, gently wiped the tears from her face. "They can't make you marry George . . . can they?" Not a novice in the ways of the world, he understood, of course, her father could. "If it's just a matter of money . . ." he began, not exactly sure how to offer her monetary salvation. He was a very wealthy man. "Maybe I could talk to your father," he heard himself saying, appalled even as he heard the words pronounced that he was involving himself in the family controversy of relative strangers. He'd spent a lifetime protecting his independence, not only from his own family, but from any susceptibility to involvement. He avoided attachments of any kind; he was comfortable with his life. Having traveled extensively since he'd come into his majority, when his father could no longer control his trust, he liked his carefree existence.

Even after his father died and the title had fallen to him, he continued in his peripatetic ways, knowing his younger brother was fully capable of taking over the dukedom should something happen to him. Actually Damien would probably have served as duke with more distinction; he was upstanding, sensible, married already with two heirs to his titles and the certain possibility of many more. There were times actually when Sinjin had considered turning all the ducal obligations over to his younger brother. Like now, dammit. When he was faced with being responsible and well bred and considerate. How the hell had he gotten himself into this wretched predicament?

By being a byword for carnal seduction, his presumptuous small voice said. If you want to know the damnable truth.

"He wouldn't take money from you, Your Grace," Chelsea murmured. "You're not family."

Unconscionably, Sinjin felt blessed relief at her words, delivered from his rash promise of help. "I'm sure if you make him understand the intensity of your aversion to George," he said, the hypocrisy of his statement obvious to them both even as he spoke, "perhaps he might reconsider . . ." His voice trailed away.

"Yes, Your Grace."

He didn't care at the moment that her answer was as fraudulent as his; he was only relieved to be removed from any further obligation.

He wouldn't have been so relieved had he known Chelsea Amity Fergusson was still determined to accomplish her mission. She fully intended to surrender the lucrative marriage prize of her virginity in order to save herself from wealthy lechers like George Prine. And now that she'd actually met the notorious Duke of Seth, his notoriety no longer figured as his principal allure.

If she was going to relinquish her virginity to gain her independence, it might as well be pleasantly done.

And Sinjin St. John, beautiful as a god, would be an exceedingly pleasant agent of her need.

"With my . . . er . . . reputation," he suggested, as his carriage rolled along the quiet lane toward Oatlands, the Duke of Sutherland's estate near Newmarket, "you'd best not be seen with me. I'll have Jed drop you off at the gate."

"Being alone with you *might* be compromise enough," she cheerfully declared, elated suddenly with the notion of achieving her end without participating in the actual physical deed. "I could simply tell my family and the Bishop I was alone with you in your carriage for a lengthy interval."

"I'll deny it," he harshly said, not about to be made anyone's scapegoat. "And your virginity's intact."

"Ummm," Chelsea murmured, not in discouragement but in contemplation.

Which intonation made Sinjin acutely nervous. "I won't be party to this, damn your sweet hide!" Did no one have control over this beautiful chit?

"No, of course not, Your Grace, you're absolutely right," she said with an agreeable sweetness that should have put him instantly on guard.

"Good. We understand each other then," he replied, beguiled by the novelty of her innocence. Young maidens were entirely outside his realm, since they possessed neither of the qualities he was looking for in a woman—availability and sexual expertise.

"Thank you so much for taking me home," Chelsea amiably declared as the gateway to Oatlands came into view.

He wished he could have done more for her, satisfying her desires and his as well. But even he wasn't reckless enough to walk into that entrapment, no matter how luscious the prize. Sinjin St. John may have earned his sobriquet The Saint for unsaintly sexual excess. But *not* with virgins. He had no intention of getting married; avoiding virgins protected him from that peril.

He knocked on the forward panel, indicating for Jed to stop.

Their goodbyes were civilized and well bred.

And blessedly final, Sinjin thought, relaxing against the soft velvet of his carriage seat some moments later, Oatlands receding in the distance. Thank God.

Chapter 4

The twilight lent a lavender peace to the bucolic landscape, shadowing the tree-lined drive, offering Chelsea the concealment she needed to approach the Priory Cottage unseen.

Only Mrs. Macaulay noticed her slip in the kitchen door, the woman's smile conspiratorial. They'd been friends ever since Chelsea had saved Cook's old tabby from Duncan's great deerhound, Mac-Beth, who was known to alleviate his boredom between hunting bouts by terrorizing smaller creatures. He did it in fun, thinking he was playing, but his huge paws even in play could knock a spoiled old cat like the tabby senseless.

A nod of Mrs. Macaulay's grey head indicated the direction of the stables. Good. Her father and brothers hadn't come in yet.

Taking the narrow dark servant's stairs with sure-footed speed, Chelsea reached the security of her bedroom unnoticed. There she discarded the riding habit she'd chosen as appropriate to Newmarket. If seen approaching the Duke's carriage, she'd wanted to look unsuspicious, as though she were one of the women who'd ridden out to view the races. She had in fact walked the few miles to the downs—sure the Duke would be chivalrous enough to drive her home after her denouement. Who would have thought the disreputable rake would have gentlemanly honor?

After changing into a simple gown of flower-strewn dimity, she descended to the parlor by the main stairs. Seated before the fire with an unread book in her lap, she calmly greeted her father and brothers when they entered some time later.

"Red Dougal came in second!" her younger brother, Colin, jubilantly declared, walking into the room first. "And Papa won five hundred guineas on him!" Colin had raised the huge chestnut from a colt, and at fourteen he was still small enough to ride as jockey.

"Only The Saint's Irish black beat us out." Duncan's voice held the mellow undertone of the Lowlands, an echo of their father's inflection although their border estates had been lost forty years ago in the rebellion.

"Damn rascal took every race today," her father grumpily muttered, dropping into the chair nearest his bottle of Fergusson-distilled aqua vitae. Reaching for a small cut glass tumbler, he uncorked the bottle with his teeth and poured himself a healthy half glass. "He breeds his racers for speed, damned if he don't," he added after setting the bottle down and recorking it. "Here's to tomorrow and another five hundred guineas." After lifting his glass to his family, he drank it down.

Duncan and Neil had settled into chairs across from Chelsea—her two older brothers, unlike Colin, were full-grown muscular men, auburn-haired like their father once was. Colin, like herself, favored the strawberry blond of their mother, dead now since Colin's birth.

"You should have come, Chel," Duncan said. "Glen Vale missed your gentle touch. He almost pulled the arms off our jockey waiting to start."

Chelsea knew how to soothe the restless nerves of Glen Vale, a splendid bay. He hated crowds, but he ran better as a two-year-old than any horse they'd ever raised. "I'll come tomorrow," Chelsea said. "Mrs. Macaulay needed help with the accounts today."

"If you were allowed to ride Glen, Chel," Neil said with a small disgruntled sigh, "we could even take The Saint's Irish black."

"I could."

"No!" Her father's roar wasn't unfamiliar, this point of dissent having been a topic of conversation several times before with their finances in need of repair.

Chelsea sat a horse as if she were an extension of the animal, her hands on the reins so light and deft that her mounts seemed to enjoy winning for her. She outrode every male in her family, a point not of dissension but of familial pride. Unfortunately, social strictures prohibited a public exhibition of her horsemanship on any of the major race courses.

A decided hindrance in the restoration of the family capital.

Having the loyalty and courage to support Bonnie Prince Charlie in 1745 and also the misfortune to have chosen the wrong side, when the rebellion was quelled, the Fergussons of Dumfries, earls since the thirteenth century, had had their lands and titles confiscated. Chelsea's grandfather retired with his clan to their dower lands in Ayrshire, where Chelsea had been born and raised. But their former fortunes were seriously depleted.

"We may have sold some horses today, too," Colin interjected, always the first to smooth over any heated words.

"To Bishop Hatfield," Neil said. "He asked for you," he added with a grin, aware of his sister's feelings about the unctuous Bishop.

Chelsea's nose twitched in distaste. "I hope you told him I'd come down with the French pox."

"Chelsea, mind your tongue. You talk like a stable boy," her father grumbled. "And he's a passable enough fellow for an Englishman."

"Rich is what you mean, Papa." Scathing derision hissed through her tone.

"Without a dowry, daughter, rich is nothing to turn your nose up at," her father pointedly noted, his grey eyes tolerant despite his reprimand. Chelsea was the image of the wife he'd lost long years ago, and he loved her in the same unconditional way he'd loved her mother.

"I'll stay unmarried, thank you," his unruly daughter crisply declared.

Duncan and Neil smiled, this argument, too, one of long standing. Personally, they would prefer Chelsea stay in the family. She saw that their lives were comfortable, and they were all close friends.

At twenty-two and twenty-five, neither Neil nor Duncan was considering marriage, so they preferred what was for them a very satisfactory arrangement.

"Rutledge is rich, dammit, Chelsea," her father reminded her, "and willing to settle a small fortune on you."

"Which will pay off *your* damned money-lenders. I'd rather lose my reputation on the race course, Papa. I don't want to marry anyone." Chelsea was, in fact, supremely content with her life. Not only were she and her brothers amiable companions, they were partners in their breeding of race horses. Her days were busy and full. She *enjoyed* training horses. And never having known the companionship of other women, she didn't miss female friendship.

"I invited him over for dinner tomorrow evening."

"Damn you, Papa! I hate that man!"

"Darling," her father gently said, genuinely concerned for his daughter's future. Without the funds to see her brought out, her only proposals would come from country gentry. She was the daughter of an earl, and however impoverished, he wanted more for her. "Just be polite . . . at least. The man's seeking you out."

"Make Duncan and Neil marry some rich merchant's daughter, Papa, and leave me alone."

"We probably will, Chel, when the time comes," Duncan reminded her. "Rutledge just happened to spy your beautiful face first."

"I've all the rotten luck! I won't though, Papa, I'm telling you. I won't be nice to him. I won't consider marrying him. He's white as a woman, Papa. Let Duncan and Neil go out and hawk their handsome looks to some whey-faced brew-master's daughter instead. I promise to treat her like a Princess Royal when she comes into the family. I won't even smile when her brew-master nabob father wears a purple waistcoat and a two-foot gold watch chain to dinner."

Her father apparently failed to see the humor in her comments, because his eyes were flinty grey. "The young Viscount is coming to dinner; as my daughter, you will be courteous to him, and that's my last word on the subject." Fergus mo Fergusson spoke in his laird of the clan voice, five centuries of command in his voice.

"Yes, Papa," Chelsea quietly said, recognizing when her father had reached the limit of his patience.

That gave her only twenty-four hours to lose her virginity.

She hoped the Duke of Seth was sleeping in his own bed tonight.

Chapter 5

With a lustrous spring moon bathing her room in shimmering silver, Chelsea lay fully clothed on her bed, her gaze drifting periodically to the clock on the mantle, its golden hands and numerals gleaming in the half light of the room. She must wait until her family was asleep so her departure wouldn't be noted. Fortunately, with the early rising necessary for the horses' morning warm-ups, her father and younger brother, at least, would retire early. Duncan had departed already for the evening festivities at the Duke's, which left Neil's presence the only unknown.

Ten-thirty. She'd wait another half hour before leaving. Even if Neil were sitting up in the small drawing room, her departure via the servants' stairway should go unobserved. But despite her intellectual resolution to the problem of Bishop Hatfield, less rational emotions continued to disturb her peace of mind. Her undertaking was reckless, rash and completely unladylike. She smiled as the last adjective came inexplicably to mind. She was decidedly unladylike by any stretch of the imagination; raised in a male household totally absorbed with racing and horse breeding, she was distinctly derelict in those feminine graces pressed on other girls of her age. She couldn't embroider or converse on the merits of lute-string or sarcenet; she didn't know how to sit demurely or be attractively self-effacing. When her father was in a temper, he would remind her that gentlewomen were expected to demonstrate those acceptable qualities.

She was, however, accomplished at painting, although unfortunately not the delicate watercolors generally considered acceptable to feminine schooling. She did in fact paint extremely well, as a result of having been horse-mad since childhood. Her first rough sketches of their horses, drawn when she was scarcely five, had been so impressively precocious that she soon advanced beyond watercolors to oils. And as a painter of horseflesh she had few equals. Portraits of all their champion thoroughbreds and hunters covered the walls of their home.

She could also play the lute with a professional grace, a talent inherited from her mother and encouraged by her father. When she played for him, as she often did, he was reminded of his beloved wife.

The distractions of contemplating ladylike or unladylike behavior aside, she distractedly thought, how exactly was she going to inveigle her way into the Duke of Seth's bed? With Duncan present, she couldn't approach him directly. And with the teasing directed at Duncan by Neil before he left for supper at the Duke's, Chelsea understood the Duke had feminine company up from London. *Experienced* female company.

How did one compete with *that*?

Seduction was definitely outside her accomplishments. Flushing in the silvery moonlight, she remembered the delicious feel of the Duke's mouth on hers and the heated sensation of his muscled body. However unquiet and disordered her emotions in terms of methodology this evening, or however inexperienced her seductive repertoire, the image of the splendidly handsome young Duke bolstered her resolve. She would not be passively bartered to George Prine with his wretched white skin and cold hands; she would instead dispose of that single commodity so avidly exchanged for money and title on the marriage mart.

And the beautiful infamous Duke of Seth would help her.

She liked the word "help." It made her undertaking more benign, more friendly, less fearful and outrageous.

She would make herself available for his pleasure, and he would help her outwit the distasteful Bishop of Hatfield.

On that generous thought, she rose from her bed, purposeful and composed. Dressed in her best new gown to further tempt the Duke if need be—hoping its allure would compensate for inexperience—Chelsea crossed the moonlit room to the armoire. Taking a dark cloak from the interior scented with the rose sachets she prepared from her summer garden, she tossed it over her shoulders and left the room without a backward glance.

She managed to exit the house without incident, and skirting the stables in a wide arc to avoid waking the stable lads, Chelsea entered the pasture bordering the Duke of Sutherland's parkland. The distance cross-country to Six-Mile-Bottom, home to the Duke of Seth during race season, was a comfortable walk of only a few miles.

The grass was damp, its scent fresh and pungent, the air warm now that the wind had faded, the moonlight bright and beautiful—a reiver's moon. She smiled at the spontaneous analogy: she was paying an unexpected visit to the Duke of Seth like her ancestors coming down to raid the borderlands in the past. She was coming to take something she wanted. His fine and bonny body.

The sounds of the Duke's entertainment reached her first across the quiet of the night: the high-pitched laughter of women, the lower tones of male merriment, the fine delicate notes of a violin and harpsichord fitfully heard at intervals over the gaiety. And the glow of lighted windows materialized next through a pale fog enveloping the bottoms, an eerie radiant phosphorescence of increasing dimension as she approached, candlelight glittering from a vast two-story facade of pedimented windows. The Duke's resplendent bachelor lodge at Newmarket bespoke his wealth; it was larger than many country homes, including their home in Ayrshire.

Standing for a moment in the shadows of an intricate wrought iron trellis bordering the terrace garden, she debated the best method of access, her gaze surveying the multitude of party-guests visible through the large windows. The women were all beautiful—*and* beautifully disheveled. They appeared animated, vivacious, disposed in varying degrees of intimacy with the aristocratic young bucks. After a prudent surveillance of the rooms, she found Duncan engaged in languorous dance with a pretty redhead; neither seemed attuned to the rhythm of the music. The Duke was in one of the other public rooms, engaged in cards, a lovely cyprian on his lap. His attention was frequently interrupted by her whispers and kisses, but he didn't appear annoyed. He'd only smile a tempting smile of acknowledgment when she murmured in his ear, and he'd kiss her then, at great length occasionally, while his partners patiently waited. His lazy application to the card game didn't appear detrimental; the pile of guineas stacked before him gave notice he was winning. He'd glance up occasionally too, as if to survey the attentiveness of his numerous footmen to his guests, and he signaled once for a fresh glass and a new bottle. Champagne, it appeared, was the beverage of choice.

Would it be possible, Chelsea debated with a slight heart-sinking concern, to detach the Duke from the stunning brunette currently ensconced on his lap? Would it *not* be possible? Would all her carefully considered plans go undone? Would she be outmaneuvered by the hateful George Prine and her father's need for money?

Not, she steadfastly reflected, in the next immediate synapse, without at least a determined offense. Surely she could find him alone for some few moments in the course of the night. Now where best to enter this brilliantly lit house?

She found a servants' door on the main floor, near a back hallway that gave her access, and cautiously making her way to a staircase obviously meant for household help, Chelsea mounted to the second floor one slow step at a time, her breathing racing like her heart. With the hood of her cloak concealing her hair and shadowing her face, should she meet someone, she would simply impersonate one of the ladies from London. Not simply, she hastily corrected, awkwardly aware of her own limitations as a courtesan. But at least with good intent.

Greatly relieved as her slippered foot touched the top step, she made her way unopposed down a long paneled back hallway to the head of the main staircase—where she secreted herself behind the window curtains of a small alcove overlooking the front drive. With the location of the Duke's rooms uncertain, she'd wait for him to show her the way.

Discreetly follow him to his bedroom.

And then . . . hopefully convince him to bed her. His earlier refusal aside, he had plainly responded to her physical overture in the carriage—or his body had responded. In the privacy of his bedchamber, she should be able to overcome whatever resistant scruples still remained— A small knowing smile spontaneously appeared on her face. Particularly . . . after a night of drinking.

Perhaps he might not even remember she was there.

For a moment she allowed the possibility to enliven her hopes of success. How pleasant a fantasy—to accomplish her aim and conceal her identity.

But what of the affectionate brunette downstairs? she suddenly thought, reality abruptly impinging once again. The Duke wouldn't likely be alone, with the number of accommodating women in the downstairs rooms, even if the brunette were discarded. Was it possible to convince a London cyprian to forgo her pleasure? With the Duke's handsome looks and amorous repute—not likely, Chelsea morosely reflected. Hell and damnation. Who'd think losing one's virginity would be so exceedingly difficult?

It should have been easy.

The Duke of Seth's well-known notoriety and his availability at Newmarket made him the perfect candidate.

He would only require a bit more persuasion, she knew—if all the people surrounding him could be eluded.

She exhaled in frustration, and if she'd not been pressed by George Prine's dinner appearance a few short hours from now, she could have selected a less daunting time and place for that persuasive effort.

Some pagan Scot's deity of old must have taken pity on her, for when Sinjin came up the stairs some time later he was *alone!* Chelsea's optimism returned—only to be immediately dashed when he opened the large paneled door at the head of the stairs. A voluptuous blonde threw her scantily clad body at him, and after the briefest moment of surprise, his arms closed around her. He kissed her there in the open doorway, a long leisurely kiss that ended in a smiling murmur, to which the woman responded by reaching for his waistcoat buttons. Gently nudging her into the room, he closed the door with a soft kick.

The libertine had women everywhere—"upstairs and downstairs and in his lordship's chamber" pertinently came to Chelsea's mind. With the extent of his amorous interests, perhaps he'd be too fatigued even if she did manage to find him alone some time before morning.

Momentarily nonplussed, Chelsea debated her diminishing options. Had she known the Duke better, she reflected, perhaps she could have introduced herself into his room regardless of his guest and somehow persuaded the luscious blonde to leave. Had she not been Duncan's sister, she needn't have concerned herself with politesse, for Sinjin St. John would have genially invited her in. And had she been privy to the more intimate gossip regarding The Saint's propensity for pleasure, she needn't have hesitated. Since his seventeenth year, Sinjin had won all the wagers at Brookes pertaining to sexual performance—duration, repetition and number of partners. He would have gladly pleasured them both.

She chewed at her fingernail, her mind in a frenzy of indecision. What to do . . . with the fiendish Bishop only hours away?

In the midst of her quandary, Chelsea was disconcerted to realize a couple was entering the alcove. She was considerably more than disconcerted when they decided the alcove offered sufficient privacy for their lovemaking and proceeded to settle in. If the Duke exited his bedchamber while she was still prisoner behind these velvet drapes, her opportunity to find him alone would be lost.

Damn!

If she'd been superstitious by nature, she might have dwelled on her dearth of luck tonight. Or had she believed in fate as a principle in life, she might have given up her night's mission as unpropitious. Raised under the Fergusson motto "Sweeter after Difficulties," however, Chelsea didn't succumb to the irresolution of lesser creatures. She still had several hours before dawn and the necessity of returning undiscovered to her bed. And she'd wait in the anteroom of hell itself if it would free her from the likes of George Prine.

Far from the antechamber to hell, her small alcove became instead the convivial chamber of love as the young couple relinquished themselves to passion. Pressed against the wall, hardly breathing, Chelsea became unwilling witness to an amorous rendezvous.

"I should make you wait for ignoring me during your card game," a breathy woman's voice reprimanded from terrifyingly close range.

"I was winning, darling, and even your"—she could hear the rustle of fabric—"bounteous charms couldn't detract me from five thousand guineas." A small silence ensued, and then the sound of kissing. "Until now . . ."

"Did I bring you luck?" The woman's voice was husky and low.

"Ummm." The soft whisper of clothing dropping to the floor accompanied the masculine murmur. "Very much."

"Oou, Will, you do feel lucky . . ."

"A thousand guineas for you too, pet, for keeping Lady Luck at my side."

The cyprian's squeal of delight pierced the shadowed warmth of the alcove, and for the first time Chelsea realized the profit in pleasure. A thousand pounds would keep the stables running for six months. Now if *she* didn't have scruples, she could help pay off her father's debts with ease. Everyone knew the Duke of Seth was one of the wealthiest men in England. And then she recalled that she'd not yet achieved the advantage of his company, which would make the bestowal of one thousand guineas highly unlikely, regardless of scrupulous principle.

Heavy breathing and muffled moans proceeded to barrage Chelsea's ears; once the lady softly chastised, "Not so hard, darling, my bubbies bruise." And then, some moments later, Will was heard to say, "I don't bruise at all, darling." His voice dropped to a teasing murmur. "But then you know that." Chelsea interpreted the muted sound of slippers and boots being discarded next. And after a lengthy interval of careful controlled breathing to conceal her presence, after a silent reckoning of the number of times a soft thudding pulsation vibrated across the floor to her slippered feet, Chelsea heard an explosive "Oh God, Liz, oh . . . God . . ." And the man's voice trailed away in a great sighing content.

A short period of silence ensued while Chelsea unconsciously held her breath, fearful the small sound might be heard. How long before they might leave? She prayed neither person would choose to admire the moonlit view out the window.

"It's a lover's moon, Will darling. Look."

Her god apparently was on holiday tonight. Should she make a break for the stairway? Step over their prostrate bodies to run down the hall? Melt into the woodwork? Such irrational alternatives indicated the degree of her panic, and whatever intrepidity had brought her this far began disappearing with the speed of the Duke's champagne downstairs.

"I'll buy the moon for you, Liz, my pet, and put it over that small house on Harley Street if you'll but say the word."

"Can I have a carriage, darling dear?" the adored Liz softly replied. And Chelsea took note of the lady's expedient sense of negotiation.

Will chuckled. "Have two, my greedy pigeon, with matched pairs to set them off. Are we agreed?"

"What of staff, dearest?" Her voice was the smallest of sweet whispers.

"All the staff you wish . . . an account at Barclay's and five hundred a month for pin money. Do you love me enough now, sweet Liz? Pledge me your heart." There was teasing in his voice, but warmth too and affection.

The giggling reply sounded very young, the previous affectation of huskiness gone. "You have my heart, Will," she softly whispered, "and everything else. Tell me *you* care."

"By the light of the moon above, I'll pledge you my heart."

And Chelsea heard the hushed sound of footsteps on the carpet. She was discovered.

A door forcefully shut very close by, very loudly, and a second later, a rich contralto declared, "I see all is reconciled with you young lovers." The smile in the female voice was evident. "He fell asleep, the beautiful St. John, and the night's still young. Come, Liz, and we'll sing for the young bloods downstairs. St. John's up early with his horses, he says, so we can sleep till afternoon. Will, let her go. I want to sing."

And as if the hand of God had interposed, within minutes Chelsea was alone.

With the Duke of Seth asleep next door.

And not another soul in sight.

Chapter 6

When Chelsea slipped through the door to Sinjin's bedroom, her heart was pounding so audibly that she covered it with her hand to still the noisy thudding, afraid the disturbance would wake the slumbering Duke.

Although her next thought—completely opposite in context, although equally anxious—questioned whether she'd be able to wake him. Maybe he wasn't sleeping. Maybe he was comatose from too much rum punch or wine, and *then* what would she do?

She stood trembling from various mutations of panic, nerves and god-awful fear.

Would it be easier after all to simply marry the white toad of a bishop? Maybe his avocation would deter him from sexual impulses; maybe she would only have to dine with him occasionally and receive his visitors and pour tea for his mother. But then she recalled how he'd tried to touch her last week out in the stables when her father had stepped away for a moment to talk to the groom. George Prine's eyes had been lustful, not pious, and his fingers had felt cold when they'd brushed her face.

No, George Prine would be the most distasteful of husbands, and she'd be sold away to him for life—regardless of what her father said about the practical considerations, the necessity of marrying a title and fortune.

Father hadn't married a fortune, come to think of it, so he

shouldn't be lecturing her on the merits of marriages of convenience. He'd married for love even when his fortunes were at their lowest ebb, so few years after Culloden.

So he could proselytize all he wished, but she intended to, first, avoid the repugnant Bishop Hatfield, despite his immense marriage settlement; second, see that her virginity was no longer a bargaining point; and third, see if she could convince Papa—once he got over his rage at what she was about to do and her reputation was in tatters anyway—to let her win them a fortune by riding their racers at the meets.

She felt better now that she'd composed her thoughts; setting her goals went a long way toward mitigating the horrendous trepidation she felt.

Her action here tonight was simply the first step in a reasonable plan for restoring some of her family's resources. Like the initial feint in a battle maneuver—an essential diversion necessary to accomplish a grander scheme.

She was careful to put out the single candelabra left burning on the console table; if the Duke thought her the courtesan returned, her identity might remain undetected. It wasn't essential to her plan that her partner be cited. It was enough to have lost her virginity. With honor she would refuse to divulge the man's name. She even debated dousing the small fire in the hearth but decided its flickering light wasn't sufficient to illuminate the area of the room near the bed, and the smell of damp ashes might occasion questions she wouldn't care to answer. But she undressed in a shadowed corner of the room, cautious not to wake the dark-haired man sprawled face down on the bed.

The bed linens were lying in a tumble on the floor, so Chelsea had only to carefully lie down beside the Duke, then wait for the frantic beating of her heart to subside once again. She could rationalize the enormity of her actions in metaphorical images of a battle successfully waged and won, but actually lying here *naked* next to the softly breathing, extremely large, nude and notorious Duke of Seth —no matter how bonny his looks—was a moderately nerve-racking experience.

And what was perhaps *most* nerve-racking was that, having brought herself to this literally exposed state, she didn't know what to do next.

As if sensing her dilemma, or more pertinently sensing the recognizable fragrance of attar of roses, the Duke lifted his arm in drowsy drifting progress, touched her shockingly—to her mind only—on the curve of her hip and pulled her close.

Half-dozing, Sinjin felt the familiar warm softness of a woman's body, sighed in content, tucked her nearer and fell back to sleep.

His breath was a fluttering rhythm on Chelsea's hair as he lay on his stomach, his head turned toward her, his arm heavy across her stomach and hip. His rangy presence was warm beside her, the heat from his body comforting in the large bedchamber, the scent of his long hair lying in disarray on the pale whiteness of the pillow tantalizing in her nostrils, faintly woodsy, like a cool fern glade or a border glen at daybreak.

He moved his leg then, shattering poetical images of nature, its weight falling across her thighs, pinning her to the bed. And then, more riveting still, that part of him for which he was notorious, and to which she intended to sacrifice her virginity, moved, grew, expanded noticeably against the curve of her thigh.

As a working member of a family seriously involved in horse breeding, Chelsea was aware of the fundamental processes of procreation . . . and the Duke of Seth was definitely beginning to emulate one step in that procreative process.

Sinjin's sense of smell responded first in his transition from sleep to wakefulness. He distinctly smelled the sweet arousing perfume of roses. "Ummm," he murmured, "you smell luscious, Polly." His slender fingers gently stroked the dip of Chelsea's waist. "Like summer."

"Thank you, Your Grace," Chelsea replied, not entirely sure an answer was required in these circumstances. Was conversation politely maintained as in other social intercourse?

"Sinjin . . . love . . ." His voice was husky and low, his eyes still closed. "Don't need titles . . . in bed . . ." His palm slid up Chelsea's rib cage, stopped for a moment where the soft roundness of her breast began to rise, then glided upward over the full pliant abundance, his fingers splaying as if to measure its size.

"Perfect . . ." he breathed in contentment.

And the length of his arousal inched upward on her thigh.

Did she say thank you again? Was his one-word comment a compliment or an assessment? Was a reply required? But his gentle fingers touched her nipple that moment, sending a burning flash racing downward to the pit of her stomach, and questions of amorous etiquette were instantly forgotten. He pinched softly, stroked, massaged the soft bud of her nipple, elongating it until it was taut and hard between his fingers and thumb.

Chelsea trembled at the fever racing through her senses, a tiny shudder, uncontrollable and curiously bewitching.

"You're awake now, love," Sinjin whispered, a smile in his voice, his own eyes opening finally as the heat of desire once again energized him. "Did you sleep?" he murmured into the grey shadows. "I think I did."

"A little," Chelsea murmured back, obliged, she felt, to answer a direct question, but the Duke's hand was tracing a downward path over her stomach and lower, obliterating any further rational thought. A flaming heat was kindling deep inside her, delicious and pulsing, radiating outward in blissful sensation. It seemed to affect her breathing. And when his slender fingers slipped through her pale silken hair, they slid over a warm sleek dampness. Her gasp trembled between them in the darkness.

"You're always ready, Polly darling," Sinjin softly declared, moving over her with an easy grace. He grinned, his smile white in the darkness. "How very convenient . . ." He shifted comfortably between her legs, his rigid erection touched the dewy moisture of her new, enchanting desire.

And Chelsea wished for a small uneasy moment—face to face with the actual consummation of her spirited undertaking—that he would continue to think she was Polly. Although she rather doubted he would for much longer.

Easing his entry into the welcoming woman beneath him with a guiding hand, Sinjin slid forward.

Only minutely. He found himself arrested.

Adjusting his position to remedy the deterrent, he moved into Chelsea's heated warmth again.

To feel this time the distinct barricade of virginity.

Absolutely, fully awake now, he said with singular confusion, "You're not Polly."

"No, sir," Chelsea softly admitted, the light weight of Sinjin's body pleasantly warm on her body, his arousal hard against her maidenhood, his astonishment evident in his arrested position.

"Harriet didn't say she was sending out a virgin." A form of query dominated his statement. "Are you my added bonus?" Sinjin's voice was teasing, blasé, his mind adjusting quickly to the altered circumstances of an unknown, grass green woman in his bed.

Harriet had charged an arm and a leg this time, his factor, Seneca, had mentioned in passing. Maybe this virgin accounted for Harriet's exorbitant fee. Not that he gave a damn one way or the other; his and Harriet's business relationship had always been exceedingly friendly.

"Are you afraid?" he suddenly asked, conscious of the utter stillness of the woman beneath him.

"No," she honestly answered, fear not one of the pleasurable feelings coursing through her body; she seemed to be floating halfway between the earth and heaven.

"Well, there's no way to mitigate it, darling," Sinjin softly murmured, intent on assuaging his desire, exploring the barrier of her virginity with a gentle finger. "There's only one way in."

"I understand, sir," Chelsea quietly breathed, strangely unconcerned now, the consequences of her act less important than the strange bewitching fever inflaming her mind.

"I hope Harriet's paying you well. This is a bit disconcerting," he added, aroused and sexually eager but out of his normal range with a virgin. He wasn't sure what she was feeling. He understood experienced women. Like his own passions, theirs followed a sophisticated, predictable course. Did he apologize now or later? Did he have to apologize at all? Harriet certainly had to have schooled the young chit in a preliminary fashion at least. Unless her customers who favored virgins liked tearful terrified young girls in their beds.

Which thought brought him to say, "Are you sure you want to go through with this?"

"Oh, yes."

No equivocation there, his heated libido gratefully noted.

"Kiss me," he said in gentle command, thinking to ease the physical hurt with an alternate sensation.

And when her soft lips touched his, an odd familiar comprehension struck a memory chord deep in his subconscious—that small stabbing impression immediately inundated by a tidal wave of passion. She felt like paradise, soft and warm and luscious, her body small, perfect, her legs spread wide to accommodate his size, her sweet mouth opening beneath the pressure of his, welcoming him.

Did one die of this shuddering rapture? Chelsea wondered, recognizing suddenly why the Duke of Seth pursued sensual pleasure with such avidity. If one always felt so intoxicated, so wildly inflamed in the throes of passion, surely the duplication of those ardent sensations would be a primary pursuit.

"I'm sorry," Sinjin unconsciously murmured the moment before actual penetration, his words a tingling breath on her lips. "Hold on." He thrust forward swiftly as her arms tightened on his shoulders, and she swallowed her small cry of pain.

"It won't hurt again," he whispered, his fingers caressing the curve of her cheek, his long hair touching her shoulders as he lay above her. His manhood filling her.

"It doesn't now," she said in a quiet sigh of pleasure, wondering if all virginity was lost so easily, if all women felt this way—flooded with a rush of wanting so strong she wished to hold on to the enchantment forever. Her warm hands lay on his shoulders, some locks of his hair twined in her fingers, the solid strength and power of his honed body hers for the moment.

He hadn't moved, content to kiss her mouth and eyelids, her soft brows, the dip of her nose, the luscious softness of her earlobes, and Chelsea wondered briefly from the dissolving haze of her sublime sensual delight if there was more.

He moved then, sliding gently upward, and she sucked in a breath of ecstasy, holding him inside her with shuddering need. When he withdrew a long moment later, she whimpered against her loss . . . a small needy sound he found intensely provocative.

Was she acting? he wondered, mildly amazed at her mercurial passionate response. Weren't virgins supposed to be undemonstrative until properly tutored? But he tested the extent of her dramatic skills by gliding forward again, and if the bite of her fingernails in his shoulders was acting, she was effectively schooled.

He settled into a rhythm of arousal he'd perfected in numerous variations over the years, bringing his own orgasmic consciousness to peaking sensation—the young virgin in his arms matching his need and desire, clinging to him with a wanton intemperance that intensified his own hot-blooded urgency.

She wouldn't release him had he wished, which he didn't—a unique and novel circumstance after a decade or more of playing at love with a cool, jaded sophistication. And when he felt her climax begin, he met it, filling her with an ejaculating rush of carnal release he hadn't experienced in years.

He felt like an adolescent again, so feverish his orgasm, his mind dissolving, the world dissolving, a low groan of pleasure coming from deep in his lungs. Chelsea cried out at the end, not even aware of her high keening scream, the sound filling the darkness of the high-ceilinged room. Filling his mind as well with sweet pleasure.

And when she lay panting in his arms, he kissed her wet lips with his own trembling mouth.

They lay as if washed ashore by a tropical typhoon, their breathing ragged, their bodies damp with sweat, exhausted in that wondrous sweet exhaustion unduplicated in human experience.

But reality eventually intruded into their idyll of sensual repletion, and Chelsea made a small movement of withdrawal.

"No," Sinjin only said in a barely audible tone, tightening his grip on her shoulders.

"I have to go," Chelsea murmured, her mind beginning to relate to the practicalities of the world.

"Where?" Casual puzzlement infused the single word. Harriet's cyprians were up for the fortnight. He should know because he was paying the charges—and gladly after the explosive climax he'd just experienced.

Was the young maid planning on sharing her extravagant passion with some other of his guests? Not likely, he possessively reflected, feeling very much the ducal potentate at the moment. "Seneca tells me Harriet raised her price another thousand guineas. If I'm paying for your maidenhead, sweet child, I might as well get my money's worth." His voice was soft, but his hands on Chelsea's shoulders were steely hard, and the weight of his body, although lightly supported by his elbows, wasn't about to be moved. "Give me dessert, sweet duckling," he whispered, licking the full perfection of her lower lip. "I like the taste of you."

He was rigid inside her almost instantly, filling her, forcing her wider once again, arousing her sensitive nerves and need and desire as though she'd never climaxed short moments ago.

"Tell me you want me," he softly demanded, surprised he was asking, but strangely impelled. Did one become possessive with virgins, as if one purchased them entirely for the price of their submission? He didn't know—but he knew what answer he wished. "Tell me," he prodded.

"I want you . . . desperately . . . Sinjin," Chelsea whispered on a small caught breath.

And his name on her lips brought a smile to his jaded soul.

"Tell me your name," he murmured, pressing deeply into her sweetness, his eyes shutting against the exquisite friction.

"Flora," Chelsea whispered because she couldn't command the necessary breath to speak with bliss flooding her heating body. Her mother's name sprang easily to her mind.

"I should have guessed," Sinjin teasingly breathed, nibbling on her ear. "Sweet, scented and fertile with passion. You're not leaving." At least not until he'd had his fill, he selfishly thought. "Let me show you," he offered, his deep voice husky with desire, "the perfumed gardens of paradise . . ."

And he did, with skill and tenderness, with gratified thankfulness to whatever Harriet had in mind when she'd sent him this delectable untouched flower, with fevered hunger and urgency. They explored not only the gardens of paradise but the friendly environs of teasing silliness and playful games and open, warmhearted giving. Some hours later, with promises yet to keep, they fell asleep in each other's arms, sated, smiling, mutually content.

The Bishop of Hatfield was checked.

Chapter 7

The party cheerfully continued apace without its host until, some hours later, one champagne-saturated guest suggested a race on the downs behind the house. An inebriated consensus of opinion heartily concurred that Warwick had a capital idea, and someone immediately said, "Get Sinjin down. He's always ready for a wager."

"Leave him," another man suggested, slightly more sober than the rest. "He said he meant to be up at dawn when he went to bed."

"Don't say The Saint is upstairs *sleeping!*"

"The pretty boyo *is* sleeping, and I should know, since I left his warm body between the ducal sheets." The wonderful contralto voice of Sinjin's earlier companion hadn't lost its beauty despite the late hour.

"I say get him. He loves to race and he loves to win."

"I say fifty guineas, he'll growl at being wakened. He's serious about his horses, and the morning runs come early."

"I say fifty guineas, he'd rather have a chance to take one of his sweet racers to the winning post. Let's wake him."

"I'll fetch him," Duncan said brashly after a night of drinking champagne, light stuff compared to the Scottish aqua vitae he and his family distilled. "He's slept long enough."

"He's only slept a few hours. Don't disturb him."

"Bring him down," a pretty blonde in peach silk purred. "I like to see him drowsy-eyed."

"More likely shooting fire from his Irish blues," another man gruffly added. "He's got the devil's own temper when he's crossed."

"It's almost morning," Duncan pointed out with a clarity that had escaped most of the assembled guests. "Look at the sky."

They all did with varying degrees of alertness. Indeed, the black of night had been replaced by the soft dove grey of pre-dawn. And it was agreed then, while Sinjin and Chelsea lay asleep upstairs unaware, that Sinjin should be wakened with the sun nearly risen.

Duncan mounted the stairs to fetch the Duke of Seth for some fun.

It was with resentful umbrage that Sinjin felt himself being shaken awake in what seemed only minutes later, and from the profound depths of a pleasant dream, he woke enough to growl, "Fuck off."

But the hand on his shoulder only tightened its grip, and he heard an answering growl. "Wake up or die in your sleep!"

Even half-dozing, Sinjin's mind effectively absorbed the pointed sentiment.

His eyes snapped open.

Duncan stood over him holding a candelabra in his brawny hand, his face black with rage.

Sinjin blinked twice, trying to interpret the startling scene. "What the hell's wrong with you!" Sinjin's voice registered his own outrage. This was his house, his party, and if he chose to sleep, dammit, he would!

"Welcome to the family, Sinjin," Duncan said with grating sarcasm, "or would you prefer a bullet through your head?"

By this time the commotion had wakened Chelsea as well, Duncan's voice her first ominous clue of disaster. She debated briefly holding her breath until she expired on the spot, but at seventeen and three quarters, life still held promise, albeit slightly blighted at the moment. So she opened her eyes, looked up at her brother from the uncomfortable state of complete nudity and said, "It's not his fault, Duncan. Kindly lower your voice."

Sinjin's head whipped around, Chelsea's voice already stimulating profound discomfort in his brain. He looked at her for a stark moment. "You!" he exploded. Then he glanced up at Duncan again, who was standing over him like a militant Thor.

"Oh, fuck," he murmured. Where the hell had she come from? Diane . . . Deeana . . . merde . . . what the hell was the name of the woman who had last shared his bed? Although it didn't matter particularly with disaster looming. But then a kindling suspicion ignited in his brain.

Had he been set up?

Was all this arranged?

Was he the financial salvation for the lost fortunes of the Lowland Fergussons? He tried to gather a semblance of sobriety after a long night of celebrating his racers' successes at Newmarket.

"I'm sorry," Chelsea whispered.

"Sorry?" he roared, staring at her as though she were an apparition.

"Goddamit, Sinjin, that's my sister," Duncan hotly interjected.

"Stay out of this, Duncan," Sinjin snapped without turning his head. And then his voice dropped to a chill whisper. "Was this all planned?"

"No, Duncan didn't know . . . no one did. It's not a plan . . . I mean . . . not the way you think." Chelsea spoke rapidly, trying to waylay the explosive rage in Sinjin's cold eyes.

"What didn't I know?" Duncan fiercely demanded. "Damn you, Chelsea. Damn *you*, Sinjin. What the hell is going on!"

"Is he a good actor too?" Sinjin softly inquired with a nod of his head in Duncan's direction, his voice laced with ice, his eyes boring into Chelsea.

"No," she whispered. "No one's acting. I'll leave now and you'll never see me again."

"Like hell you will," Duncan growled, uncertain of the exact choreography of this assignation, but certain of the sight before his eyes. Sinjin St. John was naked in bed with his sister, buck naked herself, and if that scenario didn't conjure up wedding bells, he wasn't Duncan mo Fergusson, heir to an earldom. "You're marrying her, Sinjin, or calling out your seconds!"

"I'm not marrying anyone," Sinjin spat.

"I'm not marrying anyone either," Chelsea cried, angry at being put in the exact position she was trying to avoid with the reptilian George Prine. Sitting up in a flurry of apricot hair, she shouted, *"You* don't seem to understand, Duncan. You don't order my life. No one orders my life. I'm not marrying George Prine or the Duke here or anyone else. Now get the hell out of here or I'll scream down the house and bring every curious party-guest into this room in under five minutes!"

. . .

"Would you have?" Sinjin casually asked once Duncan had left with a quiet "I'll be right outside waiting for you, Chel."

"Called down the house," he added in clarification, pushing himself up against the headboard into a half-reclining position, un-self-consciously nude, relaxed, the light of the candelabra that Duncan left behind modeling his musculature in subtle gold.

"Maybe," she said as casually, beginning to leave the bed.

"Wait," Sinjin quietly ordered, grasping her wrist.

"Why?" Her purple eyes were direct.

Sinjin shrugged but didn't release her wrist.

"Are you thinking of proposing?" she sardonically inquired.

He gave her high marks for audacity, but then she was audacious in bed as well. "What if I want to see you again?" he quietly said.

"Fuck me again, you mean."

He didn't hesitate. "Yes," he said, releasing his grip on her wrist.

"Look," Chelsea replied with a small sigh. "I came here tonight out of desperation. I didn't want to be forced into a marriage with George Prine, no matter how generous his marriage settlement. Having solved that problem with my virginity and ostensibly George's interest gone, I'm finished. I didn't come here to embark on the career of a cyprian. I couldn't do that to my family." She grinned. "They know me well enough to accept this one irrational act. Anyway, you don't need me." She shrugged then, her smooth white shoulder lifting gracefully. "You've still a houseful of women to keep you company. So—thank you," she said, putting out her hand as a man would on concluding his business.

Taking her hand, Sinjin debated for the briefest of flashing moments the word "marriage" in regard to Chelsea Amity Fergusson before the selfish principles of a lifetime quickly intervened.

"Thank you, too," he pleasantly said, her hand warm in his. "I enjoyed your company."

"I'll see you at the races."

"Yes . . . the races."

Sliding her hand free, she smiled politely and left the bed.

He watched her move away in the shadowed room with the drapes drawn, the light from the fire limning her slender form, burnishing the delicate curve of her waist, the perfection of her legs, enhancing the fullness of her breast visible in delightful profile. Her cloud of golden hair took on a singular beauty, seducing one to touch it, reminding him vividly how it had felt under his hand. Like gossamer sunbeams. And warm like her skin.

A curious possessiveness overcame him as he gazed at her, as if he wished to lock the door and keep her, as if his guests had suddenly become de trop. As if he wished to be alone with this strange young woman, this wild creature of the night. And he spoke then because he thought for a moment that his imagination had gone mad and all that had transpired was mere fantasia.

"I don't suppose you can stay."

She didn't answer, and for a brief moment he believed in dreams and shaman magic. But she smiled then and her voice reached him across the flickering golden light in the room.

"I don't suppose Duncan would approve." Her smile lifted into a teasing grin.

How extraordinary, he thought. No weeping vapors. More pertinently, no threatening demands. Instead, that luscious grin made to be kissed. Made to be kissed by him, he covetously reflected. "Duncan *is* going to be a problem, I expect," Sinjin replied, his mind racing through possible means of satisfying Duncan's outrage. "And your father too," he added with a twinge of discomfort. Despite Chelsea's acceptance of full culpability, he knew how society would view the incident.

"And my father too," she softly agreed, sliding her arms into her chemise. "But I take entire responsibility," she quietly went on, "so you needn't concern yourself. You were a necessity to me, and I'll make certain Father understands."

A humbling turn of phrase for a man sought after and patronized, but one of relief as well if she could indeed control her father's sense of revenge. For retribution would be demanded; Duncan was proof of that—standing outside his door. And how much more, he wondered, not with pressing concern, because he was a "prince" of England. The Earl of Dumfries' family had chosen the wrong side at Culloden, and Sinjin was fully capable of defending himself.

But his passing concern over vengeance was abruptly curtailed, for Chelsea suddenly bent over to pick up her petticoat from the chair where her clothes had been left, and he unconsciously held his breath. With her chemise still partially undone, the swell of her breasts quivered in the firelight, a tactile lush image of seduction. For the smallest moment, poised on one foot, dipping forward, she offered the sensuous curve of breasts and satiny bottom in graceful juxtaposition, and Sinjin had a sudden urge to keep her in this room in her luscious state of half-undress for an endless time.

Innocent of the fetching image she projected and the unusual state of Sinjin's thoughts, the beautiful Miss Fergusson lifted her petticoat, slipped it over her head and wiggled slightly to help un-catch the sheer fabric tangled on one shoulder.

Only supreme self-restraint curtailed Sinjin's impulse to leap across the bed and physically detain the voluptuous young lady.

"I'm caught," she murmured with another tantalizing joggle. And when she innocently came over to the bed for assistance, his breath caught in his throat. It had been years since he'd been obliged to restrain his sexual urges, and he wasn't sure . . .

"I can't reach," she said, turning her back to him. Without seem-ing regard for her near nudity, she smiled at him over her shoulder.

A small shudder traveled down his spine, his hand poised just short of her smooth white flesh. And then his hand closed over her shoulder; he tumbled her onto the softness of his bed, covered her with his hard, lean body and kissed her with lazy, warm seduction.

"Five minutes," he whispered across the curve of her lips. "Stay for five minutes more . . ." Shifting slightly, he traced the warm palm of his hand up her thigh, his touch skilled and sure.

"I'd love to," Chelsea breathed, the weight of his body on hers triggering newfound senses.

"Perfect," Sinjin murmured, a lush smile in his words, his mouth trailing a path of kisses down her jaw. His hand moving higher, nearer to the honeyed sweetness he sought.

She could feel his arousal, hard and blatant, and her own sense of need was strangely exhilarating. Like a new toy, an infinitely perfect pleasure was being offered her. Chelsea took a very deep breath to bring her emotions in check and said, "But I can't."

She expected a heated reply, a stark remonstrance to her refusal, but Sinjin only murmured, "Of course you can," and touched the dampness of her need.

Desire shimmered upward. The delicate contact of his fingertips was so light; she shouldn't feel it this intensely. But he seemed to know exactly where to touch her . . . and how deeply. Ummm. Her small luxurious sound was pleasure. And bewitching.

How perfect she seemed beneath him, how soft and warm, en-chanting too in the rose-scented tumble of her petticoat and che-mise. Dipping his head, he kissed the downy arch of her brow. "Stay a month," he murmured, "or a year . . ." Sliding her petticoat over her head, he tossed it aside, and when he brushed the golden tumble of her hair back with gentle fingers, she smiled up at him.

"Or at least until the race meet is over."

His grin was enchanting, small-boy wicked, but he gallantly whispered, "I meant it." Adjusting her body with the deftness of much experience, he entered her just as her arms curved around his neck.

I shouldn't, she thought for the briefest moment before overwhelming sensation inundated her senses. Nothing mattered but the feel of him inside her, penetrating so deeply a small cry escaped her. His strength and power seemed to fill her, surround her, the heat of his skin beneath her hands, the silk of his hair laced through her fingers firing her sensibilities. He was potent and vital, like schoolgirl dreams of heroes come to life. But a thousand times better . . . because her young-girl dreams hadn't included the Duke of Seth and his virtuosity.

Sinjin had never dreamed of heroines; steeped in reality, he'd always preferred the immediate satisfaction offered by willing females. Experienced females who understood the subtleties and nuances of the game. A sport, as it were—where skill was a requirement.

A new beneficiary of The Saint's extraordinary sexual talents was currently leaving small half-moon marks on his broad shoulders and uttering breathy sighs of pleasure. He smiled at her bewitching abandon. Withdrawing a fraction to give pause to sensation, he waited a pulse beat for the hysterical pressure of her hands before he slid back in with infinite slowness. She whimpered in trembling ecstasy.

He cupped her rosy face in his hands and whispered, "Soon," the muscles in his back and legs and powerful arms sustaining the delicately measured progress.

"Now," she pleaded in a heated suffocated sound.

"Later," he whispered back, licking the lush fullness of her bottom lip. *"Now* you can kiss me . . ."

And when her mouth lifted that fraction in submission to his soft command, he gave her what she wished for and felt the beginning of her expiring sigh drift into his mouth.

He met her breathless release with his own explosive climax, pouring into her in a strangely fevered paroxysm. And he held her gently for long moments, in grateful homage to her splendor.

"You live up to your reputation," she whispered into the silence of the room, the sound warm on his face.

He didn't pretend he didn't know he had one. "Thank you," he simply said, lifting his head to gaze into the violet of her eyes. "And you live up to the provocation of your beauty."

"Thank you, milord," she teasingly replied, as a young country girl might.

"Are you really Duncan's sister?" he asked, incredulity prominent in his tone. Clearly he was hoping for a more digestible answer.

And if Duncan hadn't been guarding the bedroom door, she would have gladly lied. "I'm sorry," she murmured, a small shrug expressing her apology. Mention of Duncan recalled to her the rather unorthodox circumstances of her current position under His Grace, the Duke of Seth, and untwining her arms from his neck, she gently pushed at his chest. "I *do* have to go."

He looked at her for a considering moment, selfish motives playing havoc with his tenuous regard for good manners. What would happen if he kept her? She was ruined—unequivocally, should word get out of her sojourn in his bed. And having courteously refused her first advances, how chivalrous need he be? Her family no longer had their fortune—and with power directly related to wealth, he held the advantage.

"What if I didn't let you leave?" he quietly said.

"Whyever not?" Genuine surprise colored Chelsea's tone.

"For dishonorable reasons, of course." His faint smile lifted one corner of his finely modeled mouth.

"Oh." Her expression mirrored the small revelation for a moment, and then her smile lit up her beautiful face. "I'm flattered, Your Grace," she teased, "and if we could live like Rousseau's savages in a state of nature, I'd be most pleased to stay. But I can't and you can't keep me."

"I could." His eyes were shuttered suddenly, his deep voice hushed.

"Not for long." She, too, spoke very low, but a new firmness infused her voice, and he was reminded of their initial encounter, when she'd bluntly propositioned him. Miss Fergusson was a woman of extraordinary self-sufficiency.

But she was a woman, after all, and no match . . . a reflection supported by tradition, culture and social mores. He *could* keep her —if not here with her family dangerously close, somewhere else, remote. She fired his passion, his imagination; she touched some inexplicable, anachronistic sense of possession. And a hushed silence lengthened as Sinjin considered the possibilities.

"If I scream, Duncan will kill you."

"If he could get through a locked door, he might."

"He would eventually."

Sinjin's smile discounted any sense of apprehension. "Eventually would be too late, darling. My grandpapa had need at times of a hidden staircase. We would simply vanish."

Lying still, as undisturbed as her companion, Chelsea calmly said, "You don't mean any of this, so kindly let me go."

"How do you know I don't mean it?"

"Because, my lord, you'd grow bored with me in a few days' time, and what's the use of all the fuss for that?"

Damn chit was right, he ruefully noted, her perception of his threshold of boredom astute. "Maybe I could convince you to fascinate away the boredom," he suggested with a seductive grin.

"After the pleasure of your bed . . . If not for my family, I would and willing, Your Grace." Her purple eyes held laughter in their velvety depths. "No convincing necessary."

Her honesty was startling, plainly spoken, sincere. And damned attractive. "Come and visit then. I can be discreet." At the skeptical arch of her brow, he added, "I haven't needed to until now. There. An open invitation. Anytime, anyplace. If you're more than two days' ride away, allow me time to reach you, although my mounts are the best in England and damned fast."

"*My* mounts are the best."

This time the Duke's brow arched dubiously.

"If I could ride them at all the meets, we'd always win."

"You ride? At meets? I would have heard of it."

"Incognito, of course, and never at Newmarket."

"You're a fascinating little piece."

Her smile was unconsciously womanly and self-assured. "I know."

"How can I let you just walk away?" His lazy drawl seduced her, as did his great beauty and smile.

"Because if you do, you'll see me ride Thune against your Mameluke in the Arcadia Stakes tomorrow."

He rolled off her then as though she'd burned him with flame, and half-reclining on one elbow beside her, he pleasantly said, his grin devastating, "Perhaps you'd be interested in a small wager."

"I can't afford to wager."

"You can afford this," he softly murmured.

"I anticipate you, my lord, and the answer is no."

"I knew your horse couldn't win."

He was baiting her and she knew it, but he was impugning their bloodstock, and racing was her life too. Sitting up abruptly, she surveyed the lounging young lord who was a byword for masculine beauty and notorious for his horses and women. In the shadowed room, his great sleek length, his inherent power, the stark classic definition of his features, his utter masculinity seemed to challenge her. "Name your wager," she said.

"You, of course," he drawled.

"Be more definite."

"I'd like to say forever, but you reminded me to be practical and it's only one race, so . . ." His faint smile disappeared, and his voice took on the authoritative crispness that accompanied his wagers. "One week with you this month. You name the place, I name the pleasures."

"And if you lose?"

"Your choice, of course," he coolly replied.

"I prefer coin of the realm."

"Suit yourself." He inclined his head slightly, and a dark silken lock of hair fell across his forehead. "Name your price."

"Fifty thousand guineas." It was an enormous sum. He could refuse and her honor would be intact. He could accept and the money would redeem her father's racing debts.

"Agreed," he softly said and his smile was restored.

"Am I free to go then?"

"Until tomorrow. I look forward to the race."

"My identity as a jockey—"

"Will be secure with me. My word on it."

And he watched her with contented pleasure this time as she dressed, confident he would have the pleasure of her company soon. He helped her tie her sash and button a small row of buttons at the back of her neck—and he thought, as he helped her straighten the skirt of her simple white dress, how different she looked from his usual female guests. The contrast was startling, as were his curious feelings or the fact that he had feelings at all. He usually was beginning the practiced dialogue of polite withdrawal at this point, not contemplating their next meeting with anticipation.

He kissed her gently when each ribbon was in place and said, "I'll see you at the races."

"I'm going to win," she said cheerfully.

"We'll see," he quietly replied, his courtesy intact.

She didn't stand a chance against Mameluke and Fordham. The big bay hadn't lost a race in a year.

"Have your guineas ready," she only said with a grin and, blowing him a kiss, turned the key in the lock and opened the door.

Chapter 8

"What the hell were you doing in there?" Duncan exploded the moment she exited the room, his voice a low growl.

"Not marrying George Prine," Chelsea snapped. "Now I'm going home, and you can come or stay as you please."

Following her rapid stride down the back hallway, Duncan heatedly said, "Sinjin's going to pay. You know that."

"Not after I tell Father what I did. And not after you tell Father what the bonny Duke said about marrying. I don't think he's the kind you can bludgeon to the altar. I don't wish to marry in any event." She spoke with a hushed vehemence. And she refused to say another word on the subject until she was standing before her irate father some thirty minutes later.

He roared and threatened, Duncan and Neil adding their reasonable and unreasonable comments to the fray. Chelsea stood firm, her hair disheveled, her gown stained at the hem from the damp meadow grass, her spine rigid.

"You can't *make* St. John marry me. Unless you drag him tied and bound to the ceremony, and then you'd have to tie me as well, because *I'm* not marrying him. I don't care if you scream the angels down from heaven."

"He ruined you, girl," her father bellowed, "and no damned Englishman is going to get away with that!"

"He didn't even know who I was," Chelsea patiently said for the tenth time. "He thought I was some doxy up from London. I told him stopping George Prine was my objective, and *that* situation is *your* fault, not St. John's. I won't be bartered for your damned racing chits, and if you won't tell the Bishop his courtship is over in diplomatic terms, I'll tell him in graphic detail." For ten minutes, she'd been subjected to masculine affront, masculine rage, a male view of honor and the practicalities of marriage. She was tired, her temper frayed, her own sense of affront sharpened. "Perhaps some women can be forced into marriage, but I can't," she went on, controlling her moderate tone with difficulty. "I don't know how to say it any plainer."

Her father's eyes held hers for a long moment, as if he had finally comprehended her words. He *had* suddenly, reminded of his young wife in all her youthful pride and candor. "Forgive me," he murmured, contrite and saddened by his memories, "for my selfishness." And turning away, he walked to the window. Looking out across the first pink of dawn, he said, hushed and low, "I'm sorry it came to this . . . that you had . . . to . . . do what you did because I wouldn't listen."

"It's not so terrible, Papa," Chelsea softly replied. "No one knows save St. John, and he won't tell."

"He won't, Father," Duncan agreed. "I'll talk to him too."

"You don't have to talk to him for me," Chelsea interjected. "I take issue with this council-of-war mentality when I'm very capable of taking care of our household, the stables, the bloodstock books and the accounts, and yet somehow I'm considered unable to speak clearly to one man regarding my reputation."

"His own reputation is what concerns me," her father quietly said, his gaze returned to them. "His amorous scandals are legion and a constant subject of gossip."

"He can be trusted, Papa." She didn't choose to mention that his interest in her would temper his discretion.

"A word with him would assure his silence," the Earl sputtered.

"I'd prefer you direct your threatening words toward Bishop Hatfield and leave well enough alone with the Duke of Seth. My escapade surely can't qualify as significant in his rakish life, and the less said the better." She was hoping to avoid some masculine challenge against which Sinjin might feel required to defend himself. "If you do threaten him, Papa, and he calls you out, my name will surely be the subject of gossip then. Please . . . he won't remember me when he wakes; his house is filled with—well . . . female guests."

"Duncan, you talk to him. I only want assurances of his silence."

And with that Chelsea had to be content. Her father wouldn't be dissuaded. He promised, though, to send regrets to George Prine for their dinner that evening and guaranteed her the Bishop would be made to understand that his offer of marriage was declined.

"Thank you, Papa," Chelsea replied, grateful her worries about George Prine were over. "And now, if you'll excuse me, I'd like to sleep." She blushed, as the reason for her fatigue was so obvious to all, and mumbling something about skipping the morning warm-up, she hastened from the room.

Beyond her embarrassment, though, agreeable feelings of contentment and enchanting memory filled her mind. The Duke of Seth was all he was reputed to be in terms of seductive expertise, but he was more—he was sweet and amusing. And because of that, she ruefully reflected, he was extremely dangerous.

To her peace of mind.

She expected to find sleep elusive, so sensational had been her evening and so turbulent, but she fell asleep immediately, exhausted from the excitement, from the late hour, from the strangely blissful afterglow of making love.

The Duke of Seth dressed instead of sleeping, knowing he would be receiving visitors from the Fergusson family soon. He would have done the same; he took no offense.

Calling for his secretary, he walked with him to his library, where they had an early breakfast while waiting for the envoys from the Fergussons.

What had happened was unfortunate but not irreparable, and he was willing to make amends any way short of marriage. His secretary was in attendance to scribe the settlement offer. At the very least, the Fergussons would require some monetary recompense.

His wager with Chelsea was another matter—one separate from her denouement . . . a racing bet. And he smiled in anticipation of the afternoon's meet.

Duncan was announced a short time later, his mood less benign than the Duke's, and at his request, Sinjin's secretary was dismissed, and the two men sat down.

"We've been friends since Cambridge," Duncan said, his voice gruff, "so I came to try to deal with this in a reasonable way." His dark brows creased into a scowl. "Chelsea tells us you're not to blame."

"I didn't know who she was. It was dark; you know the number of women Harriet had sent up . . ." Sinjin shrugged his shoulders apologetically. "Although I'm not excusing myself for what happened. Your sister is, however"—he cleared his throat in momentary unease—"a determined young lady."

Duncan had heard Chelsea's story too many times in the last hour to disagree. "She is . . . unfortunately," he disgruntledly agreed.

"Tell me what you want me to do," Sinjin said, his friendship with Duncan important enough to have precipitated his refusal of Chelsea that afternoon. "Had I known, Duncan," he went on, a touch of weariness evident in his careful articulation, "I would have bundled her back home. You know I don't ruin maidens as a rule." He didn't; he never had, and his conscience was troubling him slightly, for he wanted Chelsea now, still. When he shouldn't.

"I told Father. But gossip follows your affairs so closely that he wants your assurance of silence concerning this night."

"Of course. Your sister's name is safe."

"He's furious, you know. And dammit, Sinjin, so am I, but Chel has a mind of her own and . . . bloody hell, I wish Prine had never come sniffing around her."

"She perhaps misinterpreted your father's interest in the marriage settlement."

"More likely the old man misinterpreted her damned determination not to have him."

"So Prine's refused?"

"He will be today, formally."

Why should it matter that the lecherous Bishop of Hatfield was rejected? It shouldn't, but it did, and Sinjin felt a felicitous satisfaction. He told himself he would have been as pleased if any young lady was saved from conjugal intimacy with the brutish Viscount Rutledge. But had he been honest with himself, he would have recognized altruism had nothing to do with his satisfaction. He preferred not sharing the delightful Miss Fergusson, if truth be told. And then, to assuage his newfound conscience, he said to Duncan, "Let me make some monetary amends for the unfortunate circumstances of this night past. Since I was the instrument of Prine's refusal, at least allow me to cover a portion of that loss."

"Lord, no, Sinjin, you don't have to pay for Chelsea's audacity."

Without embarrassing Duncan, Sinjin couldn't further press funds on him, so he said instead, "Seneca saw your strawberry roan on the downs yesterday morning and said he's a beauty. Is he for sale?"

"Thune? No, he's Chelsea's pet, but come take a look at the stables sometime if you like. You might be interested in the grandson of Eclipse; he'd make a good match for those Herod mares you bought at Tattersall's last fall."

And their conversation turned to the familiar topics of horses and racing, Duncan's duty done, Sinjin's silence ensured, the beautiful young Miss Fergusson's reputation intact.

Chapter 9

By noon, Newmarket course was frantic with activity. Spectators were beginning to assemble; carriages parked on the perimeters of the course were surrounded by groups of men drinking and discussing the merits of their favorite horses, while an occasional landau or barouche with ladies interested enough to brave the vicissitudes of Newmarket weather in March added a note of color to the scene. Stable lads ran on their errands while jockeys solemnly listened to the trainers' instructions and reserved judgment until the actual race—whether they would adhere to those orders. Bookmakers had been at their posts since midmorning for some of the early trials, their constantly changing odds communicated in a cacophony of unintelligible shouts, decipherable only to the initiated.

Sinjin had been at the track since seven, watching the morning runs and early trials, then helping ready the horses for the afternoon meet. He and Seneca had rested briefly, napping for a short time on the scented hay newly delivered from his stud, but he'd hardly felt the need for sleep. He felt irrepressibly alert, thoughts of the lovely Miss Fergusson like adrenaline, anticipation of the afternoon race between Thune and Mameluke riveting his attention.

He'd bet heavily on the race; he intended to win. And he'd already discussed strategy in detail with Fordham. He'd remained reticent on the identity of Thune's jockey, but Fordham would know soon enough. Miss Fergusson's delicate beauty, even unadorned and concealed in masculine attire, would be evident up close.

The first two races of the day were easy wins for Sinjin's stable, the competition mostly provincial horses. With very close odds, Sinjin didn't make much money, but he won enough to satisfy his sense of sportsmanship. The Fergussons hadn't put up any horses in the earlier races, although he'd noticed their arrival at their stable block an hour ago. And he chided himself for his diligent interest in Chelsea's whereabouts when he'd scrutinized their approach. She wasn't with them.

Her younger brother, Colin, wore their blue silks. Had she reneged on their wager? Had her father refused her permission to ride at Newmarket? A female jockey would have caused a furor, although occasionally one rode in lesser stake races or on the personal whim of some noble lord. But apparently not Miss Fergusson today.

As if in conjunction with his lowering mood, the clouds billowing across the sky took on a greyish cast, the wind picked up and a hint of raw weather hovered in the air. Olim only looked askance when Sinjin questioned his orders to Fordham on the start with an unusual curtness and Fordham soothingly said, "Mameluke runs with or without a jockey, gov'nor. Don't worry none."

Sinjin apologized then for his brusqueness, his smile rueful. "I'm probably tired. Forgive me." His words only brought renewed images of the unforgettable Miss Fergusson to mind, further discomposing his serenity. Harshly taking himself to task, he reminded himself that pretty little country misses were vastly available, even country misses with clouds of sunshine hair and a notable expertise with horses. She had simply decided—with female prerogative—to change her mind about their wager.

He was past the schoolboy stage with women. They were a pleasure but never a necessity.

But when the horses were called up ten minutes before starting time and he glanced over the field moving toward the starting line, a transient glimpse of blond curl drew his rapt attention. Thune's jockey came under his intense scrutiny, and with recognition, a slow smile of satisfaction curved upward, his genial mood restored.

"I'll be gone for a week after the race meet's over here," he said to Seneca, who stood beside him near the rail separating the private stands enclosure from the betting ring. "Could you go down to London for me and pick up that Irish filly coming in from Bobby's

Waterford stud? She needs special treatment and I don't want to send a groom."

"Certainly. But why the change of plans? Yesterday *you* were going down. Cassandra's recent note, I thought, added inducement."

"Cassandra will wait. Damien had written some time ago about some estate matters he needed signatures on. If you don't mind going down to London, I'll see to Damien," Sinjin said, his tone without inflection. For the first time since he'd known Seneca, he wasn't able to share a confidence, but his promise of discretion to Chelsea took precedence. As did his intense interest in a week of passion with the exceptional Miss Fergusson.

"Damien'll be pleased," Seneca casually noted, watching the horses lining up at the starting post. "You've some heavy bets on this race, don't you?"

"Mameluke's unbeaten in a year. I thought I'd might as well make some money, since the odds are divided between him and that Fergusson roan some touts saw scorching the earth a week ago."

"Might it win?"

"It better not."

Seneca turned to him. "So emphatic?"

Sinjin grinned. "A personal side bet."

"For much?"

"It depends."

"On?"

"On your point of view."

"You're obviously not going to tell me."

Sinjin shook his head.

"She must have a jealous husband."

"She's not married."

"You fool."

"The thought crossed my mind . . ."

"But?"

"But it didn't stand a chance." Sinjin's gaze was trained on the starting line.

"I didn't think you were that stupid, with every eligible and ineligible woman in England angling for your name and title."

"I didn't either. There's no explanation. Believe me, I tried to find one."

"I expect I'll be hearing of a quiet wedding soon."

"No, you won't. We're agreed."

"She's very bright then—to cozen you so easily."

"I hope like hell you're wrong . . . because I'm not in the market for a wife."

The flag came up at that moment and conversation abruptly ceased, both men engrossed in the start of the race.

As the two youngest in the family, Chelsea and Colin were close, and when Chelsea told her brother she had a chance to win fifty thousand guineas if she took his place as jockey on Thune, he immediately cooperated.

Colin had suited up in the Earl of Dumfries' blue silks, as had Chelsea at home. Arriving late at the race course, her cloak covering her attire, she had taken Colin's place in the saddle just prior to the call for the Arcadia Stakes. Her father and brothers had been placing their bets at the betting post, and only their groom, Ross, knew of the deception. A youth of eighteen, half in love with Chelsea, he'd willingly acceded to her wishes.

"Ye ride him better anyways," he'd said with a shy smile as he gave her a leg up. "But when your pa begins screaming, I dinna know nothin'." He'd been the one to lead her through the tangle of mounted spectators crowding the starting area, and he'd stayed with her, helping to calm Thune until the last moments.

"Just give him his head," he'd said, as a last word of advice. "But then ye know this beauty verra much better than me," he'd added, touching Thune's nose for luck.

And Chelsea had been alone with the jostling mounts, her heart pounding, adjusting the reins for the tenth time so they slid through her fingers like silk, checking her stirrup buckles one last time, relaxing her thigh muscles for a count of three so Thune wouldn't feel her tension.

She had a chance to win enough money to buy off her father's creditors. She had a chance to buy her own freedom as well, from the need to consider a suitor for the measure of his wealth. But an errant part of her brain suggested in a small whisper that losing wasn't really losing either. Was it? Not with the bonny Sinjin St. John as the consolation prize.

During the coarse and ribald mockery generally prevailing at the starting post, Fordham cast a glance at his opponent seated on Thune and began to understand the seriousness of the Duke's interest in winning. The rider was a young lady or an extremely beautiful young boy, and given the Duke's amorous preferences, the former choice was more likely. She kept her mount slightly away from the restless mob without apparent effort. Either the horse was extraordinarily calm or she was a first-class rider. And rumors had it the huge roan wasn't calm.

When the flag fell, Fordham saw that he was the first off, Mameluke preferring not to follow.

Chelsea, jostled by the Duke of Beaufort's jockey at the start, thought at first it was only because of the massed start until, three lengths later, his mount brushed against Thune again. Glancing up, she saw his wicked grin as well as his raised whip, and she swerved to avoid its slash.

"We don't woant no bitches riding, I tell 'ee," he shouted, racing past her.

"Sully damn near hurt her!" Sinjin muttered, gripping the rail, utterly helpless where he stood.

Coaxing more speed from Thune, Chelsea caught up to the Duke of Beaufort's Petronel, and cutting back in front of him, she forced the jockey to pull up or crash into her.

"I'm not a bitch," she said at the moment he jerked his horse aside, no more than ten inches separating them. And she smiled sweetly, as a lady would.

Thune had fallen into his immense stride at last, and fully extended, he was truly scorching the grass with his speed. Riding without whip or spur, Chelsea drove at the hindquarters of Sinjin's powerful racer Mameluke. The Duke's bay was four or five lengths ahead, with three other horses between her and the lead. And she talked to Thune then, in a low crooning murmur, the sound of her voice familiar to him.

She had trained him, and he ran better for her than anyone. His ears dropped back a fraction, and she felt beneath her the lengthening of his stride. Thune passed the first horse on the outside as if the racer were standing still, and coming up on the second one, he seemed to pick up speed. Thune sped by the last horse just at the base of the hill, but Mameluke was charging uphill as though his energy were boundless.

"Damn him," Chelsea murmured. "He's not going to win everything. Come on, Thune my beauty, you can do it . . ."

"Damn her," Sinjin breathed. Her horse flew uphill. She's close behind you, Fordham, he silently warned. Bloody hell, move it! The Earl of Dumfries' daughter could ride like an angel, or like the Devil, he reflected with a chuckle—if you were to ask the Duke of Beaufort's rider up. Sully had tried to drive her off the course, and she'd fought back and damned near taken him down.

"Fordham's got a race on his hands," Seneca softly said, watching Thune slowly overtake Mameluke on the last uphill stretch.

"I think he just realized it," Sinjin murmured, wishing he were in the saddle, wanting to win this race himself.

The two racers had drawn level now with fifty yards to the finish. Neither rider was using the whip or spurs, the driving strides of the two horses thundering toward the winning post.

What won in the end had to do with personality.

Mameluke liked to "come home" first.

And he did, with heart, two strides ahead of Thune.

The roar of the crowd erupted into the gusty grey sky, and the mass of spectators surged toward the winning circle.

With the entire focus of the throng on Mameluke, Chelsea easily slipped away to a pre-arranged area where Colin and Ross waited.

"Great race, Chel!" Colin cried, his face a wreath of smiles.

"Well done, Miss Chelsea," Ross said, his praise too accompanied with a wide smile. Putting out a hand, he helped her down; Colin handed her her cloak and was up. And a second later Ross was leading Thune away.

Tossing her cloak on her shoulders, Chelsea pulled off her cap and sank to the ground behind the changing shed in a billow of burgundy wool. Her adrenaline was still pumping, her breathing rushed, the exhilaration of a race well run still a fever in her blood. She'd almost won . . . against Sinjin's great jockey, Fordham. She'd *almost* won! Which meant Thune *could* win against the best, if an experienced jockey were up on him. She'd lost valuable time fighting off the Duke of Beaufort's jockey because she wasn't familiar with his style. She might have won if not for that. A personal sense of accomplishment brought a ravishing smile to her face.

"You're damned good." The voice was warm and familiar and very close.

Swiftly looking up, her violet gaze took in the smiling countenance of the man who had monopolized her thoughts since morning. He hadn't changed—her memory was excellent—down to the colorful beaded ornament on his fringed jacket. He was too handsome, she thought, for any woman to resist. And her second thought echoed his, although the "goodness" encompassed different talents.

"But you lost," he softly added. Bending down, he slid his hands under her arms, lifted her upright and pulled her close. "And I'm here to collect my wager."

"Give me some time," she whispered, her breath rushed now for reasons other than exertion, the feel of his body exquisitely familiar too, like his voice and teasing eyes. "People will see us," she nervously warned, fear of her family catching sight of them second only to her heating senses.

"No one can see us here," he calmly replied, that fact already carefully scrutinized before he followed Chelsea behind the changing shed. Standing on the rail after the race, he'd watched her progress, had seen her ride behind the shed, had observed her brother and groom exit the area with Thune. "So tell me, sweet Chelsea, when and where?"

"I can't think so swiftly," she evasively said, her mind searching for some possibility of escape. How honor-bound was she to a racing bet?

"You have till Monday afternoon by Jockey Club rules to honor a racing wager," Sinjin quietly said, as if reading her mind. "I'm perfectly willing to wait until then." But his tone, however quiet, suggested he wouldn't wait any longer.

It was only Tuesday; she had practically a week to find a solution to her impulsive wager. "How do I know where to find you on Monday? I'm not allowed in the Jockey Club rooms."

"Don't worry, darling," he murmured, bending his head to brush his mouth over the softness of hers, "I'll find *you* . . ."

And dropping his hands, he walked away.

Leaving her breathless and warm and wanting something she shouldn't.

Chapter 10

That evening Chelsea was obliged to withstand a severe lecture from her father, but his temper had been calmed by the money Thune had won for him and by the lapsed time between the race and his arrival home some hours later.

"While I appreciate the winning, lass, I'm not letting you out of my sight on race days. If you'd won, everyone would have known you rode, for your chucked-up hair wouldn't have been enough under the scrutiny of the stewards in the winning circle." He sighed then, more stern than angry, and reached for his aqua vitae. Pouring himself a large portion, he lifted the glass and, with the tumbler just short of his mouth, gazed at his daughter over the rim with a twinkle in his eye. "It's a damn shame you can't ride for us, girl, for you took that great brute home like a whirlwind."

"Why *couldn't* I, Papa?" Chelsea instantly replied, taking advantage of her father's benign mood. "You saw today how easy it was . . . even in the winning circle . . . I could pass. I'll cut my hair. I can speak like Colin—his voice isn't very deep yet." When she saw the minutest hesitation in her father's expression, she quickly added, "I can do it, Papa. I can!"

"Lord, darling, I wish you could," he said, dropping into a comfortable chair. "But your mama would never forgive me. She probably wouldn't even approve of all the work you do with the horses."

"She would so, because Grandpapa said she was the best rider in the family. You see, she *would* approve."

"But not at Newmarket, Chel," Duncan interposed from his comfortable sprawl on the window seat. "It's just not done. I know you don't give a hang for things like reputation, but the world unfortunately does."

"Amen to that," her father quietly agreed. "And the last scrape you got yourself in was very near disastrous." Although tempted by Chelsea's talents as a jockey, he straightened his shoulders, paternal duty stronger than his inclination to win the meets. "I wish I could say yes, darling, but what man would want a rowdy tomboy who rides at Newmarket? And you have to think of your future. Aunt Georgina should see you out next season." Another sigh escaped the firm line of his mouth. "She should have seen you out this season, if I wasn't so selfish to want you with me another year."

"Papa, I don't want to marry. I'm happy with you and the boys and the horses. Lots of girls don't come out."

"Daughters of earls do, though, Chel." Duncan's voice was soft, low, as though he wished not to remind her.

"No one will want me anyway without a portion. And I'm going to have to be polite to rackety young men who probably don't know the first thing about horses."

"You can't talk about horses anyway, Chel," Colin piped up from his prone position near the fire. With his chin propped on a faded needlework pillow, he grinned at his sister. "It ain't ladylike."

"Bloody hell on ladylike!" Chelsea irritably retorted. "I'll be a spinster and wear mucking boots and smoke a pipe with the stable lads. And stay with my horses."

Less naive than his daughter, Fergus mo Fergusson had kept his daughter off the marriage mart this year, although her age was more than proper, because he knew that, even without a dowry, her fair sweet loveliness would have the whole of London at her feet. And at base, he didn't wish to give her up yet.

Bishop Hatfield, on the other hand, had offered his proposal with a deference and humility sure to please a father; he had also offered a pre-nuptial settlement of staggering proportions. Perhaps she could have done better in London, but all her father had asked her to do was have dinner with the man. He'd not agreed to anything. But the thirteenth Earl of Dumfries had spent too many years without his fortune, and he wanted better for his only daughter. The restoration of titles and estates had been passed by Parliament in 1782, but many of his properties had been taken over by Tory noblemen in 1746 after Culloden, and act or not, they weren't going to be relinquished.

Perhaps he'd been wrong to consider the Bishop of Hatfield's suit in terms of money, but society viewed marriage exactly that way; one consummated the very best arrangement possible. Love wasn't all. He'd lived too many years without the advantages of his former wealth. He knew the difference.

So Chelsea could abhor the thought of marriage.

And disdain the notion of marriage settlements.

But she couldn't continue running wild—and the near calamitous episode with the Duke of Seth reinforced his judgment.

If she must run wild—a distinct possibility, considering her independent nature—then she must do so within the conventions of society. That is: marriage first, an heir, then a discreet freedom to choose amenable companions.

"Find a lord with a racing stable, Chel," Colin suggested, "and you can have your horses and marriage too."

"Don't have to find anyone till next season," her father gruffly said—content, though he wouldn't admit it, that the Bishop Hatfield situation had been taken out of his hands.

"St. John has the best stud in the country," Colin went on with youthful enthusiasm. "You could throw your bonnet at him, Chel, and be rich in the bargain."

A sudden silence descended, so the firelight seemed to take on a presence in the candlelit room.

"What did I say?" Jolted by the abrupt change of mood, Colin gazed curiously at each member of his family.

Chelsea looked as though she'd seen a ghost, while Duncan and his father both had black scowls on their faces.

"St. John's a rake, son," his father finally said, "and not suitable."

"Not the marrying kind, anyway," Duncan muttered.

But still the ladies' favorite lord in England, for all his notoriety, Chelsea reflected. And now she knew why. With effort she forced aside the vivid image of his teasing smile and heated kisses, the feel of his body on hers, the ecstasy he offered with infinite skill, in short the perfection of England's most disreputable young duke. A tiny shiver ran down her spine.

"What of Bonham then?" Colin suggested. "He's got a nice string of racers and lives with his mama. Goes to church too, even during race meets."

Chelsea giggled, picturing herself married to sweet Billy Bonham. He was fine and honorable, kind to his mother and younger sister, a saint to his local parish, but without a spark of vitality. "He'd divorce me in a fortnight," she said with a grin. "On his mama's orders."

"I think," Duncan remarked with an answering grin, "he might think twice about following his mama's orders. But he would in the end."

"And there—I'd be disgraced anyway. You see, Papa, I'm not meant to go along the conventional path. I won't marry for money, I won't be a biddable wife and I fear that changing gowns four times a day would inconvenience me greatly. I'll stay with you to keep the stud books and make your life comfortable instead."

"We'll all stay with you, Papa," Colin enthusiastically proclaimed. "Duncan is forever saying he can't abide marrying a brewer's daughter. Neil don't even drink ale. And I don't intend to marry because Chel takes care of us just fine, so what do I need a wife for?"

"Talk to me in a year or so, Cub," Duncan teasingly said, "although you're probably right about a wife."

"Does this mean I'm to be plagued by you all into my old age?" the Earl facetiously asked.

"Think of it as the bond of family—unbroken . . ." Chelsea blew her father a mocking kiss.

"Speaking of unbroken family—where's Neil?" Duncan inquired, shifting his tired body into a more comfortable lounge. His sleep, like the Duke's, had been minimal.

"Seeing that Thune has his nightcap." Conventional wisdom apropos race horses favored an exotic diet and goodly portions of brandy with the mash.

"You're running him tomorrow, then," Chelsea remarked.

"With Chiffey up. He has a good chance of winning."

"How much do you need, Papa, to get out from under the money-lenders?" Although Chelsea kept the accounts, her father's racing wagers were separate from their household.

He didn't answer for a moment until Duncan said, "Tell her. If Thune performs during the meet, you can see a lot of it paid off."

"Eighty thousand."

Chelsea could feel the blood rush from her face, and while she tried to hide her shock, her voice held a slight tremor at first. "Can you win enough at Newmarket to make a difference in eighty thousand?"

"If Thune brings in some firsts, we could."

"And if he brings in those firsts, he could be sold for a tidy sum," Duncan said. "O'Donnell got thirty thousand pounds for Ormond last month."

"I didn't know you were planning on selling Thune." She did, of course—all their stable was bred for sale—but she had thought perhaps next year for Thune, since he was only three.

"If he runs well, the time would be advantageous."

Chelsea understood the process, but she always had favorites when the foals were born, and Thune had been one of them. He kicked his heels up only a few minutes after his birth, and Chelsea had known he had spirit. He seemed to understand her when she spoke to him; she could call him in from their most distant pasture by whistling the first bars to "Lass of Lochroyan." And while he was a brute in size, standing seventeen-two, he cantered as light-footed as a small Barb filly.

"We'll have to put bonny blue ribbons in his mane then to show him off," she said. "I'll get up early."

"You rode like a cossack today, lass, and no one's prouder of you than I." Her father's smile fairly beamed.

Stretching as she stood, she looked boyish in faded tan breeches and a Sheltie sweater she'd worn to work with the horses. "I'll win you some money up north, when Newmarket's over. And if you don't sell Thune, he'll be happy to oblige you at York and Doncaster." Her smile was assured, and when she strode out of the room, were it not for her long golden hair, she could have been a stable lad. But her mind was less assured. Eighty thousand, eighty thousand, eighty thousand . . . a merciless litany in her brain. She'd never realized the extent of her father's debt.

Was it possible to win that much racing?

Or was it not?

Thirty thousand for her handsome Thune, she noted in her mind.

Leaving fifty thousand.

The sum strummed through her brain like a vibrating lute string.

Now last week, she wouldn't have known how to get the enormous sum of fifty thousand guineas. Or two days ago.

But now she did. And while she wasn't actually due that sum, for Mameluke had won and Thune had lost, she rather thought she might be able to make some arrangements amenable to both herself and the very attentive Sinjin St. John.

Chapter 11

She noticed the flower scent immediately when she opened her bedroom door, because roses were out of season on a blustery March day that still held a hint of winter. With one hand lingering on the door latch, she slowly surveyed her bedchamber. A small bouquet of white moss roses, placed on the table near her bed, drew her eye in the shadows of her room.

As she walked closer, a familiar awareness touched her, as if the investiture of white roses in her bedroom brought as well the presence of their bestower. There was a card—although she had no need of one—tucked into a fuzzy green branch, deep in the arrangement.

I'M COUNTING THE DAYS TILL MONDAY.

No signature accompanied the brief message, but the ducal crest on the border was evidence enough.

How nice, she thought with a gratified smile, that the beautiful St. John was interested. She was not a mercenary woman by nature —in fact, she'd led an austere existence in terms of luxuries—but the thought of helping her father in such a pleasant manner held distinct charm nevertheless. Had she been more in society, had she been raised to consider the cultural controls on young ladies' sensuality, had she understood that young ladies' sensuality did not, in fact, exist in the rarefied world of noble young misses, she may have considered her undertaking with less joy.

Fortunately, she was not, and she did not, and she fell asleep with a happy smile.

The young Duke of Seth's bedtime pleasure was similarly joyful, although his was not precisely sleep, nor had it direct relation to the blissful dreams of the Earl of Dumfries' beautiful daughter . . . although his bedchamber suite served as site. As was customary for him and his licentious young friends, they were passing the night in various forms of sexual play, the particular amusement of the moment having to do with placing gold guineas in the aptly named honey-pot of an acrobatic young lady standing on her head.

The record had been passed amidst much shouting and exclamation one guinea ago, and the young lady was encouraging more donations with a lascivious account of her sensations.

"Are you tired?" whispered the young lady seated on Sinjin's lap, her dimpled cheeks and rosy lips only inches away. Noticeably inattentive to her or the roguish entertainment, he'd been remarkably quiet all evening.

He looked at her blankly for a moment, her words heard but unregistered in the pleasure of his musing. But he smiled when awareness intruded, and he said, "Yes . . . very."

"Should we go to bed?" Her voice held warm suggestion; her arms, wrapped around his neck, tightened slightly, and she lifted her pretty mouth for a kiss.

Instinctively, Sinjin bent to kiss her, but her lips suddenly didn't feel right. Raising his head, he gazed at her for a second in surprise, as if expecting another face in place of hers. "I *am* tired," he murmured with a small shake of his head. "Forgive me, darling," he added with a gracious smile, "but I'm off to my solitary bed tonight."

"I'll keep you warm," she softly breathed.

"Maybe later, Molly sweet . . ." Sinjin said, setting her aside with an easy strength. "Right now, I prefer my own company." And rising from the padded chaise, he congratulated Lucy—who was seated now, counting her guineas—and bid goodnight to his guests.

"You can't. It's only midnight," protested his cousin Rupert, who slept till two each day.

"I believe in a good night's sleep," Sinjin waggishly said.

"A good night's fuck, you mean," his cousin corrected with a grin.

"The frolic's just begun," another young buck protested as Sinjin moved toward the doorway to his sleeping chamber.

"Have fun," Sinjin cheerfully retorted, "without me then." And he shut the door behind him with a decided firmness.

"What was that all about?" Warwick remarked, his gaze on the closed door to Sinjin's bedroom. "The Saint never sleeps alone."

"He's tired is all," the lady he'd set aside replied. "The man never sleeps during race meets."

"Which is the point," the Duke of Warwick gently said.

"Is The Saint unmanned?" a lazy drawl suggested. And when all eyes swiveled to make out the lounging figure in the unilluminated bow window, the Bishop of Hatfield inclined his head slightly and smiled.

"Not likely, Rutledge," the heir to a Yorkshire earldom snapped.

"It'll give the gossips some new tattle," one of Harriet's ladies said with a grin. "A first now—at least since his sixteenth year—and none of you men with a bet on it in the wager book at Brookes."

"Who would think it possible?" a young cub said with a certain awe in his voice, Sinjin's celebrity with women making him a figure of hero worship to all the young bloods.

"Leave him be," Molly said. "Can't a man be tired?"

And he was, Sinjin realized, falling into his bed, but wearied as well of the lascivious amusements. And curious too to see that George Prine, the blackguard Viscount Rutledge, had joined his party tonight.

Not enemies, but never friends, they knew each other, of course, for the aristocratic world of titled peers was small in number.[3] Still— why had he come?

The question lingered in his consciousness as he fell asleep, adding an unwanted character to his pleasurable dreams of Chelsea. It brought a frown to his brow in his sleep, caused disruption to his normally sound slumber, brought him awake very early with a start.

The damnable Bishop of Hatfield had been standing there in Lucifer's ears and tail, laughing at him.

Chapter 12

The morning was crisp and cool, the puddles in the stable yard covered with a thin sheen of ice. The sun would soon melt away the chill, its warmth already causing an unladylike shine on Chelsea's face as she vigorously rubbed down Thune after his morning run.

"You're on show today, my beauty," she murmured to her favorite pet, sweeping the soft-bristled brush over the roan's silken coat. "So we're to braid pretty ribbons in your hair. And wait for all the bucks to want you for their own."

Thune nickered as though in understanding and tossed his head, showing off his fine profile.

"If you win against the bonny Duke's stable, you'll bring in some gold for Papa's money-lenders . . ." But could he, she wondered, Chiffey or no? Fordham wouldn't be so blasé today, not after their last race. And her brow creased in thoughtful speculation—the eighty-thousand-pound debt a constant in her mind.

How could she politely approach the Duke concerning a sum of that magnitude? What was the normal rate for a week of . . . well, intimacy, and did one send a bill or negotiate in advance? How outrageous would her inquiry seem? Would eighty thousand be pin money to the wealthiest peer in England? She certainly hoped so— although, having taken care of their accounts since childhood, she rather doubted that anyone, regardless of their wealth, would consider eighty thousand pounds a trifle. Minor monarchies probably ran their courts on less.

Preoccupied with her thoughts, she failed to notice the Bishop of Hatfield's entry into the stable yard until Thune turned his head. Her start of recognition was obvious, as was the small scowl crossing her brow. The man had a habit of sneaking up on one.

"I thought I might find you with . . . your horses," the Viscount said, his hesitation emphasizing instead the fact that she was alone.

Having risen earlier than her family, she'd taken Thune out before the rest of the horses had gone for their morning runs, and she was indeed alone, although her father, her brothers and the stable lads would be back soon. And while she wasn't precisely afraid of George Prine, he did give one a sense of unease. As if he were a stalking cat after a mouse. His eyes were cool, calculating grey and watchful, without a hint of warmth. Why would a man like Bishop Hatfield want . . . a wife? Why was he willing to offer such a large sum to her for a marriage settlement when no indication of affection or even friendship shone in those remote grey eyes? And what was he doing here, now, this early . . . after her father had formally refused his suit?

"You're up early," she said, taking note of his disheveled appearance, "or up late."

"I thought I'd take a slight detour on my way home from St. John's at Six-Mile-Bottom and wish you good morning."

"Good morning then." She stood, cautious, her hand on Thune's halter. His ears had gone back at Hatfield's approach as if he'd scented danger. Was the man a friend of Sinjin's after all?

"Sinjin sends his regards," he said as if reading her thoughts. His voice was soft; he stood no more than a few yards away, regarding her. By the merest chance— He'd seen them behind the changing shed yesterday after the race. And watched their embrace, the whispered exchange, their tender kiss. Had Sinjin known, he would have understood the Viscount's appearance at his celebrations last night.

"Sinjin?" Chelsea evasively responded, wondering how much he knew.

"I saw you together at the races." Sly, wicked, predatory, his faint smile struck Chelsea with terror.

"You must be mistaken." She managed to steady her voice although her nerves were on edge like the hackles on her favorite hunting dog.

"You wore a burgundy cloak, I believe, and St. John was in his usual barbaric attire."

"It must have been somebody else, Bishop," Chelsea replied in cool even tones. There was nothing to do but brazen it out; to admit to their intimacy, their kiss, Sinjin's teasing . . . And her heart quickened as the possibility of their conversation's having been overheard struck her. Did this steely-eyed man know of the wager? Had he heard them discuss the repayment? Or perhaps Sinjin couldn't be trusted after all; had he gossiped about— No, she abruptly decided. Not at least to Rutledge.

"Ah . . ." The soft sound implied deliberation, not acceptance. Gazing at her for a considering moment, he responded with one quirked brow and a patently false cordiality, "My apologies, Lady Chelsea, for my error." His voice dropped to the merest of murmurs. "The Duke of Seth is no particular friend of yours then?"

"I only know *of* him."

"As does the world." Her irritation must have showed, for his voice took on an ingratiating smoothness.

"Yes, I'm sure," she noncommittally murmured. "If you wish to see my father or brothers," she went on, determined to terminate further conversation about the Duke of Seth, or anything else for that matter, with a man she despised, "they should be back shortly from the morning runs. Mrs. Macaulay will be happy to serve you coffee or tea, but I'm afraid Thune won't stand quiet much longer. Excuse me." Her requisite duties as hostess accomplished, she tugged on Thune's halter and began moving away toward the paddock.

"You're very lovely, Miss Fergusson."

The small menace in his voice drifted across the sunshiny morning air, incongruous in the peaceful country setting, but distinct and tangible for its discordant note. She turned back to him, intent on concealing her disquietude, and found herself irrationally thinking how heated Sinjin could make one feel uttering those same words. What perversity existed behind Rutledge's chill grey eyes to make one shrink instead from his simple statement?

Standing very still, comforted by Thune's enormous size, she said with the barest civility, "Thank you."

"Your father said you didn't wish to wed any time soon."

"My father has decided to wait another season before seeing me out."

"A shame. Does St. John know that?" His inquiry was delicate, almost a whisper.

She wished suddenly to run from this man, feeling stalked, cornered. His sharp features were sinister, his skin whiter in the bright sunlight, his size ominous.

"You're impertinent, sir," she snapped instead, refusing to show fear to a Sassenach poseur of a bishop who had his lucrative sinecures because his family held political power.

"And you have a devilish fine temper, my lovely. Very heated, provocative . . ." He took a step nearer. "Fascinating . . ." When his hand came out to touch her, she backed away, glanced swiftly across the pasture to see if any help was in sight and, finding none, took a firm hold on the halter and swung herself up onto Thune.

The huge roan curvetted briefly at the unexpected burden until Chelsea settled on his back and gathered up the lead rope. Then, responding to her nudging heel, he wheeled in a flurry of gravel and galloped away, leaving the Bishop of Hatfield alone.

She shouldn't have run she thought, cantering over the downs; she should have stood her ground. But he was about to touch her with those icy cold hands. Ugh. "Ugh," she said aloud to Thune. "You felt it, too, didn't you, my darling brute? The man's cold as a corpse." And when Thune tossed his head in answer, she laughed, relieved to be away, gladdened by the beautiful spring morning, by her escape and by the feel of her favorite horse under her. She rode bareback without a bit, Thune trained to an inch, the slightest pressure on his neck sufficient to direct him. And in the sheer pleasure of riding out on a fresh spring morning with the wind in her hair, the smell of new grass perfuming the air, exhilarating speed pleasurable as the cloudless blue sky, the Bishop of Hatfield's threatening presence dropped away.

They'd be leaving for the races at York after Newmarket.

Chelsea smiled, satisfied and at ease with her life. Her gladsome feelings segued into memories of other feelings of bliss, only recently discovered, memories having to do with a beautiful man with an angel's touch, teasing eyes, a young god's body . . . And she laughed out loud in delight.

It was an era of social change, with the philosophies of Rousseau and Locke and Burke infecting the imagination and culture (which accounted in part for Chelsea's shameless liberality), a time when the Tories were forced to defend age-old policies of political conservatism, a decade in which revolutionary doctrines of democracy had wrested a colonial empire from Britain's grasp. A chrysalis stage of Romanticism in literature, poetry, gardening and the arts, a stage in which the cult of the individual and the concept of personal freedom were touching every segment of society.

Chelsea's father had been educated in France, as had many Scottish nobles over the centuries. So after his wife had died giving birth to Colin, he'd taken his family abroad to escape his poignant memories. They'd lived four years in France before he could find the courage to return to the home he'd once shared with his beloved wife. The tutors had returned with them, some French, some Scots, an Italian doctor from Bologna as well; Chelsea was well read in the newest literature and educated, like her brothers, in the classics.

She was a product of her age and also an anomaly, intensely aware of the new winds of freedom.

But she was still a woman raised in a man's world, with a spirit of independence traditionally allowed only men, preoccupied as well with masculine pursuits.

It was natural for her to disregard the strictures subduing women of lesser spirit.

"He's very bonny, Thune my darling, like a powerful war chieftain of old," she softly murmured, as though Thune were confessor to her emotions. "With eyes blue as the sky . . ." She leaned forward, throwing her arms around Thune's great strong neck, hugging him like the pet he was. "And he makes me laugh."

She stopped Thune on the crest of a hill several miles later to let him rest, and leaning back on his broad haunches, she surveyed the rolling countryside below. Like a pastoral scene depicted by Claude or Lorraine, with a touch more elevation, perhaps, she mentally assessed—the green intensely verdant as only an English landscape in spring can be, the sun bathing all in radiant splendor. She let the peace and tranquility seep into her senses, and savored a sense of security and profound content.

Soon they'd be gone from Newmarket and away from Viscount Rutledge's unwanted familiarity. Thune promised some lucrative winnings this afternoon; the Duke of Seth would no doubt be obliging in terms of some money—although fifty thousand seemed rather too much to expect. All in all, the future appeared rosy indeed. Born and bred on an estate devoted to horse breeding, Chelsea viewed intercourse in rather more mundane terms than the majority of sweet young misses. She'd always considered it a physical act, although Sinjin St. John had rather convincingly altered her conception away

from the mundane. She understood suddenly why centuries of poetry exalted the act and enthused over the subtleties of performance.
There was indeed a great deal to be said for those subtleties, and the
laddie St. John seemed to be proficient in them all.

And as a small sigh of pleasurable memory escaped her lips, a
rider appeared in the distance—a small flash of movement at first far
down the hill-side. But as it progressed nearer, she recognized the
horse, her eye for horseflesh honed to a fine pitch, and as the large
bay and rider began moving up the slope, she caught the gleam of
beaded leather across the rider's shoulders.

She waited then because she had something to ask him.

Not knowing her mind, Sinjin spurred his mount when he first
caught sight of the shining gold of her hair, a telling attribute even
high on the distant hill top. And he coaxed his stallion to more speed
for fear she'd run.

But she didn't.

And when she didn't, he knew . . . she'd decided on the when
and where. An arch-realist, he wondered next what her price would
be, for he'd learned very young all women had their price. Actually,
she'd already set hers before the race, he recalled, a smile forming as
he considered the extravagant sum she'd established as valuation.
Although he supposed the prize of an earl's daughter's virginity came
high.

When he reached her and brought Mameluke to a halt, she spoke
immediately, forgoing any polite social amenities. "Will next week
do for you?"

He would have relinquished the remainder of race week had she
said, "Tomorrow," and such unprecedented eagerness surprised
him. But his feelings didn't show when he said, "Next week is fine."

"Your racing stud at Six-Mile-Bottom will do."

She was certainly plain-spoken, but he preferred a residence more
distant from her family. With her three brothers and father all capable of retaliation, a more discreet locale would be less constrained—
emotionally. "I've a small hunting box at Oakham that would perhaps be less . . . conspicuous . . ."

"My family will be going on to York for the races, so Six-Mile-
Bottom will suit as well. I'd prefer not having to travel and take the
risk of being seen."

"What will you tell them?" he asked, not sure politesse gave him
the right to inquire, but curious when she seemed so complacent.

"I'm visiting a cousin in Uppingham."

"Why not go to my hunting box then? We can travel at night—to avoid being seen."

Chelsea bit her lower lip, and he thought she was debating the venue. She was instead debating how to broach the subject of money. Fifty thousand pounds, to be exact.

Mortifyingly exact.

But then she recalled the dozen or so ladies at Six-Mile-Bottom who were up from London, and she decided the Duke was familiar with the expenses of pleasure. Still she stammered slightly as she began, "If you prefer your . . . hunting box . . . I'm amenable—but—I was . . . wondering—that is . . ." She took a deep breath, looked out over the panorama of Cambridgeshire before her, returned her gaze to Sinjin's face and quickly, before she lost her nerve, blurted out, "Would it be possible to consider this a business arrangement?"

"How much?" he presciently said with a faint smile, familiar with "business arrangements," beguiled by her sudden agitation. How charming she looked, blushing and flustered, riding bareback in a worn skirt and boy's jacket, her booted legs exposed with her skirt hitched up, one pink knee close enough to touch.

She inhaled and held her breath for a moment while he admired the fullness of her breasts constrained by the green velvet boy's coat. Then, exhaling in a great sigh, she admitted, "I can't say it."

"Fifty thousand?" he graciously suggested.

She glanced up sharply. "How did you know?"

"Your wager, darling. Obviously you're in need of fifty thousand."

"I'm not," she quickly interjected, "but my father is, you see," and then it all tumbled out—the eighty thousand he owed the money-lenders, the hopes to sell Thune if he won tomorrow, the deduction for that sale, then the remainder she was hoping she could raise from her . . .

"Business arrangement," Sinjin gently offered when she hesitated over the wording.

"I'd be ever so grateful," she added touchingly, and for the briefest moment, Sinjin considered giving her the money, as a gentleman would, without requiring her company for a week.

The brief moment passed, however, and more selfish motives intervened, having to do with the bewitching young lady short inches away, with rosy cheeks, golden wind-blown hair, an unearthly beauty and a warm spirited nature that somehow seduced more boldly than the most celebrated belles of the Ton.

He would have her. On ungentlemanly terms. At any price.

"Would you like a down payment . . . now?"

"Oh no, I trust you."

Her words were so naive that he experienced a transient pang of conscience—quickly overcome. "In that case, consider the fifty thousand yours at next week's end."

"Thank you very much, Your Grace," she softly said. Her smile was angelic and dazzling at the same time, typical of the curious power she possessed to project both innocence and the most disarmingly opulent sexuality.

And at that moment, only heroic gentlemanly restraint—which proved, he thought, that he at least had a conscience, albeit infrequently used—kept him in the saddle. Of course, it would have been extremely embarrassing for him to stand at the moment, doeskin breeches more a second skin than enveloping raiment. "The pleasure's mine," he softly said with a certain degree of sincere feeling and smiled back at her.

Should she tell him she was flattered? Chelsea wondered, forcing back the chuckle that threatened to explode, aware of the Duke's arousal, equally aware of his unutterably beautiful smile that lit up his eyes, crinkled across his graceful cheekbones, tilted the corners of his mouth. Seductively.

"You're one flashy lad," she said with a grin, her gaze drifting downward suggestively. "Do you think you can wait a week?"

"Hell, no," he lazily drawled, his own grin in place. "Do I have to?"

She leaned back, propping herself on one elbow, looking very small on Thune's broad frame. "I'm verra tempted," she teased, dropping into a soft Scottish burr, her dark-lashed violet eyes traveling slowly down Sinjin's powerful body.

"How opportune . . ." he murmured, his deep voice amused, "for I'm way past tempted. Eager would apply. Avaricious comes to mind . . . just slightly before—attack." And he moved Mameluke up so he could reach her with a caressing hand on her soft pink knee.

The contact of his hand, warm and gentle, sent small tremors through her body. "He saw us," she said, remembering suddenly the man's touch she'd so recently fled. "Hatfield," she added, her voice hushed as her senses responded to Sinjin's palm sliding slowly up her thigh.

The single word arrested Sinjin's progress, and gazing down at her from under his dark lashes, he inquired very softly, "Where?" Rutledge's presence last night was explained.

"At the races, behind the changing shed. I denied everything."

"He came to you?"

"This morning—a short time ago."

"Did he hurt you?" He asked it gently, his hand still warm on her skin, but his voice held a whisper of harshness in its undertone.

"I rode away . . . here. Would he have?" She hadn't realized her own instincts had a basis in fact.

"Will Thune stay?"

At her nod, he threw a leg over Mameluke's neck, slid to the ground and, reaching up, lifted her off Thune. He didn't ask permission and she felt no constraint. His concern was obvious; in fact, he scanned the horizon with a minute scrutiny before taking her hand and leading her toward a small flat table rock. Initials had been carved in the soft sandstone by generations past, and he contemplated them with a brief distracted look before lifting her up and seating her.

"Is he that bad?" she asked as he absently stroked her hands.

Having known George since Eton, Sinjin understood more than he cared to about the perversions of the Bishop of Hatfield. "He was never a normal child," he said at last. "I think his Nanny beat him, or his older brother . . . I'm not sure."

"Father didn't know."

"No . . . I don't suppose he did." His eyes came up and held hers for a long moment. "He likes to hurt things."

"Things?"

"Animals, people who are weaker."

"He shouldn't be a bishop."

"He isn't except for the designation. He only takes the livings. George isn't interested in spirituality."

"We won't be at Newmarket past the end of the week."

"I'll watch you when I can . . . at the races, but—you should tell your father and brothers he came by when you were alone. I'll warn Duncan and tell him some of the stories."

"Tell me."

He shook his head. "Not for lady's ears."

"Do I look like a lady?" Chelsea retorted, piqued at being treated like a child.

Sinjin gazed at her for a long moment in her old tan serge skirt and short boy's jacket, his blue eyes as azure-luminous as the sky. "Oh, yes," he said, low and husky. "Definitely. Absolutely. From a mile away."

His voice touched her like the summer sun, warmed her skin, heated her blood. His fingers stopped stroking her hands and curled protectively around them. "Are all Scottish lasses like you?" he whispered, his question tentative, inquiring beyond the simple query, for he wanted her like a schoolboy, without discipline or reason.

"Are all Sassenachs like you?" she whispered back, lifting her face for a kiss, feeling as he did . . . overpowered and out of control.

His mouth was smiling when he kissed her, and he murmured against the softness of her lips, "All the mamas hope not . . ."

But all the young ladies would be willing, Chelsea didn't doubt—mamas or not. And she swayed into the kiss, wanting to take what he offered.

He moved swiftly to steady her from falling, his hands gentle on her shoulders, and lifting his mouth, he murmured, "You ride the same way . . . recklessly."

"And fast," she softly replied, reaching for the buttons on his breeches.

"And wild . . ." He had the top three buttons on her jacket loose.

"And wild." She wanted him inside her, now, this instant; she wanted to feel the bliss, the hot, drenching rush of sensation.

He lifted her down then, for despite his carnal urgency, he preferred a less exhibitionist position than atop a table rock on the crest of a hill visible for miles. Perhaps too he was protecting himself, an ingrained instinct for the most eligible bachelor in the kingdom.

The grass was soft, the huge sandstone monolith a shield from prying eyes, but Sinjin swiftly surveyed the surrounding landscape like a wolf scenting the wind before he returned his attention to Chelsea.

"There's no one about," she whispered, her jacket undone, her skirt flared out around her, a lush, nubile young maid fresh as spring green grass wanting him.

He recognized that look in a woman's eyes, that heated stage that ignored husbands or too observant servants, the kind that considered garden houses at breakfast routs sufficiently private. The kind that required he keep one foot against the door—which he was eminently proficient at. So he smiled his agreement instead of pointing out that someone could ride up from the far horizon in very short order. And reaching out, he brushed her opened jacket away from her breasts. "You're not cold." A hint of smile played across his mouth.

"Au contraire," Chelsea whispered. She was so warm that the cool breeze was comfort to her bared flesh. Desire burned through her body. He had only to approach her and she wanted him; he had only to smile that slow lazy smile and she melted.

"Are you in a hurry?" He was asking how much time he had, but the lingering trail of his fingers circling her pink nipples distracted her, excited her, conferred a certain ambiguity to his query.

"Yes," she whispered, "and . . . no . . ." A small, languorous smile curved her lips, touched her eyes, lent a bewitching sensuality to the delicate beauty of her face. "And I hope you can accommodate both answers."

"With pleasure," he softly replied, "and beginning with the— yes . . ." he added, his dark lashes half-covering his eyes as he unbuttoned the remainder of the closings on his doeskin breeches. "I'm at your service . . ." His gaze came up and he smiled, warm, open-hearted, beguiling.

She felt a surge of greedy lust travel downward at the sight of his enormous arousal, free now from restraint; she felt herself open for him as he stripped the soft leather of his breeches from his slim hips. His skin was bronzed, his erection pulsing against his stomach, and without preliminaries, accommodating her wish for speed, he pushed her skirt aside, moved between her booted legs and, while she was almost entirely dressed, entered her.

She had dreamed of him last night, she realized as the rigid length of him filled her with tantalizing slowness. The suppressed memory was triggered by the exquisite intoxicating friction, and she trembled at her physical need for him.

Sinjin didn't believe in the supernatural or spiritual, but the level of sheer unmitigated ecstasy bombarding his senses seared his brain, and a tingling shiver of revelation slid down his spine. How did she do this to him? How did this golden-haired lassie so tellingly inflame his sensibilities? Was she some nymph from the Lowlands or a sorceress with magic to make him feel so intensely? But she lifted her hips to meet him then, her hands drifted down his spine and nothing mattered but the feel of her hot and slick around him. Whatever her magic, he wanted it. He wanted her. He wanted this incomprehensible, penetrating, extraordinary ecstasy.

He drove into her deeply as if the answer to his unease could be physically assuaged, as if the powerful rhythm of thrust and withdrawal would clear away the enigmatic conundrum, as if his strength could overcome her bewitching allure.

But she welcomed him, exquisitely soft and wet and hot, her head thrown back in rapture, her breath little panting moans, as though voicing each powerful, surging invasion of her body at the deepest point of penetration.

Each small whimper of sound brought the horses' heads up from their browsing, Thune restless at her familiar voice, which was agitated and unusual to his pricked ears.

Sinjin noted the horses' unease with a swift glance, but simultaneously he felt Chelsea's first tentative shudder of release. She clutched at his face as he began pouring into her; she pulled him down so she could taste his mouth and share the feeling of him from her head to her toes. And she screamed at the last against the soft cushion of his lips, her climax intense, shattering.

Sinjin had experienced orgasm too frequently to dismiss the savage ferocity of his release.

She was a danger to his peace of mind.

She was also sheer unadulterated sexuality—like a pagan rite of spring.

And at the moment peace of mind wasn't even in the running.

She should get up this minute, Chelsea guiltily considered; she should push the irresistible Duke of Seth off her glowing body, straighten her clothes and ride away from this man who exercised his well-known skills too competently, too blissfully and altogether too easily. Her behavior shocked even her own unshockable, vigorous sense of freedom. What would he think of her? It was enough to climb into his bed and seduce him; at least she'd had a perfectly reasonable excuse for that. But to fall so willingly into his arms with no more than a lazy look from those impudent blue eyes . . . well . . . even her liberated sensibilities questioned the inexplicable haste with which she fell to the ground under him like some randy tart. She kept her eyes tightly shut while she tried to think of some suitably blasé statement with which to greet a man known as The Saint for his sexual repertoire—a man currently braced above her.

Nothing came to mind in her disquietude, but she was forced ultimately to open her eyes, because it was even more disconcerting to lie beneath him while pretending he wasn't there. She did then, eventually, timidly.

"I thought you may have fallen asleep," he said with charming grace and that boyish smile she found so adorable. It was obvious that he was lying to put her at ease.

"You must be very used to this," Chelsea found herself saying because he looked so very comfortable and friendly and not at all as his reputation would suppose.

He swallowed the impulse to laugh aloud and said instead, curiously honest for a man who prided himself on suave disclaimers, "Actually, I'm not used to this at all." His dark brows drew together in an uncertainty not too different from Chelsea's. "You're very unusual," he said and, so saying, rolled off her onto his back, tucked his hands behind his head and stared at the bright morning sky with his scowl still in place.

He hadn't covered himself, immune apparently to his half undress, or immune at least to Chelsea's belated sense of propriety. She didn't look at him at first as the silence lengthened, but when he still hadn't spoken after some time, she surreptitiously glanced at him from under her lashes while she brushed her skirt down a fraction to cover her thighs. He was powerfully muscled, strikingly so—a fact she hadn't had time to fully assess the night at Six-Mile-Bottom— and deeply bronzed, so his native fringed jacket seemed appropriate. And, she noted with a small flurry of excitement, immediately repressed, he was still partially aroused; she could see the slow pulsing of the blood in the distended veins of his penis.

"Are you angry?" Her voice was hesitant with his expression so forbidding. But she was curious too about his mercurial mood shift.

He turned his head to look at her, although he remained perfectly still except for that small movement, and his gaze traveled slowly over her body as if suddenly taking note of her. At last, he quietly said, "I'm not sure."

"Did I do something?" Sitting up, she covered her legs and smiled tentatively. "Or not do something?"

He took a considerable time to answer, his gaze dwelling briefly on her breasts, visible beneath the opened jacket. "I'd say you did something." He spoke very slowly, as though still considering the meaning of the words as he uttered them.

"Should I go?"

"No." He answered so sharply that his voice seemed to pin her to the ground.

She smiled then, assured at least her company wasn't disagreeable. "What did I do? Something forgivable, I hope." She unconsciously licked her full bottom lip, a tentative gesture, a small apology in body language.

"Oh hell," Sinjin exclaimed with a swift and dazzling grin. Rolling a half turn toward her, he grabbed her around the waist and pulled her close. "It's not your fault. It's my problem, not yours, and it's not my problem anymore either. It's a grand spring morning, you're the most beautiful creature on God's green earth and I'll consider the practicalities of life when I'm ninety-two."

"If you live that long, you disreputable rake," Chelsea whispered into his cheerful face.

"At least I'll die with a smile."

And he did, and she did, numerous times that morning in the poetical "little death" of the French. And neither allowed thought to intervene—both only recognized blissful sensation. There would be a time later, Sinjin decided, to debate the dangerous attraction of the provocative Miss Fergusson; Chelsea had soothed *her* conscience by placing an arbitrary limit on the singular pleasure Sinjin St. John dispensed. She would enjoy every second, every graceful nuance of his charm, every astonishing new discovery of sensuality, each smile and outrageous impudence of the bonny young Duke until the end of next week.

And then she'd try and forget him, as he would certainly her.

As they parted later that morning at a point midway between their two residences, Chelsea cautioned Sinjin, "Now don't come near me at the races. I mean it. Father will scowl or worse. Who knows about Duncan." She smiled at his mock schoolboy expression of submission and added softly, "Just don't."

A graceful rider, he sat Mameluke with an air of lounging ease, in shirtsleeves now, his fringed jacket looped behind his saddle, his dark hair untied and loose on his shoulders, his smile suddenly appearing as if in obliging capitulation. "I won't talk to you, I won't say a word, I won't even consider the possibility of seeing you. I'll stay in the purdah of my viewing box—far away."

"Are you always so accommodating?" she teased.

"Always." He grinned.

"Which accounts no doubt for your reputation." A touch of unnatural jealousy colored her tone—unwarranted, considering their brief association, and unwanted, but prominent in her thoughts, for she knew exactly how accommodating he could be.

He shrugged, not about to fuel the flames of that combustible subject. "I wish you luck with Thune," he pleasantly said into the small silence that had fallen between them. "Will you be riding?"

Chelsea snorted, the effect disarming for its lack of pretension. Her motley miscellany of clothing suited her, imparting whimsy at the same time it clothed her in a fresh naturalness. "Not likely, unless I can hog-tie the lot of my family. Chiffey's up today on Thune."

"He's the very best. Perhaps you won't need my luck."

"I'll take it just the same." Her voice went very quiet suddenly as she recalled how important each win could be. "You're used to winning. It's not so usual for us."

"Then you're due, I'd say." His tone was light, but his eyes, beneath their shadow of lashes, were purposeful.

Chapter 13

Sinjin came walking up to them after the first race, his expression angelic, his eyes, when they met hers, entertained.

"I couldn't stay away," he immediately said—and Chelsea unconsciously held her breath, bracing herself for catastrophe—"without congratulating you, Lord Dumfries, on Thune's record-setting win."

He'd understood the risk he was taking coming over, but he had to see Chelsea, was thinking and feeling like a lovesick boy. He tensed for a heartbeat, noting the unconscious turn of phrase. No, he promptly corrected, not lovesick, but something close.

And close wasn't love.

"I hope you might be thinking of selling that prime one," Sinjin added, always alert to improving his stable.

"Perhaps," the Earl gruffly replied, any attempt at serious anger toward Sinjin frustrated by his high good spirits after Thune's win.

Turning to Chelsea, Sinjin bowed gracefully, and she was struck with the curious thought that, however close their physical relationship, they had actually never met in public before. Formally dressed in contrast to his customary beaded leather, he wore a forest green coat, impeccably tailored to fit his broad expanse of shoulder. A portion of fawn satin waistcoat, embroidered in citrine and creme, showed beneath it. His linen was crisply white with a casual knot to his neckcloth; fresh doeskin breeches without the grass stains of their morning encounter covered his muscular legs, and gleaming Hessians completed his sartorial elegance. The wind blew a lock of dark hair across his cheek, reminding her of the feel of his hair on her face, and she found herself blushing.

"Your Thune," he said, his smile for the very briefest moment intimate and for her alone, "is a remarkable horse."

"Thank you," she said, fighting to subdue the flush on her cheeks, forcibly suppressing the memory of their morning together, where Thune was a spectator to their amorous play. "I'm sorry your bay didn't win. I hope your wager was modest."

Her father was regarding Sinjin with a watchful eye; both Duncan and Neil had closed ranks like a palace guard when he'd approached. Only Colin gazed at the Duke with open cordiality, unaware of the circumstances relating to Sinjin and his sister.

"In this case it was," he replied. "In others I've been more fortunate."

Duncan caught the suggestion of intimacy and swiftly looked from one to the other.

"How nice for you, Your Grace. You must be lucky."

"I am indeed, Lady Chelsea."

Some friends of her father joined them then—two horse breeders from Yorkshire, another from Lincolnshire—and after congratulations went around, the discussion centered on the next race. The finer points of all the horses in the field were heatedly debated, her father's and brothers' attention drawn away as the handicaps and past performances of various horses were analyzed in minute detail.

"Did you like the flowers?" Sinjin asked, taking care to speak quietly, keeping his gaze trained on the group of men noisily comparing past histories of bloodstock.

"You shouldn't have," she softly replied, her glance cautiously switching from her family to Sinjin. She chanced a smile. "But thank you."

"Do you like violets?"

"Don't." Her whisper was guarded.

"Mrs. Macaulay took a liking to one of my grooms. He's from Scotland. Aberdeen, I think. Do you like violets or not?"

"You're vastly spoiled," she murmured, but her eyes held his for a moment, erasing the rebuke of her words.

"It's a yes then." He was also a discerning man.

"Chel, did or did not Dungannon beat Plutus at Doncaster in '85 in the St. Leger Stakes?" Her father's face had taken on that rosy hue synonymous with the wrangling disputes always going on over racing bloodlines.

"He did," she said. "Over two miles in 3 minutes 45 seconds, Plutus in 3:55, Mayfly third at 4:02, then Javelin and Dorimant."

"I told you, Ballard," the Earl triumphantly said, turning back to the heated debate. "Anyone knows that Tremaine's offspring—"

"Very impressive," Sinjin quietly said.

"Raised in my family . . ." She shrugged. "You live and breathe horses."

"Your father's going to miss you when you . . ." With the word "marry" slightly awkward under the circumstances, he substituted, "Leave home."

"I don't plan on *leaving home.*" Chelsea emphasized the last two words and then smiled up at him. "Every woman isn't looking for a husband, Your Grace, so rest easy."

She was out of her rough clothes now, dressed in a riding habit of scarlet velvet that set off her voluptuous form, the golden hair that he'd tumbled in disarray only short hours ago now coiffed and topped with a small plumed hat, dainty pearl earbobs in her ears, her lips pink from his morning kisses. He rather thought the Earl's beautiful daughter might change her mind when she came out in London next season and every man in the Ton, eligible or not, besieged her. As surely they would.

Which thought immediately served to annoy him.

"No doubt you'll change your mind in London," he said, an unmistakable surly undertone to his comment.

"If I have my way, I won't be going to London. I'll be staying with my family in Ayrshire, taking care of my horses."

"Your father will want you—"

"He may have learned his lesson," she interjected. "Don't you think?"

"Chel, come here. Tell Hart what you were saying yesterday about the tonic for Thune, the one you give him after his run."

"Excuse me," she said to the Duke, her smile polite.

He watched her enter the group of men with a casual familiarity, her explanation instantly garnering everyone's attention.

She was infinitely intriguing, he thought. Not only as a woman, but as an equal. Astonishing reflection. He'd never known a woman before so capable. A faint smile lifted his mouth.

Although what fascinated him, he realistically noted, had more to do with sensation than capability.

. . .

The Earl of Dumfries' horses won all four races that afternoon, the Duke of Seth's stable contenting itself with second place. Sinjin took a certain amount of ribbing, which he amiably accepted. "You can't win all the time," he pleasantly said. But since he normally did, the odds were very favorable for the Fergusson horses.

Chelsea surreptitiously blew him a kiss as she left the course, aware of his part in their victories.

Fordham grumbled a little, but Sinjin praised his virtuoso riding which kept his mounts precisely in second place. A fine line there at a full-out gallop over two miles.

"And it's not for long," Sinjin promised. "Only till the end of the week."

Seneca had perceived the direction of his friend's amorous interest directly after the first race that day, and he only said in caution as they were traveling back to Six-Mile-Bottom, "When you go next week to Oakham, take Jed for your driver. He can be trusted."

"How did you know?" Sinjin sat opposite him in the carriage, his gaze startled.

"You sent staff ahead to ready your hunting box. The hunting season is over, you're like a buck in rut and you've never had Fordham or any of your jockeys pull a race. You lost four races this afternoon. You haven't lost four races in a month before."

"She's worth it." The smile of a satisfied man met Seneca's eyes.

"I hope you don't get shot."

"I can take care of myself."

"Do you want a guard?"

Sinjin shook his head. "Her family's off to the races in York next; she's ostensibly going to visit a cousin in Uppingham. It's only a week—nothing will go wrong."

Seneca pursed his lips, opened his mouth to speak, thought better of it. And then changed his mind. "You're never this . . . irresponsible," he softly said. "All sorts of things can go wrong with a young unmarried woman. You're going to find yourself trapped at the altar. Is she worth that?"

"Trust me. It won't happen. I just can't tell you now . . . why."

"I'd take a guard." After nearly two years of fighting King George's War, both men understood survival, but Seneca had lost his family in the war. It tempered one's defensive responses.

"I don't want a guard. I don't want anyone there. I'm sending Jed back for the week."

"You're going to cook?" Seneca's shock was evident.

"Oh hell, I hadn't thought about that." He was familiar with households run by armies of staff; food wasn't a consideration. He assumed kitchens existed in all his homes, although he'd rarely been in them. "I'll bring food."

"How can she be that good?" Seneca spoke with a masculine bias and vast knowledge of Sinjin's preferences in carnal amusements.

Sinjin's wide grin was a form of answer, albeit general. And then he shrugged. "I don't know. I should know . . . considering—"

"You've entertained a good share of the women in England and on the Continent."

"And in the colonies," Sinjin cheerfully added. "She knows horses."

"And?"

Sinjin smiled again, his mood supremely joyful for a man who'd just lost the only consecutive races since opening his stud ten years ago. "And it wouldn't matter if she didn't know a horse from a badger, to tell the truth."

"There's no hope for you," Seneca resignedly said.

"Probably not." Sinjin's smile was pleased.

Chapter 14

The remainder of the week went equally well.

Sinjin's horses lost by so little that it didn't look obvious.

The Earl of Dumfries won. Money.

Sinjin, too, considered the last days of the Newmarket meet extremely lucrative. In terms of future *quid pro quo* gratitude.

When Thune was offered for sale on Friday, Sinjin purchased him through an agent, not sure the Earl would sell him the horse otherwise. And he left orders to have the roan shipped north to one of his properties.

Flowers were delivered into Mrs. Macaulay's care to the Priory Cottage every day, at times when the Earl and Chelsea's brothers were sure to be attending the races. Violets on Wednesday, with a whimsical note that brought a smile to Chelsea's lips. Rare orchids on Thursday, brought down from the orangery on Sinjin's home estate. Frilled tulips on Friday, arranged in a seventeenth-century blue and white Chinese porcelain tulip vase from his family collection. And on Saturday, after the race meet was over, when Chelsea entered her room very late, flushed with victory and the improvement to their finances, she found yellow roses, delicate single-petaled Austria Copper roses blooming weeks before their season.

A small pouch in white silk, hardly bigger than a fragile rose, was tied by its drawstrings to the neck of the Sevres vase. Slipping the silken cord down, she lifted it free of the vase and opened the gathered top. Inside reposed a natural violet diamond mounted as the center of a thistle-blossom brooch. Turning it over, Chelsea read the small script engraved on the polished gold mounting:

TO MATCH THE EYES OF A SCOTTISH BEAUTY . . .

And on a card tucked deep within the rose blossoms, Sinjin had written:

MY GUESTS WILL BE GONE SUNDAY MORNING. COME TO ME WHEN YOU CAN.

A certain amount of effort was required to see his guests off by Sunday morning. Unprecedented effort, in fact—for Sinjin's Newmarket entertainments generally continued long after the race meet concluded. Often days past the end of the races. Occasionally weeks past.

So when he announced after dinner Saturday night, when the cloth had been removed and the men were sampling his port, that all carriages would be ready in the drive at nine, the clamor of shock and protest was vociferous.

Lounging in his chair at the head of the table, idly stroking the stem of his wine glass, his gaze amiable, he patiently waited for the uproar to subside.

"For those of you who find early rising unattractive," he gently began. Then he went on, "My staff has made arrangements at the Red Lion and the Ram Inn for those who prefer their sleep uninterrupted by a morning call." He'd already given instructions to his steward and housekeeper to see that the staff packed each guest's belongings by this evening, and Harriet's girls had been apprised of the new schedule. "My apologies for this change in plans."

"Some relative die, old man?" Freddie Arbruster inquired, his brows still registering his surprise.

"Not that I'm aware of," Sinjin replied, his smile cordial.

"What's up then," Warwick asked, "to cut short your revels? You ain't liverish?" He wasn't the only guest having noticed Sinjin's withdrawal the last few nights. And Sinjin's style of amusements the decade past could take its toll.

"My health is fine."

"You're not blue-deviled about losing so many races?"

"Not at all." He was obviously cheerful.

"Getting old, old man? Can't take it?" one young blood said.

"If you must know," Sinjin said at last, "I'm leaving in the morning."

"Don't need you here. We'll stay on then," Freddie said.

"No." Sinjin's soft voice held infinite authority.

"Why not?" Freddie questioned. They'd been friends since childhood.

"For my own reasons," Sinjin quietly replied.

"Must be a lady, although that's no reason to keep us in the dark. Don't say you've become discreet." Freddie was clearly shocked.

"None of this is open to discussion. I thank you all for your entertaining company this week past." Sinjin's gaze swept down the table, his smile benign, his expression unreadable.

"We'll have a farewell drink this evening . . ."

Chelsea had broached the possibility of visiting her cousin, Elizabeth, several days past, had mentioned her desire to see her yesterday again and chose an opportune moment after the family celebration round of aqua vitae Saturday evening to say, "Since the journey north with the horses will take some time, I've decided to spend a few days with Elizabeth in Uppingham. I'll meet you in York on Monday next." Horses traveled under their own power to meets, although the hardship of long journeys between race tracks generally kept most horses in their home area. But Newmarket's reputation drew more than its share of outside entries. Chelsea knew the time necessary for travel and subsequent rest for their stable. If she was in York a week from Monday, she'd still have plenty of time to help ready their race entries.

"You're not real partial to Liz, Chel," Neil noted. "If I recall, you usually refer to her as bubble-headed."

"Uppingham's practically on the way. After I help Mrs. Macaulay pack following your departure tomorrow, I'll only have to stay a day or so with Elizabeth. You know she's been issuing invitations for almost two years."

"All of which you've managed to refuse."

Duncan's grin over his glass reminded her of Sinjin's suddenly, and she wondered frantically if he had discovered her subterfuge. "Which also means I can't continue refusing forever. She is, after all, my only female cousin on Mama's side. And I can stand her frivolous chatter for one or two days."

"Your sister's been working hard these past weeks, Duncan," her father interjected. "She deserves a short holiday." Turning to Chelsea, who was seated on the floor near the fire, he kindly said, "Stay longer"—he grinned—"if you can stand the silliness of Elizabeth and your Aunt Georgina."

A small pang of guilt struck Chelsea momentarily; her father's concern and kindness added onus to her own deception. But she considered the fifty thousand that would rid her father of debt reasonable excuse for her pretense. She didn't allow herself to admit that the lure of Sinjin St. John far outweighed fifty thousand gold guineas. Honesty re-asserted itself, however, when she replied, "I don't think my patience will allow a longer visit, Papa. Aunt Georgina is bent on making me a proper lady, for Mama's sake, and she's years too late. And don't feel to blame, Papa," she went on at the sudden anxiety overcoming her father's expression, "I like my life very well."

"Take two of the grooms with you and Mrs. Macaulay, and old Andrew for driver. And don't travel at night," her father said. "I know you're not stupid, but two women traveling are more vulnerable."

"We'll travel only in daylight, Papa," Chelsea dutifully replied.

Her heart was beating so rapidly that she was afraid the sound would be heard, so she began talking about the packing as though any of her family were interested. Very quickly the topic was changed, back to the normal one of horses, and she was able to sit back and only listen, the sound of masculine voices drowning out the pounding rhythm of her heart.

Sunday morning, Sinjin had said in his note.

Impossible . . . with no circumspect way to send a reply until later. Her father, brothers, grooms and horses couldn't possibly be on their way before ten. She would have to arrange all the packing with Mrs. Macaulay; then it would take another two hours at least to issue the necessary instructions to see that the grooms who were left behind knew their duties. Further time would be needed to pack her own things that she'd need for a week with Sinjin. When her family was well on their way with the horses, she intended to tell Mrs. Macaulay of the revised plans: Mrs. Macaulay and the grooms could stay on at the Priory Cottage for a few days more while she went ahead to help Elizabeth nurse Aunt Georgina, who had come down with the smallpox. Since Chelsea had been inoculated as a child, she was in no danger, but she knew Mrs. Macaulay was terrified of the pox. She would tell them Aunt Georgina would send a carriage and groom to escort her, so Mrs. Macaulay could keep their two grooms and Andrew for her needs. On Sunday, Chelsea would meet them at Grantham, whence they would proceed to York.

Now—to have the carriage come and fetch her.

A note to the Duke, sent by a village lad tomorrow morning, would set her plan in motion.

The rest of the evening passed in a blur, her mind devoted to her own tantalizing plans, while her brothers and father talked of York. She answered briefly when addressed, or not at all, and finally when Colin impatiently said, "Chel, are you asleep?" she looked up, said, "I *am* very tired," and escaped to her room.

Chelsea sent the note to Sinjin when she took her morning ride through the village, then returned to ready the horses for their trek north. As she suspected, it was nearer eleven than ten when the stables were cleared of the Fergusson racers and the last sound of hoof-beats had disappeared down the lane. A last wave and some of the tension at the back of her neck eased. The servants would need explanations when "Aunt Georgina's carriage" arrived, but as old family retainers, they were familiar with sudden changes of plan. They were also acquainted with Chelsea's particular style of independence, and a certain down-to-earth practicality was bred bone-deep in the Scots mentality. They would understand her need to go and accept Aunt Georgina's servants as sufficient escort. She turned then to her instructions to Mrs. Macaulay and the grooms and next left to pack her own things, one ear tuned for "her aunt's carriage."

When Sinjin received Chelsea's note, he'd already seen Harriet's ladies off, several grumbling about the early hour until he'd distributed his usual generous gifts of guineas, at which point drowsy-eyed muttering had been quickly replaced by a cheerful alertness. His few remaining guests who'd decided to remain overnight despite the departure hour of nine were still abed.

Taking the note into his library, he threw open the curtains and, dropping into a chair at his desk, ripped open the seal. Chelsea's instructions, written in a small clear script, were comprehensive but coherent, and he smiled as he read her precise definition of each step required of him. He was to send a carriage, two grooms, a driver and a note from Cousin Elizabeth no earlier than noon. The servants were to be coached in their roles, although "relying on servants to sustain this charade is risky. Tell them to converse as little as possible." Since his staff was extremely well paid, the Duke had no fear they would carry off his instructions to the letter. His major problem was finding a carriage not bearing his coat of arms. But since he had till noon, there was time to send to Newmarket for a suitable vehicle.

Any of Sinjin's friends would have been astonished at his deference to a woman. He uncomfortably realized himself that his interest in Chelsea had overstepped his normal casualness. Perhaps forbidden fruit tempted him, he thought. Then, rejecting further refinement on the subject, he decided, hell and damnation, what did it matter as long as he had her?

His guests were roused before times, for he was impatient to see his residence emptied of occupants. They were served breakfast in their rooms to expedite their departure, and finally, at eight thirty-six, he stood alone on his drive, a genial smile of satisfaction gracing his handsome face.

"You certainly drove them out, sir," his major domo remarked with a smile, aware of his master's restless, quixotic elation.

"I did, didn't I?" Sinjin said with untroubled cheer. "Is the carriage here from Newmarket yet?"

"No, sir."

"Tell me immediately it arrives. Have the liveries been modified?"

"Finished, sir."

"I want fresh flowers in all the rooms and everything aired out after last night. Is my traveling coach ready?" His blue eyes seemed to snap for an instant. "Did some of my new shipment of claret get sent on ahead?"

"Absolutely."

"And some of the Hungarian Tokay?"

"Done."

His relief was obvious. "And everyone understands if any gossip issues beyond the boundaries of this lodge about the lady presently arriving as my guest, my wrath will make hell seem a paradise."

"Positively understood, Your Grace." When Somerset had assembled the entire staff to impress this fact on them, his words had convincingly conveyed the Duke's feeling on the subject, enough so that several members of the Duke's household had shivered at the graphic illustrations.

"Good. Thank you, Somerset." And then he grinned. "It's a beautiful morning, isn't it, Somerset?"

"Very beautiful, sir." Somerset chose not to mention that the only times he'd previously seen the Duke up at this early hour were when Sinjin's entertainments had continued through the night—and on those occasions, quite frequent in number, Sinjin rarely viewed the morning with similar enthusiasm. This new lady had wrought some startling changes in his master's life.

The young Duke had slept alone the past week, almost cause for alarm or concern for his health, had not his valet, Pims, mentioned to the steward that His Grace had taken a fancy to someone new. Possibly a lady from the neighborhood, Pims thought, for His Grace had come back from a morning ride in smashing good humor, with the knees of his doeskin breeches discolored from grass stains.

Scanning the horizon in the direction of Newmarket, Sinjin next glanced up quickly at the sun, as if estimating the time.

"It's not quite nine, sir," Somerset offered.

"Yes, it's still early." Sinjin exhaled, paced a few feet, turned back and checked the direction of Newmarket once again.

"Would you like me to send Tom to check on the carriage, sir?"

"No, no . . . I can wait." Flicking a dust mote from the cuff of his buff coat, his gaze lifted again to the Newmarket road. "Oh hell," he exclaimed with a small exasperated sigh. "He can't possibly be back yet, can he, Somerset?" Sinjin murmured, his observation the kind not requiring an answer. "I think that houseful of guests set me on edge," he went on, his impatience evident in his restless soliloquy. "Damnable bunch of rackety people. Can't even get up in the morning without someone hauling them out of bed. I'm going to take a short walk," he abruptly muttered. "Summon me when the carriage arrives." And shoving his hands into his coat pockets, he strode off.

For a man who had devoted a great deal of his leisure time to amusements centered around housefuls of guests and had spent considerably more hours in bed than most of his contemporaries, albeit not sleeping, this new rationale required a moment of assimilation for his major domo. Somerset stalwartly digested his master's new vision and, rising to the occasion, obligingly murmured, "Quite, sir, and I'll summon you directly the carriage arrives."

His words drifted away on the morning breeze, his master already halfway across the gravel drive.

A few moments later, over tea in the housekeeper's parlor, Somerset speculated on the identity of the lady who had the power to so alter the Duke's existence.

"He's not taking staff with him," Mrs. Abbeton archly said, her round little face and button eyes alive with curiosity, "so she must not be a lady. A lady can't manage without a dresser." Sinjin's housekeeper at Six-Mile-Bottom—inherited from his father, as was the estate—knew down to an eagle-eye preciseness the various permutations of gentility or its deficiency regarding the women Sinjin brought to his stud. She mentally charted even the doxies according to rank, several of the leading courtesans of the age having been guests at Six-Mile-Bottom. And Sinjin would have been astounded to know that a record of his celebrated "vigor" lay hidden directly after Genesis—a symbolic placement—in her prayer book.

Mrs. Abbeton, like so many of Sinjin's retainers, held the young peer in slightly awe-struck esteem. He was a distinct opposite to his father, who, while not precisely misanthropic, cleaved to a distinctly formal vision of ducal prestige—the source of much friction between father and son. Sinjin in contrast exuded a warm informality that charmed all ages, genders and social strata.

"Whether she's a lady or not," Somerset reminded Mrs. Abbeton, "our instructions are very clear. She is to be treated like the Queen herself. Have the lilies His Grace had sent down from Kingsway been arranged in the withdrawing room set aside for—her?"

"In the silver vases. Himself has already looked in. 'So many,' he said, but didn't say to take any away. There's a wagonful of lilies in there."

"Well, the room is large and the windows are to remain open, His Grace ordered. We can only hope the lady is pleased."

Intent on following Sinjin's orders precisely, they failed to take into account Sinjin's casual overview.

In the end, Sinjin's racing box resembled an indoor garden, each room, as ordered, displaying large bouquets of flowers, the spring air wafting in through the opened casements, the scented perfumes mingling in welcome.

The anxiously awaited carriage finally arrived from Newmarket, its attendants in newly altered liveries rehearsed their speeches, the specious note from Cousin Elizabeth was placed in the coachman's care . . . and the matched team, prancing in their traces, was at last given its head. Rompish in light-footed excitement for a few steps, they broke into a congruent trot and moved with a rhythmic symmetry down the drive.

Selecting a small summerhouse of Grecian style set on a grassy knoll, its commanding view of the countryside ideal, Sinjin waited, pacing the inlaid marble floor like a caged animal. He checked his

French watch a dozen times before he forced himself to sit down. Only to jump to his feet a moment later. He couldn't deal with the waiting; he had never, in fact, had patience—another bone of contention with his father, who had considered haste a plebeian quality.

Conscious of his extraordinary interest in the young Lady Chelsea, Sinjin had attempted numerous times to mitigate his unnerving desire. He'd even taken one of Harriet's London ladies to bed one night, as he would have unthinkingly in the past—in an attempt to quiet both his uneasy psyche and his friends' increasingly pointed jibes. He'd excused himself instead just short of the bed with a gruff apology to the surprised courtesan and gone outside for a walk.

After much soul-felt deliberation that night, in which he'd scrutinized his entire style of living, he'd come to terms with his uncommon attraction to a young untried maid. Sinjin had pragmatically decided his overwhelming craving for the voluptuous Miss Fergusson need not be over-intellectualized. What was the point, he concluded, in marshaling arguments against wanting someone as lush as Chelsea when he was to have her completely at his disposal for one week? A monk he was not, although, he considered with a wicked grin, the lovely Chelsea Amity Fergusson might strain even a monk's vow of celibacy. And as far as his unusual disinterest in Harriet's ladies—that too had a great deal to do with the delicious Miss Fergusson. She was particularly lush; they in contrast seemed less so. Not a difficult equation to understand. He chose not to take note of the fact that in the past, while female beauty was a consideration, his own libido was rather more interested in consummation. And the concept of sexual abstinence for even a few brief days would have been incomprehensible.

So he paced because it assuaged the excitement he was feeling and perhaps distracted contemplation of the inexplicable. And he contemplated instead—with the gifted genius for inventive sensuality he'd honed to a fine pitch over the last decade—a number of discriminating ways he could please the beautiful Miss Chelsea.

Chelsea, in the meantime, was undergoing a similar intoxicating madness regarding Sinjin St. John, although her feelings were by necessity forcibly suppressed since she was arranging packing with Mrs. Macaulay. But her attention was less than focused, and after Mrs. Macaulay found herself posing the same question for the third time, she asked, "Are you coming down with something now, lass? You've scarcely heard a word all morning."

Jolted out of her familiar reverie—the one with Sinjin's teasing smile only inches away—Chelsea quickly improvised. "The excitement of winning so often at Newmarket is still in my thoughts, Mrs. Macaulay. Forgive me my preoccupation." She *was* thinking of Sinjin, of course, and his part in those victories gave a touch of verisimilitude to her response.

"Well, if your mind is off with your horses, as usual," Mrs. Macaulay replied with an understanding smile, "you might as well get out from underfoot, so I can get about this packing. Shoo, now . . ."

"I should help."

"And if you were helping, girl, I'd let you, but you're more in the way than useful, so scat. Go bother the grooms packing the wagons," she cheerfully suggested. Since Chelsea spent most of her time at the stables like her father and brothers, Mrs. Macaulay was familiar with doing the household duties alone.

So Chelsea walked down the driveway toward the gate, Sinjin's thistle brooch pinned inside her pocket so she could touch it unseen. Her fingers smoothed over the rose-cut diamond, glided over the warm gold mounting, picked out the thistle design with the pads of her fingers, ended atop the small bee perched on the thistle flower. The Fergusson badge adapted to a jeweler's design was an extravagant gift, the natural violet diamond extremely rare, and by rights she should return it. Unmarried women couldn't accept expensive jewelry from men; it suggested something improper. As if anything about their relationship was politely correct. She smiled then at the host of shameless improprieties surrounding their relationship, beginning with her initial proposition in his carriage. So she had every intention of keeping his thoughtful gift—as a memento. His fifty thousand pounds—a shocking impropriety, had she concerned herself about such things—would, by necessity, soon be gone.

Then a sudden unrelated thought struck her as she considered shocking improprieties in general and those of a sexual nature specifically, and she wondered naively whether she should bring some books along. In the juxtaposition of fantasy and romantic idyll, her thoughts drifted over the prospect of seven days together. And she suspected—even the Duke of Seth's reputation notwithstanding—there would be periods during the course of the week when he wouldn't require her immediate presence. She also doubted whether a hunting box in Leicestershire would offer many diversions.

Running back to the cottage, she chose a few of her favorite books and packed them into her portmanteau. She'd just returned downstairs when the spaniels began barking, and a moment later a lacquered blue carriage crested the small rise, making for the Priory Cottage at full speed.

How like Sinjin, she thought with a flare of excitement coursing through her senses; his driver drove as though he was racing for a purse at Newmarket. And typically, too, Sinjin had sent them early.

Pandemonium reigned for several minutes as the coach careened into the yard and came to a spectacular halt in a spray of gravel. The spaniels barked as if their noise alone would hold the rearing horses at bay, while Mrs. Macaulay shouted at them for quiet. The grooms came on a run from the stable yard to investigate the uproar. Chelsea stood in the shadow of the doorway for a moment, gathering her courage. And if the prize of fifty thousand guineas hadn't been pledged her, she doubted for a frantic minute whether her bravery would have sufficed to play out the drama. It was one thing to plan out a deceit; it was quite another to brazenly act out the fraud. But her goal was quite plain. The Duke had guaranteed a debtless future for her father; for that she could act on the stage at Drury Lane.

"I'll see what they want, Mrs. Macaulay," Chelsea said, walking out onto the porch.

She showed the proper amount of surprise, she thought, when the driver handed her the note from Cousin Elizabeth. She read it thoroughly with all eyes trained on her, then announced the serious content of the note in a suitably grave manner.

Immediately backing away, as if in fear the pox had traveled from Uppingham, Mrs. Macaulay and the grooms stood well off. Even the dogs seemed to sense the servants' apprehension, scuttling back under the porch for security.

"I'll finish packing my things," Chelsea mendaciously said. "Mrs. Macaulay, would you ready a basket of food for the road?"

The grooms carried her portmanteau down a short time later, but only to the top of the stairway. From that point, Sinjin's servants took over, assisting Chelsea into the carriage and strapping her small trunk onto the back. The arrangements to meet at Grantham had been discussed swiftly in the kitchen while Mrs. Macaulay packed the food.

"Wait for me here and I'll send you a message with the exact date to meet at Grantham."

"What if the poor woman needs you, miss . . . beyond next week?" Mrs. Macaulay questioned, knowing the Earl was expecting them at York. "Or maybe—your aunt might . . . die."

Chelsea immediately soothed her fears, no acting necessary to sound convincing. "Cousin Elizabeth says Aunt Georgina is past the crisis already, so she won't die. Elizabeth is simply in need of another nurse to help her after caring for her mother so long."

"Very well, Miss Chelsea, we'll wait for your message," Mrs. Macaulay quietly agreed.

How well she deceived, Chelsea thought with a stab of remorse.

"Or I . . . could come . . . with you—if you have need," her housekeeper added with an unselfish charity, considering her morbid fear of smallpox.

Another wave of guilt at her subterfuge inundated Chelsea's thoughts, only to be overcome almost immediately by an irrepressible elation. And while the money for her father offered newfound security for her family's finances, she was honest enough to admit that, now that her faint-heart had been overcome, she was *vastly* looking forward to seeing the charming Duke of Seth.

Handed into the carriage by a groom whose eyes she dared not meet, Chelsea sat back stiffly, her hands clasped in her lap, until the door snapped shut and the carriage began to roll. Then she let out a stifled breath of deliverance and, leaning out the window, waved to her retainers.

She didn't smile unduly, for it wouldn't be proper under the circumstances, but beneath the white lawn of her bodice, her heart was beating a wild tattoo.

Chapter 15

The sun glinted off the blue lacquered carriage as it broke from the trees into the open road fronting the pastures some distance away, giving Sinjin sufficient time to return to the house and summon his staff. When Chelsea stepped down from the carriage to Sinjin's outstretched hand and welcoming smile a short time later, he greeted her as he would an honored visitor.

She was surprised at first, and then touched, as he introduced her to his entire staff lined up before the house like crack troops. In very much the manor born, he conducted the welcoming ceremonies as he would with any peer of the realm, offering her in that studied gallantry, the respect of a guest. He could have done otherwise; he could have treated her as his paramour.

"Lady Chelsea will need to refresh herself," he said to his housekeeper, who immediately snapped to attention with surprising briskness for a small chubby woman.

"Do you beat them?" Chelsea inquired sotto voce, her violet eyes twinkling up at Sinjin. The Fergusson retainers, more family than servants, were apt to give advice sooner than take orders.

"Never in front of guests," he murmured back, "so they're safe as long as you're here. Show Lady Chelsea to her withdrawing room, Mrs. Abbeton," he said aloud.

"Do I have to go alone?" Chelsea breathed, half in jest and half in earnest, the full phalanx of Six-Mile-Bottom retainers daunting.

"You don't need privacy?" Sinjin asked.

"Darling," Chelsea said in a normal voice—her endearment causing even the imperturbable Somerset a moment of breath-held shock, for Sinjin rarely displayed affection before his staff—"I only drove three miles to arrive here. I've not been on the road for a week. I would dearly love your company"—her voice dropped into a soft whisper—"although privacy would be high on my list—later."

Sinjin grinned and, bending down, kissed her in front of his entire staggered but entertained staff. Lifting his head a moment later, he said, "Thank everyone, Somerset. You may dismiss the staff. Mrs. Abbeton, we'll have luncheon soon. Where?" he asked Chelsea, taking her hand in his.

"I haven't the vaguest idea." With her hand in his, she felt suddenly as though the universe had turned rosy and rainbow fresh.

"Do you like lilies?"

"I love lilies."

"We'll have luncheon with the lilies," Sinjin instructed Somerset, "and my usual too," he added.

When Sinjin opened the door to the parlor set aside for Chelsea's withdrawing room, she gasped.

The majestic room—high-ceilinged, painted on the walls and dome with murals by Romano depicting Neptune and sea sprites, resplendent with ormolu molding, carpeted with a Gobelin of gigantic proportions—was eclipsed by the dramatic display of lilies in shades of creme and saffron and pale yellow, disposed in lush tropical abundance on tables, consoles, tripods, mantelpieces, windowsills—in short, everywhere.

"How very lovely," Chelsea said in a small voice.

"I only said lilies," Sinjin remarked lightly.

"Were you shouting or threatening anyone at the time?"

He laughed. "Apparently. Is this too overpowering? Wait here." And swiftly turning, he strode down the hall, looking into each room as he went. Short minutes later when he returned, his smile touched his eyes as well. "They must have savaged every garden within miles. Come look. It's all for you."

And Chelsea was charmed by the concern both Sinjin and his staff had expended on her account. The entire house was splendidly adorned with bouquets of every size, dimension and color.

"Thank you," she said with a sweet smile as they stood in the doorway of the last room viewed. "I'm vastly overwhelmed."

"Well, then it was worthwhile," he teasingly replied, "for I'm definitely interested in overwhelming you."

"You do that pretty well all on your own."

Her straightforward directness enchanted. A week, he thought with enormous satisfaction. Seven days, one hundred sixty-eight hours, ten thousand-some minutes . . . His smile could have charmed the angels from the sky. "I'm very glad I met you," he said, his voice low and husky.

"I know it's not at all proper to say," Chelsea murmured, gazing up at him, "but I'm glad too." And she reached up on tiptoe to brush a kiss on his chin.

They had luncheon—salmon verte, asparagus, apricot tart, pine-apple ice ("Something a lady would like," Sinjin had ordered)—amidst the lily garden, the scent surrounding them like the anticipation that hovered beneath the serenity of their words. Neither ate much, the taste of expectation sweet.

Sinjin drank a pear brandy he'd discovered in a mountain monastery in the Pyrenees. And due to a sizable yearly donation to the upkeep of the monks' chapel, he was the recipient of a dozen cases of the eau-de-vie each season. He favored it on languorous afternoons, its perfume redolent of spring in the mountains.

Chelsea sipped on chilled champagne from a Persian glass of great antiquity. And when she remonstrated at using the fragile glass so mundanely, Sinjin only smiled. "Darius, with his eye for beauty, would approve. He knew horses too."

"Are the two critical tastes parallel?" Chelsea inquired with amusement.

"No," Sinjin gallantly replied, "but both susceptible to strong emotion."

"Are you feeling emotional then?"

"Oh definitely." His grin lazily lifted the perfection of his mouth, his voice soft as velvet. Under any circumstances she roused him, but here in the solitude of his home, lounging on a gilded Louis Quatorze settee, surrounded and framed by opulent lilies, she exuded an explicit freshness as if in contrast. She wore a simple bodice of lawn, the thistle brooch he'd had made for her pinned at her throat. Her golden hair was pulled back with a green ribbon, her ears without adornment. If the gods could fashion natural beauty to dazzle the world, they would do it in her image.

"Should we just stay here then?" she said, as if reading his mind —or, in fact, reading his eyes.

"I don't think so," he answered simply. "I can wait."

"But then," she said, like a young pagan sorceress, sweetly and genuine, "you've had more practice."

He didn't want to disabuse her. He had had no practice at all in "waiting" until she'd come into his world. She was revealing to him a character he hadn't known he possessed.

"Eat something," he suggested, his smile gracious. "This is too close to the Priory Cottage. We'll leave for Oakham as soon as the daily stir of business abandons the roads."

She thrust her bottom lip out like a young pouting child. "Entertain me then," she insisted with a hint of a moue before she smiled across the luncheon table.

"Would Bach do?"

"You play?" Her gaze took in the inlaid harpsichord near the windows.

"Occasionally, for amusement."

"Do you know any Scottish airs?"

"A few," he said, not elaborating on the reason Scottish airs were in his musical repertoire. Cassandra would practice at times in the morning when he was still abed, her husband partial to Scottish airs. Many mornings he'd wander into her sitting room and drink his coffee and listen while she perfected her technique. For their amusement, she'd parody the lyrics at times, her elderly husband of course bearing the brunt of her ridicule.

"Play 'The Broom of Cowdenknows.' "

"And then you'll be content?"

"Temporarily," she said with a grin.

He played for her, moving after a time from the Scottish airs she'd requested—his repertoire limited by Cassandra's—to Bach and then Haydn, his long slender fingers effortlessly gliding over the keys. With Sinjin dressed like a country gentleman in unornamented buff superfine and chamois, his hair sleek behind his ears and tied with a plain black ribbon at his nape, his boots polished but worn, Chelsea forgot for a moment the sumptuousness of the room and the imposing splendor of his title and fortune. She forgot for a time that afternoon, listening to his music and basking in his smile, the motive that had brought her here today.

He could do that to a woman. Make her forget everything but his pleasure and her pleasure. She wondered how long it took to master that unassuming skill.

She fell asleep like a puppy under the spell of the scented lilies and champagne and graceful music. And he kept playing so she could sleep. And he could watch her.

Somerset opened the door once discreetly, but Sinjin put a finger to his lips and shook his head. Time enough to leave when she woke. There was pleasure in the simple proximity of the rosy-cheeked Miss Fergusson. He was content.

They journeyed that evening to Oakham through a spring evening so magically moonlit, so redolent of flowering flora, so peaceful and silent that Chelsea teased Sinjin that he'd ordered the poetical world as lyrical preface to their week together.

He was aware in an unusually perceptive way that her high spirits and her envisioning of their week together in romantic terms, while different perhaps from his, struck an agreeably affectionate nerve all the same. While carnal thoughts were never far from his mind in proximity to the delectable Lady Chelsea, he found himself enjoying her company.

"Since we're obliged to travel at night, I thought a suitably silver moon of vast proportions was called for," he facetiously replied. "I'm glad you approve."

"Are you always so charming?"

"No," he answered honestly. "But you're always beautiful," he added with a grin, "so I have the advantage . . ."

"Douec gratus eram tibi," she murmured, then translated ironically, "so long as I find favor in your sight." She lay back against the padded seat opposite him, composed, tranquil, assured of her beauty.

"Where did you learn Latin?" His had been beaten into him at Eton.

"At home from my tutor."

"Lucky man," he automatically replied, sure Chelsea's tutor must have had trouble keeping *his* mind on Latin grammar. "But why Latin?"

"He was very old," she said. "And why not, pray tell?"

Infinitely lucky man, he licentiously thought, his mind taxed with the image of a young beautiful Chelsea and her Latin tutor—however old. "Forgive me," he apologized. "Why not, indeed," he graciously agreed, although the women of his acquaintance were not generally proficient in Latin. As a man of his time, he generally considered women as the lesser sex, viewing them as amusements, breeders, overseers of households, their beauty forgiving them their dearth of intellect.

But Chelsea didn't neatly fit any of the norms.

"Why should only men study Latin and Greek?" she inquired, her question oddly incongruous with her sensual lounging pose, her froth of golden hair pulled loose from her ribbon in provocative disarray.

"You know Greek also?"

"Yes. Is that so strange? My mind works as well as yours."

"Women usually don't, that's all," he simply said, stating a fact rather than being argumentative.

"Some women don't."

"Most women."

"A pity then," she dryly retorted.

He gazed across the carriage at her, his face fitfully lit by the small carriage lamp, his eyes speculative. There were blue-stocking women, of course, but he didn't move in their circles—finding them too serious. And while Chelsea displayed a remarkable independence, she didn't strike him as a woman of the blue-stocking mold . . . although she was unusual in many ways. "You breed horses, you ride at race meets—and very competently, I might add . . . you damn near took Fordham—you know the classical languages . . ." As if trying to place her somehow within the normality of her sex, he asked, "Do you have any of the usual feminine accomplishments? Besides that," he added with a grin in response to her arch glance.

"Meaning?" She wasn't adversarial, only curious about what he considered feminine accomplishments.

"Embroidery, for instance."

"Does Cassandra embroider then?"

He was nonplussed for a moment at both her candor and his inability to answer her query.

"You don't know," she said after a small silence. "Which only goes to show," she added with a dazzling smile, "how unimportant embroidery is."

"Touché," he admitted, his own smile warm and inviting.

And they chatted then about the interests that were important to them: their horses; the race meets; the hunt season; salmon fishing in Scotland. The Duke had a small barony, inherited from his grandfather, where he went for fishing. Chelsea, he discovered, played the lute. He would have one sent up, he said, and they could practice Mozart together. She painted—mainly horses—and following Stubbs' methodology, she'd once dissected a horse that had died in order to improve her technique.

A singular woman, Sinjin found himself thinking on more than one occasion as they conversed in easy friendship.

He was totally unassuming, Chelsea discovered, although he was accomplished in so many areas. His estates were experimenting with the rotation of crops. He'd traveled extensively on the Continent, as had any young man of fortune. They compared their memories of Paris. He was organizing the dredging of a canal connecting three of his estates so he could more easily move his horses between meets. He'd spent almost two years in the colonies during the campaigns and had traveled the Near East and North Africa in search of bloodstock.

"I'm planning on going again to Tunis . . . perhaps in the fall. A friend sent me word of a phenomenal Barb owned by one of the desert chieftains. Perhaps I can persuade him to sell the animal where others have failed."

"How old is the Barb? Have you been there often? Are there lions in the wilds and harems for the women? Do desert chieftains look like the etchings in the travel books?" Her questions came in a rush of curiosity.

All of which he answered, with anecdote and colorful detail that brought the North African landscape vividly alive. She sighed a little when he finished. "I envy you your travels," she said.

While her sex wasn't a deterrent, for English women traveled everywhere in the company of their servants, she'd never had the necessary financial resources. "Perhaps someday . . ." she wistfully murmured.

He told her more of his travels then, describing in some detail his journey from Acre to Tunis. It seemed, when they arrived at Sinjin's hunting box, that they'd known each other for a very long time.

When the carriage came to a halt before a rambling red brick structure of Elizabethan design, with high peaked gables and dozens of chimneys, with the morning sun gleaming off its mullioned windows, and the soft green hills of Leicestershire gently falling away to the south, Sinjin pushed open the carriage door and leaped to the ground.

"Hurry," he directed, spinning swiftly around to take in the bright morning scene. And when Chelsea stood at the door of the carriage a moment later, he opened his arms, smiled and said, "Jump. I'll catch you."

She fell into his arms in a flurry of tartan plaid and rose perfume. Swinging her up so she was comfortably settled in his arms, he kissed her, a gentle welcoming kiss.

"I know you," she murmured, her words an assurance of her unspoken feelings of delight, her dark eyes joyful beneath his gaze.

"You're perfection, lass," he whispered, his mouth touching the tip of her small straight nose, the simplicity of his compliment voicing his own content.

He grinned then in his familiar roguish way. "I think you're going to like this place."

"I already do." Her own smile was bright as the morning sun.

Chapter 16

His hunting box was like his race house at Six-Mile-Bottom—grander than most, larger than most, filled with centuries of exotic furniture and art brought back by wandering St. John forebears. Unlike the newer Palladian structure at Six-Mile-Bottom, though, Sinjin's Elizabethan hunting box had cozy small rooms with low ceilings, linen-fold paneling exquisitely preserved and a rabbit warren of hallways, stairways and meandering additions attributed, too, to former St. Johns with a love for building. Light through colored window glass illuminated the interior with a jewel-like iridescence which flickered over the rich reds of Turkey carpets, catching the gleam of gold, brilliant indigo, deepest carmine and the greens of summer in the embroidered upholstery, casting a soft sheen over the polished floors and ornate woodwork.

A richness imbued the atmosphere; an imperishable sense of place whispered through rooms that had housed generations of St. Johns and would be home to generations more.

"This wasn't always a hunting box," Chelsea said much later after their tour of the house, after their luggage had been carried in and the drivers had left. They were seated in a small parlor with a breathtaking view of the green valley to the south, sipping steaming tea—Sinjin's laced with brandy—smiling at each other, feeling an untroubled serenity.

"Long ago it housed the first St. John to travel to Russia for the

Queen. Needless to say, after his voyage to Muscovy, he returned a much richer man and built himself a more majestic residence at Stamford."

"Kingsway." Everyone knew of Queen Elizabeth's minister who continued to add to his Renaissance palace during forty years of service to the Queen.

Sinjin nodded. "I prefer this old house when I'm in Leicestershire. My family oversees Kingsway."

"You don't live there?"

"I have an apartment there."

Apparently he didn't choose to elaborate on the fact that his ducal residence didn't serve as his home. Disinclined to pry, Chelsea instead commented on his skill with tea. "I didn't think an august duke would know his way around the kitchen so well." He had in fact surprised her.

"Steeley, my nanny, let me wander into the kitchen as a child. I think she had a *tendresse* for the butler. I think, too, he was married, which just goes to show"—his mouth quirked sportively—"that amorous liaisons aren't the prerogative of the beau monde."

"And you learned how to make tea when you were three," Chelsea teased, not about to touch the subject of illicit liaisons.

He shrugged. "Among other things. Cook took a liking to me, and my parents felt their duty was accomplished once the nursery staff was in place." He smiled a smile of remembrance, its faint melancholy not wholly concealed. "Although," he went on, the good nature in his expression restored, "we're going to have to acquire some staff. While our food has been more or less arranged, no one apparently dared to make mention of the necessary cleaning."

"I'll help."

His surprise showed. No women of his acquaintance would know how to wash a dish. "Thank you," he graciously said, "but to be perfectly honest, I don't want to take the time . . ."

Chelsea understood immediately, for his voice had grown husky at the end and his vivid eyes held hers now in a familiar inviting look. "We could have some local people come in for a few hours a day. That wouldn't be too intrusive. Do you know anyone?"

"Normally there's a staff here." He grinned. "You see how besotted I am . . . I wanted you only for myself."

"I didn't want to appear . . . unladylike," Chelsea replied, setting her teacup aside, "but I . . . well . . . It's very hard to be near you for hours—the closeness of the carriage . . ." She stopped, not knowing how brazen she was allowed to be before even the infamous Duke of Seth might think her shameless. Her dark lashes dipped for a moment in an ingenuous brief shyness, for she was away from home—alone with a man for the first time in her life.

"Go on . . ." Sinjin softly prompted, charmed by her manner, by her fresh natural beauty, by her artless wanting of him.

Her lashes lifted at the sound of his voice. Gazing at him across the low-ceilinged room, she told him her feelings in the simplest way possible. "I've wanted to be held in your arms ever since you left me last. Please hold me again . . ."

Never since Catherine years ago had he been petitioned so sweetly, and shaking away the small poignant stab of memory, he gently said, "Let me show you the view from my bedroom." Rising, he held out his hand.

The splendid state bed almost filled the small room, the canopy and headboard intricately carved, the hangings embroidered for one of Queen Elizabeth's visits.

The silk bedcurtains were creweled in flamboyant flowers and vines, the colored silks still brilliant against the navy silk, the inside of the curtains more subtly shaded in a soft gold. Enormous milkweed puffs as delicate as nature's own adorned the corners of the canopy— a tribute to the exquisite talent of a master woodcarver.

And a pair of gilded steps offered access to the enormous bed.

A cabinet, two stands and a table in the finest of French floral marquetry had been purchased by an ancestor from the Gobelin's workshop of Pierre Gole, the principal furniture maker to Louis XIV. Their elegance complemented the state bed, lent further richness to the small room, embellished the jewel-like character of the interior.

"How cozy," Chelsea said, thinking even as she uttered the words how incongruous her emotional reaction was to such splendor. But the room was a chamber rather than a public room, the bed like a lush silken flower, the furniture not so much objects as objets d'art—everything resplendent with rainbow colors and rich surfaces.

Standing just inside the door, she turned back to Sinjin, who stood on the threshold, his gaze not on the room but on her.

"I've often thought so," he said with a smile, amused at her descriptive word but understanding the essence of her feeling. He'd chosen this room years ago for the colors and the human dimensions. "You should try the bed," he added, his voice oddly calm. "It was Queen Elizabeth's when she stayed here."

"Oh . . ." Chelsea's mouth formed the soft round sound, her

lush lips immediate temptation to her host, who found his tranquility abruptly shattered. "Do you think of her when you sleep here?"

He hadn't, of course, virgin queens outside his emotional sphere. "Sometimes," he lied because her breathless response seemed to expect an affirmative answer.

"I knew you would." Chelsea's smile appeared with such suddenness it generated a strange excitement, as though her vitality touched him across the small distance. "Are you going to hold me now?" she quietly said, standing very still, a blush coloring her cheeks. She'd tried to be more blasé; she'd tried for a moment to match Sinjin's composure, but this was all very new.

And Sinjin St. John excited her.

"Oh yes," he said, his voice strangely hushed. He moved toward her soundlessly like a great dark panther and lifted her into his arms. Smiling into the violet depths of her eyes—only inches away—he whispered, "I'd like to lock you away . . . and keep you for myself alone. And I'm raving mad, I think," he went on, his smile so close it warmed her, "to be saying this."

"Feel me . . . I'm trembling," Chelsea murmured, "because I want you so. And I must be mad too, because I shouldn't be here at all."

"But you are," he said, the words oddly a statement of possession.

A shiver ran through her—of anticipation and need, Sinjin's strength and power, his casual holding of her without effort an aphrodisiac. "And I can't leave . . ."

Their eyes met, the message one of mutual desire—more—feverish, vaulting urges trembling on the brink.

"I wouldn't let you go," Sinjin said, a peremptory sovereignty beneath the hushed reply, "even if you wanted to." He was moving toward the bed, wondering if he could indeed keep her somehow, astonished at his outrageous sentiments, but astonished more at the overwhelming violence of his feelings. "I don't know if I can be gentle," he warned, an uncustomary wildness flaring through his senses.

Her answer was a fierce kiss that ate at his mouth, captured his tongue and, greedy for the feel of him, drew it into her mouth, her hands on his face as compelling as her kiss.

And when her mouth lifted long moments later, she murmured, "I *know* I can't be gentle, so be warned."

They were like wild young animals that afternoon in the jewel of a room—frenzied, rapacious, insatiable, their need for each other unquenchable.

And much later, when Sinjin left the bed to open the window and let in the cool evening air, he stood before the casement, his sweat-sheened body gleaming in the twilight, his breathing ragged, his mind in tumult.

Languid from sexual excess but heated still from within, Chelsea gazed at Sinjin's tall form outlined against the lavender sky and understood the meaning of enchantment. She hadn't known before how desire could command one's mind and body, could make one burn with such need that the world disappeared. She hadn't known until today just how much Sinjin St. John could make her want him.

"Come back to bed," she softly said to the man braced against the window frame.

No, he thought, I shouldn't. It unnerved him that he wanted her so, still, yet . . . after half a day. An out-of-control feeling . . . and this from a man who had always considered women in the plural as a diversion—a *temporary* diversion.

"Come back to bed," Chelsea said again, moving so he heard the sound of her legs brushing against the sheets—the legs that wrapped around him and kept him deep inside her, the slender pale legs that tasted of rose water and heated passion.

He stood for a moment more with the damp air cooling his face and body, knowing he should break away because no woman should be this important. "Please?" she whispered, and he relegated reason to temporary exile, forcing away his unease because he wanted what he wanted. And he went to her like an adolescent driven by lust, pulled her into his arms and just held her while he willed his hands to stop shaking. "Will it ever end?" he whispered, uncertain of everything but his obsession for her.

"Ask me later," she whispered back, driven by her own urgencies, lifting her mouth to his, opening her legs to him. "I don't know now, I can't think, all I know is I'm on fire and I need you inside me . . ."

They lost track that night of who needed whom, when and how and to what degree, but they understood the finite nuances of sensation by morning and the incredible wonder of passion in accord.

When the sun first colored the sky, with both of them dressed only in robes, Sinjin carried Chelsea through the quiet corridors, down the stairs to the kitchen door and out to the stables . . .

Very early . . .

When the dew-drenched grass was cool on his bare feet and the sun still clung to the horizon . . .

"I have a present for you," he said, stopping by the pasture fence.

"For me," she said, in coy teasing affectation, kissing him with lingering warmth on his neck as she snuggled close to his warm body.

"You deserve it," he said, thinking she deserved the treasures of Aladdin's cave as well and the gold of Peru and the entirety of the pearls of the Orient for her rare exquisite sensuality. His smile was the smile of a contented man who no longer questioned every rule in paradise.

He turned her slightly so she could see the rolling field to the west where Thune was grazing. "He's yours," he simply said, and her eyes opened wide for a moment before her violet gaze lifted to his.

"It's too much."

She was right. It probably was, but her face was alive with joy and it was money well spent.

"Maybe I could pay you back someday," she said.

He grinned. "Maybe you could."

"I didn't mean that." His grin was infectious, though, and she found herself smiling back at him. "Does everything have a sexual connotation for you?"

"This week it does." And he meant it not only in a teasing way but in the disquieting way that had plagued him all night. Despite his reputation for sexual excess, women had always played a relatively minor role in his life. Certainly in his thoughts. But not Chelsea: his consuming need was insatiable, her image perpetually in his mind.

"From what I hear," she said, reminded of his dissipation, "it's *every* week. According to gossip, your largesse is limitless." And after last night, she should know. The cold light of morning perhaps tempered her mood or the practical reminders of his fame.

He sobered at the sudden distance in her eyes.

"Don't believe everything you hear," he quietly said.

"Even if I believed only half of what I hear, your exploits are . . . monumental."

"Then don't believe that much." He was tired in general, physically fatigued and weary as well of defending his life from the gossip and tattle of the broadsheets and the righteous. "Look," he said with a small sigh, "I don't know why my life is of interest to so many

people. I never deceive anyone or dissemble or pretend. My friendships with women are mutually agreeable"—his lashes lowered
briefly in deference to the past night—"cordial and"—he paused,
searching for a benevolent word—"non-exclusive. Why my love life
should be of such consuming interest to every tabby in town aston-
ishes me."

But not me, Chelsea thought. He was truly unaware of his potent
attraction, and she suspected even those old tabbies would purr un-
virtuously if Sinjin were to look their way.

"There's no need to take issue," she said, aware of their brief
time together, reminding herself why she'd come to Oakham.
"Whether you keep every woman of beauty in London happy is your
business."

"Don't," he muttered, his voice rumbling deep in his throat. "I
tell you, it's mostly idle gossip."

At least he had the honesty to qualify his statement, and apparently he didn't keep count. She had overheard Duncan telling Neil
last week that The Saint was the stud of choice for every woman over
fifteen, that the scented billets-doux arriving at Seth House each day
kept one secretary busy sorting them into appropriate designations
for the Duke's perusal.

There was no argument why he was in such demand. She had
come to him knowing what a week at Oakham implied—wanting
what a week at Oakham offered. It was a little late for piety. And
while she might resent his universal appeal, she understood perfectly
the overwhelming measure of his charm.

"Forgive me," she said, "for speaking out of turn. Your life is
your own and I've no right to comment. Friends?" she inquired,
smiling up at him.

Her sincerity always staggered him; he'd been too long in the
brittle world of the Ton, where no one meant what he said—or at
least not for long. "Definitely friends," he quickly agreed, his grin
playful. "Now shall we go for a ride?"

In that simple phrase he was offering her a degree of pleasure
only superseded by the pleasure she found in his arms, for riding was
her life, Thune her favorite horse. And Sinjin St. John the most
pleasant of companions.

They rode often that week, sometimes in the pale mist of morning, sometimes slowly in the heat of the afternoon, occasionally very
late at night—to cool their bodies from the heated glory of their
passion. They raced too at times, matching Thune against Sinjin's

magnificent Mameluke, trading victories on the valley flat with wildly racing hearts and an intoxicating exhilaration.

Sinjin's size was a handicap when pitted against Chelsea's slight weight, but Mameluke was used to carrying him and Mameluke liked to win, so the heats were democratically won over the course of the days—both riders generous in victory, indulgent in defeat, their affection for each other unselfish.

Sinjin *had* refused to clean when the actual necessity arose, his privileged background unfitting him for the mundanities of the world. So his staff was recalled almost immediately, and his life settled into the comfortable ease to which he was accustomed.

"I really don't mind washing the dishes," Chelsea had said at the time.

"No," Sinjin had abruptly retorted that first morning, searching for a fresh shirt in a bewildering array of clothing still in his portmanteau. "I didn't rearrange a dozen people's schedules to be with you this week in order to watch you wash dishes. Lord God, where the hell is a clean shirt!"

"You look like you need help," Chelsea had cheerfully noted from the comfort of the bed, her gaze following the trajectory of numerous items of clothing as they landed on the carpet.

"I also need a bath, but I have to find a shirt first so I can go into the village and retrieve my staff. Aha!" The missing shirt was found, he was dressed in quicksilver time and within an hour, the hunting box was a humming hive of activity.

"I hope you don't mind," Sinjin had said over a steaming hot breakfast a short time later, "and I'd never have thought lust would lose out to a good cup of coffee and a hot bath, but I stand corrected." His smile over the rim of his coffee cup was open and boyish and smugly content now that he was clean and well fed.

"I expect the maxim 'The way to a man's heart is through his stomach' would be pertinent to the occasion," Chelsea teased, seated across the table from him, looking scrubbed and rosy clean in a plain silk wrapper, pale yellow like her hair.

"More than pertinent . . . essential," Sinjin agreed, thinking he would buy her some negligees of Mechlin or Alençon lace. Something more feminine. An unconscious thought, it didn't take into account the brevity of their time together. But it took into account, perhaps, enigmatic considerations of a future.

Chelsea sighed theatrically. "To be displaced in your heart by a bowl of porridge and a hot slice of ham."

"Look at it this way, darling," Sinjin had said over her second mocking sigh. "If I keep my strength up, I'll be able to"—his smile was shamelessly cheeky—"keep my strength up."

Agreement was instant and cheerfully forthcoming from his breakfast companion. And in the course of the following days, Sinjin proved the merits of eating well to a grateful Scottish lass, several times a day.

Their last morning together, Chelsea woke very early, as if some inner voice had wakened her, warning her of fleeting time. And as she had so many times before in the sweetness of their days together, she gazed at Sinjin asleep beside her in a casual sprawl, one hand thrown over his head. He always slept easily, like a child without cares—falling asleep in mere seconds. A clear conscience there, she'd facetiously speculated the first time she'd seen him go from wakefulness to sleep in an instant. Or perhaps no conscience at all.

He'd given her the fifty thousand pounds in new crisp notes yesterday because he didn't want her to worry, he'd said, and he didn't like goodbyes. She could understand why he didn't like goodbyes. She didn't suppose any woman ever wanted to let him go. For beyond his essential beauty, which would be reason enough to desire him, Sinjin offered a world of pleasure, laughter and open-hearted friendship. His celebrity was well founded.

Her gaze drifted over his sleeping form, the fresh morning sun bathing him in glorious light, gilding the bronze of his body, burnishing his sleek black hair adrift down his corded neck, touching his high cheekbones, his straight nose, his slashing jaw. He looked like his mother's family, he'd told her, and Chelsea distinguished the legacy of a long-ago Viking forebear in his great broad-shouldered frame. Extremely large and powerful, he reminded her of a warrior from another time, out of place in an era of fops and dandies. But elegant also, she reflected with a slow smile, when he had cause to be, and refined in the symmetry and classic perfection of his features.

She touched him then because she couldn't help herself in the presence of such fluent beauty, her fingers lightly tracing the slender grace of his long-boned hand. And he came awake with a start, accommodating and polite, his smile coming to life at the sight of her.

"Good morning," she murmured, a small sadness in her heart that she would never see him again like this.

His lashes lifted and fell twice, the drowsiness of sleep not completely shaken off. "Good morning," he breathed on a small exhalation of air.

"I'm sorry . . . about waking you." She spoke in meaningless phrases so she wouldn't have to utter the less palatable words this last day would bring.

He shook his head once, trying to be alert for her, gracious even in his torpor. "It's fine; I'm awake." He raised himself swiftly on one elbow, his glance stabbing toward the windows. "What time is it?"

"Early. Go back to sleep."

"No . . . come here instead." Reaching for her, he rolled on his back, pulling her with him in a great swinging sweep. "There now," he whispered, his eyes shut again, her soft nude body lying on his. "That's better . . ."

The heat of his body made her skin feel cool, his internal temperature degrees higher, his energy too indefatigable. He slept less than she, played harder and, gentleman that he was, devoted endless hours to pleasing her in amorous play.

Without experience, she didn't know whether all men were as gracious, but she suspected a portion of the demand for Sinjin's services had to do with the selflessness of his expertise.

"Ummmm," he murmured, his hands running down her spine, "kiss me awake . . ."

In some ways he was awake already, Chelsea knew, feeling his arousal pressing into her stomach. And when she kissed him gently, a small sadness reminded her she wouldn't ever be kissing him good morning again.

"Don't go," he said a moment later when her head raised, his eyes open now and very close, his voice teasing, casual. She responded in kind, as though jest insulated them from reality.

"Never."

"Good. I like it here."

But they made love that morning with a special tenderness, the fleeting moments of their remaining time together an internal ticking . . . a constant reminder. Chelsea had to be in Grantham by afternoon or significant problems would arise.

Their week was almost gone.

Each sensation seemed enhanced, a touch, a kiss, the fever racing through their blood, their climax that lingered long exquisite moments. And the instant renewal of their passion, as though their bodies conspired to keep them at Oakham.

"I have to go," Chelsea finally said, reaching up to push Sinjin's hair behind his ears as he lay above her, the gesture intimate, possessive, her fingers slipping through his sleek hair, sliding around his ears, gliding down his powerful neck. Mine, she inexplicably thought, although she didn't speak.

Gathering her left hand in his and bringing her fingers to his mouth, Sinjin kissed the warm soft pad of each finger with a gentle caress. Lord, he hated to let her go. But she wasn't available, he knew. If she were married or a common woman, he could continue seeing her, but an unmarried lady of good family was off limits. He knew it; everyone knew it. And by bringing her to Oakham this week, he'd already pressed reckless conduct beyond the pale.

"You're very charming," he said, his courtesy automatic, all the polite phrases instinctive. "And extremely—beautiful." Another word had come to mind, a sensual amorous word no longer appropriate. He was grateful for her company this week, but their time was at an end; more suitable words were required.

"Thank you," Chelsea softly replied, blushing like a schoolgirl at the compliment, "and thank you too for . . . everything." Her voice trembled a moment before she steadied her emotions. She knew she'd never forget Sinjin or this enchanting week, but sensible people understood parameters of behavior. She'd allowed herself a week with him—a personal prize, as it were, beyond the money he'd given her—but she understood the insupportable danger in continuing to see him.

Not that he'd ask her anyway.

And he didn't, the habits of a lifetime standing firm against his novel partiality for this woman.

They were standing beside Thune, Chelsea about to mount. At Sinjin's suggestion, she was taking Thune as far as Grantham, where she was to meet Mrs. Macaulay.

"Thank you very much for an enjoyable holiday," Chelsea said into the small silence that had fallen between them.

"You're welcome. And once you think of a reasonable way to explain Thune to your family, send me word and I'll have him brought up to you." The words should have come easier. Normally they did; normally he was impatient to be free of a woman. Normally he didn't have to force back softer words of farewell. But since he had no intention of marrying—and that was the only honorable option should he choose to continue his relationship with Chelsea—he refrained from expressing any affectionate sentiments.

She smiled ruefully. "That may take some time, although I'm selfish enough to want him."

"He's your horse. I bought him for you." He shrugged. "Consider him in place of jewelry . . ."

His words, meant to mollify, reminded her instead of the casual gifts habitual to his libertine pattern of life. Dr. Johnson's phrase—coined to describe Sinjin, a friend he loved—sprang unwanted to her mind. "Thy body is all vice, and thy mind is all virtue."

A small shiver raced up her spine at the thought of all the women, and new resolution steeled her emotions. It wasn't wise to care; it was, in fact, extremely unwise.

"In that case," she said, her face schooled to a bland politeness, "when I concoct a creditable story, I'll send instructions for Thune's destination." Her smile, at least, was sincere. "Thank you very much for Thune."

They had both been as polite as the situation warranted, though neither was at ease. All the courtesies were accounted for, the thanks, the compliments, the kind words, the gallant cavil. There was no more to be said, short of the truth.

And that of course would not suit.

Sinjin made the first move toward her leave-taking, inactivity more disturbing to him, prone as he was to action. Cupping his hands, he bent down to give her a leg up into the saddle.

It was over, she thought for a flashing moment, and then she placed her foot into his cupped hands.

He lifted her without effort, helping her settle comfortably into the saddle. "Jed's trustworthy," Sinjin said, placing Thune's reins into her gloved hands. "Ask him for anything you require."

"You're very kind."

She looked an angel, Sinjin thought, the forenoon sun gleaming over her golden hair, her round hat tilted gracefully, the green ribbon around its brim matching the green superfine of her riding habit. He should have given her jewelry too, or more jewelry, he reflected, for she wore his thistle brooch at her throat. Rubies would have done justice to her fair beauty, or emeralds. But he hadn't and he wouldn't, nor would he see her again. Short of marriage, she was no longer available to him. And that extremity didn't bear contemplation. So he said in a moderate voice without inflection, "You should reach Grantham in two hours. Au revoir." He would have liked to kiss her goodbye; with women who affected him less, he would have. But he didn't. He only nodded to Jed, then said to Chelsea, "Pleasant journey."

"Goodbye," Chelsea said. There was nothing more to say that wouldn't embarrass her. Smiling down at Sinjin, she nudged Thune with her heel.

Sinjin didn't watch Chelsea and her escort canter down the drive. His unsteady nerves drove him inside to his eau-de-vie. It was damned near afternoon, and he enjoyed the fruity brandy in the afternoon. He didn't admit that he was hoping to drink away the golden image of the only woman since Catherine to affect his emotions.

Chapter 17

Chelsea arrived at Grantham in time to engage a room at the Angel and Royal before Mrs. Macaulay arrived. Jed was sent back to Oakham with Thune, and Chelsea lay down to wait for her household to appear. More tired than she imagined, she fell immediately asleep, her dreams a young girl's fantasies of love.

Mrs. Macaulay's strident tones and banging fist on the door brought her awake with a start, and the first of her lies began, although once her initial story had been related, she avoided discussion of Aunt Georgina as much as possible. And Mrs. Macaulay's steady round of chatter relieved her of the burden of conversation. Mrs. Macaulay's familiar presence, too, drove away her powerful fantasies, mitigated her vivid sense of loss, helped ease her re-entry into a familiar, comfortable world.

By the time they reached York the next evening, Chelsea almost believed the past week with Sinjin had been a dream. With her father and brothers waiting to greet them at their rented house near the track, their smiles and immediate discussions of training schedules effectively erased any remaining sentimental images of the past week.

But she didn't dare be alone in the following days, because then Sinjin would be standing beside her bed or at the door of the parlor, or smiling at her in the dimness of the stables. And her infatuation, her longing, would devastatingly reappear. How many times during the ensuing days did she remind herself their time together was over?

A thousand times each day—each minute, it sometimes seemed? Then she'd throw herself into her training work with single-minded purpose, forcing her thoughts back to the business of racing. Luckily the work was unending; she rose early, rode many of the trial heats herself, helped with the stable work, rode out on the evening runs, saw that the racers were put to bed and only then returned to the house.

She should have slept better—and sometimes, from sheer exhaustion, she did—but there were many nights when sleep eluded her because her thoughts of Sinjin were more powerful than her fatigue.

On the day before the race meet began, her father came into the parlor late one night and, dropping into a chair near the fire, reached for his decanter of scotch whiskey. An envelope fell onto the carpet from the jumbled contents of his overstuffed frock coat pocket, and bending over to retrieve it, he tossed it to Chelsea, who was seated at a nearby table adding up the feed accounts.

"The Duchess of Hampton sends her regards."

Chelsea caught the smudged and muddied envelope, turned it over to study its disreputable state and, with an inquisitive look, said to her father, "How long have you been carrying this around?"

"A day or so, two maybe, three at the most."

Chelsea swiftly broke the seal, intrigued by a note from the grand Duchess of Hampton. Quickly perusing the invitation, she saw with a small frown of consternation that the breakfast she was invited to had taken place that afternoon.[4]

"I'll have to send my apologies. And next time, Papa, if you prefer not offending the Duchess, you might consider delivering my invitations on time."

"Hmpf . . . well, forgot, as you can see. Tell Betsy 'tis my fault entirely."

"I will, you can be sure, although I'm not sure I would have had a gown grand enough anyway for the Duchess's coterie."

"Buy yourself some, then, lass. You know how much Newmarket helped our fortunes."

Which comment gave her the opportunity she'd been waiting for all week. "Are you wagering much during this meet, Papa?"

He hesitated marginally, knowing how Chelsea felt about his outstanding racing debts. "Some—not any plunging, though," he quickly added.

"I've been feeling inclined to bet a few guineas on Minto this meet, Papa. He's been running like the Devil's chasing him. Yesterday he took me an extra two miles before slowing down."

"Suit yourself, lass, so long as you don't gamble away your honor like some of the ladies of the Ton."

"I'll be cautious, Papa," Chelsea replied, the false words troublesome on her tongue, her honor long since sold for fifty thousand pounds. But so willingly given, she reflected, without guilt. Her only regret was having to give up the bonny young Duke.

The first day of the race meet bore the promise of idyllic spring, the air balmy, the sun warm, the breeze from the south scented with apple blossoms. Chelsea's sleep had been restless, but the perfect day swept away her drowsiness, and she watched the morning runs with notable cheer. Minto stood a very good chance of winning this afternoon, as did Bally, and if she were seen to bet on both, her subterfuge with the fifty thousand pounds would soon be over.

She dressed with more care than usual, taking time to tie blue ribbons in her hair. Her mother's pearls were taken out of her jewelry box, the necklace and earrings perfect complement to her cerulean lute-string closed gown. Sinjin's brooch on the revers of her gown took pride of place in her ensemble.

She turned eyes as she walked from the paddocks to the viewing enclosure, a familiar sight at York with her family so involved in racing, but everyone agreed that the Earl of Dumfries' young daughter was absolutely dazzling today.

Perhaps her satisfaction in knowing that the deception about Sinjin's money would soon be over showed in her face; perhaps she'd come to terms at last with the brief interlude at Oakham, assigning it its rightful place in her memories; or perhaps balmy spring days brought that special radiance to her face. Whatever the reason, her stunning good looks were especially high, and every man jack at York wished her smile were for him.

Her suitors swarmed around like bees around their queen, and she laughed and smiled and teased them all back with a new confidence that was marked. The look of a nubile maiden still clung to her, so dew fresh was her beauty, but she tantalized with a new coquettish air and mocked with a teasing accomplishment lacking before. She knew exactly how to raise her dark lashes so the suggestion of intimacy lured like Circe, and when she laughed at some drollery, her lush bottom lip curved with a fascinating sensuality.

And when their horses won that afternoon, all of them in record times, her jubilation was only matched by the beauty of her smile. Colin shouted and Neil hurrahed and Duncan and her father counted their winnings with the satisfaction of a hard-earned reward. The aqua vitae began flowing with a vengeance, and by the time Chelsea excused herself from the festivities, her father and brothers were well on their way to floating home. Leaving her family to their masculine celebrations, she drove her small tilbury home through the gathering dusk, her own spirits high.

Mrs. Macaulay, when told the news, burst into tears. "It's been a wee long time since such gladsome news," she sniffed, wiping her eyes with the corner of her apron. Loyal to the Earl's family through the years of privation since Culloden, she understood the significance of such winnings. "An' now the horses will no be sold so cheap," she said with a hiccupy smile.

"And Papa can pay you some wages at last."

"I do na care about that, lass. But the laird will smile a wee bit more now, I ken."

Her own smile was added reward, Chelsea thought, Mrs. Macaulay as much a part of the family as they.

"The grooms are all down at the White Hart if you're in the mood for a wee dram. I've had my share already and left Papa and the boys to drain the whiskey dry." Chelsea had had a drink or two, but when the revels began to escalate, she was safer at home. Aware of Scots' appetite for whiskey, she knew that soon the brawls would start, or the challenges, and a young woman would only add to the trouble.

"Weel now, perhaps I might just have a nip." Mrs. Macaulay was already untying her apron strings, her eyes sparkling with joy.

And within minutes, Chelsea was left alone.

Chapter 18

Hungry after an afternoon when she was too busy to consider food, Chelsea went into Mrs. Macaulay's larder to find herself something to eat. Finding some venison pie, figs, oatmeal bread and butter, she took her small tray into the parlor and set a place for herself at the table near the window. Unloosening the braided trim fastening the neckline of her gown, she pulled the silk scarf from her neck and kicked off her low boots. Seating herself on a sturdy wooden chair—their rented house near the track furnished for masculine tenants—she faced the windows to enjoy the bucolic view overlooking the track. The evening twilight streaked the sky with orchid and mauve, the smallest fringe of golden sunset hovering on the horizon. A peaceful scene; the perfect end to an eminently successful day.

Chelsea ate slowly, savoring the tranquility, the silence, her mood of well-being. Her father's debts would soon be paid; their racers had won enough to sustain the up-keep of the stables into the foreseeable future, and she could even have Thune back soon. She would "buy" him back with her "winnings."

A shame, she thought with a brief smile, that she couldn't "buy" the sweet Sinjin St. John as well. What a bonny prize that would be. She could keep him in a pretty little house for her pleasure alone, as all the lords did their mistresses. Grinning out the window, she contemplated for a moment, her chin propped on her hand, how long someone like the scandalous Duke of Seth would remain docile in a pretty little house. Not above a day or so, she suspected.

At which point, her musing turned to the harsher facts of life regarding Sinjin St. John. He wouldn't, she knew, be willing to limit his sexual appetites to one woman, familiar as he was with a full stable of women to service.

And that was the rub, she reflected with a sigh, in pining over her memories of the infamous Duke of Seth. Desiring her, he'd been willing to pay fifty thousand for a week of her time. But he didn't want her beyond that. So the sooner she forgot him and put aside the exquisite fantasy of the days at Oakham, the sooner she could get on with her life.

Briskly collecting the used dishes into a neat pile on the tray and whisking the crumbs off the cloth into her palm with a meticulous vigor, as if energetically whisking away her images of Sinjin, she forced her thoughts into more productive channels. Now, in what order would they arrange their racers for tomorrow? Minto should rest after his illustrious race for the finish today, which brought her father an extra five thousand. They could put Broadland into the first stake race, and perhaps Tripoli would do well for the Queen's Ribbon Stakes . . . Carrying her tray into the kitchen, she contemplated the proper placing of their horses.

Ascending the shadowed stairway short moments later, the white faille of her collar a shimmer of light in the gloom, Chelsea wondered how long her father and brothers would celebrate their victories. She smiled. They'd be home before midnight, she didn't doubt, for they knew the necessity of early rising with another day of racing ahead. But they'd be a noisy crew after their hours of celebrating, and they'd be complaining of aching heads in the morning.

Walking down the narrow hall, she entered her room and crossed the carpeted floor to her small dressing table, which was placed in the crescent of bow window facing the stable block. There was still activity in the yard, she noted, as the grooms saw to the horses, settling them in for the night. Lanterns were hung at each stall, the lights muted in the half light of twilight, some stalls still open, others closed for the night. Minto was being washed, standing content as he always did for the dousing in warm water he favored. She'd left instructions for an extra measure of port with the horses' mash in celebration of the occasion.

Sitting down before the mirror, she took down her hair, laying the pins in a silver box that had once been her mother's. Then she leisurely brushed her hair the ritual one hundred strokes, her face a pale image in the gilt-framed mirror. Replacing the ivory-handled brush on the polished tabletop, she unclasped the thistle brooch on her lapel, undid her mother's pearl earrings from her ears and took off the pearl necklace, systematically placing each piece of jewelry in her cloisonné jewelry case. Her movements were languorous, as if the waning light of twilight cast a spell of lassitude over all.

Unbuttoning the closures on her gown, she slid it off her shoulders, the silk lute-string slithering over her skin as she pulled the narrow sleeves down her arms. Standing, she let the gown drop to the floor, and with a laziness she attributed to the two whiskeys she'd drunk and the long day of bustle, she picked up her dress and tossed it on the chair, promising herself she'd hang it away first thing in the morning. Framed against the faint light from the windows, she stretched leisurely, the excitement of the day slowly draining away.

"You neglected Betsy's party today," a soft familiar voice murmured.

Chelsea spun around, her gaze sweeping the dimly lit room.

Sinjin was seated in a chair set against the far wall, the shadow of the bed-hangings further obscuring his form. His long legs were stretched out, his booted feet crossed at the ankle, his hands gently resting on the chair arms, his slouched form casually disposed in the depths of the Queen Anne chair.

"And congratulations on your horses' wins." He spoke as though they met in the park on the daily promenade, his voice carefully bland, a practiced pleasantry infusing his tone.

"Ah . . . she's *your* friend," Chelsea softly accused, ignoring his pleasantry. She'd wondered at her invitation to the Duchess of Hampton's tonnish world. The Duchess was older, unalloyedly modish and moneyed. And while her father knew the lady well, because she was not yet out in society, Chelsea was not a habitué of the Duchess's beau monde.

"We missed you."

"You were there then." How easily he fit into the Duchess's milieu she didn't doubt. How easily he fit into any world of beautiful women.

"In a manner of speaking . . ." He had been, in fact, waiting for Chelsea in the Duchess's suite.

"In what manner?" She shouldn't have asked; she certainly

shouldn't have asked in such an acerbic tone. She should have had better control over her ridiculous flashes of jealousy. But she could just picture him in the midst of the Duchess's admiring female friends.

"I was waiting for you upstairs."

He was waiting for *her!* A series of golden chimes, angel voices and birdsong from the gardens of paradise exploded in Chelsea's head for a flashing moment until her better judgment regained control of her senses. Sinjin St. John was hardly interested in romantic flights of fancy.

"The Duchess plays procuress for you often?" She kept her voice light, as she imagined those sophisticated ladies of the Duchess's circle did as they flirted and coquetted.

There was no mistaking the steely undertone despite Chelsea's feigned levity. Sinjin didn't, of course, have need of procuresses with so many ladies ardently interested in him, but that would never do to say, so he said instead, "She's a friend—of my mother—and she agreed to do me a favor. No implication of indecency intended."

"Your mother? Really." Chelsea's tone was arch, incongruous with her fresh luminous beauty and long flowing hair, the purity of simple chemise and petticoat adorning her like innocence and blameless virtue.

"Really." Avoiding dangerous ground, he didn't elaborate.

"Why?"

"Because I wanted to see you," Sinjin replied, understanding the meaning of her ambiguous inquiry. Not necessarily understanding his *own* reasons for being in York.

"How long have you been here?" How long before the invitation was extended? her rational mentality questioned. How long? her heart wished to know, as though she could recount her steps of the days past and savor his then unknown presence.

"Three days."

"And where are you staying?" That jealousy again, as if she had a right. But she could no more contain it than hold back the tides.

"In town."

"How deliberately vague."

"Are you angry?"

"Answer my question."

"At Hampton Manor."

"I thought so."

"You're wrong."

She knew him. She knew the rumors. "Have I always been wrong?"

He had the grace to hesitate. "Should I move my lodgings?"

"Don't do it for me."

"You're the only one I'd do it for."

"Why me?" She shouldn't have been so bold. And if she hadn't already spent the better part of the week convincing herself she could live without Sinjin St. John, she wouldn't have been so daring. She would have fallen into his arms long since. She would have accepted any reason for his presence. She wouldn't have insisted on the words.

He moved then from his position of ease, himself disturbed at the complexities of his presence in York, miles from where he intended to be, infinities away in terms of wisdom from where he *should* be. He straightened his posture, although he crossed his legs again and relaxed against the padded chairback. But his eyes were alert, and his voice, when he spoke, was bereft of its habitual charm.

"Because, if you must know," he said, each word relinquished reluctantly, "you've been in my thoughts persistently." His voice dropped to a hush. "Particularly . . . at night."

"I know." Although the smallest breath of sound, Chelsea's utterance dropped into the quiet of the room like an explosion.

Sinjin's brilliant gaze altered with predatory speed, impaling now in its intensity, holding Chelsea's dark gaze with mesmerizing force.

Neither spoke for a lengthy moment, and then he smiled, that slow lazy heart-stopping smile.

"Well then . . . you're glad I came—"

"No." Her hands were clenched at her sides, the cambric of her petticoat cool to her touch, her heart beginning to race.

"Tell me the truth," he softly said, uncrossing his legs and rising from the chair, looking very tall in the low-ceilinged bedchamber.

"No." She moved a step back.

He stood very still, as though he knew he needn't move, as though he knew very well what her no meant.

"I saw you at the races today." His voice was low, conversational, without threat. "You look very nice in that shade of blue lutestring."

He would know, of course, Chelsea reflected, the nuances of female fabric, but she found herself unable to conjure up a suitable resentment at the thought. She found herself instead thinking of the particular delicacy of his touch, and the inexplicable way he had of smiling when he kissed her, so she tasted happiness with his kiss.

Touched with a sudden alarm when she thought of his kissing her, she firmed her wavering resolve. "You really should go."

He began moving out of the shadows toward her.

"My family will be home soon."

"I'll be very quiet."

She should have been alarmed at his unthinkable response, but instead a shiver of need coursed through her senses.

"They'll be coming upstairs to bed," she remonstrated.

"They won't know I'm here." He was very close now.

"My father sleeps in the room next door."

"We'll lock the door."

This is impossible, she thought, lunatic. I shouldn't even be carrying on a conversation with this arrogant libertine who casually appears in my bedroom and intends as casually to stay. But she didn't tell him to leave again, which he and she both took note of.

"You're not alarmed?" she inquired, as if her question or his answer mattered when the inevitable consequences of his appearance palpably hovered in the air.

"Should I be?"

"This is very dangerous . . ." she insisted, trying to assert some semblance of prudence to the extraordinary scene.

"Really?" He said it so calmly that he could have been questioning the impossibility of Somerset refusing him.

"Really," Chelsea retorted somewhat heatedly, annoyed suddenly at his calm when fear of discovery left her nerves in a state of shock, and because, too, he could *not* casually intrude into her life again, she thought, conveniently forgetting who had intruded originally into whose. "Now I don't know how you came in," she said in an officious tone, as a teacher might lecture one on muddy boots in the schoolroom, "but I would appreciate it if you'd leave the same way."

"I walked in."

He was mad. She expected him to have climbed onto the porch roof or up the ivy on the walls or jumped onto the windowsill from one of the huge trees in the yard. "You're insane," she blurted out.

"Not presently," he quietly replied, his smile the kind that could charm one out of purgatory. "But I'm mad for you. And I rode across a good part of England to see you again." His expression was angelic and open, without a trace of cultivated politesse or pretense. And he moved forward, closing the last small distance separating them, and gently brushed her cheek with the back of his fingers.

As he'd advanced, Chelsea had unconsciously waited, and she found herself waiting again, her breath held.

It was one thing to consider the liabilities of succumbing to the seductive lure of Sinjin St. John when two counties separated one from desire. But when only inches remained as barrier, no restraint, however strong, proved powerful enough.

She lifted her face to him and, with a small rueful smile, said, "If I could, I'd make you leave . . ."

"If I could leave," he softly replied, "I would."

And for a moment more they stood without touching in a final attempt at constraint, both struggling with feelings they would have preferred didn't exist.

Then Chelsea swayed toward him, infinitesimally—a small fragment of movement only one acutely attuned would have noticed.

It was enough. It was all.

And Sinjin folded her close in his arms and held her for a shuddering moment before he lowered his mouth to hers.

He felt adolescent again, quickening even as his lips brushed hers, dangerously out of control with wanting her, not caring if there were a firing squad outside the door. Jubilant to have her in his arms, he pressed her close to his fiercely roused body, unaware, as in the midst of battle, of anything but the need to conquer. He felt that way again, as if he must have her through miles of enemy territory and battalions of adversaries. The feeling was unprecedented, bizarre, completely out of character and so brutally powerful that he felt the weight of it on his chest.

He was already pushing her backward toward the bed, his mouth eating at hers, the feel of her soft body beneath his roving hands forcing his heedless senses into ramming speed.

Lock the door, lock the door, Chelsea's mind was screaming, because she wanted Sinjin with the same relentless fury, wanting to open herself to him . . . now . . . wanting to feel him inside her, wanting to instantly still her monstrous need.

Shameless, her hands came up to tear at his coat, wanting his nude body touching hers. "I want to feel your skin," she whispered. And he dropped his arms from her shoulders in instant response to shrug himself free of the garment.

"Take your petticoats off," he ordered, low and fierce, his fingers ripping his waistcoat buttons open, his eyes never leaving her.

And she frantically tugged at her petticoat ties with trembling fingers, tearing the fine linen when it wouldn't come loose speedily enough, brushing the frothy fabric and lace over her hips and crushing it underfoot with a mindless unconcern that would shock her was she not so obsessed with longing. Her chemise came off as quickly, cast aside without thought, her body pulsing so powerfully with desire that she wondered if the rhythm of lust was visible to the naked eye.

"Don't move," Sinjin commanded in a husky deep voice, his gaze traveling down her nude body. His body was clad only in buckskins and boots, and his fingers worked the buttons of his breeches.

Chelsea couldn't move had she wished, her gaze trained on the enormous bulge under his buckskins. Sinjin's erection stretched the soft leather of his tight-fitting breeches from groin to waist.

One top button on the leather breeches came free and then the other. Sinjin's slender fingers were moving down to the second row when Chelsea whimpered and his blue gaze came up quickly, an animal gaze of sensuality incarnate. A pulse beat later, his mouth lifted in a smile of tempting allure, and he said in a velvety voice that touched her across the dimly lit space, "Would you like to help?"

She went to him because she couldn't stop herself, even though his knowing smile followed her. He knew how the size of his erection affected women; the amusement in his eyes gave indication of that awareness. But she didn't care, for her need to feel him was overwhelming.

She released the last three gold buttons, took him in both her hands and stroked the rigid length of him with trembling fingers. She heard him suck in his breath and, looking up, saw him breathless, eyes closed, still. She smiled, assured she had his attention, and bending her head, she took him in her mouth and slid her tongue gently around the pulsing head of his erection.

It was too much in the current state of his desire, and he abruptly pulled her away from him, lifted her under her arms like a child and deposited her on the bed in a blur of movement, following her down a flashing moment later, oblivious of his boots and breeches. He was inside her a second later, deep inside her with a force that stopped both their breathing for a staggering length of time.

When she eventually found the breath to speak, Chelsea frantically whispered, "The door . . ."

Sinjin looked up, a swift assessing glance, but he could have no more left her hot, welcoming body than he could have stopped his heart from beating, so insensate was he to reason.

"Please . . . the lock . . ." Chelsea pleaded, terrified her father might come in.

"Hush, darling," Sinjin murmured. His mouth covered hers and the rhythm of his penetration deepened.

Orgasmic sensation overwhelmed sense and sensibility. The world disappeared for Chelsea—only flame-hot desire mattered as she arched up to meet the next powerful downthrust. She melted around him. He could feel the shimmering heat surround him, the soft tissue part then yield as he buried himself inside. She cried out— a muffled, low-pitched sound of restraint in her father's house. But her hands clutched him, her nails dug into his back and he recognized the erratic breathy respiration of her peaking orgasm. He smiled at the lush recognition and withdrew partially against her unyielding hands.

"Noooo . . ." she pleaded, fiercely drawing him back, and he drove in again, moving her at the last a small measure upward toward the headboard.

As her climax began to tremble through her body, he poured into her, as impelled to haste as she, as greedy for release, as deprived as she had been the days since Oakham.

They both lay prostrate, Sinjin's face buried in the pillow near her shoulder, Chelsea smothered under the braced weight of his large form, their bodies beyond recognizable feeling for brief moments, as though sensation existed outside the perimeter of the mind.

Until gradually the boundaries of reason and feeling merged, and their heartbeats slowed, and bliss and reality met in some common ground.

"Now lock the door," Chelsea whispered, knowing she couldn't let him go tonight, regardless of danger or fear or family.

"*Now* I'll lock the door," Sinjin said, his voice muffled by the down pillow. A moment later, he lifted his head, grinned down at her and said, "I thought I'd died." He kissed her very gently on the curve of her upper lip and added, "I'll be staying tonight."

She didn't argue and he said, "Good, that's settled," and he kissed her again, less tenderly, less gently, more thoroughly, with great attention to detail.

She had to remind him twice more before he finally locked the door, but he did in the end, and they were at least protected behind the barrier of one wooden door when her father and brothers came tramping up the stairs an hour later.

Her body went rigid at the first footstep on the stairs. Her breath caught in her throat for a moment before she whispered, as if it wasn't too late already, "You have to go!"

While she pushed at his chest, Sinjin just shook his head and put a finger to her lips. But his gaze swiveled to the door, and his head came up like that of a wolf sniffing the wind.

"Chelsea! Are you still awake?" her father bellowed as he reached the top of the stairway.

She froze. The sound of her father's voice—separated from her by scant feet and two inches of oak door—brought terror to her soul.

"Hey Chel!" Duncan shouted, "We're running Minto again to-morrow!"

"Chelsea!" The Earl pounded on the door. "Wake up, lass, and help us celebrate. We won eight thousand guineas today!"

"Answer," Sinjin murmured.

"I'm sleeping, Papa," Chelsea said, her voice a whisper of fear.

Sinjin grinned and motioned for more volume.

"What, gel? Can't hear you!"

Sinjin's brows rose as if to say, "See?"

And clearing her throat with telling effort, Chelsea managed to croak in a voice loud enough to carry to the hallway, "I'm sleeping, Papa."

"Don't sound like it to me!"

Sinjin moved in her, and Chelsea sucked in a treacherous breath of arousal. "You're drunk, Papa. Go to sleep." She tried to sound purposeful but only managed to sound breathy. *Lord,* he felt good inside her, filling her.

Grinning, Sinjin bent his head to nuzzle her ear and whispered, "If you don't get rid of them, I can't fuck you . . . properly."

She should have taken affront, and if his stiff rigid length wasn't impaling her, and were not her desire additionally inflamed by his leisurely small movements—and strangely too by her family's prox-imity—perhaps she would have. But she couldn't think . . . only feel. "What should I—"

He slid upward a fraction more just then, cutting off her words as flame tore through her senses and an inadvertent cry ruptured the silence—immediately muffled by Sinjin's mouth descending on hers.

"Chelsea! Are you all right?" The Earl's roar was punctuated by agitated pounding on the door.

Would she climax before or after they broke down the door? she transiently wondered, her body on fire—peaking.

"I'll see you in the morning," Sinjin murmured.

"No!" she breathlessly objected, clinging to him more tightly, shameless in her desire.

"I mean," Sinjin whispered, his smile more sound than image, "tell them that."

He was too casual, Chelsea thought, a fleeting resentment flaring through her mind—too blasé, too used to taking his pleasure in other men's homes. And if she didn't so desperately want what he could give her, what he gave other women—if she wasn't degrees beyond reason—she'd take issue with his nonchalance.

But overcome with passion, she followed his instructions, crying out, her voice strengthened by her pique, "It's *late!* I'll see you in the *morning!*"

Breathless with fear and sumptuous flaunting need, she waited to see if she would be discovered. Scraping feet . . . murmurs, then footsteps, and as the treads receded down the hall, she whispered, "I hate you."

Sinjin's face above her was very close, the sparse candlelight in the room enhancing the shadows under his brows, concealing the amusement in his eyes. "I can tell," he said, his voice low and husky. "But remember, I rode across half of England to see you."

His words served to remind her that his nonchalance was perhaps one of habit, not feeling, or he faced danger with more sangfroid than she. And he *had* ridden a very long way.

"Thank you then," she said, easily appeased in her present state of passion, her arms twining around his neck in languid repose, "for coming."

"I didn't know if I'd be welcome." He did, of course, based on past experience, but he was a courteous man.

"And maybe the world is square," Chelsea cheerfully replied, acutely aware of his universal appeal but infinitely pleased at his need for *her*.

"And maybe you're too damned desirable for your own good," he teased in return.

"Or yours."

"Or mine," he softly acknowledged.

"You probably shouldn't have come, though," Chelsea said. "This is very risky." But she said it with pleasure in the words, as one would say, "You shouldn't have" to a gift of diamonds.

"In the morning," Sinjin perceptively noted, "it might seem risky. At the moment I find you infinitely alluring . . ." And then his head dipped and his mouth drifted down her cheek. "I think," he murmured, his voice like velvet, "I'll let you climax *next* standing up."

She was going to die of bliss tonight, she thought as the throbbing between her legs intensified at Sinjin's whispered words.

"But you have to be *quiet,*" he added, his mouth warm on her skin, "or your father will kill me."

He had to wait for the third time to have her climax standing up.

Sinjin left very near morning, lingering so long that Chelsea was panic-stricken her family would wake, or else the servants or grooms.

He kissed her goodbye, then came back before he opened the door and kissed her again, holding her face gently between his palms, his mouth lush, sweet, tender.

But he spoke no words of love or commitment.

She knew better, of course.

She knew he never would.

Chapter 19

The next week found Sinjin in London, for the season was gearing up. Families were in from the country, his included; town homes were being polished from top to bottom—luckily, his mother was on hand, he teased her, to see to the proper use of his servants. And with the masculine element of the aristocratic families in town, although otherwise uninvolved in the social arrangements, a great number of male entertainments transpired—to which Sinjin contributed his congenial person.

In the stir of activities, Cassandra petitioned him for some exclusive use of his time. As did his mother, brother and son.

So while Sinjin didn't forget the delightful Lady Chelsea Fergusson, the picturesque memory of their pleasurable diversions tended to fade under the sheer number of social commitments constituting London's season. She'd be recalled on occasion when a female with golden hair struck his visual field, and at those times, he experienced an elusive sense of loss. But then it was immediately shaken off and as quickly forgotten, for he was much in demand.

His mother required his escort, and as a dutiful son he complied. His brother's wife entertained large parties at Seth House, which sometimes also demanded his presence. Cassandra often wished him to escort her to small private parties. His own amusements occupied considerable time. And he spent most of his daytime hours with his young son, Beauclerk St. Jules, now that the boy was in town.

. . .

Chelsea's family had returned to Ayrshire once the races were over at York, and she spent the month of April enjoying the peace of the country. Springtime was her favorite time of year with the new foals gamboling about, and she found herself spending long hours lying on the hills overlooking the pastures, watching the youngsters test their new legs.

A month's hiatus intervened before the Doncaster races, when they'd take Minto and Thune south to test their mettle against the northern horses. In the meantime, their racers were on a schedule of rest. She'd had Thune sent to her two weeks ago, her account of having bought him back with her winnings at York accepted by her family. Since the original buyer was unknown, with Thune purchased through an agent, her explanation that Thune's new owner had to sell his stable for gambling debts wasn't untoward. Everyone agreed that Chelsea's luck had been phenomenal.

Chapter 20

"Papa, hurry or we won't be at the auction in time to bid on the best jumper for me."

"We looked at them yesterday, Beau," Sinjin calmly replied, tying his neckcloth before the pier glass in his dressing room, Pims having been dismissed so he and his son could visit, "and Tattersall will save him for us even if we come late." He grinned down at his anxious nine-year-old son, a sturdy young replica of himself at that age, and added soothingly, "But we're not going to be late."

His son smiled back, reassured to know Tattersall wouldn't sell the big Irish jumper before they arrived. "I'm riding Mameluke today. Jed said I could." He was shifting from foot to foot, trying to be patient while his father took what Beau considered an inordinate amount of time to dress.

"And what does Mameluke have to say about it?" Sinjin teased.

"He likes me, Papa. I feed him carrots every morning and he remembers me."

"Take some sugar bits for him too," Sinjin said, indicating a Sheffield cachepot on the top of a bureau near the door. He always carried some in his pockets when he went down to the horses. "Mameluke particularly likes sugar."

Beau was already racing across the carpeted floor toward the dresser. "Do hurry, Papa! Your tie is fine enough for the men at Tattersall's. There's never any ladies there."

Following his son's flight in the mirror, Sinjin smiled.

"In that case," Sinjin ironically replied, looping the final fold in place with practiced skill, "I've spent a great deal too much time on this neckcloth."

"I'm not going to cater to the ladies when I grow up like you do, Papa," Beau asserted, pulling up a chair to reach the top of the bureau, "and then I won't have to worry about neckcloths and such. Sahar says anyway that women are treacherous to a warrior's duty. Not Grandmama or Auntie Viv, of course. Sahar says women of the family must be treated with every respect."

Sinjin grinned at his son's typically boyish disinterest in the female sex. "While Sahar's advice is excellent, there are occasionally lady friends to whom one can't be rude. Sahar will no doubt clarify that for you someday . . ." Shrugging into his blue superfine coat, he added, "Sahar's advice on horses is equally good. Listen to him and you'll be a *mekhazeni* someday."

"I am already, Sahar says," Beau proudly replied, standing arrow straight in the way that Sinjin's Bedouin groom had told him warriors face their enemies.[5]

Sinjin's smile reflected the pride in his eyes. His son, almost lost to him once, was growing into a fine *mekhazeni* indeed. Thanks to Sahar, who had been with Sinjin since his first trip to Tunis years ago, Beau rode like a desert horseman already. Sinjin's mother saw to his son's tutors, and Damien's family offered the companionship of cousins and playmates; Beau was loved by all, but most of all by his father, who publicly acknowledged him in an age that rarely did. And while Beau couldn't legally inherit Sinjin's dukedom, he was already heir to his wealth.

"Are we ready then?" Sinjin asked, standing dressed in blue and buff, his boots polished impeccably, his linen brilliant white, his hair dressed in a simple queue by his valet when he'd been shaved earlier that morning.

"I've been ready since seven, Papa, which is when you came in, Steeley said. She saw you from the nursery window."

There were disadvantages to having all the inhabitants of Kingsway in residence, Sinjin thought, his old Nanny still keeping watch over him. "Did she pray for my soul?" he asked with a grin.

"For certain, Papa." Beau's young face broke into a tentative smile. "Steeley says she has to keep on living because someone has to pray for your disrep . . . u . . . table"—he struggled over the unfamiliar word—"soul and for all your harlots. What's a harlot, Papa? Sahar won't tell me."

"And well he shouldn't," Sinjin said, trying to suppress an urge to chuckle. "When you're older, I'll explain."

"Sahar says Steeley's God doesn't understand men."

"Perhaps Allah does look at certain aspects of . . . er . . . living slightly differently than Steeley," Sinjin blandly agreed, although Steeley's Methodist prayers had been active in keeping him out of the devil's clutches for a decade at least—for which he was deeply grateful, Sinjin facetiously reflected. "Now let's see about that Irish jumper," he quickly added, moving the topic to safer ground.

And Sinjin's days continued apace as London's season offered amusements and entertainments in unlimited profusion. He refused to go to Almacks and be polite to masses of simpering misses up on the town for their coming out, but he did his share of being polite at private parties to numerous daughters, nieces and sisters of his friends. Needless to say, he was much in demand as the largest prize on the marriage mart any time these last ten years.

Cassandra was his companion most nights, for her special brand of practiced vice appealed to his profligate soul, but he was by no means constant to her, as she in turn was not to him. They were both creatures of pleasure, beguiled by the unusual, diverted by change, entertained by variety in their sport.

"Tell me what you possibly can see in Jane Bentwin," Cassandra was saying, one finger traveling slowly across Sinjin's chest as she lay in the crook of his arm one night—or actually morning, for Lady Wentworth's ball had lasted till three.

"If you tell me what Willie Chenowith does to entertain you, for I'm told he has the finesse of a rabbit."

"And who told you that?"

"Sally Stanley," he said with a grin, gazing down at her from under his long lashes.

"Maybe Sally doesn't know how to properly *charm* Willie."

Cassandra's azure eyes held Sinjin's in suggestive insinuation. "And you still haven't explained the particulars of Jane Bentwin's appeal."

"A gentleman doesn't discuss the particulars, darling; you know that."

"You should write your memoirs someday."

"I should, should I? For what purpose, pray tell?"

"For the diversion of the populace."

His lashes only lowered slightly more over the placid blue of his eyes. "Why don't I," he gently said, "leave that for the courtesans of the age?"

"Are you implying I'm a courtesan?" Cassandra's voice held no affront; a practical woman, she understood labels were of little consequence if one was titled and wealthy. A Queen could be a whore, but she was still first a Queen.

"Not at all. You are, I believe, the devoted wife of the Duke of Buchan."

"You're so utterly polite, darling." She stretched up to kiss him lightly. "Now if that politeness could be extended to, say, one additional service . . ." she purred.

"You haven't been serviced enough tonight?" Sinjin murmured, a teasing note in his voice.

"You're an addiction, darling. Humor me . . ."

"If you humor me in turn."

"Tell me."

And when he did, a tiny shiver thrilled through her body. "Do they really do that in harems?"

"Some, apparently . . ."

"Have you done that before?"

"Does it matter?" His eyes had gone blank suddenly.

He wasn't going to tell her, she could see, so she said, "No."

"Well then, let's see if you like it."

Chapter 21

Now while Sinjin was entertaining and being entertained by a great number of England's peers and peeresses, the latter in the majority, Chelsea was passing the weeks of April in contrasting solitude.

Feeling strangely lethargic, she excused herself from a sizable portion of her stable work. Since her father had always felt slightly guilty over Chelsea's unusual involvement in their racers, he excused her with his blessing. Maybe she was finally coming of age as a woman, he thought, and leaving her tomboyish ways behind. Perhaps, with spring in the air, she was turning to romantic sensibilities like her Cousin Elizabeth. Perhaps some of Georgina's incessant harping about ladylike ways had rubbed off.

Regardless of the reasons, the Earl was grateful that Chelsea had turned to less masculine pastimes. She would have to marry someday, and no prospective bridegroom considered horse breaking a necessary qualification in a wife.

But while Chelsea's father was being gratified at his daughter's less rough activities, Chelsea was actually spending most of her leisure time sleeping. At first when she'd felt constantly tired, Chelsea had physicked herself with spring tonic and rose hip tea, thinking she was overfatigued from their busy racing schedule of the past month. The tonics hadn't mitigated her lethargy, however; in fact, she was sleeping more. And eating with the appetite of two men.

Her unknown malaise came to public exposure one morning in

May when, concerned with her absence at breakfast, Chelsea's father entered her room to find her green-faced and vomiting into her chamber-pot.

"I must have eaten something that disagreed with me," she said some moments later as she lay in bed with a cool cloth on her forehead, a maid seated at her side and her father standing very still at the end of her bed.

"Let me check with Mrs. Macaulay and find something to settle your stomach," he gently said, although it took tremendous effort to keep his voice steady.

His daughter looked so young and innocent in her white nightgown, with her pale hair spread out on the pillow, her violet eyes reminding him poignantly of his wife. He was to blame for this, he thought, assailed with guilt. God forgive him, he was accountable. Because of his pressure over the Bishop of Hatfield, his daughter had found a way to compromise herself.

And now this. With the father that disreputable rake, Seth.

He calmed himself for a moment, cautioning himself against suspecting the worst. Perhaps she really *was* sick with a stomach ailment.

An hour later, however, after he questioned Chelsea's serving maids and Mrs. Macaulay, that tentative hope had died. She'd not had her menses since Newmarket.

And he was back to the bitter conclusion that Sinjin St. John was about to become his son-in-law.

Fergus Fergusson waited until afternoon to speak to his daughter, when she was feeling well again, after a lunch she'd done such justice to that her morning stomach upset appeared a negligible memory. As they sat in his wife's rose garden, carefully preserved and nurtured since her death, the May sunshine warm and benevolent, he debated a diplomatic opening to a delicate, disconcerting conversation. A breathtaking array of blooming roses surrounded them, the heady scent of attar fragrant on the light breeze blowing in from the Firth of Clyde short miles away, the beauty incongruous contrast to the awkward discussion about to take place.

"Do you feel better now?" the Earl gently asked, his gaze on his daughter, who was seated across the small flagstone terrace from him. Lounging on a wrought iron settee, she looked very much the feminine lady today in a white dimity summer frock and green silk slippers.

Chelsea looked away from the hills bordering their valley home, her lavender gaze swinging back to her father. She smiled. "I feel wonderful. You needn't sit with me like an invalid, Papa. I'm perfectly fine."

"Mrs. Macaulay tells me you've been napping in the afternoons the past few weeks."

"That doesn't make me sick, Papa. I think it's the spring air making me lazy."

"Or something else," he quietly said.

Her father's voice held such a hushed resonance that Chelsea focused her gaze on him with a pointed regard.

"Like what?"

He swallowed once before speaking, the words stuck in his throat. "Do you think you could be pregnant?" he said at last.

Chelsea's stomach seemed to have heard the question too, and she felt a flip-flopping twinge of nausea grip her. "I hadn't thought of that." Her voice was barely audible.

Her father's face turned pink beneath his tan, and he wished some female relative existed who was close to Chelsea and could have this discussion with her. But one didn't, and at base it was his responsibility to resolve the problem which had begun with his own selfish demand of his daughter.

"Mrs. Macaulay and your serving maids, er . . . mentioned . . . that . . . your menses haven't appeared since Newmarket."

"It's only six weeks, Papa," Chelsea quickly replied, her own face flushed with embarrassment. Although well aware of breeding techniques, she had never discussed the intimate details of her femaleness with her papa. Mrs. Macaulay had been her surrogate mother for conversations of that nature.

"Your sickness this morning . . . and your napping and—"

"Papa, please! I think you *must* be wrong!" He had to be, she frantically thought, even while a consciousness beneath the contention of her words ruinously took into account all the unusual changes in her activities. For someone who had never napped since early childhood, her fatigue now had a probable cause. And even she'd been surprised at how rapidly her morning nausea had passed, to be replaced by a vociferous hunger.

Although the Earl wished to place the entire blame on St. John, as an honest man he knew that censure couldn't be fairly placed on the Duke alone. His own obstinacy had been the initial impetus for Chelsea's outrageous undertaking. He didn't know, of course, of the ensuing events at Oakham or York.

Chelsea, however, was well aware of those pleasurable times, as she was equally aware of the substantially increased possibility of conception after a week at Oakham. Sinjin hadn't always been prudently cautious—nor had she, in all honesty, even though Sinjin had taught her the function of Greek sponges. And certainly none were available that night at York.

"Perhaps you're jumping to conclusions, Papa," she offered, swinging her feet onto the ground and sitting up very straight. "Six weeks is very early."

"We'll wait two weeks more," he quietly agreed, "but if there's . . . no change . . ." His dark brows drew together in a frown. "Then you must marry St. John."

"No!" She shot to her feet, outraged at her father's statement. "I won't be married off like that. It's no different than forcing me into Hatfield's hateful company." She began pacing, feeling caged, the same future awaiting her that she'd so diligently tried to avoid. She stopped in midturn, facing her father. "St. John won't marry me, in any event. He doesn't wish to marry."

"I don't suppose he does, with an heir already to his wealth."

The shock of his statement showed on her face. "He has a son?"

"I thought you knew. He openly acknowledges the boy."

"How old is the child?" As if it mattered, her agitated mind recognized, as if it mattered in the smallest way that he had a son or ten sons—which was a distinct possibility as well.

"The boy's nine. The scandal of his birth marked the event in the mind of the world."

"Who's the mother?" She *had* to know, even though she knew already there were hundreds, thousands, of rivals for Sinjin's notice.

"No one knows. But he broke with his father over the affair and never spoke to him again."

"Who does the boy resemble?" She shouldn't care about all the details; she should be aloof from the man who had entered her life for a brief time and left with the same charming casualness.

"He's the spit of his father. St. John keeps him at Kingsway with the Dowager Duchess. He won't have him at Eton, rumor has it, because he dislikes the bullying and wishes to protect his son. Enough tutors reside at Kingsway to populate a school."

But Sinjin didn't stay at Kingsway, Chelsea thought, recalling Sinjin's comments on his ducal estate. Because of the bad blood between his father and himself? Did he have his son come to

Oakham? Had the boy lived in the same rooms she'd occupied? Had he basked in the pleasure of his father's charm as she had?

"What is the boy called?"

"Beauclerk St. Jules, after Seth's barony of St. Jules."

Chelsea sat down then with a small sigh, another facet of Sinjin's life revealed, another reason for his disinterest in marriage—beyond the usual ones for a young bachelor of wealth and title. He didn't need to marry for money, and he didn't require a title through marriage. Nor did the Duke of Seth want for an heir. He had one, as well as a brother to inherit the dukedom in the event of his death.

"Papa, if . . . well . . . if I should prove pregnant, you know how I feel about being married to a virtual stranger." Granted the word "stranger" stretched the truth, but not completely, considering she'd only known Sinjin for a total of nine days. "And he won't be amenable to marriage either. Let me go to our border farm. Other women have children outside marriage. I don't mind, Papa. My life is with my family."

"I don't want you shamed in the eyes of the world. Whatever the circumstances . . . you're my daughter and he must marry you."

"I'm opposed. Now, later, always." Chelsea's voice was very soft, but an obstinate core attested to her feelings. "Don't you understand how much I despise the aristocratic marriages of convenience? How can you force me to give my life away to a man I scarcely know, a man who doesn't wish me in return?" A flicker of hope struck her as she spoke. How could her father force Sinjin to comply? He couldn't. So she discontinued her futile argument and said instead, "Perhaps none of this is necessary, Papa. Perhaps everything will resolve itself and we can all go on with our lives."

"I hope so," her father gently said, but he was already planning for the escort of clansmen he'd need should the bridegroom prove recalcitrant.

Two nerve-racking weeks passed in which the state of Chelsea's health was prominently on everyone's thoughts. And the certainty of pregnancy increased with each passing day. Her morning sickness intensified, augmented by bouts of nausea in the late afternoon as well. There was no longer any doubt about her condition.

She had attempted to persuade her father of the feasibility of rearing her child alone at one of their small estates, but no arguments succeeded against his masculine principles of honor. She had finally shouted at him one day, after another fruitless go-around, "If I were some farm lass or common woman, money would suffice to solve the dilemma, but I'm an earl's daughter, so Scots honor demands he marry me! Damn your honor! It's my life!"

"But you're an earl's daughter, lass. And that won't change. So he'll marry you, for I'll not have a grandchild of mine born in shame."

"Think of me, Papa! Good God, what kind of marriage will I have?"

He didn't answer, for there was no palatable response. But he'd been raised with a clear understanding of the distinctions of honor—inherent traditions of Scottish culture that required recompense for a wrong, predicated on a warrior code that defended one's principles and protected women. He could no more consider his daughter living in isolation with a bastard child than he could think of disowning his ancestors' Church of Rome.

The discussion was over . . . again.

Chelsea tried enlisting her brother's aid, but Duncan and Neil supported their father in principle. It was inconceivable that their sister bear a child out of wedlock, despite the fact she'd been the seducer at Six-Mile-Bottom. Only Colin shared her distaste of marriage to a man she scarcely knew, a man likely to abhor the thought of marriage as violently as she.

And he offered to run away with her and help her take care of the child once it was born. Chelsea almost considered resorting to Colin's offer until reality intervened. Neither she nor Colin would be allowed to flee to one of their lesser holdings, and even if they were able to reach their remotest property in the Highlands, pursuit would be instant.

"Thank you, Colin," Chelsea said with a smile for her young brother. "Perhaps you can help me to run away from my husband later."

"He owns the best horses in England, Chel. Maybe you can learn to muddle through with him," Colin said with a young boy's logic that discounted obstacles like affection and feeling.

It wasn't that she had no feeling for the charming rogue; she just didn't care to be married against her will, nor did she wish marriage to a man who not only objected to matrimony in principle but would continue to live as though he had no wife.

"They say he's very pleasant to women," Colin went on, his face reddening as he considered his sister's particular knowledge of that quality. "Oh hell, Chel, maybe he won't be so bad," Colin finished in a sympathetic rush of words. "And if he *is* dastardly to you, tell me and I'll take you away. I'll begin thinking of places Papa can't find us."

"I'll bring my jewelry and we'll run away in style," Chelsea teased, knowing she wouldn't be ready to run any time soon in her present state or when her child was small. And she knew, too, that if the Duke did mistreat her, her father would take her home. Enough of the scandals of the peerage reached even the north in Ayrshire for the Earl to understand there were limits to miserable marriages.

One morning after the two weeks had elapsed, Colin was sent north with a message for the Fergusson clansmen, and Earl Dumfries and his two older sons set off on the road to London. Chelsea didn't realize she was left alone with Mrs. Macaulay and their staff until she came down for breakfast.

"They're gone then," she resignedly said to Mrs. Macaulay, who waited for her in the deserted breakfast parlor.

"Aye, child, they're off to fetch your bridegroom."

"I hope they bring him back alive," Chelsea morosely replied, knowing the extent of Sinjin's resistance to marriage.

"He'll have breath enough to say his vows at least, lass. Your pa will see to that. Now tell me what ye want to eat, child, for the coming days will test your strength."

"He's going to hate me," Chelsea said, her face bereft of color. Walking to the table set near the window, she sat down like someone doomed to the scaffold.

Mrs. Macaulay knew better than to offer platitudes. Cognizant of the heated arguments during the past two weeks, she rather suspected Chelsea was right. "He'll change his mind, lass, when he comes to know ye," she soothingly replied.

"No, he won't," Chelsea murmured, feeling trapped and helpless and condemned. "Not ever."

Chapter 22

The season was well under way, and in deference to their long friend-ship and Cassandra's particular coaxing, Sinjin was to play consort to her role of hostess at the coming-out ball of her niece, Lavinia Wroxley.

The Duke of Buchan preferred salmon fishing to coming-out balls; he had not, in fact, graced a season with his presence in three decades.

"Before you were born, darling," Cassandra had teasingly noted, her explanation of this absence in answer to Sinjin's query concern-ing her husband's disposition toward other men usurping his place as host.

While Sinjin and Cassandra's liaison was common knowledge within the small world of the Ton, to publicly flaunt this relationship by his standing beside her in a receiving line required at least a polite nod from her husband. Which had been forthcoming, along with a generous quantity of smoked salmon for the festivities.

"He's not a selfish man," Cassandra had said at the time, reassur-ing and coquettish as she discarded her robe on her bedroom carpet.

"How very convenient," Sinjin had answered, the Duke of Buchan's absence *and* generosity particularly obliging at the mo-ment.

"It doesn't have to do with convenience so much as age, dar-ling," she observed, standing at the foot of the bed and taking the pins from her hair. "A man of seventy has different interests than you."

"Admit though, Cassandra," Sinjin replied from his comfortable sprawl on the bed, "he allows you more license than most."

"For which he's well repaid." Her sultry voice defined the manner of payment.

"Ah . . ." Sinjin softly murmured, "and yet Buchan should be congratulated for such unusual selflessness."

Their voices drifted lazily across the scented chamber, lovers of long standing in familiar conversation.

"You misunderstand, Sinjin my sweet. He is, in fact, the most selfish of men."

"Ah . . ." Sinjin said again, understanding completely. "What does he like best?"

Shaking her hair free, its heavy black weight—unpowdered to please Sinjin—falling on her bare shoulders, Cassandra smiled. "I shouldn't."

"A bit late for scruples between us, pet. I'm curious."

"About sex? *You,* darling?"

"I was just wondering," he gently said, his voice amused, "what price you paid to have me stand beside you at Buchan House?"

She hesitated for a fraction of a second. "Your word now, for I tell you in confidence."

He nodded, then grinned. "I'm breathless with curiosity."

"Buchan has a young footman," she said, climbing into bed beside him, her smile matching his.

"Yes?" He anticipated, his mouth curving wider in merriment, but he wished to hear her account.

"And we act out a particular performance for Buchan."

"He watches?"

"Of course."

"Does anyone else watch?"

"Sinjin!"

He suspected others did; Buchan had a reputation for voyeurism. Perhaps she didn't know. "What's the lucky young man's name?"

She shrugged. "I'm not sure."

"And does he like you?" he drolly said.

Lying on her side, propped on one elbow, she traced the line of Sinjin's jaw—shadowed at this late hour with a dark stubble. "He gives that impression." Her smile resonated in her voice.

Blocking the leisurely drift of her fingertips with a gentle grasp, he took her hand in his, lacing her fingers companionably in his. "I've never been a footman," he murmured with a grin. "Are you a demanding mistress?"

"You're a scapegrace rogue, Sinjin," Cassandra playfully said, trying to pull her hand free.

"I suppose I'm not humble enough." He gazed at her cheerfully over her firmly imprisoned hand.

"My arrogant darling, you don't know what the word means."

He suspected Buchan's footman had been carefully selected for his physical attributes and, footman or lord, a man knew his capabilities. "And neither does your footman, does he?"

He'd never seen her blush before.

"Tell me what he says."

"I don't know, *Sinjin* . . ."

But her nipples had peaked, he noticed, and a warm flush had pinked her skin. "Tell me," he murmured, bringing her fingers to his mouth and nibbling gently, "and I'll see what I can do . . ."

He did, as it turned out, a very good Scot's accent, and he was no more humble than the well-endowed Buchan footman. For which Cassandra was well pleased. And much later, just before she fell asleep, she drowsily whispered, "You're an adorable rascal . . ."

Half-asleep, Sinjin lazily replied, "And you're the most delightful tart I know . . ."

So two nights later, he stood at the top of the stairway at Buchan House beside Cassandra, her silly young niece, Lavinia's country baronet father and disapproving mother.

Lady Wroxley, not comfortable with the accepted infidelities of the Ton, took exception to Sinjin's role in the family party, but since Cassandra was the benefactress who made young Lavinia's bow to society possible, her condemnation was restricted to cool rejoinders and lowering looks directed at the infamous Duke of Seth.

Within the elegantly incestuous world of the haut Ton, however, Sinjin's presence at Cassandra's side proved a drawing card of the first magnitude.

He was shameless—everyone agreed. And brazen.

Impudent too, with those eyes that could turn blankly angelic in a flash.

Unabashedly bold—like Cassandra, gossip tittle-tattled.

And they all came to see the insolent sight of Sinjin and Cassandra publicly playing husband and wife for a night.

Young Lavinia Wroxley's debut was the biggest crush of the season.

"Never thought to see The Saint domesticated," one of his friends sardonically commented as he passed down the receiving line.

Sinjin's bow was exquisite, his smile benign. "Cassandra can be persuasive," he said.

"Playing the gentleman, Sinjin darling?" a woman of his acquaintance archly purred when she made her curtsy to her host and hostess.

"I'm trying," he replied with a grin.

"George is going down to Kent for a week," she went on, her message unclouded.

Cassandra turned her head and scowled. "Really, Caroline, could this wait?"

"Have you met Miss Lavinia, Caro?" Sinjin smoothly interjected. "She seems a charming girl."

Caroline Danford's gaze held Sinjin's for a moment longer than necessary. "I'm sure she is. Remember now . . ." and with a light tap of her lace fan on Sinjin's cheek, she moved along.

"Good God, Sinjin," Cassandra hissed, her smile in place for her guests, "that woman has nerve. Can't she write you a note in the morning?"

Lady Wroxley's expression had turned glowering. Seth was a by-word for vice; women propositioned him openly. If Cassandra wasn't spending a fortune on Lavinia, she had half a mind to give that too handsome young blade a piece of her mind and let him know there were respectable people left in the world. And then her eyes opened wide, her jaw dropped and she forgave Sinjin St. John all his sins, for she recognized the man bearing through the crowd to greet the Duke of Seth.

"Evenin', Sinjin," the young man dressed in the height of fashion murmured as he approached, "you seem to have everyone in town here tonight."

"Evening, Prinny," Sinjin casually said to the young Prince of Wales, a companion in many of his revels. "And now that you're here, of course, the party is a sure success."

"Where's the chit you're doing this for?" the Prince inquired, his gaze drifting down the receiving line.

"Not doing it for a chit."

Prinny's glance swung back, the men's eyes meeting in understanding. "Cassandra," he said as she turned to him with a smile and curtsy, "you look eighteen yourself tonight. How can you possibly have a niece coming out?"

And when Lady Wroxley, cognizant of the great honor bestowed on her daughter's debut, swept her future king a deep bow a moment later, Sinjin glanced at the clock and said to Cassandra under his breath, "How much longer?"

Hours later, a thousand pointless social comments later, hundreds of cases of champagne later, a full repertoire of Maestro Longhi's dance music and dances later, buffet food and cards and gallons of shrub punch later, Sinjin and Cassandra walked into her boudoir.

"Vastly amusing," Sinjin mockingly exclaimed, falling onto Cassandra's bed, the last guest bowed out, the sun just beginning to rise over the garden wall, bathing the Palladian facade of Buchan House in rosy pink.[6]

"Vastly *successful,*" Cassandra more pertinently remarked, both ironically wielding the current adverb of choice in the Ton, "for young Tremaine and Georgie Cecil took a fancy to Lavinia."[7]

"So it's all been productive," Sinjin placidly said, kicking off his diamond-buckled shoes and beginning to unbutton his creme satin waistcoat. "Tremaine or Cecil will be shackled to—pardon my bluntness," he added with a grin, "your very dull niece. And worse," he went on with a swift rise of his dark brows, "they'll become son-in-law to the dull and *righteous* Lady Wroxley."

"Hush, Sinjin," Cassandra said, her own smile self-satisfied. "I've done my family duty."

"And the hell with Tremaine or Georgie."

"Of course, darling. If they're that—"

"Stupid?"

"I was thinking more benignly of—gullible . . ."

"Are we reeling in fish here?" Sinjin had gone still for a moment, his own escape from numerous manhunts over the years leaving him cynical, gun-shy and mildly resentful.

"Now, sweet, don't take it personally." Accomplished at reading Sinjin's moods, Cassandra prided herself on sustaining his interest for so long by never pressing. At the first whiff of constraint or obligation, Sinjin St. John generally disappeared. "You can warn off Tremaine and Cecil if it will make you feel better. The dowry I've given Lavinia will bring her a husband. It need not be them if it pains you," she remarked with a smile, and having finished untying the sash and drawstring neckline of her silk muslin gown, she let the sheer frothy garment drop to the floor in a whisper of silk.

"You do have a tantalizing way of expressing yourself, Cassandra," Sinjin said, his voice a husky murmur.

Cassandra stood in the middle of her Bessarabian carpet clad in a diminutive silk chemise, more sheer than opaque. She was the only woman he knew with breasts that large who had no need of corsets.

"To hell with Tremaine and Cecil," he said with a grin. "Come here."

And the sun had risen high over the garden wall by the time Sinjin and Cassandra fell contentedly to sleep.

They woke in the drowsy heat of afternoon to an altercation taking place below the opened windows.

A door banged open, or shut—the sound was indistinct. And in the torpor still clouding his mind, Sinjin registered briefly a word or two in Scots. But a second later, the angry voices quieted, and the spring afternoon outside resumed its lazy somnolence.

Cassandra rolled away from Sinjin with a blown kiss; he murmured something unintelligible to her before falling back to sleep.

Waking again short moments later, he realized the raised voices were closer now, although still muffled. Half-rising, he lay back on both elbows and, after swiftly casting a glance at Cassandra sleeping beside him, turned his head toward the door.

Distinct footsteps sounded now—heavy, determined strides moving down the corridor in their direction . . . and the unmistakable metallic rasp of a swinging scabbard—several scabbards!

He was out of bed in an instant, his black satin breeches almost buttoned when the door crashed open.

And the Earl of Dumfries, flanked by his two sons, all armed with broadswords, dirks and pistols, stood in the threshold.

Even had he a weapon, which he didn't, Sinjin swiftly reflected, the odds would be decidedly against him.

"We've come for you!" Fergus Fergusson bellowed, his voice rousing Cassandra from the hazy stupor occasioned by the crashing door.

"For what purpose?" Sinjin asked, his voice too harsh with affront.

"Ye can dress if ye wish," the Earl said, in his anger the Scots coming to the fore, "or ye can leave bare-assed. It makes no mind to me."

No answer there, but Sinjin wanted shoes at least wherever they were taking him, and from the rage emanating from Earl Dumfries, Sinjin didn't have to guess Chelsea figured somehow in this scene.

"Is there something I can do?" Cassandra quietly said, sitting up, awake now, clutching the bedclothes to her bosom, the action unfolding before her recognizable at least in terms of content. An armed, irate father and his two sons coming to take Sinjin away had of course to do with a seduction. She recognized Duncan. Who was the lady?

"Tell Seneca," Sinjin tersely replied, pushing his arms into his shirtsleeves. Wrenching the shirt swiftly over his head, he added, "And Sahar."

"You might tell them St. John is going on his bridal journey," the Earl growled, "and not likely to return any time soon."

Sinjin's head snapped around at the word "bridal," and he stood now, shock-still, his waistcoat at elbow level.

"You're mad," Sinjin said in a voice so cold that Cassandra shivered in the heat of the afternoon.

"You're right there, St. John," Fergus Fergusson rapped out. "Mad as hell. Now say goodbye to Lady Buchan, for ye won't be back to warm her bed."

"How quaint," Cassandra said sotto voce, but the sound traveled in the absolute silence of the room, and the Earl's scowl deepened.

"Quaint and farcical it may be in London's beau monde, but marriage is binding to the Fergussons, my lady, so ye'll have to find a new stud to amuse you."

She didn't think it possible to curb the Duke of Seth's propensity for vice, marriage or no, but the Earl's tone precluded voicing such observations aloud.

"You're way out of bounds, Dumfries, coming here," Sinjin declared, roughly dressed, seething with rage, "but you're a fool if you think you can force me to marry."

"You'll marry with the last breath in your body if need be, but marry you will." The Earl of Dumfries had his pistol pointed dead center at Sinjin's chest, his hand steady, his eyes flinty hard. "Tie him," he ordered his sons.

"Bloody hell, this is medieval," Sinjin said as Duncan and Neil approached. But he was wondering how much they knew. Had

Chelsea admitted all? Did they know of Oakham and the night in York? He couldn't in honor deny his part in the seduction of their sister. But Lord, marriage?

"Medieval it may be," Duncan said, gruff and curt, his face set, his eyes expressionless, "but she's my sister." And in that irrevocable statement of fact, no issue of culpability or blame mattered. Family honor demanded justice.

They differed on the matter of justice, Sinjin thought as Neil unlooped a coil of rope from his belt, and he was damned well not going to go like a lamb to slaughter. Striking out, he slammed his fist into Neil's startled face and straight-armed Duncan out of his way with an adrenaline-induced power that sent Duncan sprawling across Cassandra's brilliant floral carpet. Sprinting full out, Sinjin made for the open window. They could discuss the particulars of Dumfries honor in a venue less disadvantageous to him, one where he wasn't unarmed and outnumbered three to one.

A pistol ball narrowly missed his face as he lunged for the open window, and Sinjin had one leg over the sill when the Earl coldly said, "The next shot is for your mistress."

The portico roof was only six feet below him, and for a fraction of a second Sinjin weighed the sincerity of the Earl's threat against the sight of freedom. But he had no choice of course; even the remotest possibility of harm to Cassandra was unthinkable.

He swung his leg back inside and sat on the wide sill surveying the sight of Cassandra, who was no longer blasé, but terrified in her position of hostage to Sinjin's impulses. "Your protection of women," Sinjin drawled, "doesn't extend beyond your family circle, I take it."

"Let's just say in terms of priorities," Chelsea's father replied, his voice as rude as Sinjin's, "your presence at the altar outweighs the Duchess of Buchan's current good health."

"Chivalry apparently has a price."

"And perhaps you weren't aware of its exact cost when you entertained my daughter."

His daughter! Who was the chit? With Cassandra's personal danger passed, her gossiping mind reverted to type, racing through all the possible young misses down from the north. Why hadn't she heard of the Earl of Dumfries' daughter? Leave it to Sinjin to find a pretty thing no one else had seen. But she pitied his unfortunate discovery, for Dumfries was dead serious. And while duels were still a means of settling masculine affront, Sinjin wasn't being given a chance to defend himself. He was going to be manhandled to the altar like some common person.

"Your daughter never mentioned this particular price," Sinjin insolently said, finding himself still curiously honor-bound about Chelsea's confidential fifty thousand.

"Well then, we'll have time to discuss it on our journey north."

"Do you really think you can get by with this?"

"I know I can. Look out the window. You wouldn't have gotten far."

Sinjin turned, his gaze sweeping the drive and garden that had a moment ago been vacant, save for some droning bees in the flowers. A platoon of Scotsmen, their kilts the green and blue of the Fergusson clan, weapons in hand, surrounded the entrance and guarded the gate.

"So you wouldn't have shot Cassandra," Sinjin said, turning back to face his assailants.

"Probably not." The Earl's voice was as equivocal as his reply. "But don't make the mistake of thinking my courtesy extends to you," he added, "for I'd shoot you in a minute. In fact, I'm finding it increasingly difficult *not* to shoot you."

"But then your daughter would lack the husband you're so assiduously pursuing," Sinjin lazily drawled.

"I didn't say I'd kill you."

A certain inevitability suddenly struck Sinjin, as though a door had closed in his face. Swiftly looking out the window again, he mentally counted twenty-five—enough, he thought, to nicely force the issue. He was caught, and securely. "Your daughter may rue this choice of yours," he quietly said, his blue gaze swinging back to the Earl. "Have you considered that?"

"Constantly," Fergus Fergusson brusquely said, his own gaze uncompromising. "Now tie him."

Chapter 23

Cassandra sent for Seneca as soon as the Scots rear guard left her home, but it was many hours after Sinjin had been taken away, giving the Fergussons considerable lead time.

Cassandra greeted Seneca in the entrance hall, obviously concerned for Sinjin. Guiding him into the nearby library, she already had filled him in on the general sequence of events before she beckoned him to a seat.

"Dumfries took him?" Seneca questioned, dropping into a large Jacobean armchair. "You're sure now?"

"I know Duncan. I'm sure." Cassandra paced, unable to relax after being held captive for six hours by polite but barbarically large and reticent Fergusson clansmen. For a woman prone to chatty conversation, the long hours of silence had been distressing.

"And you think they're heading north?" While Seneca displayed no apprehension, his questions were succinct, swift and to the point. He had every intention of leaving London within the hour.

"Dumfries said north, so I'm assuming to his estate in Ayrshire."

"A troop that large will cause notice. They should be easy to follow."

"They've been gone over six hours . . ."

"We'll be on our way shortly. Sahar's mounting the grooms now."

"You'll need more than a few grooms against the army of Dumfries' clansmen. He *means* to marry Sinjin to his daughter. And post-haste."

"I'm bringing the Bedouins," Seneca tranquilly said, "who should be adequate." He smiled in that calm way of his that seemed to regard any crisis as manageable. "And perhaps the ceremony won't take place the minute they arrive in Ayrshire."

"If you're bringing those burnoused cutthroats with you, Sinjin's as good as free, but not in time, I suspect. The bride has had plenty of time to arrange the 'festivities,' and Dumfries is assuming pursuit, or he wouldn't have left a rear guard to stave off word to you. I expect the ceremony will be expeditiously done."

Seneca shrugged, conscious of his friend's adamant position on marriage. "Well then, there's always divorce."

"If Dumfries' daughter is some virtuous young maid, the courts and Parliament may not be amenable to a divorce. If she's pure, Sinjin won't have just cause . . . Derby lost his case because his own infidelities were held against him."[8] Cassandra swatted at her silk-tasseled drapes in passing, vexed at Sinjin's being taken away. "Sinjin may have finally bedded the wrong woman."

Seneca sighed. "He knew it too—damned fool."

Cassandra came to an abrupt stop in her restless perambulation. "Is she so beautiful then?"

Seneca paused, having caught the undertone of envy. Cassandra was one of the beauties of London, but in an exotic fashion—dramatic and dark.

"She's different," he kindly said.

"She must be *very* different to bring Sinjin to his knees."

"The girl likes horses," he said, using the words Sinjin had answered with once to avoid closer introspection.

"What the hell does that mean?" Her dark brows suddenly arched in inquiry. "Are we discussing some perverse depravity?"

Seneca shook his head, a faint smile enlivening the serenity of his features. "I very much doubt it; I'm simply repeating a comment of his. But you'll have to ask Sinjin."

"I surely will when he comes back to town with his new wife." Cassandra's smile could not be characterized as pleasant.

Seneca and Sahar set out immediately with a small number of grooms to track Sinjin, their best hope of rescue a stealthy raid with a few men rather than a frontal attack. In any event, even ducal establishments no longer maintained armed fighting men, so a sizable force wasn't feasible on such short notice—although Sinjin had an advantage in the style of his grooms brought back from Barbary. Warriors from the desert tribes, they were trained from the cradle in the only two pursuits considered appropriate to a man: horsemanship and combat.

The Scots' clan system, while theoretically broken forty years ago after Culloden, still maintained the ties of family obligation undiminished. The Earl of Dumfries, as titular and functional laird of the clan, had at his command the allegiance of his clansmen, who were a formidable army.

The size of the Fergusson troop precluded concealment, so their route was obvious beginning at Cassandra's doorstep. The Scots were riding hard, not concerned with hiding their trail. Even with Sinjin's best bloodstock in pursuit, Seneca and Sahar set out at a disadvantage of several hours.

Seneca knew that the Earl of Dumfries would be traveling on prime horseflesh as well, so the possibility of gaining on them was limited. Neither party stopped to sleep or rest, the Fergusson horses replenished with mounts left at posting stations on the route north. Seneca and Sahar had taken Barbs from Sinjin's stable, their endurance and speed legendary, the chosen Haymours considered the fastest horses in the world, capable of galloping days without tiring.

Desert-bred, the *chareb-er-rehh,* poetically defined as "drinker of the wind," boasted a beautiful conformation, excellent wind and the strength to travel 320 miles in twenty-four hours.[9] With the fleet, courageous Haymours, Sinjin's posse hoped to close in pursuit, for English horses weren't bred for endurance.

Each horseman in Sinjin's employ, whether from North Africa or North America, experienced an exhilaration long denied them as they rode to save their friend. Reared in cultures of austerity, they carried enough barley to feed their mounts, frugal stores for themselves, lethal unsheathed blades and pistols tucked into their belts, rifles slung across their backs. There was no need to stop.

They swept north, this black-robed troop mounted on lean, long-legged bays with flaring nostrils and huge black eyes. A red Indian in fringed, beaded leather commanded them, the exotic host causing excited comment as they raced through the villages and towns on the Great North Road.

Sahar rode point, setting the murderous pace.

·   ·   ·

Meanwhile Sinjin, surrounded by Fergussons, his hands bound before him, continued pounding north with only short delays for fresh mounts. A new horse was always brought to him by one of the Fergusson clansmen at a point some distance outside the villages through which they passed.

With the number in Sinjin's guard, no one would have been foolish enough to help him anyway, but curious spectators were avoided by this method and also any awkward need to shoot him—should he attempt to call for aid. Escape was continually on his mind; he had no intention of being married off without a struggle, and without Cassandra's welfare in jeopardy, he had only his own health to hazard.

He stayed alert, familiar with the route they were following, watching for an opportunity to flee. Just as evening fell, they reached a bridge that had been narrowed for repairs, so only two mounted men could ride abreast—the road ahead bordered with forest. His chance had come. Impatiently he sat on his horse as three pairs of riders preceded him, his gaze on the landscape ahead, searching for the best cover. Finally his turn came, and escorted by only one clansman, he urged his mount forward. Counting the hoofbeats—hollow echoes on the wooden planks—he reckoned the approach of freedom, and as his horse stepped back onto the road, Sinjin broke away, lashing his horse, wrenching its head sharply toward the trees lining the road. Charging into the thicket, he entered the shadowed tree line twenty yards ahead of instant screaming pursuit.

"Stop him!" the Earl of Dumfries cried, still on the opposite side of the river, whipping his pistol from his saddle scabbard and taking aim.

Crashing through the underbrush, Sinjin spurred his horse, viciously jabbing his heels into the big chestnut's flanks. Snapping branches slashed at his face as he urged his mount to speed, the huge beast plunging through the heavy cover like a battering ram.

The pursuing guards thundering behind fired at him, their aim erratic at such speed, the thirty yards separating them sufficient screen in the heavy growth.

Dappled light shone ahead, Sinjin thankfully noted, the possibility of being unhorsed disastrously real in the thick timber, and in fifty more yards, patches of open sky beckoned. He could pick up speed across the open country ahead. Breaking from the thicket at a full gallop, he swiftly studied the landscape ahead: to the left the river, directly in front the gentle rise of fallow field, far to the right—the church spire of a village.

Wheeling to the right, he dug in his heels and, grateful for the Fergussons' excellent stable, felt his mount gather himself for more speed. If he could reach the village before his pursuers, he might be able to reach the sanctuary of the church—or, considering the Earl's sense of mission up against unarmed religious refuge, he'd perhaps find better protection behind a musket at the nearest tavern.

The full cry of his hunters exploded into the calm of evening as they bolted from the trees, and moments later, renewed firing exploded around him now, his body a prime target in the open. Bending low over his mount's neck, he gauged the distance to the possible safety of the village. A quarter mile at most, and he might stand a chance. Fifty yards less now . . . could he be lucky enough to find a sheriff in residence? The Scots' method of procuring bridegrooms was illegal in the civilized world.

Closer . . .

Closer . . .

Only two hundred more yards . . .

The hedge bordering the road to the village was near enough to touch when the shot hit him.

The Fergussons must load their own charges, he thought in fleeting acknowledgment as the powerful impact knocked him from the saddle. But he wasn't able to immediately determine the point of entry, for the convulsive shock seemed to detonate in his body and brain with indiscriminate explosive force.

How good was their aim, he facetiously thought, surprised that humor survived under such incapacitating agony. Would Chelsea's bridegroom be delivered to the wedding dead or alive? His bound arms didn't seem to work properly anymore, an indistinct premonition judgmentally assessed as the ground spun toward him with violent speed and he found himself unable to muster the strength to break his fall.

He heard an ungodly scream as he hit the ground—a scream detached somehow from his person, yet obstinately vibrating through his body in horrendous torturous spasms. The racking pain concentrated a lifetime later into an excruciating core of unbearable agony where his arm joined his left shoulder.

Aha, he mildly reflected, already drifting toward a welcoming darkness.

A shoulder shouldn't be fatal.

The Fergussons were excellent marksmen.

And Chelsea Amity Fergusson had not been cheated of a bride-groom.

They carried his bloodied comatose body to an apothecary in the nearby village.

"A hunting accident," the Earl said, his voice suggesting that any further questions would be unwelcome. The wounded man was to be cleaned up and bandaged. They had some distance yet to ride that night, the Earl succinctly added. So the shoulder should be tightly bound.

The apothecary worked over Sinjin, grateful that his patient was still unconscious, for the pistol ball had shattered and the laborious extraction would have felled a conscious mind.

"He should be allowed a night's rest," the surgeon cautiously declared as he knotted the last bandage in place. "The wound could putrefy with agitation."

"He can rest tomorrow," the Earl sharply replied. "Wake him."

And when the hartshorn was placed beneath Sinjin's nostrils, he came awake with a start, still half-absorbed in a curious dream, thinking he was in the colonies. A moment later he groaned at the shocking pain and opened his eyes to recall that, instead of suffering from wounds sustained at Saratoga, he was the victim of his future father-in-law's displeasure.

The night ride was almost intolerable, the swift pace an excruciating torture that, Sinjin felt sure, gladdened the Earl of Dumfries' heart. So he set his teeth against the pounding rhythm cruelly jarring his mutilated shoulder, gave thanks to the dose of laudanum the apothecary had given him, which kept him from fainting away completely, and reflected on ways he might someday retaliate against the man destroying his life.

Never a vengeful man, Sinjin discovered during that long, seemingly endless night of grating pain that he possessed a capacity for personal violence directed at another human being. Not the generalized soldier's duty necessary to defend one's country from its enemies, but rather a gut-deep hatred sufficient to feed a vendetta of revenge through several generations.

A pity his blood lust was directed at his future father-in-law.

· · ·

They arrived at Holybow in Ayrshire early evening the following day. Without ceremony, Sinjin was escorted to a first-floor bedchamber held in readiness for him with a hot bath and clean clothes.

He saw no one save an elderly manservant who they must have considered too feeble for him to throttle in cold blood. When he was bathed, rebandaged, dressed and fed, the old man carried away the remnants of his meal and bath. Neil arrived at the threshold of his room a short time later, his face bruised from Sinjin's recent well-placed blow, and said, "You've five minutes with my sister to put affairs in order between you."

The door closed behind Neil, the sound of the key turning in the lock a reminder of his captivity. And he awaited the next act in the horrendous drama of his newly obstructed life.

Disgust, and an anger so powerful that only another man of unlimited authority would understand, inundated his brain at his unnatural predicament. He was coerced, confined, captive. Unheard of for a peer of his rank, unconscionable for a man like Sinjin, who hadn't subjugated himself before even that most dutiful of obligations—his father. He had instead, years ago, when forced to submit, broken forever with his parent.

And now he was wounded and a prisoner, about to be forcibly married.

All because of a golden-haired bitch.

Chapter 24

Sinjin was standing in the middle of the room, his eyes trained on the door, his rage so intense he had to clench his usable fist to keep from hitting something. Preferably a Fergusson.

She looked very pale when she entered the room, her green and blue tartan—pinned on her shoulders with a silver brooch bearing the family arms—sharp contrast with her ashen face. He almost felt a pang of sympathy for her, so tragic an expression gazed out from her deep purple eyes. But the inclination instantly dissipated at the grating sound of the key once again being turned in the lock, his forced marriage only minutes away.

"You bitch," he growled. "This is what you've been after from the first, isn't it? The fifty thousand wasn't enough for you god-damned Lowland bandits. You want my title too."

Twin spots of color pinked Chelsea's pale cheeks at his brutal words, and were her unhappiness less vivid, she would have answered as heatedly. But she was as much a prisoner as he. "I'm sorry about everything that happened, about your shoulder, and . . . Father's —rage. And regardless of what you think," Chelsea quietly said, "I'm not a willing participant in any of this. I understand your anger," she went on, pressing her hands against the door as if to support herself against his diabolical stare, "for I'm equally offended by Father's heavy-handed methods, but you can't deny your part . . .

at least . . . in terms of partial responsibility. This child is yours, after all."

"Perhaps," he said, his voice softly vicious, his large form utterly still, his eyes as unrelentingly chill. "As I recall, the Greek sponges I gave you at Oakham *were* used."

"Then it could have happened before or after Oakham—although," she added with a thistledown touch of sarcasm, not prone to passively accept the role of adventuress, "as *I* recall, on numerous occasions at Oakham, you were too impatient to give me time to make use of the Greek sponges."

She always managed to sound so reasonable, and were he not a captive about to be married under duress, he would have willingly accepted that reason. "You could have lain with someone else between Newmarket and Oakham or now," he bluntly said. "I dislike being selected as the father of your child."

"You're accountable for what you do despite your high rank." Each word was uttered with an even modulated restraint, but Chelsea's violet eyes were touched with resentment. "A new concept for you, perhaps." She sighed suddenly, a soft sound of regret. "Look," she quietly went on, "I'm not arguing about who's more responsible; I wholly accept my part in the conception of this child. And were I not vulnerable to the force my father and brothers employ—as you are—I wouldn't be here now speaking to you. I'd be in hiding somewhere, awaiting the birth of our child. Without you, without even informing you of the event. Without demands of any kind. I wasn't interested in anything more from you when we met, save a means of escape for myself from Bishop Hatfield. I still don't want anything of you, but my family disagrees and I'm powerless to oppose them." Her chin lifted a small fraction, and her eyes surveyed him with a degree of criticism previously absent. "But other men take responsibility for their children . . . surely it's not unheard of in your rarefied world."

Sinjin looked at her from under mockingly lowered lashes, the throbbing of his shoulder adjunct to each harsh word. "Like Devonshire, you mean, who keeps his wife and mistress under one roof, with his mélange of family underfoot. Or our illustrious royal dukes who have children by many women but marry none." His tone was cold as ice. "Maybe you mean Topham Bolingbroke, who's bred two children on Chester's wife. Or you're probably thinking of Leveson-Gore. He just married Leicestershire's young daughter after impregnating Diana Fowler for the third time. Don't talk to me about responsibility like a Methodist," he snapped. "I'm Seth, and that precludes your kind of responsibility."

He was right, of course. No peer of illustrious rank was ever forced into marriage. Nor should he be, if she had her way. "If I could, I'd run," Chelsea whispered, weary of the weeks of fruitless argument with her father. She'd never wanted a husband. This awful predicament had all been begun to escape that very trap. "I don't want you for a husband any more than you want me for a wife." Her voice was no more than a wisp of sound at the last, and she sat down suddenly on a nearby chair, her head spinning.

Sinjin stood aloof, suspicious, too familiar with female ploys. Chelsea's tartan shawl, trailing on the floor, was symbolic to him of a world still operating with medieval custom. In his sophisticated world, overt scandal was avoided. An unconventional pregnancy didn't require marriage, or at least not necessarily marriage to the responsible party. Often children of noble families owed their patrimony to a variety of fathers. Pregnant aristocratic ladies traveled abroad to have their lover's child and returned from their "holidays" with a "cousin's" child, who would be reared by a relative removed from society. Everyone understood there were manageable solutions. And marriages were ultimately consummated for dynastic reasons, for required heirs, for profitable alliances, occasionally for love, but not because of a pregnancy.

Contemplating her growing pallor, he was about to ask if she needed help when she gasped, "The basin," and put both hands to her mouth.

He moved with lightning speed, snatching the washbasin from its stand near the window, and lunging forward, he slid the porcelain bowl under her mouth just in time to catch her expelled dinner. She looked so miserable that he felt his bitterness abate slightly. "Do you get sick often?" he asked, offering her his handkerchief.

She nodded, her stomach not entirely free of nausea yet.

Setting aside the basin, Sinjin squatted down, gently wiped her eyes and mouth, then sat back on his haunches watching her while she shivered.

"Are you cold?" He wasn't a cruel man by nature, his voice familiar again, deep, rich-timbred, without antipathy.

She shook her head no, even as another trembling spasm vibrated through her body.

"Poor thing," he murmured. Rising, he walked over to the bed, ripped off the coverlet and, returning, wrapped it securely around her.

He smiled a little and hunkered down so their eyes were parallel, the first smile she'd seen since entering the room. "Will I have to play nursemaid from now on?"

"We won't be together," Chelsea said.

His surprise showed; he hadn't known.

"They're taking you north to a fishing lodge."

"Why?"

"They think you might harm me . . ."

A flicker of something unearthly—terrible and ferocious—shone in his eyes for a moment, and Chelsea wondered if her family was right to show caution. But he seemed to regain his composure, although his voice, when he spoke, was guarded.

"For how long?"

"Until the baby is born."

"Impossible!" he exploded, standing in a fierce rush of muscled power. He glanced down at her for a moment; then the fury returned to his face. Twirling about, he stalked to the window.

The arithmetic sliced through his brain. Six months! No, seven! Bloody fucking hell! Did these Scottish brigands realize what century this was? His fingers, braced on the windowsill, were white with the pressure of his rage.

Whirling around, he said, clipped and terse, "What if I refuse?"

"It won't matter. Papa's called down more of his clansmen already for the escort north. There's thirty additional Fergussons to see that you don't refuse."

"I wish," Sinjin said, dead cold and pitiless, "I had never met you."

She shrank from his savage hate, not strong enough at the moment to fight back. She had, in any event, been battling her family for over two weeks, with little success—with *no* success—and she was weary. "I too wish," Chelsea murmured, her eyes smudged with lavender shadows of fatigue, "I had never heard your name." He took no blame; he blamed her, as if his seductive charm, his easy friendship, his impatient pursuit were separate somehow from the circumstances that brought them here today.

"How convenient for men," she said, passion in her words, "to be able to walk away."

"How convenient for women," he growled, "to set the trap."

. . .

They were given a choice a few minutes later by a grim-faced Earl of Dumfries to be bound or unbound at their marriage. But married they'd be. And he waited silently for their answer.

"How far would I get?" Sinjin grimly said, not inclined to say his marriage vows in servility.

"Why offer the pretense, Father, when I'm being forced like chattel to do your bidding? Tie me," Chelsea said, each clipped word falling like poison into the deadly silence.

"Very well," her father snapped, his patience lost two weeks ago, his headstrong daughter not about to bring a bastard into the world, no matter her preference. He was laird; he would be obeyed as the lairds of Fergusson had been obeyed since the dawn of history, and if she wished to play the martyr, she could.

A curt nod a moment later to the family priest and the ceremony began, fifty armed Fergusson clansmen witness, the glitter of weapons brilliant in the candlelit chapel.

Dressed in borrowed Fergusson clothes, a jacket found that was loose enough to slide over his bandaged shoulder, Sinjin stood rigid, letting the words wash over him, his gaze unfocused above the priest's tonsured head. He didn't often acknowledge the importance of his family and name, but he was struck with a sudden sense of solemnity at his marriage, no matter its unorthodox nature. The next Duchess of Seth was standing at his side, another St. John wife in a lengthy history that went back to early baronies in Normandy. St. Johns had come over to England with William the Conqueror; they had stood by their king, strong and valiant, through the vicissitudes of the Plantagenets and down through the centuries. His son, this child perhaps, would inherit his title. A sobering prospect for a man who had never seriously considered marriage.

He glanced down at his bride, tied like a trussed chicken at his side, and felt, for the first time since his abduction, the urge to chuckle. Whatever their differences (and they were many), whatever the iniquities of this forced marriage, the Earl of Dumfries' daughter would certainly not bring docile blood into the family.

She must have felt his eyes on her, for she looked up that moment and, seeing his suppressed smile, frowned at him. "Do you see some ghoulish humor in this situation?" she hissed, the flowers in her hair quivering with her indignation.

"I find the means of your obedience rustic, my darling Duchess." The white tabby of her dress was incongruously ornamental against the rough rope binding her.

"I'm not your damned Duchess yet," she whispered, ignoring the frowns of the priest and her father.

"Do you, Lady Chelsea Amity Fergusson of Dumfries," the priest intoned, the brief ceremony almost over, "take this man for your lawful wedded husband?"

"No," she snapped.

"She says yes," her father blandly remarked. "Go on."

The small priest looked cautiously from face to face, but short of serving as pincushion for the fifty-odd broadswords desecrating the Lord's chapel, he had no choice *but* to go on.

"Do you, Sinjin St. John, Duke of Seth, take this woman as your lawful wedded wife?"

Sinjin looked down at Chelsea's small set face, gazed briefly at the array of warriors surrounding him and decided he would speak for himself at his marriage. "I do," he said, his voice clear.

Awkwardly pulling his signet ring off with his left hand, his injured shoulder painful enough to cause an unconscious grimace, he slid the huge ring on the fourth finger of her left hand, then gently closed her fist over the ring that had been his father's and grandfather's and beyond—a gift to a St. John ancestor for loyalty, tradition said, from King Richard on his return from the Holy Land. "It lives in you, my Duchess," Sinjin murmured, the St. John family motto especially apt on this occasion.

It was over, he thought as the priest shut his prayer book, two months after he first found Duncan's sister in his carriage.

He was married.

It was over, Chelsea thought. Sinjin's ring, still warm from his finger, curled within her fist, like his child in her womb—the thing she wished least in the world.

She was married.

As in all the nuptial arrangements, neither bride nor groom was consulted, and immediately after the abbreviated ceremony, Sinjin was bustled into a closed carriage with two armed Fergusson clansmen, the remaining guard accompanying the vehicle front and rear. And his journey north began.

Chelsea was untied and escorted to her room, where she was locked in.

Their honeymoon night proved sleepless for both bride and groom, but not for normal reasons of romance.

They were both planning their escape.

Chapter 25

Chelsea had been left with a guard at Holybow, but the bulk of the Scots, along with the Earl and his sons, had accompanied Sinjin farther north. Sinjin's people would be more interested in freeing him, Dumfries had concluded, and the Earl had divided his force accordingly.

The stables were almost empty of horses, the house lit in only a few rooms, when Seneca and his men arrived. And after further reconnoitering, it appeared as though only Chelsea was left at the country house with a modest guard.

The new bride alone? And guarded? Apparently she and her relatives were not in accord, Seneca concluded. But he was forced to wait until the servants had all gone to bed, until the routine of the guards' patrols had been marked, until deepest night enshrouded the old stone country home in concealing darkness.

Then the taking of Chelsea from her bed was accomplished by Seneca and his cohorts with no bloodshed and a minimum of difficulty. Since their style of warfare was predicated on raiding and surprise, all were well trained in the necessary tactics; the guards on patrol were silenced, one by one, and Seneca and two Bedouins went up the granite wall of the house on a rope conveniently lassoed around a gargoyle drain spout.

Chelsea didn't even hear the three men come through her window, which was slightly open to the warm night air. All moved soundlessly on the carpeted floor, their heelless footgear silent, their weapons—tucked into the sashes at their waists—noiseless. And her initial shock and fear at the feel of a hand covering her mouth were quickly dissipated when she opened her eyes and saw Seneca's face in the gloom.

She waved at him to indicate her friendliness, and when his hand tentatively slid away, she whispered, "I know where they've taken him."

"Where?" he asked, his voice raised only enough to carry the small distance to her ear.

"I'll show you."

"No, just tell me. You'll slow us down." Then, recalling her near win over Fordham, he said in modification, "My men aren't used to traveling with a woman."

"Well then," Chelsea softly said with a smile, "they're about to experience it for the first time. You don't know where Sinjin's being sent. I do. And unless you take me out of here, I shan't tell you."

Seneca hesitated only the merest fraction, debating the merits of threats, but his two henchmen, tall dark shadows at the foot of her bed, didn't seem to deter the Earl's daughter. So, unless he wished to use more lethal means . . . And she *was*, from all appearances, Sinjin's new wife.

"Did Sinjin marry you?" he asked as a matter of clarification.

"Yes."

"Willingly?" Although the answer was fairly obvious, he needed a definitive answer.

"Of course not."

"And you?" It was grossly impolite, but it mattered if she wanted to come along.

"I was bound during the ceremony."

No equivocation there. Should he take her? Seneca sighed, his better judgment screaming dissent. "The guards are to keep you in then," he tentatively said.

"And you out."

When she smiled, Seneca immediately realized how she'd dazzled even a jaded man like Sinjin. "Dress comfortably," he said, relenting. "We don't stop often."

Chelsea was already throwing the bedcovers aside before he finished speaking, no prudish modesty curtailing her desire for freedom. "Give me five minutes," she said, throwing her bare legs over the side of the bed without a thought for covering her limbs with her nightgown. "My dressing room doesn't have another exit," she went on, striding toward the small chamber adjacent to her bedroom, her blond tresses and white gown flaring out behind her. "And you can be damned sure I won't take my own life."

Seneca grinned. The new Duchess would give Sinjin a wild ride, he didn't doubt, and for the first time since hearing of Sinjin's abduction, Seneca marginally relaxed. He didn't know about the Earl of Dumfries' plans, but his daughter at least was unobjectionable, and more—an independent young lady of beguiling character, a distinct improvement over the superficial beauties of the Ton that Sinjin customarily entertained.

Short minutes later, Chelsea came out booted and dressed for hard riding, a small leather satchel slung over her shoulder. "I'm not coming back here," she said. "And if Sinjin doesn't want his wife in close proximity, which," she went on with swift smile, "I expect he doesn't, I've my portion in hand to live on . . ."

Seneca didn't perceive that the Duke of Seth intended for his wife to live as a pauper somewhere, but under the bizarre circumstances of his marriage, he'd reserve judgment on Sinjin's feelings until he spoke with him. He might, in fact, want her to the devil and out of his sight without a shilling.

Chelsea led them down the back staircase, out the terrace door and through the kitchen garden to the open ground of the stable yard. At that point Seneca and his men rechecked the bound guards, led Chelsea to their hidden mounts and men, saw her up on one of the sinewy Barbs. Seneca mounted and the troop fell in behind him. Without a command or gesture or word, they cantered out of the small copse and regained the road.

Chelsea maintained the pace without effort, the steady gallop a familiar pace after riding relays of racers out every morning and evening at their stables. Occasionally she'd pat the soft leather of her satchel, slung over her pommel, reassuringly, the money sufficient to maintain a small household for several years. Sinjin's thousand pounds saved against an undetermined financial emergency had turned out to be *her* emergency.

Hers and her child's. For the first time since she'd acknowledged her pregnancy, she faced the prospect of a child with pleasure.

She had independence once again, too—at least she would after Sinjin was rescued and returned to London. Neither of them wished for this marriage, the absurdity of her father's actions ruinous to them both; surely living apart would prove amenable to Sinjin. And since he already had a son, this child she carried should be of no interest to him.

I'll teach you to ride, she silently said, as though she already had the company of her child. And you can teach me about babies, she reflected with a smile. She'd find a small cottage near Newmarket, for she planned on continuing to do what she did best—raise racers.

Chapter 26

Two days later, they reached the desolate seacoast off Rattray Head and concealed themselves in a deserted crofter's hut on the isolated shoreline of the North Sea. Dressed for the cool weather coming down with the winds from the north, Chelsea tramped the familiar terrain of her family's landhold while Seneca and Sahar reconnoitered Sinjin's prison.

A small lodge built of native stone, its slate roof glistening smooth from a century of punishing wind and rain, the residence serving as gaol for Sinjin stood stark and solitary on a rise overlooking the River Dean. Stunted pines, planted by generations past, gave mute evidence of nature's unfavorable rule, nothing taller than marsh hay thriving on the windswept coast.

Their arrival had been recent, for supplies were still piled in the stables built into the lee of the hill. Seneca's scouts stayed on watch around the clock, monitoring activities, detailing the pattern of the guard schedule, looking for evidence of Sinjin's position. They discovered he was being kept in a second-floor room; they had caught a glimpse of him once. But apparently, even in his room, guards attended him, for he wasn't seen at the window again.

The Earl came to see Sinjin in the morning, an invariable pattern since their arrival, with the marriage settlement drawn up by Fergusson lawyers in hand. On each of the four mornings he'd ordered,

"Sign these," and for four days Sinjin had refused. Their conversation this morning had lost even the slender pretext of civility previously maintained, both men openly hostile after four aggravating days, both furious at the impasse in their lives, neither inclined to offer even the barest of courtesies.

"If you don't sign," Earl Dumfries curtly said, slapping the document on the table near Sinjin's chair, "you'll rot on this desolate shore, my word on it." The Earl's sense of affront mounted each time he dealt with the arrogant Seth.

"Then I'll rot, for your family won't get a penny more than prescribed by law. *My* word on that, Fergusson!" Sinjin was tied to a chair after he'd lunged at his father-in-law's throat the previous day. "And your daughter better damn well have a child who bears some resemblance to me, or you won't even get that."

The Earl struck Sinjin with a lashing straight-arm, the blow delivered with such force that Sinjin's head snapped back. "Mind your tongue about my daughter," the Earl softly said, massaging his stinging hand, "or she won't recognize you when she sees you next."

"One can only hope it won't be soon," Sinjin softly said, his voice sounding strangely far off with the ringing in his ears. "I don't think I can afford her. She cost me eighty thousand already for your racing debts," Sinjin insolently added, licking away the blood welling from his split lip.

The Earl, while clearly struck by the startling news, wasn't in a frame of mind to acknowledge a debt of any kind to the man who had ruined his daughter. "You're a liar," he growled, "as well as a libertine. She won the money at the York races."

"She *won* it at my hunting box in Oakham," Sinjin softly drawled, "in the usual way . . ." Gentleman's honor no longer operated under his current conditions of durance vile, and if Fergusson intended to beat him into signing the marriage settlement, he might as well understand the extent of his daughter's "cooperation" in the matter of her pregnancy. "To satisfy your money-lenders, I believe . . ." he cuttingly added. His shoulder was worse today, the throbbing extending down his arm; his wrists were raw from being tied to the chair arms, and he didn't give a damn if the Earl of Dumfries choked on his stunned disbelief. Right now, if he could break free, he'd choke him himself.

Slowly advancing toward Sinjin, the Earl wore an expression of such black fury that Sinjin braced himself for the coming blow. But the Earl didn't strike him when he neared. He bent slightly forward until his face was very close to Sinjin's; then, deliberately grasping him on both shoulders with a punishing grip intended to inflict pain, he said in the barest of whispers, "If you're right, *you're* to blame for seducing my daughter, and if you're *lying,* I'll beat you like a black-guard cur for disgracing my daughter's name. I detest you for plant-ing a child in my daughter's belly, and you'll pay for that, St. John . . . dearly. With this settlement, with your skin, with your peace of mind."

Pale under the Earl's harrowing grip, Sinjin grimly clenched his teeth, determined not to disgrace himself by fainting. His gaze locked with the Earl's. "Fuck you," he weakly said.

The Earl's hands tightened.

A buzzing hummed in Sinjin's ears, his vision danced with dots of light and only steely nerve wrenched his mind back from welcom-ing oblivion. Perspiration beaded his upper lip; his fingers curled dead white over the chair arms, and his teeth were bared in a ghastly grin. "Could our lawyers discuss this?" Sinjin whispered, "because I'm losing my concentration."

"Everything's a game with you," the Earl flared, "including my daughter's seduction . . ." Incensed at the useless debacle of his daughter's life and at his iniquitous son-in-law's shameless insolence even in extremity, he wished to kill the notorious rake who had destroyed Chelsea's life.

He could crush him, he thought, squeeze the life and blood from him and save the world from the corruption of his casual transgres-sions. The pressure of his fingers increased, and a sense of pleasure inundated the Earl's mind as Sinjin's pain intensified, as he fought to endure the agony racking his body. The cords standing out in Sinjin's neck defined his anguish; sweat ran into his eyes, and his legs were braced hard against the floor as though holding him upright in the chair.

No sound broke the silence of the room except the tortured rasp of Sinjin's breathing.

"God help me," Fergus expelled on a rush of heated temper, releasing Sinjin's shoulders, "I can't . . ." He stood abruptly, glar-ing down on Sinjin like some god of retribution. He couldn't kill a bound man, no matter how sorely tempted.

A moment passed before the ravaged pain centers of Sinjin's brain reacted, and another moment before the message of salvation registered in his nervous system. His teeth unclenched, his fingers relaxed their death grip and he found enough air in his lungs again to say with his familiar quixotic insolence, "If this is a game, Fergusson, when do I get a turn?"

"Perhaps after your child's born," Chelsea's father sharply retorted. "And you can name your weapons."

"Why the sudden chivalry, Dumfries? Why not just whip me to death?" Sinjin's voice was weak under the edge of his anger.

If truth be known, the Earl was acutely disturbed at Sinjin's disclosures. Previously unaware of assignations between Sinjin and his daughter beyond the single night at Newmarket, he was forced to face the renewed possibility of Chelsea's culpability. And his, if Seth's statement of the money given to Chelsea was true. His mind refused to neatly sort the chaos into order; he was sick at heart and dispirited at his daughter's wretched future. The Duke of Seth, a byword for vice, standing stud to half of London, notorious since adolescence, under normal circumstances would have been his last choice as husband to his darling daughter.

"Don't press your luck, St. John," the Earl snapped, and turning abruptly, he walked from the room.

Chelsea would have the answers to his questions.

The Earl and his sons were seen to depart the morning of the fourth day, and when Seneca was told the news, he said, "At last," and was gone the rest of the day.

Reluctant to take on Sinjin's in-laws with Chelsea along, Seneca had assumed they must leave eventually to return to their estate in the south. He hadn't thought they would have lingered so long.

Chapter 27

An exotic troupe of performers slowly advanced across the grey, rocky landscape, the sea-birds swirling above them, cawing at their invasion, or perhaps at the colorful banners tied to the covered cart being pulled by two magnificent bays. Four horsemen, enveloped in great black capes whipping in the damp breeze off the North Sea, followed in the cart's wake, their dusky faces shadowed by the voluminous hoods of their capes.

The cart driver offered exotica of another kind in his costume of fringed leather, his spiked hair dressed with feathers and brilliant strands of beaded leather. On the seat beside the driver sat a fifth caped man playing a strange flute of carved ivory, its haunting tone sweeping before them on the capricious winds.

As they approached the grey granite lodge, armed Scots appeared to take note of their arrival, and the members of the troupe took surreptitious notice of the guards' positions: four at the stables; three spread out on the crest of the hill above the house; two at the front; two on the porch; one at the window of Sinjin's room; two more at windows on the main floor. One missing of the fifteen-man twelve-hour shift taking the day duty. But otherwise all the positions were accounted for.

A tall dark-haired clansman, already recognized as one of the leaders, stopped them a hundred yards from the modest entrance gate. Flanked by two lieutenants, he looked over the odd assemblage before him for several silent moments before he said, a martial quality to his voice, "State your business."

"We're traveling the Highlands for the gratification and entertainment of the populace, Colonel," Seneca replied, tipping his feathered head in courteous obeisance.

"Doing what?" the Scotsman asked, but since he'd been upgraded to colonel, his voice was less gruff.

"Offering the entertainments of the Pasha's Maghreb, excellency, acrobats and tumblers, snake-charming, feats of horsemanship to astound and delight . . ."

The man hesitated, but duty prevailed and he said, "No, ye'll have to be on your way. We donna have time for entertainments."

"We have scented liquors from the fruit of the Sahara, your graciousness, that bring paradise to the mind and body of those who taste its nectar."

The two lieutenants showed immediate interest, one even speaking to his superior in his excitement. "I've heard tell of that heathen liquor, Dougal. From McTavish who once knew a man had come back from that land. 'Tis smooth as Highland spirits, he said."

"We're on duty here, and not here for pleasure," his superior reminded him, although his tone was by no means unyieldingly firm.

"We have a treasure from the Pasha's harem as well," Seneca quickly interjected, understanding their last card must be played to gain the equivocating leader's assent. "Beautiful Leila has danced for the Pasha himself . . . privately," he added in an insinuating murmur.

"Where is she?" The man's interest was obvious now, but he was still cautious.

"The delectable Leila is resting inside the cart, for she danced to exhaustion at Peterhead last night."

"Show her."

"She only dances under the moon, excellency," Seneca protested, "and sleeps all day to conserve"—he paused significantly—"her necessary energy for the evenings . . ."

Such potent promise breached even the most rigid sense of duty, and the Scotsman, after looking at both his companions, who were visibly moved by their anticipation of the evening festivities, said, "You can set up camp over there." He pointed at a corner of the stable yard. "But the dancing girlie better be awake by sunset or you're gone."

"You won't be disappointed, Colonel. The lush flower Leila dances like Bathsheba herself."

Thank you very much, Chelsea nervously thought, huddled inside the cart, disastrously aware of her deficiencies in harem dancing. And while she'd been coached in abbreviated fashion by the Mussulmen of the troop, they were nearly as ignorant as she—seeing as how their interest in the dance was visual rather than practical.

She adjusted her cramped foot and mentally counted the hours till she could step free of the small cart. Although appearing before her clansmen in the guise of a harem girl would be perhaps more uncomfortable than her present position.

The men spent the day preparing a rough stage for their performances. Since their task required a variety of materials—some gathered from the Scotsmen after a dialogue of sign language and Pidgin English or Seneca's interpretation—the construction offered considerable opportunity to survey the house and grounds. Every guard's position was documented, door locks noted, the weapon supply counted, the swiftest route south determined.

By late afternoon, with their plan essentially in place, Seneca and the Bedouins relaxed, joking among themselves and occasionally with the Scots guards, only Chelsea still panic-stricken with nerves. Warriors by profession, they faced the evening's operation with cool self-possession.

When Seneca had disappeared into Peterhead for supplies the previous day, he'd purchased the materials for Chelsea's costume—numerous silk scarves which would be attached to her chemise like so many flower petals. Her face would be completely concealed below her eyes by another scarf serving as veil. And she spent the better part of the day, when she was ostensibly getting her beauty rest for her evening's dance, sewing her costume. Luckily her sewing technique would be visible only under the moon's illumination, for it wouldn't bear closer scrutiny.

She'd never reached Mrs. Macaulay's standards of needlework, her finished products generally bloodstained, knotted and wrinkled, and lack of practice hadn't improved her poor skills. As she sat in the cart constructing her costume, it seemed as though she speared her fingers with the needle almost as often as she managed to pierce the fabric.

The mood of Sinjin's men abruptly altered late that afternoon, when one of the guards coming off duty from Sinjin's room mentioned that the prisoner was sickening badly from his wound.

"We might be going home early," the guard had cheerfully remarked, "if the poison keeps spreading in his blood."

And a new determination seemed to grip the men.

The cart they'd driven up in had been brought along against such an eventuality, for they knew Sinjin's shoulder wound could be dangerously compromised by constant travel. No one, however, had considered the awful possibility of death.

Seneca didn't discuss the new revelations with Chelsea in order not to alarm her, but he and his men understood their time had clear-cut limits now. Sinjin would have to be taken out tonight without fail. That meant no aborted plans to be re-formed another day; that meant their performances tonight wouldn't be repeated another night with a second opportunity for success. That meant they fought their way in and out if necessary.

The moon shone with a special brilliance that night, as though it knew the importance of the performances taking place under its light.

The flutist performed first, charming a local reptile into a swaying approximation of the snakes in his homeland. The music had a mesmerizing effect on the snake curled within the warmth of a small basket, drawing the attention of the guards as well.

Four Arab grooms bounded onto the stage next, dressed in brilliant white pantaloons, tunics and low red boots. They stunned the audience with their acrobatic feats. As though made of supple rubber instead of human flesh and bone, they rolled and tumbled and jumped over each other's heads as easily as children jumped over puddles.

Beguiled and amused, glad for a respite in their duties, the clansmen cheered and shouted, the sounds of their uproarious enjoyment rising into the cool night sky.

Although, since Seneca had been moving through the small audience pouring his desert nectar into waiting cups during the performance, the noisy appreciation of the guards may have been augmented by Seneca's libations. His exotic beverage was a potent combination of Highland whiskey purchased in Peterhead liberally laced with date liquor and opium.

The dispensing of the drink required strategic restraint, however. While Seneca wanted the guards incapacitated, he couldn't have them fall into a drugged sleep before Sinjin had been spirited from the house. The Scotsmen's leader had assigned a skeleton crew on guard tonight over Sinjin. And they weren't drinking. If those men noticed all the guards in the audience falling over drugged, they would be alerted to danger.

All depended on Chelsea.

She'd been prompted. She knew her role in the escape attempt.

In the meantime, the trick riding entertained the men, and Seneca continued his careful dispersal of liquor.

It was almost nine when the make-shift curtains on the back of the cart parted and Chelsea stepped out on the rough stage.

An utter silence fell over the small audience for a moment, each man open-mouthed at the sight of her, and then the screaming applause began, erupting into the moonlit sky like fireworks.

Chelsea's golden hair fell down her back; her eyes were kohled above the veil covering her face, her shoulders and arms bare, gleaming in the moonlight, the round fullness of her breasts visible above the décolletage of her altered chemise. And she wore gold bangles around her ankles and rings on her toes.

An apparition of every man's dream of far-away harems, she was lush and beautiful and . . . no more than ten feet away.

Taking a deep steadying breath, she lifted her arms gracefully above her head, waited for the first note of the flute and prayed Seneca and Sahar accomplished their mission.

As the music began, the bells on her ankles tinkled in the cool summer night, a delicate suggestion of exotic seraglios, of submissive women and carnal pleasures. And she moved across the small stage in a gentle swaying rhythm, her smile promising heavenly delights, every man's attention riveted on her. Her lashes lifted seductively, she twirled to clamorous applause and over the heads of her audience she saw Seneca and Sahar slip through the back door of the house.

She danced then, an age-old dance of seduction and allure, her body offering intemperate passion, her small bare feet gliding over the rough lumber as if it were the silken carpets of Kairouan, the music of the flute a bewitching siren song to Chelsea's sorcery.

No man stirred, every one obsessed by the delicious female, her pale flesh only partly concealed by the shimmering veils, each languid drift of her supple body offering added glimpses of creamy skin, tantalizing invitations to touch, to feel . . .

The red Indian had offered them paradise with the nectar, and his promise had been fulfilled. Before their eyes was the resplendent enchantress of a Pasha, the moon shamed by her beauty.

Leaving three unconscious guards hidden in a storage room near the kitchen on their passage upstairs, Seneca and Sahar reached the door to Sinjin's room and knocked.

"Come take your turn with the lady dancer," Seneca shouted, training his voice into a Scots brogue.

The door opened, as he knew it would, for the windows of Sinjin's room overlooked the stage where Chelsea danced.

Before the surprised guard had fully crumpled to the floor, felled by a powerful blow from Seneca's pistol butt, Sahar was already halfway into the room attacking the second guard. He carried a small lead pendulum swinging from a leather cord, and the second guard dropped in his tracks, falling heavily with a thudding vibration that shook the floor.

Sinjin's head came up, his feverish eyes trying to focus, the sharp noise and flurry of movement registering vaguely through his pain and febrile senses. Hearing Seneca's voice, he forced his reluctant mind to function and shook his head in an effort to bring the images before his eyes into focus. Sahar! A slow smile spread across his face, and he lifted his head fully.

The effort brought forth an unconscious groan, an animal sound guttural and low, as the small movement shifted his left shoulder and arm. He clenched his teeth against the stabbing pain a moment later as the sensation reached the cognitive centers of his brain, and he said in a voice forced from his lungs by sheer will, "Your timing's propitious." He smiled faintly. "Tomorrow might have been too late."

"Can you walk?" Seneca quickly said, understanding the extent of his injury if Sinjin recognized his weakness.

"I'll walk." Sinjin's words were resolute, his courage willing, but his voice was weaker, even his brief effort at speech a drain on his impaired strength.

"We'll help. If you can stay upright for five minutes, we'll be out of here."

"To get out of here," Sinjin said in a whisper of sound, "I'd sign a pact with the devil. Lift me up and I'll stand."

Both men considered for a moment how best to lift him. His left arm was streaked down its length with angry red, swollen twice its normal size, the bandage on his shoulder yellow with pus.

Seneca cut his bonds as gently as possible, but it brought sweat to Sinjin's brow, the small movement too much for his ravaged arm. But he repressed the moan coming up from his throat, his senses marshaled to bring him to freedom. And when Sahar and Seneca slowly lifted him upright, he fought back the scream tearing through his mind. The degrees of endurance would soon be defined, he thought, struggling to maintain self-mastery over an incoherence blurring his mind as the corrosive agony of standing vibrated through his body. Both men braced themselves against Sinjin's unsteady weight; Seneca's gaze held Sahar's for a moment behind Sinjin's back, each man's compassionate sensibilities engaged by the devastation to their friend's powerful body. Time was an essential consideration, they knew; Sinjin's limited strength gave them an escape threshold of mere minutes.

"You've had too much to drink," Seneca quickly said, "and we're taking you out to the cart to sleep it off . . . if anyone should ask."

"A drink would be damned helpful now," Sinjin said through clenched teeth, his legs keeping him upright through sheer willpower, the agony of his wound almost beyond bearing.

"I've some outside," Seneca replied, "seasoned with opium."

"Incentive then," Sinjin whispered, "to get me down the stairs. Give me a weapon," he added. "I'm not coming back here."

Seneca wondered where he'd find the strength to use it, but he gave him a small dagger, placing it in his right hand. Sinjin's fingers curved around the carved bone hilt with a satisfied smile, and taking a slow look around the room that had been his prison—and possibly would have been his dying place had not Seneca arrived—he said, "At last, a bit of equity."

They concealed him in a long black burnoose, pulling the hood well down. His face bore the beginnings of a beard, the days since his abduction allowing no opportunity to shave, and the black shadow of beard matched the look of the Bedouins.

Each step was torture for Sinjin on the laborious trek down the hall, any movement, however slight, jarring his shoulder and arm; they had to halt for a moment at the top of the stairway to give Sinjin time to rest. Struggling to still the trembling of his legs, he whispered, "Go" after only a few moments, his need for freedom intense.

Take a step, he silently said, willing himself to move one more time. And now another, he mentally commanded his reluctant body.

Another . . . and another, he resolved with an iron will, each tread requiring a stubborn courage to keep himself upright—until the three men reached the bottom of the stairway.

"We're going out through the rear door to the cart in the stable yard. Fifty more yards," Seneca encouraged, "and it's over."

"Point me in the right direction," Sinjin murmured, leaning heavily on Seneca with his good right arm, the small dirk partially concealed in his large palm.

"You've drunk too much now, should anyone inquire," Seneca reminded him, not sure Sinjin's present state of mind sustained thought for any duration.

"I'd like my poppy juice straight," Sinjin facetiously replied, "if I make it to the cart alive." And he tightened his grip on his dirk, understanding the next fifty yards would be a test of both his nerve and strength.

Sahar opened the door, and they felt the evening air on their faces.

Blessed freedom, Sinjin gratefully thought, if he could cross the gauntlet of Scots filling the open ground before him. They rose up into his field of vision, like an apparition in a dream, his senses absorbing information with a languorous disregard for his peril, and he blinked twice to steady his vision.

The music struck his senses next, as if another door to his consciousness had slowly opened. Then his mind cleared, and he saw a veiled dancing girl performing on a rough stage under the brilliant light of the spring moon.

Chelsea! So fundamental was his reaction to her that, beneath the stupor of his fevered mind, she was instantly recognizable even under a veil and heavily kohled eyes. Even beneath the ridiculous arrangement of fluttering scarves.

Those bare arms, the lush fullness of her breasts etched on his memory, the feel of her pale hair on permanent recall in his mind, however befuddled by pain and fever, the opulence of her slender form, her feet—bare as they were when she slid them down his legs to draw him closer in passion.

Unconsciously, he'd come to a stop, and it took a moment more to understand that Seneca and Sahar were urging him forward.

He tried to sort through the tumult in his brain and comprehend Chelsea's place in this bizarre scene, but deductive reason eluded his grasp. He felt hate and joy at the sight of her, pleasure and betrayal and a burning anger that matched the burning pain streaking down from his shoulder.

It was too late, or too early, he thought in a premonition of doom; it was too dark to distinguish her completely . . . or not dark enough to know her only by her scent in his nostrils—or not private enough, he decided, looking out over the heads of her avid audience, his mind racing down mindless paths without coherent responses to the paradoxical sense of frustration and happiness filling his brain. There were *too* many Scots—that was perfectly clear, though, regardless of his pain or fever or disordered senses. And he forcibly cast aside any reflections save those pertinent to his escape.

The short range of steps was behind them a moment later, and they were moving in a straight path toward the cart, placed conveniently in the shadow of the stable wall.

"Hey there!" the Scots' leader shouted.

And they all stopped in their tracks, tensed and waiting.

"I want some more nectar!" And he held out his cup upside down.

"My friend has had a drop too much, your excellency. Let me put him to rest and I'll return immediately with your nectar."

"Now, man! Now!"

If Seneca moved from his position of support, Sinjin would collapse, his weight too much for Sahar to hold alone. If Sinjin fell, there was a good likelihood he could be exposed. His size alone wouldn't bear close scrutiny.

"Now, dammit, you red-skinned heathen!" the Scotsman growled, belligerent in his cups.

Chelsea stood motionless on the stage, her gaze, like everyone's, turned on the trio of men. It was obvious Sinjin was desperately ill. Even concealed beneath the voluminous burnoose, his shoulders slumped, his head hung awkwardly, his feet were braced as though to steady his weight.

With her heart hammering in her chest, her palms clammy, a sharp pain of calamity stinging her lungs, she understood she was the cause of his brutal deterioration. Would he die now because of her?

In extremity she reacted with primeval instinct, her fingers seeming to move of their own accord to the bow at the neckline of her chemise. She could save him, perhaps, or at least gain him the few moments he needed to reach the cart undetected.

"Leila will show you all," she proclaimed, her voice tantalizing, offering more, its lush husky undertone drifting out into the audience . . . turning every gaze back—to the pink satin ribbon she held between her fingers.

"See what the Pasha of the Maghreb adored. See all that the Sultan's harem nurtured and enlightened . . ." A sharp tug on the ribbon brought an audible gasp from the audience. The bow fell open, four inches of her chemise parted and a luscious valley of shadowed cleavage lured each masculine eye.

The Scots' leader instantly forgot his need for liquor; each guard as readily relinquished his duty, for on a jerry-built stage in the desolate hinterland of the Highlands, an eternal male fantasy offered fulfillment.

Immediately forgotten, the three men covered the distance to the cart as swiftly as Sinjin's weakened state allowed. But climbing into the small confines of the cart was more than Sinjin could endure, the pressure on his shoulder and arm excruciating, what strength he'd possessed exploited on his journey from the house. He lost his fight with the encroaching blackness he'd held at bay by strength of will, and he allowed the soothing mantle of unconsciousness to still his pain. But his grip on the small dagger remained firm, as though a fragment of his mind knew he wasn't yet out of danger.

In rapid-fire dialogue, Sahar and Seneca marginally altered their plan for escape: Sahar would stay with Sinjin to administer adequate opium to quiet him and ease his pain; Seneca would return to the performance and continue to dispense liquor, a mixture now *liberally* blended with poppy. Seneca understood that the rapt male audience wouldn't be completely satisfied by passively watching Chelsea discard her costume, however seductive her dance, so a necessary speed impelled him. Once the beautiful Duchess of Seth was nude, Seneca knew it wouldn't be long before the guards would require some physical fulfillment of their fantasy.

Collecting the other tribesmen, Seneca set everyone to serving the "desert nectar," the men moving through the audience, generously dispensing the opium liquor so each guard's cup was constantly full.

Aware of the plan to drug the guards, Chelsea disrobed as slowly as possible, keeping her gaze above the heads of the men staring at her, unnerved by the hungry looks on every face. With her veil concealing her face, she maintained her anonymity at least, but the thought of being nude before so many lascivious gazes tested her intrepidity. She understood too the effects of liquor on men's restraint, and she hoped the opium did its work quickly. But she had so little clothing to discard that she was already bereft of all but her last silk scarf, her nerves taut as she gracefully twirled and swayed to the clear melodic song of the flute.

And when the first clansman fell asleep, she inwardly sighed with relief. The progression of slumbering Scots followed like ninepins, until her audience was all thankfully unconscious.

Her flutist stopped playing immediately when the last Scot tumbled over; he rose from his seated position, swept off his burnoose and offered it to Chelsea, with a small nod of his head in the manner of the Arabs. "Our gratitude, my lady, for saving our lord. May entire health and divine happiness be with your person. And may God cover you with His protection." His dark-eyed glance was courteous; no flicker of disrespect shone in his eyes.

Walking barefoot across the stable yard a moment later, the warm woolen cape pulled close around her, Chelsea shivered slightly in the aftermath of her perilous venture. Somehow, when the Duke of Seth had entered her life, or she his, the prosaic normality of her existence had abruptly shattered. And if someone had told her two months ago that she would be dancing nude before a troop of her clansmen, she would have considered them insane.

But she had, and perhaps more daunting, she had now to face the grim prospect that, due to her actions, her husband might not survive. How strange the word "husband" tasted on her tongue, she thought—how new and different and sadly melancholy considering the circumstances of their marriage.

If her small skills would help in saving him, she must offer them, although she felt inadequate to the enormity of the task. How awful that concept called male honor, she mused, how brutal, how defenseless she felt in its grip, a victim too as wife to a man she barely knew. There wasn't time, she hastily reminded herself, the cart short yards away, for her own grudging demurs when a man might be dying. She prayed that he didn't die. She'd not wanted her escape from George Prine to be at the cost of another's life.

And for a brief moment, she felt hatred for her father and his code.

She and Sahar stayed with Sinjin in the cart as they journeyed south, taking obscure byways, careful to travel by night. They slept when they could, taking turns nursing Sinjin, forcing broth and liquids down his parched throat, changing the dressing daily on his gruesome wound, packing the swollen, distended arm and shoulder with poultices familiar to Sahar and Seneca.

The opium dulled Sinjin's pain and kept him in a state of half sleep, only his dreams seeming to cause him distress. He felt no pain when they moved him, nor when his wound was ministered to. But no one dared provoke the gods with suggestions he was on the mend. The Arab mind recoiled at tempting the gods with personal happiness, and Sinjin had many incantations of "Tabark Allah" (may God preserve him from the evil eye) offered up for him. He'd need more than supplications, though, Seneca knew; he'd never seen a wound so putrid and festering that hadn't carried away the man.

Inexperienced, only Chelsea remained optimistic: Sinjin was too strong to succumb to infection; he had too much vitality to allow that energy to die. She didn't even think of their child in the hectic schedule of their days, but if she had, she would have wanted its father to live to see it.

Sinjin existed in a torrid, parched land, familiar to him from his journeys into the *Bled*,[10] recalled to him whenever he opened his eyes and saw Sahar's face bending over him. A blurred vision with other memories, analogous but strangely atypical, of Chelsea dancing in the moonlight, like Arabic dancing girls but robed differently— not like the women in the Moslem world . . . And very near to him at other times, as she was in their bedroom at Oakham . . .

His mouth was dry, his body raging with fever, like the sun in the desert that could kill with its heat. But he didn't want to die, he thought, his anger returning; he wanted to live. For he had vengeance in his heart that needed surcease. And in the fever burning his brain raged a simultaneous fire of revenge—against his wife's family, against his wife, against all the goddamned Fergussons for placing him here on the brink of the black chasm of death.

Chapter 28

They managed to elude the Fergusson pursuit by their circuitous route, unable to outdistance them with speed. By necessity they traveled often at night and very slowly in an attempt to cause no more damage to Sinjin's shoulder. And they arrived at Sinjin's hunting box in Hatton on the morning of the seventh day from Rattray Head.

Sinjin was carried in on a newly constructed stretcher, the housekeeper and staff told only that Sinjin had suffered his wound while out hunting. But his Bedouin grooms were deployed about the grounds of the small estate around the clock, a fact duly noted by the permanent residents of Sinjin's household.

None questioned the strange ways of their lord, though, for he paid them handsomely, allowed them time off for all the rural holidays and never lost his temper or beat them. Also, some of the older members of the staff had known Sinjin's father, so the oddities of the St. Johns were accepted, like the madness of the Townshends and the eccentricities of the Herveys.

Anyone who employed so many desert heathens had to be considered, even without a mysterious "hunting" wound, a man of irregular habits. And additionally, Sinjin had brought enough hunting companions of both sexes up to Hatton over the years for his staff to be inured to the wild ways of their young lord.

The next week consisted of continuing and punctilious care of

Sinjin's infected wound. With vigilance and constant poultices of chamomile oil, garlic juice, sage leaves and yarrow, with nourishing liquids coaxed down his throat, with substantial applications of thyme oil to the festering wounds, Sinjin's condition stabilized. The opium allowed him to dwell in a world without pain while Sahar and Seneca, with Chelsea's help, nursed him in relays.

Late in the afternoon of the eighth day since their arrival at Hatton, Sinjin opened his eyes for the first time with any recognition and spoke to his friend Seneca. "In my considered opinion," he softly drawled, "the worst is over." His grin was shaky, but touched with his familiar impudence. His eyes, although veiled with the effects of opium, glittered not with fever but with good cheer.

"And you should know," his friend happily replied, reaching over immediately to touch Sinjin's forehead with his palm. His brows rose in a mild judgment. "Better," he briefly said, but the fever was by no means gone.

"I need food." Sinjin grinned. "The women will have to come later . . ."

"You must be on the mend." Seneca's handsome face broke into a wide smile. "But let's take this one slow step at a time."

Sinjin laughed, the sound very close to normal. "As long as the first slow step is in the form of a beef roast with potatoes and peas. Where are we?" he abruptly inquired, wondering which of his chefs was in residence.

"We're at Hatton."

"That's a long way from London."

"But a shorter run from Rattray Head." And he watched his friend's expression change, Sinjin's smile wiped from his face.

"I'd forgotten the reason for this," he said, his voice suddenly chill as he attempted to lift his left arm. His effort brought a grimace to his mouth. "How long has it been?"

"Two weeks. One on the road."

"Was Chelsea at Rattray or was I dreaming?"

"She led us to the fishing lodge."

"So I suppose I should thank her." But Sinjin's voice was without warmth.

"You could thank her for that and for saving us from discovery as we came out of the house." She at least deserved credit for those actions, Seneca thought; the rest wasn't his to decide.

"Or I wouldn't be here." A begrudging declaration.

"You wouldn't be here," Seneca softly agreed.

"I'll thank her when I see her again." But Sinjin spoke dismissively, his intention plainly in the distant future.

"She's downstairs."

Sinjin shut his eyes, disturbed by the thought, not ready to deal with the complicated anarchy of their relationship. "I don't want to see her," he murmured. His lashes came up, and the blue of his eyes held a sharp-set anger. "She almost killed me."

"Her father almost killed you."

"Or one of his henchmen. What damn difference does it make," he bitterly went on, "splitting hairs over which damned Fergusson pulled the trigger? Her father rode me to death after whoever shot me. But my darling *wife* put me where I am today. Shackled for life, don't forget. Unless she starts selling her body in Piccadilly so Parliament will give me a divorce. And I doubt whether she's that stupid, considering the extent of my fortune. Actually, I *know* she's not stupid at all," he heatedly added. "No one else has managed to become the Duchess of Seth. Although her father must be given due credit. Only a heathen Scot still considers marriage a military campaign."

Seneca didn't point out that Sinjin's pursuit of the young Lady Chelsea had not been without due warning of the consequences. Time enough for that later when he was mended.

When Seneca told Chelsea that Sinjin didn't want to see her, she said, "I understand," and made no fuss, although as his wife she could have made demands.

"But tell him when he's feeling better that I'd like a short audience with him, to—well . . . clear up . . . certain . . . ah . . . situations. Tell him I can stop my family from harassing him. Tell him that."

And for the next week she took care to stay away from Sinjin's rooms. She spent time instead with the grooms, for her natural love of horses drew her to the stables, and her expertise in an area unusual to a female intrigued the Bedouins.

But their main courtesy to her was influenced by Chelsea's extraordinary bravery that night at Rattray. Arab culture revered courage, and the young Duchess had proved her fearlessness; her quick thinking and boldness had saved them all from a bloody engagement.

In the course of her hours at the stables, Chelsea learned about the Haymour breed and listened while the grooms discussed the training of their mounts. Arab training was quite different from the English manner, or the Scots. Chelsea impressed them as well with her riding skill, and when an impromptu race developed one morning across the flat stretch of pasture north of the lodge, Chelsea won. After their initial shock, for women were considered inferior, the grooms sensibly decided to overlook the fact that she was a female.

It was a natural assimilation for Chelsea, who had been raised in a masculine household and lived in the racing world, which was almost entirely male; she easily entered into the Arabs' leisure time routine of riding and training. She rode their Haymours and helped with their work, joining them occasionally in an early morning run.

After one such ride several days later, Seneca mentioned that Sinjin would see her that afternoon in the small downstairs parlor.

Chelsea arrived early for their appointment, nervous and anxious ever since Seneca had told her of the meeting that morning. She had tried to calm her apprehension, reminding herself that she had nothing personally to apologize for, except for that first night at Six-Mile-Bottom, which had been seriously exceeded in terms of guilt by Sinjin's ensuing and zealous sexual pursuit.

But rational argument proved useless against emotional distress that kept dwelling on the appalling abuse of her husband at the hands of her family. So she wasn't able to quietly sit and wait as she'd hoped, wanting to greet her husband with a polite courtesy she assumed would be normal in the world in which he lived. She was instead standing at the window when he came into the room, nervously tapping her fingers on the polished frame.

She spun around at the sound of his footfall.

Her beauty always surprised him, he thought, his expectations of a young country maid less glorious. Even dressed in her simple muslin frock, the sash tied without care, the yellow silk bow drooping, she put all the beauties of the Ton to shame. It was her hair, in part, the pale frothy halo magnificent in its luscious disorder, and her eyes . . . reminding him of great huge violets, velvety and dark in their centers.

He found himself instantly involved.

A feeling he ruthlessly crushed. It was similar feelings that had placed him in his current predicament, an uncomfortable, unwanted and unpalatable position.

"Seneca tells me you wished an audience," he coolly said, not advancing into the room, the door framing him as though holding him at a distance.

He looked much thinner, even in the full-sleeved shirt and exotic Arab breeches, but he stood calmly, his damaged arm out of its sling. He looked a stranger to her. His eyes watched her without friendship; she'd never seen him when he wasn't out to charm. Some of his father—rumored to have been an unsympathetic man—must have passed to his son, she thought, and steeling herself against those cold blue eyes, she said, "I told Seneca I can stop my family from harassing you, and I can."

"How?" He knew his danger continued; no truce had been called between himself and Dumfries.

"I'll write and tell Father that if he kills you, I'll kill myself."

"That's not necessary. I can take care of myself." Now that he knew he was a Fergusson target, he wouldn't be taken unaware again. "Is there anything else?" he briskly said. His impatience showed; he clearly didn't wish to speak with her.

"Just the child."

"Yes?"

"I was wondering if you intended to take it from me." She knew women had few rights to their children; if a husband wanted his children, his wife had no chance to keep them.

Sinjin hesitated. The disposition of a child he wasn't altogether certain was his seemed premature. "We can discuss this after the child is born."

"Thank you then," Chelsea politely replied, hiding her relief in the event he took advantage of it. "And I'm glad you're feeling better." They could have been strangers meeting for the first time, Chelsea thought, instead of two people who had shared the most impassioned intimacies.

He had turned to leave when he apparently reconsidered, and swinging back around, he said, "Where will you go?"

"Does it matter?"

He found himself impetuously, without reason, saying, "Yes."

"I'm not sure," Chelsea carefully said.

"You'll have to stay in England." He told himself he wished to know where his child was—if it was his—but something more aberrant drove him to add, "As my wife, you're under my command."

His words struck her as though he'd hit her with his hand in violence.

"No," she simply said, every fiber in her being taking offense.

"No and never and if you try, you'll be sorry." She should have acquiesced with deceit; she should have shown more sense. She shouldn't have caused his jaw to clench like that.

Perhaps it was an unconscious form of revenge, he reflected, his inchoate need to detain her. Perhaps he wished to make her a prisoner, as he had been. Perhaps it was something more sinister and depraved. A yet unmeted punishment for what she had done to him. But whatever it was, he didn't wish for her to casually walk away from the ruin of his life, however polite she'd appeared. He wished her to pay . . .

"I've already been made eminently 'sorry' by your family. Can you do more?" he mockingly inquired, but his eyes were flint hard and cold.

Having realized her mistake, Chelsea instantly took measures to ameliorate the effect of her unwise reply. "Please accept my apology for my temper, but my family coerced and dragooned me with no less sympathy. I overreacted. I simply would prefer the freedom to live quietly where I choose. I have no intention of bothering you again." After weeks of wrangling and intimidation, she longed only for peace and solitude.

"On second thought," Sinjin said, "with your family's flair for violence, your presence here might deter a holy war at least. Consider yourself my guest until I return to London."

She wished to scream her dissent, but the arctic chill of his eyes deterred her impulse. On his estate surrounded by his phalanx of armed guards, he was in possession of the key to her freedom. And she cursed her ungovernable temper for putting her in this new untenable position. "Yes, Your Grace," she said, but she couldn't tamp the trace of insolence in her tone. Damn his black soul. She'd stay only so long as it took her to find a way through his guards. And with the friendships she'd developed in the last week with the Arab grooms, that interval might be pleasantly short.

"You're confined to the house," he curtly said, as though reading her thoughts.

And when her brows flew upward in surprise, he added, "I heard of your race with Jahir. Riding might be a temptation." His voice gentled in insolent drama and he went on to say, "It's probably not wise in your condition. You must think of your child."

"*My* child? How convenient. If memory serves, this is *our* child I'm carrying." If she was to be treated as a captive, there was no longer any point in politesse. "*You're* the father, husband of mine."

He winced at the word "husband," and his voice when he spoke was empty of emotion or emphasis. "That remains to be seen . . ."

"You're much too familiar with whores, my lord. It tempers your judgment."

"As I recall, you learned their ways in record time. With your natural bent for amorous adventure, allow me my reservations on the paternity of this child. Two months elapsed before your father so thoughtfully informed me of your condition. Two months is a very long time . . ."

"Enough for a hundred women, no doubt, for you, my lord," Chelsea sarcastically noted. "We country lasses possess a touch more modesty."

"And you entertained no men in that interval?" Clearly, his tone expressed skepticism.

"I prefer my horses," she heatedly retorted.

He laughed, diverted at her prim rejoinder, his own perverse allusions less virtuous, and the smile curling his mouth showed a glimpse of his familiar charm. "Well then, your innocence will be exonerated in due course. In the meantime, you're here, and here you'll stay. Until I state otherwise."

"You bastard," she hissed, her temper—which had been held leashed for expediency—exploding at his arrogant gall.

"As you wish," he softly said, not responding to her explosive expletive. "But consider, dear wife," he unctuously went on, "at least your child won't be." His smile was fixed for a moment, no longer charming, then he turned and walked away.

He left as though she weren't significant beyond his injunctions, Chelsea resentfully thought, as though she existed only as an object of his decrees. It took some moments for her to quiet her agitated breathing and suppress the violence of her emotions. And some moments more before she walked over to the window, her mind filled with new resolve. How best might she make her escape? she considered, gazing across the lawn to the stable block.

How the hell long would it take her to find a way out of Hatton?

He could have been less autocratic, Sinjin reflected as he returned to his room to rest. Although his appearance gave little indication of his injury, particularly while he wore the loose costume of the desert, standing for any length of time still debilitated him. His strength wasn't fully returned, nor was the use of his left arm. It would take time to regain both, although he'd begun yesterday lifting his weighted arm to shoulder height.

Seneca had denounced his stupidity when he'd found him collapsed on the bed some twenty minutes later, unable to garner the strength to loose the leaded saddle weight from his wrist.

"Damned fool," Seneca had exclaimed. "You'll reopen that shoulder."

"I was careful," Sinjin had murmured, but he was smiling despite his weakness.

"Is there some fitness timetable I'm unaware of?" Seneca had sarcastically inquired, unstrapping the weight from Sinjin's wrist.

"If the Fergussons come, I want to kill a few," Sinjin had said with a grin.

"They won't get past the Bedouins, guaranteed, so you can desist from trying to put yourself into an early grave. We just pulled you out of the last one, with some great difficulty, I might add." Seneca rarely raised his voice, but he had then. "And with your wife as hostage, you're safe from their raids," he'd added.

Which was probably the reason he'd insisted that Chelsea stay, Sinjin decided, mounting the stairway to the second floor with the help of his good right arm. A practical decision based on sensible military tactics. It had nothing to do with her violet eyes, or full red lips, or with the fact that the sun had shone through the light white muslin of her dress, outlining her slender form in fascinating clarity. It had better not, he abruptly warned himself a moment later, determined to ignore both her allure *and* the fact that he had a wife. Other men—hell, most men—ignored their marital state; he could do the same with impunity.

No, he wished her here because she was part of the debt he intended to repay. And she was the first installment in his punitive vendetta.

Chapter 29

Three nights later, Chelsea slipped from her room, dressed for riding, her boots in her hand. Quietly traversing the upstairs hall, hugging the shadows of the wall, she stole down the servants' stairway. Sinjin had come downstairs for dinner for the first time that evening, and he had sat up late over port with Seneca. She had listened from her bedroom above the dining room, the hum of the men's conversation audible through her open window. She hadn't been able to distinguish the words, but there was more laughter as the evening progressed, so she suspected that Sinjin would sleep deeply tonight.

Additionally, the new moon cast little light, the thin crescent useful to her escape. She took the time to pull on her boots outside the kitchen door, and still cautious, moving from shadow to shadow, she covered the distance from the house to the pasture. Retrieving the bridle she'd hidden under a privet hedge, she scaled the pasture fence and approached one of the four mares fenced off from the stallions. With the warm spring weather, the horses preferred the new green meadows to the stable.

Safy lifted her head from her browsing as Chelsea neared, even nickering softly in greeting. Chelsea had ridden her most often, and the young mare knew her scent. Impeccably trained, she stood quietly while Chelsea slipped the bit into her mouth and slid the leathers over her ears.

Remembering to mount from the off side, Chelsea vaulted onto

Safy's back and, settling comfortably into place, spoke to the pretty bay in a soothing murmur. "I'll send you back, sweetling, once I reach Newmarket . . . you won't be gone long." She gathered the reins and gently turned Safy's head toward the far fence line. "We're going over, darling, and you're taking me away. Now," she commanded at the same time her heels nudged the mare's ribs.

The bay moved into a fluid canter almost immediately and, sighting the fence in the distance, began gathering speed, her instincts faultless. They approached the fence at a hard gallop and soared over as if the mare had wings.

Free! Chelsea exulted as the mare landed on the opposite side, her hooves already digging into the soft pasture sod in response to Chelsea's booted heel. "Thank you, fleet, winged creature of the desert," she purred, bending low over Safy's neck. "Thank you, thank you, thank you . . ."

The sound of her words had barely drifted into the dark when a piercing whistle broke the night air and her mount came to a careening stop. Before Chelsea had fully restored her seat, the mare wheeled around, churning up clods of sod, and broke into a loping gallop back toward the pasture.

Immune to Chelsea's reined or spoken commands, Safy retraced her path, leaping over the pasture fence without hesitation. And short moments later, Safy was happily munching from a sugar block held in Sinjin's open palm.

"Hazan will escort you back to the house," Sinjin said, stroking the mare's silky nose, his voice casual, his attention occupied with Safy's dainty nibbling.

The slim Arab groom stood ready to help her dismount. "And if I don't *care* to go back to the house?" Chelsea was seething; he'd toyed with her, letting her think she'd escaped, knowing he could call the horse back with ease.

"You don't have a choice." He glanced up at her briefly, a faint smile lifting his mouth. "Do you?"

"I could wipe that smug look off your face," she snapped. "I have that choice!" Raising her quirt in hot-tempered rage, she lashed out with her arm.

Sinjin easily side-stepped, ripping the quirt from her hand with a twist of his good right hand. "Take her down," he brusquely ordered Hazan.

"Can't you fight your own battles?" Chelsea taunted, as Hazan momentarily hesitated.

"I might hurt you," Sinjin said, his voice hard and ruthless, handing over the block of sugar to a groom who had materialized at his side at a small gesture. "So henceforth you'll be confined to your room." His gaze rose to hers for the first time, and he softly added, "Like a recalcitrant child."

It was an unfortunate turn of phrase, for he was reminded instead of how unchildlike she was—how womanly . . . how heated . . . and as her scent washed over him, he took a step backward as though in need of conscious withdrawal.

Chelsea slid down of her own accord, for she wouldn't be humiliated before Sinjin's cold, grim gaze, nor would she embarrass her new and recent friends—the Arabs. They would have collected her from the mare's back, for their warrior code set distinct parameters on female privilege, but it would have been awkward for them and for her.

They escorted her to her room in a benevolent fashion rather than in a martial way, but she was indeed confined, she realized as the heavy door shut behind her and the scraping of the key locked her in.

Was this ironic justice? Chelsea reflected, staring out her window a moment later at the two guards stationed below. Or was she a double victim of male privilege? First her father and now her husband chose to imprison her for the outrageous impudence of wanting to be in command of her life. Granted, her father had been as unconcerned with Sinjin's freedom as he'd been with hers, but his odious disregard didn't excuse the fact that she was chattel to both men. And dammit, she was *tired* of forfeiting her independence!

Was a rational conversation too much to ask for from a man? Could she and her husband not amiably resolve the living arrangements of their marriage? After all, they were in agreement in general terms. Neither wished to be married. Neither wished to live together. Surely, with those fundamentals agreed on, the less pressing issues could be resolved.

It took her only a moment to decide on an effective method of attracting her husband's attention. And she regretted briefly the "childish" action, but only briefly, and then she smiled a smugly complacent smile, similar in many ways to that recent one of her husband's.

. . .

Seneca and Sinjin had just settled into the library for a cognac when the first crash exploded into the quiet night. With the windows open to the spring air, the vibrations of sound seemed to issue from a multitude of directions, although the locale was soon established.

"Women," Sinjin muttered in disgust.

"Have you talked to her?" Seneca asked.

"About what? About her family nearly killing me? I don't think so. Her neck's too slender for my current temper."

"How long do you intend to keep her there?"

"Until her family's neutralized."

"That could be indefinitely."

Sinjin looked at his friend over the rim of his glass, shrugged and, tipping the goblet to his mouth, drained it. He sighed then and said, "Once my strength is back, I'll challenge the lot of them and shoot the bastards."

"Duncan was once your friend."

"Was. Almost dying stretches the bonds of friendship—in his case, snaps the bonds."

The destruction of Chelsea's room noisily continued: breaking glass, crashing pottery, smashing wood echoed throughout the house, the major domo coming in once to question the Duke's wishes on the subject.

"Clean it up in the morning," Sinjin complaisantly replied. "The lady's temper will cool by then. Send the staff to bed. There's nothing anyone can do."

But Sinjin did go upstairs sometime later when one of the Arab guards came to fetch him, concerned that Chelsea might have hurt herself. Sinjin listened for a moment, his face expressionless, and then only said, "See that she doesn't come out," and walked away.

But ten minutes later, when the dressing table came crashing down on the terrace below, narrowly missing one of the guards, Sinjin reluctantly said to Seneca with a sigh, "It looks as though she's not going to wait till morning."

Refilling his glass, he tipped the liquor down his throat, set his glass down, groaned theatrically and rose from his chair.

"If I don't return," he said with a grim smile, "send in the reserves."

Chapter 30

Sinjin entered the room and stood observing Chelsea for a moment
after shutting the door, as though his presence alone would subdue
her. The pearl buttons of his green striped waistcoat gleamed in the
candlelight; his doeskin breeches took on the softness of velvet in the
saffron light; the whiteness of his shirt bleached to alabaster; his
riding boots were planted firmly on the carpet, as though he had the
right to be standing there silently surveying her.

In retaliation for his nerveless tranquility, she threw the last piece
of pottery at him.

The small pierrot figurine smashed against the door only inches
off target, shattering into splinters, then falling in a shower of
brightly colored porcelain to the carpet.

He didn't even flinch, although a small drop of blood appeared
near his jaw. Reaching up, his eyes still on her, he extracted the sliver
of china from his chin and dropped it to join the litter on the floor.

"Oh hell, I'm sorry," Chelsea said, not tantrumish by nature, her
drama enacted for a specific reason.

"And well you should be," Sinjin softly replied, surveying the
extent of the damage. Nothing in the room remained untouched.
What wasn't broken was damaged; she'd even managed to wrench
several spindles from the headboard of the bed.

"I didn't know how else to get your attention," Chelsea said,
and while several less destructive methods ran through Sinjin's mind

—like sending down a note—she added, "Even with this, it took you long enough to respond. You must be inured to female tantrums."

He was, although not fool enough to admit it, and perhaps, if he were honest with himself, a note wouldn't have sufficed. He would have been reluctant to speak to her under any circumstances because he didn't know if he was capable of controlling his anger. He also wasn't altogether certain he wouldn't have found it extremely tempting to punish her for the cataclysmic changes in his life. He'd felt safer avoiding her. Even now, he found it necessary to quell his urge to strike out at her, and he only beat back the impulse with enormous self-control.

"So now you have my attention." His gaze swept the room littered with debris, and he added with a grim smile, "This will come out of your pin money."

"Do I have pin money?"

She said it so delicately, it struck him suddenly that they indeed existed as a couple, legally. And allusions to that conjugal state disastrously stirred his senses.

"You sound like your father," he curtly said, the terms of the marriage settlement etched on his liver, recall of his torture in the Highlands sufficient to block any fonder sentiments.

"Can we talk like reasonable people about our—situation?"

"Our marriage, you mean." He ground out the hated word.

Chelsea didn't flinch either. "Yes."

He mentally measured the distance between them, the width of the room not much protection for the slender woman still dressed in her mannish riding clothes. But he'd never laid a hand on a woman in anger, he thought, with an inward sigh, and much as the idea of beating her for her father's transgressions gave him pleasure, he couldn't bring himself to do it.

"What would you like to talk about?" he quietly said, looking for a place to sit. But nothing was undamaged or unstrewn with china shards, so he remained standing.

"Mostly about how long you intend to detain me."

"I'm not sure . . . probably until my health permits me to call your father and brothers out."

"All of them?"

"That depends on your father."

"What do you want from him? Could I help?"

"I want my freedom, but you haven't seemed to have had much luck to date."

He was right. "So until then I'm a hostage."

"Something like that." And it occurred to him then that, should the child clearly not resemble him, an annulment might be possible. He certainly had enough money to buy off the Vatican. "Perhaps until the child is born," he added.

Chelsea suddenly felt faint, her pregnancy making her very susceptible to heightened emotion. And the thought of captivity for that length of time made her slightly breathless.

"Are you nauseous?" She had that same pale look he'd seen before.

"Just a little dizzy," she whispered and sat on the windowsill, not trusting her legs to hold her. The cool night air helped as the shock of his statement subsided. She smiled faintly as her dizziness receded and said, "I wouldn't have had to ruin this room. I thought I might be able to convince you to let me go."

"I can't. I'm sorry. You're my guarantee against your family's retaliation. It won't be for so long."

"Over six months is long." She looked at him, at his calm detachment as he leaned relaxed against the door. "You don't think this child is yours, do you?"

He debated for a moment the degree of courtesy required. "In my position," he finally said, "I want to be as sure as possible. This child could be heir to my dukedom."

"Could be?" She knew the legalities as well as he.

"If it's mine."

"If it isn't?"

He might as well be honest, he thought. "I'll divorce you."

It wasn't as though she too didn't wish a way out, but his answer was so completely without feeling that she felt a degree of resentment. He had, after all, been an active participant.

It was an era in which men assumed little responsibility for their amorous adventures. Some few did on occasion, if they felt affection for their lovers, but their sympathy rarely included marriage.

And the only women who could demand accountability from their lovers were women who had something with which to negotiate. This generally meant either fortune or extreme beauty.

Also, in order for this option to exist, the lady's lover must be open to negotiation—meaning he was in need of funds or much beneath her in looks.

Neither of these conditions applied to Sinjin.

He knew—outside of force majeure, already attempted by Earl Dumfries—he was *untouchable*.

"You won't be able to divorce me," Chelsea said just to be obstinate, piqued at his dismissive assumption.

He knew what she meant, and whether she spoke the truth or was a consummate actress, she seemed assured.

"We'll have to see then."

"Which brings us back to the beginning once again. Will I be free to leave after the child is born?"

"Of course."

"Even if the child is your ducal heir?" He hadn't brought up the fact that he already had a son. Perhaps he assumed she knew, since he'd acknowledged the child for years.

"Of course."

"And the child?"

They were back to that question—one he didn't wish to consider, or answer, or think about now. Too many other priorities took precedence. "I don't know," he honestly replied and was disconcerted to see Chelsea burst into tears.

"Forgive me . . ." she gulped a moment later, "I seem to . . . cry . . . so easily . . ." Even though she had anticipated his reply, his answer was distressing, and with the current shaky state of her emotions, everything seemed to overwhelm her.

"At least you're not throwing up," Sinjin kindly noted.

"That . . . seems to have . . . passed," Chelsea hiccuped, trying bravely to hold back her tears.

She looked so small and forlorn suddenly, sitting on the window-sill, her feet inches off the floor, her face streaked with tears. She was still in her riding clothes, her booted feet swinging back and forth as a young child's would. Her innocence touched him.

"Do you cry often?"

"All the time now, I'm afraid."

He couldn't help but smile at her apologetic tone.

"I wish I *didn't* cry so easily; I'm not looking for sympathy."

"And I'm the last person likely to give it to you," he replied, but his glance had lost its coldness and he abruptly said, "You can't sleep here."

His mind seemed to stop for a moment, as though giving pause for an addendum to his spontaneous remark. And into that small void, a thought emerged—as an actor from the wings arrives suddenly on stage.

She could sleep with *him*.

The normal functioning of his mind resumed then, but that revealing notion was center stage now—a spotlighted prima donna.

Why not? he thought; she was his wife.

Why not? he further considered; she couldn't get any more pregnant.

Why not, when he was alone in exile while he healed?

Why not indeed?

"You'll need a clean room to sleep in tonight," he said, as if in further explanation.

"I can brush off the bed. I seem to be able to fall asleep anywhere these days."

He'd forgotten how outrageously candid her personality was . . . and how unassuming. Pushing away from the door, he began walking toward her, the evening having taken on sudden promise.

"Are you still angry?" She viewed his approach with a degree of apprehension.

"About this?"

She nodded, tensing as he approached.

He shook his head and smiled. "Your temper will give the staff some gossip for a few days. Would you care to redecorate the room?"

"Why are you being so understanding?"

He shrugged, his feelings too muddled for him to easily reply. He was standing before her now, and her face, lifted to his greater height, seemed all huge liquid eyes. Would her child have the same deep purple eyes? he suddenly wondered, struck for the first time with the reality of this new life she carried.

"How do you feel?" he quietly inquired.

"Tired." She grinned. "As usual . . ." If he was going to pretend he'd have come upstairs without her turbulent invitation, she could be as agreeable. And she was tired, not only physically but emotionally, after the last few weeks, which had been reminiscent of full-scale war. If Sinjin was offering her a temporary truce, she was more than willing.

"I'll find you some better accommodations," he said, touching her shoulder first as if not to frighten her. Then, slipping his arm under her legs with only a minimum of pain, he picked her up. Holding her lightly so she barely touched his chest, he said, "You don't seem any heavier."

She liked the reference to their past, as though he were acknowledging those happier days when they had been together by choice.

"I'm not very much; I just feel like sleeping all the time . . . and I'm sorry," she softly continued, lifting her hand to the disarray. "I wish I could pay for the damage."

As his wife, on her name alone, she could probably get funds—he thought, although, since he'd never signed the marriage settlement, she had no specified jointure or pin money. Maybe she *was* still poor.

"There's no need for apologies. I should have been less autocratic. Do you need anything?"

"My brush," she said, so he carried her over to the bureau, the top empty except for a brush and mirror.

"You're superstitious?"

Looking up at him, she ruefully smiled.

Then he noticed all the mirrors in the room were intact. When he looked down at her, his eyes were warm again, as she remembered. "We'll work out some compromises tomorrow," he said.

"The fairies of the glens must have heard me." She grinned up at him. "And I almost got away."

He didn't want to suppress her small good spirits when she'd admitted how much she'd cried lately, so Sinjin said, "Yes, you almost did."

But as he carried her down the hall to his bedroom, he found himself curiously pleased in a convoluted way that she hadn't.

Not knowing precisely what to do once in his room, his feelings still in flux, Sinjin walked to a small settee near the fireplace, a light blaze taking the chill from the night, and sat down.

"I suppose I'm a burden on you," Chelsea quietly said.

He *supposed* so, amused at her benign expression for the total disruption of his life. "Not too heavy a burden yet," he facetiously replied, her weight incidental on his lap.

The room was suddenly intensely silent, so many unresolved issues still separating them.

He was thinking himself a reprobate for wanting her regardless of all that had passed between them.

She was thinking she felt protected sitting on his lap, his arms lightly enfolding her, his size alone security.

And the hush lengthened, neither sure how to open a dialogue without touching on all the animosity.

"I'm tired."

"Are you tired?"

They spoke in unison like a Greek chorus and then laughed at their discomfort.

"And I'm hungry too," Chelsea added, "if you don't mind."

He almost said, "For what?" in the wrong tone of voice, for his mind was distinctly focused on the feel of her in his arms, on her soft bottom warming his thighs. But he caught himself in time and said instead, "Of course I don't mind. We'll ring for the chef."

And their informal picnic, eaten in the middle of his simple wooden bed, helped restore their friendship.

Chelsea ate pickled eggs and cold pudding and warmed scones with sultanas. She drank Hatton mead, cool from the still room. She ate a goodly portion of the grilled beefsteak Sinjin had ordered, and she sent her compliments to the chef for a puffed pastry filled with marzipan and clotted creme.

She finished with two China oranges while Sinjin watched, amazed.

"This child will weigh a stone at least, my darling wife, if your appetite continues."

"Isn't it terrible?" she replied, warmed by his affectionate designation for her. "I can't help it. I'm hungry all the time. I don't suppose a man would understand."

"Maybe he would . . ." he said, his voice suddenly a half octave lower, and Chelsea's gaze came up from the brilliant orange peels she was piling back on the tray.

"You're not mad anymore? You don't hate me?" And even as she spoke, she questioned her lack of judgment. Men, she'd discovered very young, rarely appreciated probing questions. They preferred not discussing their feelings. "Could I retract that?" she hastily interposed, her smile tentative.

"Gladly."

She was right. He didn't wish to answer, the single word almost a rebuff.

And then he sighed, leaned back against the headboard, ran his hand over his jaw and said, "I don't know how I feel. But I'm pleased you're not crying, and I'm pleased to have your company."

"And I'm pleased your arm is healing. And now that we've exchanged all the requisite pleasantries, would you mind if I wiped the blood from your chin? For you've just reopened that cut from the crockery."

He laughed. "You don't bore me."

"Is that unusual?"

"Very."

"In that case I'll consider not changing my ways."

"Would you have?"

"I might have liked to but I couldn't, I'm afraid, after so many years of, well, hoydenish ways."

"Is that why I like you?"

"I don't know. *You* don't know, my lord, if I dare be outspoken, what it is you like about me, because you've always only liked one thing about women."

He thought for a minute that she was remarkably perceptive for seventeen and three quarters.

"It's my family, Your Grace . . . nothing but men. One learns."

"Sinjin," he said.

"I didn't know if I dared."

"Dare away."

It was the wrong thing to say to a young girl who had been in charge of her life for many years. Or it was the absolutely right thing to say, considering Sinjin's current desires.

And she found a highly combustible way to wash the blood from his chin. Moving very close, she leaned closer still, and steadying herself with her hands on his shoulders, she licked it away.

Needless to say, no one slept much that night, and the stay at Hatton took on a new rosy cast.

Chapter 31

Spring rains unfurled new leaves and sweet blossoms, greened the hills and vales in fresh beauty, brought the sunshine of spring in its wake. And a fortnight passed at Hatton in contentment and pleasure while Sinjin and Chelsea, reconciled and enraptured, ignored the world beyond their isolated valley. They laughed and talked and made love, they fed each other and read from their favorite books and made love, they walked and rode through the lush countryside and made love; they dwelt in paradise—and made love.

While Seneca had been sent back to London, sufficient guards remained to offer security against the possibility of a Fergusson assault. Sinjin's shoulder healed; he regained the strength in his injured arm at the same time Chelsea's body nurtured the child within. She started blooming in small subtle changes that her husband watched with increasing interest.

"Have you thought of a name for the baby?" he asked one afternoon as they lay in dishabille under an apple tree in the orchard, his head in her lap, the droning of bees overhead languorous like the warm spring day.

Chelsea tipped her head slightly and smiled, her fingers continuing their languid stroking of his hair. She shook her head, too lazy to articulate an answer. Drowsy under the warm sun, she was half-asleep.

"Does that mean I have carte blanche?" The intense blue of Sinjin's eyes held a sparkling amusement.

"Where do you get your energy when I have none?" She smiled. "And no, you don't."

"I'm not supporting a growing baby, darling . . . you're *allowed* to do nothing"—he grinned—"well . . . almost nothing . . . and," he went on, mischief in his eyes, "I particularly like Alfred."

He rolled away before she was able to strike him, and lying in the petal-strewn grass beyond the range of her closed fist, he facetiously assessed her. "Alfred doesn't appeal to you?"

"This baby's going to be a girl."

"How nice." And settling his chin more comfortably on his propped palm, Sinjin reflected on the perfection of a family with Beau and a new daughter. "You're *sure* now . . ." He enjoyed teasing her, just as he enjoyed the sight of her beauty and the feel of her in his arms. Just as he was beginning to enjoy the prospect of this coming child . . . the enmity between them reconciled—submerged under the sweet enchantment of their days at Hatton.

"I'm positive." A curious assurance affected Chelsea, feeling a flash of her old nanny's confidence when she was foreseeing signs. Resting her head against the rough bark of the old apple tree, she softly said, "We'll name her Flora, after my mother."

"Flora was *your* sobriquet that night at Six-Mile-Bottom." In all the tumult of their first passionate encounter, he remembered the aptness of that name, and his voice took on a brief hushed quality as he considered how close he had come to never meeting her.

"Flora—really? I said that?" In the angst and tempestuous delirium of her first night with Sinjin, details blurred, burned away by sensation. She remembered only kisses and aching need and abandonment.

"I remember distinctly," he said very low, reaching over to touch the slender curve of her ankle, his own memory vivid of the flower-sweet virgin, perfumed, dew fresh, magnificent . . . Not a superstitious man—even at the gaming tables, he believed in skill over luck —he was struck with the blundering presumption, the sheer good fortune, that had brought him Chelsea Fergusson.

He was too close, too attractive, Chelsea thought, gazing across the meadow grass at the man who had captured her heart. Restless as flashing sunlight, elusive for all his charm, capricious as the wind catching his dark hair, he offered fugitive pleasure without permanence; and she loved him more than she should, more than a sensible woman would allow. The world diminished to elemental feeling when his eyes held hers, as now, in teasing invitation, and she wished very much to articulate her passion. But he never spoke of love directly, careful to use teasing words, affectionate indirect words. So she restrained herself with a self-control developed out of necessity the past weeks, and she said instead with a small faint smile and the merest arch of her brow, "If you're very, very good, I'll allow you to select one of Flora's lesser names." The insinuation in her voice suggested a degree of goodness immediately understandable to a man of Sinjin's repute, and her badinage drew him from his more earnest reflections.

"By all means then, Alfreda if it's a girl . . ." He grinned. "For I know *precisely* how to be good to you . . . or maybe Parthenia or perhaps Zilpha . . ." he teasingly added. Circling her ankles with his strong fingers, he slowly pulled her toward him, and when he'd drawn her close, he murmured in a low heated growl, the scent of crushed grass fragrant on the air, "Let me know when you've had your fill of . . . 'goodness' . . ." He licked the instep of her bare foot, nibbled lightly at her tender flesh. Looking up at her, he softly went on, "And if by that time, you don't care to speak at length . . . a nod will do . . ."

Delicately placing the pads of his fingers on the inside of her knees, he exerted the slightest pressure. A man of finesse and extravagant sensual allure, he had no need to importune. Women willingly opened themselves for him.

"And if I can't nod?" Chelsea whispered, his touch and voice and magical eyes, his body heat and closeness enough to bring her to quivering desire, as if she lived for pleasure alone here at Hatton.

"I'll decide then," he said, his warm palms sliding up her thighs, "when you've had enough."

She was so desperately in love with him she almost hated him for the loss of her freedom, for the invisible ties that bound her more securely than physical force. But while she might deplore her need of him and her bondage, he offered her inexplicable bliss, and she found him irresistible.

Life at Hatton was absolute heaven, Sinjin reflected, touching the dampness between her thighs with a gentle stroking finger, or as near to it as man was allowed. He was content—more, enchanted, the days of his recuperation replete with lavish passion and tenderness, with laughter and joy.

More sympathetic to affection, less chary of attachments, Chelsea recognized her feelings as love. Sinjin didn't. He didn't know what love was.

But when their lips met in a gentle kiss, with or without the acknowledgment of love, a trembling susceptibility, a responsive turbulent emotion possessed both their hearts.

Chapter 32

It rained for three days and three nights following the afternoon under the apple tree, but the idyll at Hatton continued undisturbed, the cozy rooms of Sinjin's hunting lodge serving for pleasurable pursuits as well as had the sunny environs of Hatton.

Waking on the fourth day to a continuing downpour, Chelsea rolled away from the warmth of Sinjin's body, stretched lazily and said, "Does it rain like this often?"

Still half-asleep, Sinjin answered without opening his eyes. "I've never been here in the spring." Pulling a pillow over his face to shut out the daylight, he muttered, "Nothing to hunt."

Sitting up, Chelsea brushed her pale tousled hair away from her face, her gesture ending in another leisurely stretch. How pleasant life was despite the rain . . . how blissfully lazy away from her normal busy schedule centered around home and stable yard. She felt on holiday. Gazing at her husband's inert bronzed body sprawled in a tangle of bedclothes, his arms folded over the pillow on his face as though to keep away the morning, she said in the direction of the pillow, "Let's make taffy today."

An indistinct sound emerged through layers of down.

"I'm starved."

Another mumbled response, this time even less clear.

"Sinjin!"

He opened his eyes then because the pillow was wrenched away, precipitously tossed aside, and a soft warm body installed itself directly atop him, his wife's thighs straddling his hips. Forcing himself awake with a facility acquired after years of waking in strange boudoirs after very little sleep, he smiled up at her rosy-cheeked face. "Do you know *how* to make taffy?" he conversationally inquired, as he would in the past have said, "Good morning, darling" to the lady whose bed he was sharing. He grinned. "Because I sure as hell don't."

"I know how to pull it," Chelsea said with confidence, as though leaving out the first six steps were incidental.

"Since our mutual ignorance of taffy making seems to be nearly total, why don't we just order up some taffy from the cook and sleep until it's brought up?"

"We *always* made taffy on rainy days . . ."

His eyes opened fully for a brief astonished moment before half-closing again in lazy irony. "How wonderfully wholesome," he murmured. His rainy days tended toward less tame pursuits; of course, his entire life tended toward less tame pursuits.

"Besides, I'm very, very hungry," Chelsea noted, ignoring his mild sarcasm.

"You're *always* hungry."

"I'm eating for two."

She looked enormously cheerful for such an ungodly hour of the morning, Sinjin reflected, like some chirpy woodland nymph whose boat was already prepared for the flood. *He* viewed the early hour with less bright-eyed favor after having sampled two bottles of the claret last night, not to mention a snifter or two of cognac. But his half-lidded glance was affectionate as he surveyed his wife—the focus of all his delight these days at Hatton—and he decided that, in recompense for the vast pleasure she gave him, he could participate in even an outrageous exercise like taffy making.

"I suppose then," he said with a smile, his blue gaze taking in her expectant expression, "since you're eating for two and family tradition recommends it, we must make taffy—"

"Now?" An irrepressible excitement, a young child's impatience vibrated in the single word.

He groaned, his mind more willing than his body. But with a resigned sigh and an affable grin, he agreed, "Now."

Literally bounding from the bed with an effervescent energy, Chelsea quickly crossed the small corner room set under the eaves. Gathering up her robe from the chair near the dormer window, she twirled once in a light-hearted flurry of movement and tossed it on.

Half-raised on his elbows, Sinjin smiled at her sunshiny cheer on such a wannish grey morning, the aquamarine robe she wore complement to her pale hair and the cloudy, slate-colored day. The brocade shimmered like an azure sea as she passed with swift efficiency from desk to armoire to bureau, picking up his comb and robe, her brush and mirror, her sweeping passage jolting his marginal headache.

"You're moving too fast this morning, sweet," Sinjin mumbled, collapsing back on the pillows. "Come, sit for a minute."

"Is this better?" Chelsea inquired with a grin, aware of the probable effects of two bottles of wine, instantly altering her pace to accommodate his lethargy. Dressed in his silk robe, the oversized length trailing behind her in a train, she looked queenly, her saunter theatrical. But her smile still reflected her mood, impish and fey, and her diaphanous hair reminded him of a nymph.

"You've cut your leg," she said as she approached the bed, and setting down the objects she carried, she leaned closer to scrutinize the blood on Sinjin's upper thigh.

Sitting upright abruptly at her surprising comment, Sinjin swore softly as his sensitive cranial nerve endings took issue with hasty movement. Gazing at the streak of blood on his thigh, he said, "A cut?" in precisely the tone a prim virgin would pronounce the word "intercourse." With suspicion and disaffirmation.

"I'll wash it for you," Chelsea said, turning to find a cloth.

Considering with perplexity how one could cut oneself while sleeping on a down mattress, Sinjin impatiently grabbed a corner of the sheet and wiped away the bloody smear.

There was no cut. His skin was unblemished.

The disturbing implications struck him in the next pulse beat, followed instantly by a chaotic disarray of sensation: perverse relief; concern; a strange perturbation *and* an overwhelming ignorance. Having always avoided long-term female attachments, he had only a rudimentary knowledge of miscarriage.

"I think you're bleeding," he cautiously said when Chelsea walked back from the small table that held the washbasin, his face without expression even while a juggernaut of shock and calamity overran his reason.

Dropping the wet cloth as though it were flame hot, Chelsea raised her hand to her mouth and stood motionless in the center of the room while the ramifications of Sinjin's carefully restrained statement held her terror-struck. The sound of the clock ticking seemed loud in the sudden silence, and she wondered for a moment whether her heart had stopped because she'd turned so cold.

"You should check," Sinjin quietly suggested. Easing across the rumpled bedclothes, he carefully slid his legs over the side of the bed with strangely controlled movements, as though the silence demanded circumspect actions.

And when Chelsea did check a moment later, the white linen towel held a conspicuous red stain.

Her face turned ashen.

In an unconscious reflex, she pressed her thighs together, as though that insignificant gesture could stem disaster, as though she had any control over the inexorable flow of blood. *I'll lose him,* was her first thought. *And our child.* She swallowed and shut her eyes, fighting against the pressure of her tears.

I never wanted to love him, she helplessly thought as the ache of tears in her throat intensified. And she'd struggled against the impulse for all the weeks before Hatton. But Sinjin could make one believe even in love when he exerted his easy charm. And lately, when he'd begun speaking of the baby with warmth and ease, she'd tentatively dared to build modest dreams. But now her child was in jeopardy, all her dreams were in danger and the abject terror that she might lose her child overpowered her reason, her self, even her ability to intellectualize her feelings. All she could feel was a vast sadness crushing her—limitless, oppressive, without confining dimension.

And her tears seeped from beneath her eyelids, glistening grief trailing down her pale cheeks.

Only a brief moment had passed while the world shuddered on its axis, but Sinjin had already moved swiftly from the bed at the sight of her tears, and lifting her into his arms, he held her tightly against the solid wall of his chest, the shimmering azure fabric falling over his arm to the carpet like a trail of tears. "Maybe it's normal," he whispered in comfort. "Maybe there's no need to cry."

Chelsea's muffled sobs warmed his skin; the wetness of her tears slid down his chest into the Lyon silk of her robe. "We'll call in a midwife—a doctor—they'll know. Don't cry, maybe you don't have to cry. Maybe it's nothing."

He spoke the small automatic phrases of solace, offering soothing comfort while considering the possibilities.

Personal freedom suddenly tempted him like St. Anthony's visions in the desert; his former life shimmered like a mirage on the horizon in all its unfettered independence . . . Brutal and selfish, potent as a drug in his brain, the word "annulment" invaded his consciousness.

But juxtaposed with the inhumanity of his self-interest, a genuine affection and passion for Chelsea existed, as did a deeply felt sorrow for their child—perhaps too frail already to withstand the harsh reality of life. Like their vulnerable relationship, he thought, and the crippling compulsion of their marriage.

He was afflicted and chagrined, as though the god of folly served as puppet master in his recent life. Sinjin's disordered feelings refused definition. An innate kindness and compassion prevailed over all the muddle in his mind, and Chelsea's immediate needs took precedence.

"Let me call a midwife." He spoke softly, rocking her gently like a small child. "I'll lay you on the bed—for a moment only," he added as her arms tightened around his neck.

"No." A small hurt sound.

"Please, darling . . ." he gently pressed.

"Do we have to?" Her voice trembled when she spoke, the words barely audible. And if she hadn't been so overwhelmed by bereavement, she would have marveled at her disablement. But defenseless against her feelings of loss, she wanted comfort, hope; she wanted Sinjin's arms around her.

"As a precaution, sweetheart, we should."

"Stay with me." No one else in the world could feel the warm liquid issue from her body, the drops of blood like a death warrant, unseen, merciless, terrifying. She didn't want to be alone. She didn't want him to leave her.

He understood—if not her terror, at least her woeful need. So holding her with one arm at a time, he managed to shrug into his robe without setting her down, his strength sufficient to the task. Tying the braided silk belt with his teeth and one hand, he kissed Chelsea gently on her forehead, and then with swift strides—the need for help compelling in his mind—he walked out of the bedroom.

Carrying Chelsea down the dim hallway (his hunting box a half-timbered cottage with low beamed ceilings and small mullioned windows), Sinjin stood on the landing at the top of the stairs, framed by stag-head finials and a balustrade of primitive huntsmen.

"Mrs. Barnes!" he shouted. "Forester, Ned . . . Jim, Frank!" The litany of names swirled down the ornately paneled stairwell, ringing clarion-clear through the ground-floor rooms.

And his staff came on the run, for the Duke had never raised his voice at Hatton. At the sight of Lady St. John in his arms, they recognized a crisis. The Duke's appearance this time of the morning indicated some emergency as well; he wasn't an early riser. And the lady's face, while not completely visible, was tear-stained.

"I want a doctor or doctors; I want midwives. And I want them here immediately," Sinjin said, his voice powerful and intense. "Send out as many grooms as necessary; have Sahar come to me. The Bedouins will go out too." He was taking out his guards, Chelsea's peril more urgent.

"And breakfast for my lady, *now.*"

The cadence of his commands, issued in a crisp decisive tone, scattered his staff, as did the apparent cause of his concern.

And then Sinjin and Chelsea waited.

The sluggish passage of time awful . . .

Sinjin wanted to pace, inactivity foreign to his nature, but he couldn't without disturbing Chelsea. He sat instead with Chelsea in his arms, in the chair near the window overlooking the courtyard, so he could monitor the travels of his grooms. Sahar had gone out himself with the Bedouins as escort to the staff. One troop north to Glendale for Dr. Hatch, another east to Wakefield for Dr. Gregory. Two more had been dispatched to fetch the neighborhood midwives.

When breakfast was brought up, Sinjin coaxed Chelsea to eat.

"You have to," he said, "to keep up your strength. Just try a strawberry or some chocolate, a bite of cake . . ." And selecting some morsel from the tray set on the table beside him, he fed her while he carried on a monologue of idle chatter to distract her from her heartache. "The roads are poor after the rains; it could be some time before the men are back . . . so you have to eat—open your mouth, darling, Mother used to always say spring at Hatton is wetter than Brighton, the old moat is even filling. Here—a spoonful of pudding, eat now, sweetheart, it's almond creme, your favorite. And what do you think of hanging your new painting of Mameluke in the dining room? We'll move over the cabinet of delftware a few feet to give it proper exposure. Try this now . . . sliced ham on toast points with a sauce of some kind, do you think it's Stilton cheese? Just a small forkful now . . . it's Mrs. Barnes' mother's recipe, I'm told."

His voice soothed, as he hoped it would, or distracted her for brief moments, the deep low resonance a constant like his presence, like a lifeline to reality when her own sense of failure threatened to overwhelm her in self-pity. Not a single thought survived for more than a few moments against her fixation on the blood seeping from her body. If she didn't move, if she ate, if she prayed, would it stop? Was it too late already for the baby, or could a pregnancy survive this bleeding? Please let it stop—could this be common?—did this happen to other women?—would it please *stop, please, please,* and she sent supplications heavenward because she didn't want to lose this baby. Her child had a name and gender already; she talked to it, made plans for their future. And then in contriteness, she apologized to all the gods and mythical spirits if, in her selfishness, she'd insisted on a girl and they were punishing her now for her presumption. *I'm sorry, I'm sorry,* she silently pleaded. *I didn't mean it. I take it back. Forgive me . . .*

But if there were gods or spiritual divinities listening, they chose to ignore her pleas, and Sinjin helped her stem the increasing flow of blood with a new linen towel when the first one became saturated.

"Darling," he said immediately after he'd disposed of the bloody fabric, "You *have* to lie down for a few minutes while I go and talk to Mrs. Barnes." Only extreme constraint kept his voice level, for Chelsea's loss of blood was significant. "You need a doctor; I'm helpless in my ignorance. Please, dear, I'll be gone just a moment."

Without waiting for a response, he rose from the chair, intent on bringing aid despite Chelsea's protests. Losing their child distressed him, but under no circumstances would he simply sit and watch Chelsea die with the unborn babe. And no one could bleed that profusely for long.

Placing her on the bed and covering her with a down quilt, he quickly threw on breeches and a shirt. Barefoot, he raced from the room, descended the stairs in plunging leaps and ran full out through the public rooms to the kitchen, snapping questions immediately he entered the room. He grilled the staff, wanting immediate answers: Why had no help arrived? Where were the doctors? Why hadn't the midwife come? And his scowl deepened at each answer.

Frank had been turned back from Glendale with the bridge washed out at Ongley. Dr. Gregory had left Wakefield for a meeting at Manchester last week; Ned hadn't returned yet from midwife Simond, but Ickely bridge was never passable when it rained; and James was still out. Striding like a caged animal or standing rigidly still, Sinjin questioned his servants more closely, his eyes trained on the face of the speaker as though the force of his gaze could temper the substance of the recitation. And he swore softly at each discouraging disclosure. He debated then whether he should try to bring Chelsea to a doctor, but even before the thought was fully formed, he discarded it, the roads impassable by carriage.

No help, no damned help yet, and forty minutes had passed. His staff hovered around him, but beyond sympathy they could offer no aid. Pacing for a few brief moments more, he wondered with a cold chill fear how much blood Chelsea could lose before . . . Thrusting away the unthinkable conclusion, he racked his brain for some solution. He wasn't on a dueling field now, with doctors and attendants readily at hand, or in battle, where one had come to terms long since with death. Sahar had some knowledge of medicine but more specifically gunshot wounds or sword cuts, broken bones, not miscarriage.

And all the horror stories of confinements and travails gone awry suddenly flashed through his mind: Lady Blair's death last year; Paget's young wife, who was barely nineteen; Harold's daughter, who hadn't lived to celebrate her first wedding anniversary; Callister's sister, whom he'd danced with at her debut only short months before her confinement—young women all in their prime, their lives taken away in hours or brief days. But the melancholy anecdotes had always concerned others, never him.

Until now.

And for a man who had always ordered the world to his perfection, the cold reality of death struck him intimately for the first time. He'd been in life-threatening situations before, but none where he couldn't fight his way out. But no heroics or courage, no cold calculating strategy would win the day in Chelsea's case. He couldn't command the deities or dictate the fragile elements of Chelsea's body into order.

He was powerless.

For a moment more he considered his unnerving impotence and then, reaching a decision, said, "Send word up if you hear *anything* from Ned or James." He kept his tone moderate, for apparently he'd frightened the staff before. No one had dared come to tell him of the unsuccessful attempts. "I want to know immediately." His gaze swept the ranks of his servants, one and all tense and wide-eyed.

"Understood?"

Heads bobbed and nodded in acknowledgment, but no one braved speech under the drilling blue eyes until Mrs. Barnes found voice to say, "Yes, Your Grace."

"Have Mameluke saddled."

He left then, his long-legged stride taking him swiftly through the west wing rooms. If no message reached him in ten minutes, he decided, mounting the stairs at a run, he'd go after midwife Hobbs himself. The village of Dedham Close was just across the river.

Chapter 33

He found Chelsea dozing when he returned to their bedchamber, and moving about the room with infinite care in order not to wake her, Sinjin found his low riding boots, slid the heelless soft leather footgear on, and pulled a leather jacket from the armoire. Anticipating a swim in the flooded Kinnbeck, he dressed in light garments.

Sitting down beside the bed, he alternately watched Chelsea and the clock, his gaze traveling often to the tall case clock in the corner. Ten minutes—no more, and he was on his way to Dedham Close.

And when the hands of the clock indicated the end of his purgatory, he rose as though he were jerked upright by some unseen hand. Standing at the side of the bed for a brief moment, tense beneath his motionless stance, he gazed at his wife, fear curling in the pit of his stomach, reason insufficient to leash the chaos in his mind. She looked slight and pale, dwarfed by the enormous four-poster bed, the heavy draped bedcurtains of red cut velvet reminding him for an eerie moment of rivers of blood.

Whirling around, he left then, driven to speed by the pernicious image and the pallor of his wife's face.

No one was left to ride with him, the entirety of his staff out scouring the shire for medical help. But he knew the way to Dedham Close and Mameluke sensed his urgency.

The lanes were slow going, the mud hock-deep and treacherous in spots where water ran across the road. Mameluke slipped to his knees twice before they reached the cross-roads at Syndam. The next two miles to the river ford resembled a mire bog so much that Sinjin dismounted on three occasions to lead Mameluke through.

By the time he reached Villar's farm, Sinjin was soaked through, covered with mud, Mameluke lathered from the hard going. Open fields, dense hedges, shadowed copses fringed the lane as he rode north, the surrounding landscape utterly silent under the steady drumming rain, and Sinjin felt as though he and Mameluke were alone in the universe. Even the birds and beasts no longer ventured out after four days of rain.

Straining his eyes through the curtain of mist and rain, he caught sight of the marker for Dedham Close. Another half mile to the ford.

He heard them before he saw them, the shouts of the men carrying faintly, the high-pitched squeal of the horses coming to him fitfully through the veil of rain. And when he rode from the trees bordering the river, he saw James and Jonathan trying to force their horses into the violent torrent. Mrs. Hobbs waited on the opposite side, enveloped in an oilskin, seated on an old cob that had no intention of venturing into the swirling floodwaters. Several villagers clustered around her, willing but unable to help against the mighty forces of nature.

Normally the ford ran no more than four feet of clear water over a sand bottom; today it overflowed its banks, a maelstrom of brown muddy water fifteen feet deep and eighty feet across.

Riding up to his men, Sinjin asked, "Has Mrs. Hobbs been waiting long?" He was concerned that she not be unduly fatigued. He had great need of her skills.

"No, not long," James replied. "Old Nat the ferryman fetched her when I shouted him out of his house."

"I'm going over with Mameluke. Help Mrs. Hobbs ashore when we return." Without wasting any time in conversation, he turned Mameluke, spurred the big bay upstream to take advantage of the current and, fifty yards upriver, urged the thoroughbred into the turbulent water.

Mameluke responded, sinking into the floodwaters with the same composure he exhibited on the race course, understanding what was expected of him, rising to the challenge. Slipping from the saddle once Mameluke launched himself away from the riverbank, Sinjin swam beside the huge racer, a stirrup leather wrapped securely around his hand.

As they were swept downstream, Mameluke's immense strength propelled them by slow degrees away from the violent center current, his powerful legs churning, drawing them toward the opposite shore a torturous inch at a time until Mameluke touched bottom at last. Struggling for a moment to gain his footing on the rough bottom near the bank, he surged up out of the river, stamped and tossed his head, the soft ground underfoot a cushion of mud. Pulled along in Mameluke's wake, scrambling to keep up, Sinjin stood beside him for a breathless moment, his lungs heaving, trying to draw in much needed air.

Time was precious, though, so still slightly breathless, he squished across the small distance of open ground to the group of villagers short moments later. His smile appeared between his irregular respiration. "Bloody wet out," he said—which phrase, much embroidered with the details of his spectacular crossing, would serve as the principal topic of gossip in the shire for the next month. "And thank you . . . for coming out . . . on such a hellish day," Sinjin said, turning to Mrs. Hobbs, water streaming from his clothes, his breath still rasping in his lungs. "We'll see you . . . safely over . . . on Mameluke. He's absolutely . . . dependable." Drawing a deep breath, he reached up for her.

"He looks right strong," she said, familiar with bad weather after thirty years of delivering babies, already throwing her leg over the saddle pommel to slide into Sinjin's arms.

Seconds later, Mrs. Hobbs was seated on Mameluke, her oilskin satchel tied to her shoulders, and with a courteous "Hold on tightly now," Sinjin placed both her hands on the pommel. His concern for Chelsea impelling him to speed, the Duke of Seth and his prize-winning racer plunged back into the floodwaters. Swimming when they could, swept away at times by the current, they struggled to bring Mrs. Hobbs to the Hatton side of the Kinnbeck while James and Jonathan, standing out as far as they dared in the rushing current, eventually pulled Mameluke and Sinjin ashore to a round of cheers from the villagers. Waving back, exhilarated with the success of having found Mrs. Hobbs, Sinjin pushed his wet hair out of his eyes and said in the staccato cadence of inadequate breath, "My apologies, Mrs. Hobbs, for your drenching."

His tone was pleasant, as though risking his life was incidental to Mrs. Hobbs' discomfort, and he even smiled at the end, immensely pleased he'd found someone to help Chelsea. "We'll see you warm at Hatton soon," he graciously added.

"I've been out in worse, Your Grace," the small elderly woman said, "over the years. How far along is the Duchess's labor?"

Sinjin's smile disappeared, and he felt for a moment as though he'd swum the Channel, so great a weariness assailed him. "It's not labor, I'm afraid. At almost three months pregnant she's bleeding badly."

"For how long?"

"Since morning. We should hurry, if you don't mind." A surge of fear tightened his stomach; how long had he been gone? "You stay on Mameluke with me." He gave a nod to James and Jonathan, and the three men mounted.

On the ride back to Hatton, the slogging pace too slow for Sinjin's taut nerves, he explained all he knew of Chelsea's condition.

Mrs. Barnes was waiting for them at the door, the staff at the ready with dry clothes, hot tea and welcome news that the Duchess still slept. Sinjin changed quickly so Chelsea wouldn't be alarmed at his appearance, and going up to the bedchamber first, he greeted Mrs. Hobbs when she arrived shortly after. Dressed in dry clothing and warm slippers, she briskly took charge.

For which Sinjin was eminently grateful.

He could face enemy fire, swim flooded rivers and fight duels, but he could do nothing for his wife in her extremity, and he desperately needed Mrs. Hobbs' expertise. Following her instructions, he had the servants bring the necessary linens and hot water while Mrs. Hobbs unpacked the contents of her satchel, spreading out the containers and packets of curatives on a table. When all was in readiness, Sinjin woke Chelsea.

Sitting gently on the side of the bed, he bent close to Chelsea and whispered, "Darling, wake up. Mrs. Hobbs is here to help."

Chelsea came awake to his smile and thought him just out of the bath with his wet hair, forgetful for a fleeting moment why she was in bed and in need of help.

In the next flashing beat, recognition dawned, the pain of remembrance touched her eyes and Sinjin covered her hand with his. "She'll help you," he whispered, lifting her hand to his lips and tenderly kissing her fingertips. "Don't cry, sweetheart," he murmured as her eyes glistened with tears. He wanted to cry himself at the sadness in her dark eyes—feeling bereft of adequate words to ease her pain.

He wished jewels or furs or costly gowns would diminish her suffering, and he'd buy her shops full; he wished it were possible to purchase happiness and perfect health for her, and he'd put his wealth at her disposal. But neither fortune, power nor title would divert the damage to their child, and he could do nothing but share her sorrow.

Mrs. Hobbs was gentle, thorough and sympathetic with her examination, but her diagnosis held little hope. The extensive bleeding signaled the end of Chelsea's pregnancy, and no single explanation or simple cause, no hard facts gave indication of what was responsible. There rarely were any answers with miscarriage, she said. "You're young and healthy though, Your Grace," Mrs. Hobbs soothingly went on. "You'll have other babies."

Mrs. Hobbs couldn't know, of course, how questionable other babies were, Chelsea thought. I'll divorce you, Sinjin had said only short weeks ago, if the child isn't mine. And now there was no child at all. And even weeks ago, when she was infinitely less attached to him, his flat repudiation had stung her with its finality. He wasn't a man to suffer graciously under duress; a man of action, he remedied his discomfort instead.

Sinjin heard Mrs. Hobbs' words too, a plain statement of solace offered in time of despair. And it gave hope, he didn't doubt, to many. His own feelings, however, failed to fall into regimented ranks of harmony and hope for the future.

He didn't know, to be perfectly blunt, whether he wanted more babies.

Mrs. Hobbs suggested an abortifacient then to properly cleanse the womb and eliminate the risk of fever from tissue residue. Without the drug, the possibility of fever increased; with the drug she promised a speedier recovery.

"Recovery" wasn't the appropriate word to indicate Chelsea's indelible sense of deprivation. And she initially resisted, clinging to hope, not wishing to acknowledge the loss of her child.

Taking the drug would be too final; why couldn't she wait?

"Fine," Sinjin said. "Of course. Whatever you wish," he softly added. "Let me escort Mrs. Hobbs downstairs and I'll be back directly."

In the corridor outside his bedchamber, he asked hard, pointed questions of Mrs. Hobbs, all of which she answered with candor and honesty. "Her Grace has lost the child," she said with a sigh. "I'm sorry."

"I'll try and convince my wife to take the decoction then if you're absolutely sure."

"No babe could survive that bleeding," she said without hesitation.

Experiencing a small chill at her words, Sinjin found he had to pause for a moment to steady his voice. "Very well," he quietly said. "I understand, and I'll talk to the Duchess. Can you stay with my wife until she's well?"

"I'll stay as long as I can," the midwife said, plain-spoken as always. "Forgive me, Your Grace, but Mrs. Densmore is due to deliver soon, and so is Mrs. Howard. It's her seventh. And they don't wait, those later babies."

For an instant, Sinjin was jealous of the two women who were having children, seven for Mrs. Howard, when his own child had died, and he wished to say, "No, you can't go to them because my wife needs you." But his sudden resentment succumbed to more reasonable emotion a moment later, and he said, "We'd appreciate your staying as long as you can . . . and thank you again."

After seeing Mrs. Hobbs into Mrs. Barnes' care, Sinjin sat through the night with Chelsea. Mrs. Hobbs looked in every few hours, monitoring Chelsea's progress, checking to see she wasn't developing a fever, offering to take over and let Sinjin sleep. But he preferred staying himself, knowing Chelsea would look for him when she woke, still anxious about the state of her health despite Mrs. Hobbs' reassurance.

The rain stopped near midnight, the quiet so unusual after four days that Sinjin found it momentarily distracting. Soon after, he opened the windows to let in the fresh night air, moving the fire screen to protect the candelabra from the light drafts, covering Chelsea with an extra blanket, standing for a moment before the open casement and listening to the night sounds. Running a hand over the dark stubble on his jaw, he stretched, easing the muscles in his shoulders. So much had changed since morning; a small unformed life gone, Chelsea not yet reconciled to the casualty, his own emotions unsettled. So much in his *life* had altered since first meeting Chelsea Fergusson at Newmarket . . .

Chelsea stirred then and called out his name, and he swiftly crossed the room to the bed. "I'm here," he said, taking her hand. "How do you feel?" And he spoke to her then of trivial things, of local gossip brought over by Mrs. Hobbs, of Cook's special meal of greens she'd made for Mameluke, of Sahar's good wishes to her. He stroked her hand gently as he talked, a tranquilizing soothing gesture, and when she dozed off a few minutes later, he kissed her flushed cheek.

He sat beside her all night, sunk in the armchair he'd pulled near the bed, unshaven, his neckcloth discarded, his long legs stretched out before him, weary physically and mentally—sobered by the sudden sadness in their lives, disheartened as well . . . his emotions in flux.

The only surety in all of the unhappy occurrence was that Chelsea would need his comfort.

When morning came in a brilliant golden dawn so different from the days past, Chelsea opened her eyes to gleaming sunlight and said, "The rain stopped. Could it be a sign?"

Her voice held such pathetic hope that Sinjin wished intensely he could agree, but when Mrs. Hobbs had last come in to change the dressing, the linen was thoroughly soaked with blood, so he knew better. Sunshine or not, her bleeding continued.

"I don't want you to take a fever, darling," he quietly said, reaching over to take her hand. "You have to listen to Mrs. Hobbs. The babe's gone," he gently whispered.

"Don't say that." Wrenching her hand from his, she turned her head away, angry and desperate and afraid.

"I wish I didn't have to," he honestly said, conscious of his much altered sentiments. Two months ago, a month ago, this miscarriage would have been a propitious solution to his unwanted marriage. But his feelings had begun to change in the past weeks with Chelsea's picturesque images of their child. The small daughter she spoke of so often had taken on an unmistakable reality, had become *his* baby girl . . . and he too wished very much that Mrs. Hobbs were wrong.

But even fond hope couldn't long withstand the graphic evidence of that much blood, and he knew better. "Mrs. Hobbs has thirty years' experience, darling," he softly said, the frank assessment she'd offered yesterday etched on his mind. "You have to listen to her."

Chelsea's head swung back, her violet eyes shadowed with despair. "I don't want to." Denial, without regard for logic—a small cry of pain vibrated in the morning light.

She looked very young in his nightshirt, the sleeves rolled up many times, her small hands peeking out from the oversized garment, her eyes too large in the paleness of her face, smudged with fatigue and unhappiness, her slender shoulders so small he could cover them with his palms.

He felt an enormous responsibility suddenly, a startling and novel concept for Sinjin St. John, who had long resisted emotional involvement with any of his lovers. Perhaps if his previous life had been less transient in entertainments, he would have been aware of cause and effect, of accountability, long before. Intellectually, of course, he was cognizant of the principle; he'd simply never stayed long enough to give heed to his own obligations.

The seriousness of Chelsea's health suppressing even his own considerations of freedom, he said, "Do what Mrs. Hobbs suggests, sweetheart, and when you're feeling better, we'll go down to London and finish the last of the season. No one's seen you yet." He smiled with a remnant of his glorious teasing smile. "Allow me to show you off."

He was offering her a prize—a dazzling acknowledgment before the world . . . a place at his side as his wife.

"What makes you think I want to see society?" Chelsea's voice was very small, but she understood the enormity of his offer. Until now, he'd never suggested she join him in London. Not too long ago, in fact, their conversation debated the logistics of maintaining separate lives.

"They want to see you." He noted the Ton's singularly avid curiosity regarding the Duke of Seth's new wife. "And you can meet my family," he added.

In all the time she'd known Sinjin, he'd never mentioned his family except in passing, as though he existed distinct from any of them.

"I may not be up to all of that," Chelsea candidly replied, the totality of such social obligations daunting to a young girl whose previous company had been predominantly equine.

"Then I'll hold you up," Sinjin said with a faint smile, "and occasionally you can hold *me* up." His smile was sweet as a young boy's. "Attendance at some social events," he went on, "requires substantial alcoholic incentive."

She smiled up at him, the first smile he'd seen in two days, and he congratulated himself on his stratagem. "Now be a sweet child and listen to Mrs. Hobbs."

"Is it truly over?" A breath of quiet words, an exhalation of dashed hopes, the end perhaps of her marriage.

He too found the words difficult at the last. "It is," Sinjin finally said. "I'm sorry."

And her mouth quivered for a moment before her tears spilled over. He said he was sorry, but in her melancholy the words seemed a courtesy—a requirement—not an open wound, as it was for her. They didn't feel the same way, and while she hadn't expected they would, the degree of his acceptance grieved her.

Gathering her into his arms, he held her in silence while she cried. He had no words to console her, no platitudes sufficient to ease her pain.

Having spent a lifetime keeping emotion at bay, he didn't expose the extent of his distress, but his child too had been lost, and he felt a sudden emptiness.

Perhaps her anger at Sinjin's perceived disregard helped in her decision, or maybe her fierce autonomy overruled her tears at last. If crying could have helped bring back her child, she would have cried a lifetime, but since it could not, she knew what she must do.

"Call Mrs. Hobbs," Chelsea quietly said into Sinjin's shoulder, the sound muffled against his shirt.

But he heard the words as if clearly pronounced in an empty chamber, for they echoed his own silent judgment.

And he reached for the bell pull near the bed.

Once Mrs. Hobbs had been sent for and she'd spoken to Chelsea, Sinjin followed her down to the kitchen, where she brewed a tea of tansy, rue, marigold, chamomile and hops, sweetened with honey and laced with a tot of brandy.

"It will deliver a woman of a dead child," she said to Sinjin, "and bring down her courses. You must see that Her Grace is up four times a day so the blood doesn't pool. And keep her warm. I'm telling you this now and I'll tell you again before I leave. She mustn't be allowed to lie in bed all day."

"How soon . . . after . . . will she be ready to travel?"

"It depends on her constitution."

"She *was* quite strong." He thought of Chelsea handling the brutes of horses in her stables.

"A week then . . . or ten days, but she'll feel the jarring for a time, so travel slowly."

Chelsea drank the tea that morning, and by the time Mrs. Hobbs was called away two days later, she was pronounced doing "clev-

erly." And while her melancholy still persisted in varying degrees—
for no independence, however strong, was proof against so devastating a sorrow—Chelsea's health renewed itself with the impressive
speed of youth. Meanwhile Sinjin insisted on strict adherence to Mrs.
Hobbs' governing rules, and he personally checked to see that his
cook made the recuperative broths to Mrs. Hobbs' directions.

"Did you ever think to see the Duke stirring a pot of soup?" Mrs.
Barnes said one day to the cook directly after Sinjin had left the
kitchen with orders to add more mustard greens to the stock.

"I never thought to see him up before noon, darling boy," the
cook said with a smile. "Nor was he in the past." A local woman like
Mrs. Barnes, she kept track of her master's exploits. As did many.
The Duke of Seth, famous or notorious depending on your moral
stance, was the subject of much interest.

"Married life has changed him," Mrs. Barnes said with a small
smile as she knit in her rocking chair near the window overlooking
the kitchen garden.

"Her Grace has changed him," Cook more precisely noted.

"He's taking her to London." Mrs. Barnes' gaze came up to
meet Cook's in an exchange of friendly acknowledgment.

Less romantically inclined than Mrs. Barnes, who had sighed with
fond enthusiasm for the dear Duke's charming new state of matrimony, Cook laconically said, "I expect his mistresses are sharpening
their claws."

But as it turned out, Sinjin was called to London the following
day for an urgent meeting with his factor from Tunis, who had been
unexpectedly recalled to North Africa. With an erratic but recurring
public exhibitionism, the Bey was threatening all the European facto-
ries again, Sinjin's included. So Ali Ahmed intended to return on the
next sailing.

Although Ali Ahmed's visit to London had been scheduled long
in advance, Sinjin's unexpected marriage, captivity and recuperation
had kept them from meeting. And now very little time remained.

Seated with Chelsea on a south-facing terrace overlooking an
old-fashioned parterre garden reminiscent of bygone centuries, the
afternoon sun drifting toward the horizon, Sinjin broached the subject of his leaving. "If I want to see Ahmed, I should leave tomorrow. I'd be gone five days, six at the most." Chelsea was aware of his
packet from Seneca, which had been delivered after lunch. "I
wouldn't go at all if it weren't for the urgency of Ahmed's leaving.

The Pasha periodically dislikes the infidel when it's convenient for him. Apparently another tirade against foreign intervention is about to begin. Will you manage here alone?"

"I'll be fine. I'm practically well." Dressed in a simple country gown of sprigged muslin, Chelsea had color in her cheeks again, and she smiled more often.

"By the time I return, you'll be fully recuperated and we can leave for London."

"I might go to see Father first."

Sinjin's scowl was immediate. "Why?"

"To arrange a truce."

"I don't need your protection," he growled. "Your father can damn well go to hell."

"Very well," Chelsea amiably replied, wishing to avoid any disagreement but determined to talk to her family. Too much in love with her husband to contemplate widowhood with any equanimity, she intended to arrange an armistice.

Wars ended with amnesties. The Border clans traditionally called truces in the eternal conflict with the English. Surely the men she loved could come to some workable arrangement of co-existence.

"I don't want anything to do with your family," Sinjin brusquely said.

"Do you mind if I do?"

"Suit yourself." He wasn't medieval. She was his wife, not his chattel. But his terse reply indicated the limited extent of his largesse.

"Perhaps I'll go north while you're in London. Ayrshire is only a day away."

"Hmmm." Sullen and ill humored at talk of her family, Sinjin slid down in his teakwood garden chair and contemplated the toes of his boots. If he could play the tyrant, he'd refuse her permission to go, but too enlightened, he only said in grudging temper, his narrow-eyed gaze coming up to hold hers, "Don't stay long."

"If I go," Chelsea obligingly replied, "I'll be back in three days."

And she would have been, too, except for a dreadful fatigue induced by ten hours on atrocious roads. Once in Ayrshire she posted a letter to Sinjin explaining she'd decided to stay a few days longer until she was more refreshed. "I'll meet you in London in ten days," she wrote. "I'm feeling fine again, the weather is gorgeous, the horses are winning, Papa sends his regards and Jed assures me he'll see that extra padding is added to the carriage seats." She went on

briefly to list several of the horses' timed workouts she'd witnessed—
a source of great pride for her, as many of the racers had been trained
by her hand and were now running in top form. She debated various
conclusions to her letter, uncertain if she could blithely write, "Love
from your wife" when so little time had elapsed since their disaffec-
tion and she still understood so little of her husband's feelings. So
she compromised with a cordial, non-intimate "In good health,
Chelsea."

With John Palmer's new fast mail coaches relaying mail from
Scotland to London in a record two days, Sinjin received Chelsea's
letter before his scheduled return trip to Hatton.

When her letter was brought into the library, Sinjin and Seneca
were reviewing the lists of cargo being shipped back to Tunis. Taking
the slip of white parchment from the salver held out by the footman,
Sinjin ripped open the seal with some anxiety. Had Chelsea's health
relapsed?

Reassured that she was well after the first few phrases, he read the
note with less concern, muttering, "Hmpf" when he came to the
regards from his father-in-law. After finishing it, he leaned across his
desk and handed the creased paper to Seneca rather than explain.

"She'll be here soon then," Seneca said after perusing the brief
message, "and save you the trouble of posting back to Hatton."

"If they let her go, damn barbarians . . ." Sinjin grumbled,
lounging back in his chair, his hands clasped around the volutes of
his chair arms with an unnecessary force.

"Why wouldn't they?" Seneca assumed the Fergussons had re-
lented in their opinion of their new son-in-law if the Earl was offering his regards.

"How should I know why a Scot does anything? They're bandits
and outlaws, the bunch of them."

"Your wife included?" Seneca inquired with a grin.

Sinjin returned his smile, relaxing at the turn of conversation. "In
a way," he quietly replied, recalling Chelsea's assertive introduction.
"She *did* proposition me like any canny Scot . . . but," he added
with cheer in his voice, "I'm not complaining."

"Do I detect a new note of complacency concerning marriage?"
As Seneca sprawled comfortably in his chair, his dark eyes regarded
Sinjin's lingering smile.

Sobered suddenly, his smile dispelled by recall of the liabilities of
marriage, his expression shuttered, Sinjin didn't immediately reply.

"I don't know," he finally murmured. "I'm not sure what I feel. Marriage is so damned final. And Lord knows my parents' marriage left its scars, not to mention Damien's *charming* wife, who terrifies me continually with her very indiscreet pursuit. And try and think of a damned society marriage that's not wretched." He shook his head as if in lament. He was familiar only with living for transient pleasure, so his overview of marriage and its attendant prolonged involvement with one woman—a state long discredited by males of his class—left him nonplussed.

He had no experience with either permanence or love.

"We'll have to see," he said, the royal pronoun comfortable on his tongue. Without a child, an annulment was possible. He had time to decide before Chelsea arrived. But he'd promised her the rest of the season, and he'd keep his promise.

Chapter 34

Chelsea walked into Seth House a day earlier than planned, at four-thirty on a Tuesday afternoon. Her timing was unfortunate, as it turned out.

The Duchess of Buchan had just arrived for tea.

And when Chelsea entered the Painted Room on the second floor amidst a flurry of Seth House retainers stumbling over one another in their eagerness to escort their new chatelaine, she found herself announced to a small afternoon party, two females of which viewed her with displeasure.

Chelsea stood in the center of the pedimented doorway, framed by vividly painted Corinthian pilasters, dressed in a country gown of printed linen, her straw hat hanging down her back by loosened bonnet strings, her glorious blond hair as usual in tousled disarray, a tentative smile on her face.

His wife's beauty always astonished him, as if memory were incapable of fully preserving such dazzling fairness. But she needed a dressmaker, Sinjin reflected with a smile, or the Ton would consider him more solicitous of his mistresses' wardrobes than his wife's.

Instantly rising to greet her, he saw her smile widen as she caught sight of him, and he felt an unexpected pleasure at her delight. She waited for Sinjin to cross the dramatic room, which had been designed and painted by James Stuart after Roman prototypes, thinking her husband very much more patrician when seen in such a grand setting. She'd seen him only in the country, casual and in shirtsleeves. But at the last, as he approached her, she couldn't help herself from rushing into his arms, relieved after five long days of traveling to have arrived, artlessly jubilant to see him again.

"I'm afraid I barged in," she murmured, gazing up at him past the crisp linen of his neckcloth, her expression full of cheer despite her polite disclaimer.

"Nonsense," Sinjin replied with a smile, finding he liked the familiarity of her in his arms. "I think Vivian orchestrated this tea in any event, so I'm pleased you've come to save me from boredom."

"I'm occasionally very good at that," Chelsea whispered, ingenuous in her joy.

And he laughed at her enchanting witchery.

"Although," Chelsea went on with a teasing smile, gazing up at the gilded, coffered ceiling adorned with replicas of Roman painting, "these grand ceilings could be distracting . . ."

"A simple solution comes to mind," he found himself saying, as though he'd never considered the folly of further conjugal relations with his wife.

And they smiled at each other in pleasurable memory, the neoclassic splendor of Seth House momentarily supplanted by images of country bedrooms and lush green grass and a hayloft that smelled of sweet clover.

"Bring us your little Scots bride, Sinjin," the Duchess of Buchan said, the rudeness in her voice carrying across the sunlit room, "so we can *welcome* her to London."

Cassandra's peevish invitation rent the enchanting moment like cat claws ripping through silk, and Sinjin debated for a moment whether he dared place Chelsea in close proximity to either Cassandra or Damien's wife. Cassandra's intonation of "welcome" had sounded rather more like a caustic threat.

"Should I be carrying a weapon?" Chelsea pleasantly inquired.

Sinjin grimaced, then grinned. "Come, darling," he said, taking her hand, "for your first blooding in the Ton." Moving toward the group seated in the apse overlooking Green Park, he softly added, "But don't roll over and play dead or they'll go for your jugular."

"Charming advice," Chelsea murmured, forming her mouth into a polite smile as they began moving toward the sunlit corner of the room.

"Useful advice, darling, if you want to survive in society," he softly replied and then, in a normal voice, said, "Mother, I'd like you to meet my wife . . . ," making introductions for the members of the tea party.

Sinjin's mother, Maria, the Dowager Duchess, still a recognized beauty at forty-six, was gracious and warm in her greeting. Damien, who bore no resemblance to his brother other than his height, seemed genuinely pleased to meet her. His wife, Vivian, looked at Sinjin with more than sisterly affection, Chelsea immediately noted, and said in lieu of something pleasant when they were introduced, "Riding boots? How quaint." Her gaze leisurely swept up Chelsea from the toes of her brown leather boots.

"I rode some distance today to break the tedium of travel," Chelsea explained. She probably should have changed her boots, and if the thought had occurred to her, she definitely would have.

"And your gown must be Scottish. Did you sew it yourself?"

Sinjin's sister-in-law was peering down her pert nose with such a superior sneer that Chelsea decided a small lapse in good manners wouldn't be unfair. "And I spun the thread and wove the cloth as well," she cheerfully lied. "Sinjin likes most my domestic skills, don't you, darling?" she said, looking up at her husband, who was struggling to suppress a smile.

"It's astonishing what she can do," he blandly said, giving his wife match point in that particular set.

"I'm Cassandra," the Duchess of Buchan interjected before Sinjin could introduce her next, her intonation suggesting she was considerably more to Sinjin. And Chelsea wondered for a moment at the subtle finesse required to so pointedly proclaim yourself mistress to someone's husband with two innocuous words.

It was her expression perhaps, assured, confident of her beauty, so secure was she in her position as one of the Ton's reigning belles. There was no denying her splendor, Chelsea thought, a small sinking feeling settling in her stomach at the thought of battling the gorgeous, self-possessed woman for her husband's affection. Porcelain skin, lustrous black hair, eyes so blue they rivaled the sky. Cassandra's mouth was a luscious red from artifice, but delectable, and her shapely form, clothed in a fashionable froth of white muslin and ruffles and striking Roman-striped ribbon, had lain beneath Sinjin's in amorous intimacy.

Chelsea's heart lurched briefly at the disquieting thought, and she found her smile difficult to maintain.

"Will you be staying long?" Cassandra pleasantly asked, but her blue eyes were cool and deliberate, her remark barely civil.

She couldn't have asked a more indelicate or apt question considering the state of Chelsea and Sinjin's relationship, and Chelsea immediately assumed the Duchess of Buchan was in Sinjin's confidence.

Angered at her husband's license, but unwilling to give ground to a mistress any more than to a rival jockey in a race, Chelsea replied in a mild voice that she hoped concealed her resentment, "I'm down for some entertainment. Sinjin wished to show me London, didn't you, dear?" Gazing up at him, she playfully ran her fingertip down his cheek.

"Absolutely," he quickly replied. "Now would you like tea?" he inquired of Chelsea, fervently wishing to change the subject. "Mother has some special oolong she hoards like gold, or would you like sherry? Personally, a brandy appeals to me—Damien?" he inquired in the general direction of his brother as he escorted Chelsea to a chair near his mother. Or better yet, ten brandies, he thought, if Cassandra's and Vivian's cheeky baiting continues in form. At a nod and an understanding smile from his brother, Sinjin moved toward a nearby console table, swiftly uncorked a decanter, poured a healthy bumper into a glass, instantly drank it down and then, fortified against the coming ordeal, more leisurely re-filled his glass and one for his brother. Glancing briefly at one of the clocks, he decided to carry the decanter back with him. The verbal sparring could go on for some time, and a sufficient quantity of alcohol would help him disregard at least a portion of Cassandra's and Vivian's venality.

"You know, of course, everyone will be thrilled to meet you, my dear," Sinjin's mother was saying, handing Chelsea her cup of tea, her smile reminiscent of her son's. "Most everyone's still in town. We must immediately plan a ball to welcome you. Can't you see her in a shade of rose, Sinjin, with her glorious coloring? Sinjin will bring you to Madame DuBay tomorrow," she went on, her glance dancing between her son and daughter-in-law, "and arrange everything. Or perhaps a primrose shade with silk flowers would be nice," she added, looking back at her son, who was regarding her with an amused expression.

"And then again, *Maman,*" he said with a smile, "Chelsea might prefer you not dress her to your taste. Maybe she'd like fuchsia?"

"Oh, dear, you don't, do you, sweet child? Fuchsia is for, well—"

"Women of a certain profession, Mama is trying to say," Sinjin lazily murmured. "And never fear, Mama, for Madame DuBay is fully aware of the difference."

No doubt, Chelsea thought, with the number of mistresses brought in by her male clients.

"I thought you liked fuchsia, Sinjin," Vivian interjected, her glance dwelling on Sinjin's lounging form with a fascinated interest she didn't bother to hide. "The woman on your arm at the Rotunda last week wore fuchsia."

"She was on Seneca's arm, not mine, Vivian. My wife, however, wouldn't wear that particular shade. Now, unless this conversation moves into more interesting channels, I'm afraid you'll have to excuse me. I detest talk of fashion."

"I was wondering," Cassandra said, her azure gaze trained on Chelsea with a minute scrutiny, "on a topic removed from fashion, are you expecting an heir soon? Forgive my curiosity," she blandly went on, as though she were questioning Chelsea's taste in novels rather than asking the most intimate of questions, "but with Sinjin's abrupt removal from my home those months ago by your father and his troop of Scotsmen, I assumed news of a blessed event precipitated his sudden departure."

Chelsea flushed, the pink rising heatedly up her throat to her cheeks, that particular query rife with emotion. And while she resented the worldly Duchess of Buchan for her casual malice and her friendship with her husband, she also envied her her careless aplomb.

"You'll be the first to know, Cassandra," Sinjin drawled, coming to his wife's aid, his comfortable pose unaltered, his expression urbane, only the tightening of his fingers on his glass indication of his impatience with her, "but since the Duchess is only seventeen—"

"Eighteen," Chelsea interjected as if it mattered.

"Eighteen?" He suddenly remembered her saying seventeen and three quarters that first day in his carriage, as though the added months made her proposition completely valid, and he pleasurably recalled as well the feel and scent of her. "We missed your birthday then?" And at Chelsea's nod, he broke into a smile, all of Cassandra's impertinent discourtesy overcome by a sweet and unassuming child whom he happened to be married to, who hadn't even demanded a present for her eighteenth birthday. "When was it?" he asked as if they were alone in the room.

"Three days ago." She adored him when he smiled at her with

that flaring sensuality in his eyes. For the briefest moment, she forgot Cassandra and Sinjin's vapid sister-in-law and all the tumult of their untidy relationship, and her heart swelled with love.

"We'll have a birthday ball," Sinjin asserted, his mind already sorting through appropriate gifts for an eighteen-year-old. "And you must wear white, of course, for your eighteenth birthday. Mama, where are those pearls that all the Seth duchesses wear? Unless you want diamonds," he quickly added, his gaze swinging back to Chelsea. And whether it was the warm glow of two brandies or the engaging delight in his child-bride's face, he felt a sudden cheerful animation.

"I'm sure Chelsea is more interested in dancing than having babies," Vivian interposed, determined to disrupt the irritating intimacy between Sinjin and his wife *and* any talk of the Seth jewels, which she'd considered hers now for several years. She would also be pleased if Sinjin never had a ducal heir, for then her husband or sons would inherit the title.

At the moment, Sinjin was selfishly considering an activity directly related to the subject of babies that he'd enjoy sharing with his wife. Even in the pretentious magnificence of this room, taken wholesale from some Roman temple, she was irresistible, he decided, looking like a wholesome country milkmaid in her ivory linen dress sprigged with hand-painted flowers, her unruly hair and worn half boots, her skin rosy fresh, the pale silk of her hair an invitation to touch, the rise and fall of her full breasts a nuance of motion beneath the light summer fabric of her gown. But just as his libido was about to overcome the prudent reason he'd systematically constructed during Chelsea's absence, the drawing room door burst open and three young boys barreled into the room.

"Papa! You must come and see this *perfect* horse just arrived in our stables," Beau cried, racing across the Aubusson carpet at full speed. "It's red like our Irish cousins' hair and way over sixteen hands—"

"And stamping and snorting and not letting anyone near him," his cousin Ben blurted out.

"Except he'll let Jed feed him apples," the smallest boy breathlessly added, having caught up to the two larger boys, so they all stood before Sinjin, panting and wide-eyed.

"That's Thune, I'm afraid," Chelsea said. "I thought he might be lulled into a more placid mood if Jed fed him apples. He doesn't like the city."

"Is he *your* horse, Mademoiselle?" Beau's voice indicated his disbelief. No lady he'd ever seen could handle a brute like that.

"Madame la Duchesse, Beau," Sinjin corrected. "This is Chelsea," he declared to the group of boys, her anticipated arrival having been previously discussed. "And she rides Thune like a champion jockey. She even beat Mameluke and me several times."

"You did?" Beau breathed, speaking for the group, amazement clear on each young face.

Chelsea noted the omission of the word "stepmother" or "wife" in Sinjin's introduction to his son and nephews, a cautionary judgment no doubt in the event of a swift divorce. And while she didn't blame her husband for considering a dissolution of their forced marriage, she found his manner toward her, paradoxically, also warm, friendly and charming.

But understandably protective of his son's emotions.

"Thune and I took your father and Mameluke on the straightaway near the river bottom at Oakham house, where you can pick up speed if the ground's dry," Chelsea said, which raised eyebrows among the adults in the group who knew the extreme proximity of Oakham to Kingsway. And each mind simultaneously wondered exactly when the races had occurred. Sinjin was never discreet with his amours, so his unusual circumspection regarding his wife piqued their curiosity. "And Mameluke sulked for days after," Chelsea added, casting a teasing smile at Sinjin.

"That's because he *always* wins," Beau pronounced with a degree of awe.

"We'll take you riding soon," Sinjin offered, ignoring the palpable adult scrutiny directed at him after Chelsea's candid comments, "and Chelsea can show you some of her riding style. She's very good."

Clearly Sinjin was fascinated by his wife, his mother noted with satisfaction, regardless of his casual attitude toward his marriage, *and* clearly he wasn't going to satisfy the inquisitive interest concerning his stay at Oakham. Upon his return from Hatton, he'd only described his abduction and marriage in the most general narrative, mentioning in conclusion that he'd promised his young wife an introduction to the Ton. He'd made no mention of divorce or annulment, but in his reserve she'd detected a detachment that might foresee such an eventuality.

He'd said even less to Damien. Although he and his brother enjoyed a cordial friendship, they'd chosen years ago to avoid discussing women. Sinjin had always entertained himself with a wide variety of females, while Damien, more virtuous, had disapproved of the casual concept of women as amusement. A gentleman scholar by inclination, Damien preferred his studies of ancient architecture; much of his passion for antiquity was evident in Seth House and in his Palladian residence at Chelton.

"How charming to have a jockey in the family," Cassandra said, her voice treacle sweet and cloying. "Have you made much money in your *profession?*" She enunciated the word in such a way as to suggest that another more common calling may have occupied Chelsea's time as well.

"Quite a lot actually," Chelsea said with a grin, the look passing between Sinjin and herself so intimate that even Beau noticed.

"What does that mean, Papa?" he bluntly inquired, as young children do without regard for politesse or circumstance.

"I won a bet," his father cryptically replied, "and when you're older, I'll explain the finer points of betting to you. Why don't you give Grandmama a kiss now and we'll go out to see Thune."

As the boys rushed to their grandmother to comply with Sinjin's suggestion, Vivian's lips pursed in distaste. "Do they actually allow women jockeys in the races?" she queried. "How very . . . masculine."

"The smaller county races allow female jockeys," Chelsea replied, undeterred by her sister-in-law's discourtesy, her feminine self-esteem undiluted by her riding skills. "And actually I find it satisfying to win against men."

For the first time Cassandra considered Sinjin's young wife with more than a casual regard for her youthful beauty. The Fergusson woman offered Sinjin challenge, and knowing his instinct for sport, Cassandra viewed her rival with a new degree of respect. "Do you win often—against men?" she softly inquired.

"Quite often," Chelsea placidly replied, "and I'm always learning . . ."

It was a small, perhaps unconscious warning, the benign phrase hanging in the air for a moment like one of the new faddish hot air balloons, before Sinjin stepped in to say, "I think the boys will burst with excitement if we don't show them Thune. Excuse us." He preferred not to tempt fate and Cassandra's legendary temper, and Thune gave them a perfect reason to leave. Putting his hand out to Chelsea, he helped her rise.

The boys tumbled around them like puppies, tugging at Sinjin's and Chelsea's hands, all speaking at once, asking a rush of questions impossible to answer in the steady clamor of appeal.

"Do you need riding clothes?" Sinjin asked Chelsea as they stood in the center of the hubbub.

"They can just get used to Thune today and he to them. I'll take them riding in the morning when the city's quiet."

How nice it was, Sinjin thought, to have Chelsea so harmoniously accepted by his son, so enthusiastically received.

How nice it was, Chelsea reflected, to be part of Sinjin's small family and have him smiling down at her with his familiar captivating charm.

"After all this stirring interest," Damien said, setting down his brandy glass and rising, "I'm going to have to go along and see this remarkable horse."

"He's the biggest horse you ever did see, Papa," his youngest boy, Harry, exclaimed, running over to take his father's hand. "Do you think Auntie Chel will let me sit on him?"

"Auntie Chel" had a warm welcoming sound, Chelsea cheerfully decided, thinking perhaps that some of her wistful dreams might come true here in London.

Auntie Chel, Sinjin mused. How different that sounded from his own tempting vision of his wife . . . but charming. And smiling at Chelsea, he said, "It appears you've brought considerable excitement to the St. John family." His eyes held hers for a lingering moment. "Welcome to London."

Thune was brought out into the stable yard so the boys could take turns sitting on him, but he was restless, the sounds of the city disturbing to him, no matter that they were filtered by the high wall separating Seth House from the streets. But when Chelsea said, "Thune, this is Sinjin's boy and you must behave" as Beau was lifted onto his back, the big roan thoroughbred quieted immediately.

Beau's eyes opened wide in awe-struck wonder. "He understands, Papa! Look, look! He doesn't mind me riding him!"

"He likes you, I can tell," Sinjin agreed and, turning to Chelsea, added with a smile, "As you can see, Beau's horse-mad."

Like his father, Chelsea reflected.

Like his step-mama, Sinjin noted, an unconscious designation he failed to acknowledge, for he'd never considered that relationship before.

"Would you like to ride him around the stable yard?" Chelsea asked, the sight of Sinjin's son affecting her oddly. He was a small replica of his father, and she imagined Sinjin as a child with the same enthusiasm and openness.

"Yes, yes—yes! I can hold the reins myself! He likes me!" Leaning toward his father, he whispered—as children do, in a sibilant resonance resembling normal speech—"Papa, if all women are so clever and nice as Chelsea, I can see why you spend so much time with them." Straightening back in the saddle, his expression beaming like a small sun, he nudged Thune with his heels and set the racer off around the yard.

"That was a compliment, although he lacks a certain tact at age nine," Sinjin said, grinning. "You've charmed him thoroughly, for not too long ago he told me he would *never* have any interest in women."

"Give me a horse anytime over flirtatious banter," Chelsea replied, her own smile benevolent. She had no choice in any event; horses were all she knew.

What his son couldn't know, Sinjin reflected, was that all women weren't like Chelsea. In fact, she was very different from most women: refreshingly frank; indifferent to vanity; unconcerned with her wardrobe—he still liked her best in riding breeches; as open with her feelings as she was with her smiles; endowed with a fresh natural beauty without the need of artifice.

And his son liked her. An absorbing thought . . .

Abruptly curtailed by Beau's exulted cry. "Ooowee! Look at him prance."

"Thune's showing off," Chelsea murmured. "I taught him a little dressage for discipline and he adored it. Lift the reins like this," Chelsea called to Beau, indicating the position with her hands, "and he'll back up for you with mincing steps like the minuet."

"How unusual for a racer. Does he do other tricks?" Sinjin asked, impressed at the sight of the huge roan placing his feet with such lightness.

"He can count. Only to twenty," she added at Sinjin's astonished stare.

"When did you find the time to train him so well? It must have taken an enormous effort."

"What else is there to do in Ayrshire, pray tell?" Her smile was teasing.

Instantly he was reminded of their disparate lives—and of her innocence. "What do you think, Damien? I've not only found a wife but a new trainer for my stud."

"I'd say you've a bargain," his brother cheerfully replied. "And someone Beau likes," he added with a significant underlying gravity.

"Amen to that," Sinjin said, considering the character of the previous women in his past, all beautiful and entertaining but predominantly interested in the state of their wardrobes and jewelry boxes.

"He's a wonderful boy," Chelsea murmured, watching Beau. "So full of joy . . . you're very lucky."

Although Sinjin's attention was focused on Beau's attempt to back Thune, he heard the small stricken break in her voice, and turning to her, he wrapped his arm around her and pulled her close. "He likes you. I'm glad about that." He couldn't say more; he couldn't say, "We'll have another child." He wished he could. "And I'm pleased you came down to London," he softly said, sincere at least in that declaration. He found he liked having her in his home.

"I intend to torment you with my company," Chelsea said, "since you were unwise enough to invite me." Her teasing was easier for him to accept than profound emotion, and she'd cried enough at Hatton to last her a decade. "Just fair warning . . ."

"Warned and waiting," he replied, grinning, and winked at her with a roguish gallantry she found endearing.

While Thune was the center of attention in the stable yard, Vivian and Cassandra were left in the drawing room debating the longevity of Sinjin's marriage. The Dowager Duchess had excused herself soon after the exodus to the stables, and the two women had decided to replace their tea with sherry.

Dressed very much alike in the height of fashion, Marie Antoinette's faux shepherdess silk muslin the *dernier cri* of female apparel, both women wore white: beribboned, ruffled and lace-trimmed. What Vivian lacked in dramatic beauty like Cassandra's she made up for in delicate femininity. Very petite with milk white skin and dainty features, she emphasized her diminutive stature by wearing low slippers and a simple hairstyle. No towering headdress for her, although the new romantic ideals invading culture had seriously reduced the number of powdered, four-foot coiffures seen in society.

"I give it six months," Vivian said, her finger tracing the base of her small stemmed glass.

"She might be pregnant—in which case . . . he won't be free in any six months." Cassandra had considerable time in Sinjin's absence to contemplate the ramifications of his marriage.

"Or she might *become* pregnant. I forgot."

"How could you overlook that rather pertinent factor with your husband so close to the title?"

"Sinjin's been opposed to marriage for so long . . . *and* so devoted to Beau, I suppose the thought of an heir has been dismissed from my mind. Beau *is* set to inherit a great deal of his fortune already in any event . . ." She shrugged one small shoulder. "How much inclination does he have for an heir to his title? You know how he deprecates all the pomp of his dukedom."

"Don't you think his young wife might have her own ideas on providing an heir, regardless of Sinjin's? A ducal title for one's child holds a certain cachet, you must admit."

"A circumstance too late for you, with Buchan's first family in such good health," Vivian unkindly murmured.

"Or for you, dear, now that Sinjin has brought home an eighteen-year-old. Think how many years she can bear him children," Cassandra silkily replied. "I expect Ben and Harry will be well down the line of inheritance within a few years, Sinjin's libido being what it is."

"Of which you well know."

"Yes," Cassandra said with purring memory, "pleasantly well. A shame for you he has scruples about his brother."

"Are you suggesting—"

"Come, Vivian, you fairly pant when he's anywhere near you, and the only one not aware is Damien."

Vivian viewed the world with a skewed vision conveniently focused on her own interpretation of reality. "I resent your allusion, Cassandra."

"Darling," Cassandra went on unperturbed, "what you really resent is the fact that you can't lure Sinjin into your bed. And my sympathy goes out to you; he's a not-to-be-missed experience."

"How vulgar you are, Cassandra." Vivian was sitting up very straight on the red brocade settee, as if primly defensive against Cassandra's contentions, but the high color in her cheeks acutely revealed her feelings.

"Honest, I think, Vivian darling, but enough said on a moot subject. Now—we're agreed on the fact that Sinjin's young bride may have children," Cassandra declared.

"But will he stay married?" Vivian retorted, her voice still touched with a small peevish constraint. "He's utterly faithless."

"Aren't all husbands?" Not so much cynicism as reality motivated Cassandra's reply; on intimate terms with a great number of noble husbands, she viewed with just suspicion the romantic myths of eternal love and fidelity.

A transient smugness pursed Vivian's rose-bud mouth. "Damien isn't."

"How very sweet." Cassandra took a small sip of her sherry. "But then he's not interested in women, is he? . . . I meant *other* women," she added with deliberate tardiness. It was common knowledge Damien much preferred his books to his wife. Although, in the abstract way of scholars, his detachment wasn't from aversion but due instead to his absorption in his studies. His collection of vertu at Chelton outshone any collection of antiquity in England. "Sinjin, on the other hand, will find it impossible, I don't doubt, to forgo adulterous pleasures considering his devotion to amorous pursuits this decade past. So we're back to the question: will he divorce her? . . . Or more pertinently, when will he divorce her? *Or* . . . will he simply overlook the fact that he has a wife, like so many of his aristocratic brotherhood?"

"A small wager on divorce," Vivian declared. Like most of the members of the peerage, she was a devoted gambler. "Sinjin doesn't want to be married; he never considered marriage after Beau, and according to Damien he has some aversion to matrimony because of his father."

"You might lose . . ." Cassandra murmured in thoughtful reply, more familiar with Sinjin's sentiments than his sister-in-law. His mannerisms toward his wife today were singular in her experience: unusually intimate and tolerant, benevolent too at times, like an amused guardian. And his eyes followed his wife when she moved and talked. "Although," Cassandra went on, her thoughts manifest in speech, "we don't know how long his young bride can sustain his interest."

"No woman has ever held Sinjin's undivided attention," Vivian bluntly said, her brusque comment—considering Cassandra's friendship with Sinjin—unflattering to her guest.

Immune to the small pettinesses of lesser women like Vivian, Cassandra ignored her disparagement. "I don't know . . ." she speculatively replied, her phrase drifting like a lazy curl of smoke across the sunlight that poured in through the sashed windows. "Although it's not in my best interests," she declared with a smile, "I'm going to put my money on that little Scottish girl. She's very odd, and that in itself might be enough to keep his interest. I hope I'm wrong, but wishful thinking and betting are two different matters. I say five hundred pounds you lose your bid for Sinjin's title and the Scottish brat sustains his interest in wedded bliss."

Vivian smiled knowingly, a feline smile of accomplishment. "You of all people to mistake Sinjin's lust for permanence. Five hundred it is, and another five hundred says the marriage won't last till the fall hunting; Sinjin's next sojourn at Hatton for the grouse season will be sans wife."

Cassandra hesitated. A thousand-pound bet on Sinjin's fidelity was a sizable leap of faith. But then it was Buchan's money, not hers, she decided in the next impulsive moment, and she and Sinjin had shared a great many impetuous moments over the years. Intellectual deliberation shouldn't be a consideration in betting, Sinjin always said, nor was it ever in her relationship with him, so why begin now?

"Done," she said, "and I'll collect my money in the fall."

"Are you finished with him then?" Vivian was surprised Cassandra would so generously give up her protracted liaison with Sinjin. According to gossip, they had been lovers even before her marriage to Buchan.

"I certainly hope not," Cassandra cheerfully replied, pouring herself another measure of sherry. A worldly woman, she cherished Sinjin's friendship but not in the same way his little bride did, not with such unfashionable adoration; she found she liked the excitement of variety as well as she liked Sinjin's roguish charm. "In any event," she declared, lifting her glass toward Vivian, "I win either way."

Chapter 35

Dinner was early that night and *en famille,* except for Vivian, who was resting before an evening of cards at Blake House, and the Dowager Duchess, who'd been called away earlier for a court function. Seated between Beau and Harry at a small table arranged for a view of the garden, which was lit with Chinese lanterns, Chelsea felt very much at home surrounded by men. Damien and Ben sat opposite her, while Sinjin played host at the head of the table. Conversation turned on familiar dinner-time topics as Chelsea countered a steady barrage of questions about horse training.

The food was perfection with Sinjin's two French chefs in residence, yet simple enough to appeal to children's tastes: braised ham au Bourgogne, duchess potatoes, Hampshire trout, green peas, pickles, apple dumpling, wild raspberry tart, Egyptian watermelon. Sinjin drank rather more than he ate, but Chelsea was familiar with his pattern after the time at Hatton. While he answered his share of the boys' questions, he more often deferred to Chelsea's expertise. Damien, less consumed by horse breeding and track anecdotes, nevertheless participated in a general way, offering occasional details of his and Sinjin's boyhood in the course of answering his sons' questions—precious details Chelsea stored away to examine at her leisure later.

Damien and Sinjin had both learned to ride at age two at their mother's ancestral home in Ireland, and they'd continued their training on their yearly summer excursions. She had watched while the boys laughed together over their escapades with their Bourke cousins.

"Are you bored?" Sinjin asked Chelsea over Harry's small head, his voice a low undertone in the buzz of conversation going on around them, "with all this talk of horses and small boys' interests?"

"I never knew any little girls—or big girls, for that matter," Chelsea added with a smile, "so this is all very familiar to me. And no, I'm not bored. My conversation is almost exclusively horses as well."

"We'll have to compose a suitable dialogue for you for Almacks, I think, or the patronesses will consider you unladylike." His easy smile contradicted his statement, as did his gaze, which lazily took in the particularly female portions of her anatomy.

"Will I pass?" Chelsea teasingly inquired.

"No problem here," Sinjin murmured, lifting his wine glass in salute to her beauty. "Almacks will fall at your feet."

"I may not want to go."

"Go where?" Damien interposed.

"Almacks," Sinjin answered. "Tell her she will dazzle even the oldest biddies."

"You will, my dear," Damien gallantly said, "bring every man to his knees."

"In that case, she may stay home," Sinjin said, his smile indication of his jest, but his gaze suddenly speculative.

"Will they bring me posies and presents?" Chelsea cheerfully asked, "and may I hold court in my boudoir like fashionable ladies?"

"Hell no!" Even Sinjin was surprised at the vehemence of his reply.

Chelsea affected a disconsolate moue. "I'll be considered *très* gauche if I don't; all the business of the day transpires in a lady's boudoir."

Sinjin's dark brows came together in a definite scowl, his own experience in ladies' boudoirs in the morning too fresh in his mind. "How the hell do you know that?"

"Duncan," she sweetly said. "I think you know many of the same ladies."

Sliding down in his chair, Sinjin glowered. "How did we get on this damnable subject anyway?"

"You were telling me I'd shouldn't be daunted by Almacks . . ."

Her smile was delectable, Sinjin thought, her skin touched with gold from the candlelight, and even in that rustic country gown, she'd outshine the most fashionable belles at Almacks. He foresaw a more demanding role as chaperon than he'd anticipated.

"We'll talk about this tomorrow," he gruffly said.

"Yes, Your Grace," Chelsea replied with a theatrical docility.

"You're going to blue-devil my life, aren't you?" Sinjin sighed, finding his selfish existence in violent upheaval if he was going to have to play duenna to his wife every evening. When he'd promised her the entertainments of town, somehow he'd never quite visualized his own consuming part in the scheme.

"You needn't bother yourself about my activities. I'll muddle along famously, I'm sure."

Damien, involved in conversation with the boys again, listened with half an ear to the fascinating new Duchess of Seth discompose his normally unruffled brother. Sinjin's easy detachment had been dexterously breached by this young female jockey from Ayrshire, and the remaining weeks of the little season should prove interesting. Perhaps he might even be induced to attend an occasional soiree to watch the fireworks between his modish brother and Sinjin's country bride.

Some time later, the boys were escorted back to the nursery floor, where promises were exchanged for riding in the morning, and after goodnight kisses and raucous goodbyes, the adults departed for their apartments. Sinjin's area of Seth House, an elegant suite of rooms for sleeping and entertaining, overlooked Green Park. Chelsea's luggage had been unpacked, and while Sinjin strolled around her room, opening and shutting the armoires and bureau drawers, she took a chair near the fireplace, which was filled for summer with an arrangement of ferns and lilies, and sat down to watch him.

After perusing her limited wardrobe, he said, "My room is through there," pointing at a connecting door, her question answered before she could ask it.

"So fashionable people live this way."

"Yes," he said in answer to her implied query. "You need to be outfitted immediately," he pronounced with a sigh that didn't exclusively reflect the problem of her clothes. He was struggling with his usual reckless desire for his wife—something he'd thought thoroughly subdued until she'd walked into the Painted Room this afternoon. Dropping onto a chaise some distance away, he crossed his booted ankles, sank back against the jonquil satin pillows that made him look even more masculine, crossed his arms over his chest and said, "I'm sorry, but none of your clothes are wearable." In lieu of what he really wanted to say, his statement sounded a shade more terse than intended.

"You can tell from that brief scrutiny?" She was impressed.

"I've sent a note to Madame DuBay, telling her we'll be in tomorrow at eleven. Is that convenient?"

"And if I said no?" She was clearly teasing, but his brusqueness tempted her.

His gaze came up as if seeing her for the first time since they'd entered her bedchamber, and his eyes were dark in the candlelit room.

She smiled. "Eleven is fine, but I have very little patience with clothes. Just a warning."

"We'll have some diversions, then, to amuse you." He was in control again of his rash impulses, his voice tempered with a lazy insouciance.

All I need is *you* to amuse me, she wished to say, but more prudent in the enigmatic fashionable world, where one never said precisely what one meant, and husbands slept not with their wives but with other men's wives, and mistresses had tea with the family as cozily as though it were a visit from a bishop, she said instead, "I'm sure Madame DuBay will be vastly interesting, and I promise to behave."

"It's not a prison sentence." A half smile lingered on his lips.

She smiled back. "For me it is."

"A duty then for the house of Seth."

"Of course, Your Grace, I'm at your service."

"You're an odd child." His voice held a musing note as though he were reappraising a former notion.

"But then I'm not a child, Sinjin." She said his name softly as if to remind him.

As if he needed reminding. He immediately came to his feet. "I'm afraid I made plans for this evening before your arrival. Forgive me, but I'm at your disposal as of tomorrow morning." And he began walking out.

"Are you seeing the Duchess of Buchan tonight?" Chelsea asked, not sure she was in a position to question her husband, but impelled to know.

Halfway to the door, Sinjin turned back and stood very still for a moment before he answered.

"No," he said. "The Sublime Society meets on Tuesday nights."
He wouldn't have had to explain, and it unnerved him for a moment
that he had. "Sleep well. You must be tired after your long journey."

He was polite and engaging . . . and reserved.

And the pattern was set for their days in London.

She heard Sinjin come in the following morning, his return initi-
ating an immediate commotion of activity in the adjacent room as his
valet began issuing orders to the servants. Doors opened and closed,
racing footsteps signaled haste on some errand and the sound of
running water issued from his dressing room. Seth House, newly
built by Sinjin's father in the late sixties, had the convenience of
indoor plumbing.

Where had he been all night, she wondered, and with whom?
Although, with the season not completely over and most aristocratic
families still in town, she didn't doubt that his choices were plentiful.
How did one pretend not to notice one's husband's nocturnal ab-
sences? How did one learn to be nonchalant and indifferent to such
blatant infidelity?

But at that moment the sound of Beau's voice carried through
their connecting doors in cheerful greeting to his father at the same
time that a knock on her door signaled a maid arriving with cocoa
and cake for her breakfast. Having been up for some time, Chelsea
was already half-dressed, for the boys' promised ride had been scheduled at seven-thirty in order to avoid the crowds in the parks.

"I'll send your dresser up, my lady," the maid quickly said as she
entered the room. "You needn't do that."

"I'm almost finished," Chelsea replied, slipping her arms into the
jacket sleeves of her old brown serge habit. "But thank you."

Placing the tray on a table, briefly re-adjusting the roses in the
vase on the tray before opening an embroidered napkin, the young
maid stood at attention, holding out the napkin. "Whatever you
wish, my lady," she said, although her brow was slightly creased at
the curious behavior of the Duke's new wife. Word had it she rode
race horses and came from Scotland, which might account for her
oddity, the young maidservant thought—London servants were
aware, to a nicety, exactly how the beau monde should act. "His
Grace will be ready downstairs in twenty minutes. He sends his
greetings."

How different, Chelsea thought, taking the napkin from the
maid's outstretched hand, receiving your husband's good morning

from a maid instead of his usual waking kiss and warm hug. But she schooled her expression to one suitable for a sophisticated duchess, smiled at the young girl and said, "Thank you. Please relay my greetings to the Duke."

And sitting alone in the huge gilded room, she gazed at her beautiful breakfast tray, wondering if she would ever be comfortable playing the role of duchess in the manner required. A small sigh escaped her as she stirred the Chantilly creme into her cocoa; a country girl at heart, she already found the protocol and affectations stifling. But the bustle of the city outside the high walls surrounding Seth House intrigued her as she gazed out over the busy metropolis; Beau and Ben and Harry at least spoke without pretension, and riding Thune always gave her pleasure.

As for her husband—

Some reassessment seemed necessary in her naive expectations of London society.

Or perhaps, she thought with a small smile, some alterations might be required in her husband's plans.

She'd have to think about it.

And on that cheerful note, a woman of enterprise and presumption at heart, she dipped her cake into her chocolate and ate with relish.

The morning ride further secured her new friendship with Beau, for once they were clear of the leisure riders in the park, she took him up with her on Thune and raced Sinjin and Mameluke beyond Hyde Corner to Knightsbridge.

They won, or Sinjin let them win, she wasn't sure, but Beau enjoyed himself, teasing his father unmercifully, promising him a rematch the following day.

Sinjin looked tired beneath his good-natured smile, and she jealously wondered if some woman had kept him awake all night, at which thought her spirits underwent a dismal plunging descent— disturbing visions appearing in her mind.

"Chel, tell Papa how we won by at least three lengths. He wasn't even close!" Grinning from ear to ear, Beau twisted around to look up at her. "Tell him we're the champions!"

Returned to more pressing issues, Chelsea found it took a moment to answer in a normal tone of voice. "I hope Mameluke doesn't mind that we're champions," she said, managing to smile, although it took some effort. It wasn't fair that Sinjin could live his life as though she didn't exist, unless she was allowed the same options.

Damien and his boys rode up then, and her participation in the conversation was less necessary as the boys exchanged opinions on the merits of both racers on the ride back to Seth House. They breakfasted again—or the boys did while Sinjin and Damien drank coffee and Chelsea toyed with a dish of strawberries. Vivian never rose before noon, while Maria breakfasted in her room and generally spent the morning with her secretary answering correspondence.

"You might wish to change before Madame DuBay's," Sinjin mentioned when the boys had demolished heaping plates of sausages, ham, eggs and kippers. He looked himself the perfect negligent degree of fashionable in buckskins, primrose Loretto waistcoat and a bottle green jacket exquisitely tailored to fit his wide shoulders.

Chelsea almost said no, because during the interval of breakfast, she'd had additional time to dwell on the unprincipled mores that allowed men such open freedoms, and her temper was up. Instead, she said, "This should serve as well as any other gown."

Sinjin debated responding but thought better of it. The firm set of Chelsea's mouth persuaded him not to initiate a disagreement. He shrugged and smiled.

"Or will your consequence be harmed by my costume?"

He recognized temper in a woman's voice, as did Damien, who glanced swiftly at Chelsea and then his brother before diplomatically saying, "Come, boys, Dr. Beckett requires that you do your Latin in the forenoon, and he's probably impatiently waiting your arrival."

A chorus of groans greeted his statement, but the young boys reluctantly rose, and after agreeing on a time for the next morning's ride, the troop followed Damien from the breakfast room.

"He's very diplomatic," Chelsea said with a nod at Damien's departing figure. "And he stays home at night."

"Is that what's causing this petulance?"

"I don't believe in the double-standard." And if she didn't care about him so much, she wouldn't even be angry. Which made her doubly resentful.

Chelsea's statement contradicted the entire aristocratic culture, or at least its obvious veneer. Women generally weren't allowed unreserved independence, and a variety of answers raced through Sinjin's mind, none appropriate to his wife's current querulous mood. And perhaps more to the point, *he* wouldn't allow his wife to be out all night, regardless that *some* peeresses lived intemperate lives.

"I was at Brookes most of the night," he said in partial atonement.

"Until six-thirty?"

"Are you keeping track?"

"Yes."

He didn't know what to say, short of something discourteous; he'd lived too many years without controls. "I wasn't with a woman. Is that enough?" It was an enormous concession on his part, and so distinct from his normal habits that the declaration would have staggered any of his friends.

"I don't know."

"And I don't know why I have to explain my life to you."

Both were moody and restive under the pressure of emotions not easily controlled, having been thrust into a strange relationship very different from anything in their past.

"Should I leave? Why don't I? I'll see London some other time." She didn't like the Vivians and Cassandras of the world; the social whirl held little allure, and if Sinjin intended divorcing her or annulling the marriage, there was no point in becoming close to any of his family. And even less point in pining over her love of him.

He didn't answer for so long that she'd begun to rise from her chair when he softly said, "No."

And she found herself terrified at the relief she felt.

"The carriage is waiting, Your Grace," an august butler said at that moment, interrupting their conversation, his posture so punctiliously straight his voice traveled over their heads. Sinjin gazed for a brief moment at the imposing figure framed in the doorway, as though bringing his thoughts back from a great distance. "Thank you, Edmund," he abstractly said. "The Duchess will need her hat."

And Sinjin smiled at Chelsea suddenly, as though none of the words between them had been spoken, as though they'd been calmly waiting to be called to the carriage for their appointment at the dressmaker's. "Madame DuBay is a petty tyrant," he noted, "but you only need say no to her very firmly and she recalls you're a client."

"You would know, of course." She was still annoyed at his sudden dismissal of their conversation, at his obvious knowledge of Madame DuBay, but most at the joy she felt in knowing he didn't wish her to leave.

"You don't own my life previous to our meeting, darling," he casually replied, sliding his chair back. "Although," he went on, his voice exceedingly soft as he stood, "women always want exclusivity to your soul."

"And men are benign in their possession?" Her sarcasm was pointed.

"A dual problem then," Sinjin said, coming around to help her from her chair. "Can we call a truce? I dislike public contretemps."

"Or any contretemps," Chelsea retorted, standing and turning to face him in a flurry impelled by resentment.

"Yes."

Well, that was plain, she thought—slightly autocratic, but plain . . . "What would you say if I told you I intend to spend your money wildly?" There was a wildness too in her voice, as though the tumult of her feelings had broken free and a form of vengeance had been chosen.

At last, a familiar response from his unique and complicated wife. He understood avariciousness in women. "Madame DuBay will find you charming."

She found his grin a shade too smug. "I intend to have her find me *irresistible.*"

"In that case, I shall warn my steward to brace himself." His smile lingered; he much preferred banter, however sardonic, to serious, revealing speech. "And the Ton will be dazzled by my Scottish lass."

"I'm not your *anything.*" In her current mood, she wasn't beyond childish remarks. Maybe she cared too much to be serious; maybe only avoiding her feelings would let her function in a relationship with Sinjin.

Her retort, however childlike, touched an intrinsic male nerve in Sinjin, a throwback to cave-man days. "We'll see about that," he said, without even thinking.

Chapter 36

"Your Grace," Madame DuBay said in warm greeting as Sinjin and Chelsea walked through the unpretentious entrance of her shop, which was tucked away on a quiet street in St. James. "How *nice* to see you . . ." The "again" was implied in her warm greeting; he was obviously no stranger to her establishment.

Her cool grey eyes quickly swept Chelsea, a swift assessing glance, and Chelsea felt as though she were being placed in some specific ranking on Madame DuBay's list of customers. Elegantly dressed in charcoal silk lavishly ornamented with lace, London's most fashionable dressmaker was younger than Chelsea had expected. Small, trim, with light brown hair, a composed expression and dark gypsy eyes, she couldn't be over thirty-five.

"I'd like you to meet the Duchess," Sinjin said, drawing Chelsea forward and making the introductions. "And we need a gown first for her birthday ball. White, I think."

"Actually I'd prefer green, emerald, I think," Chelsea said, parroting her husband's phrasing, her smile bright even as she wondered how friendly the relationship was between Madame DuBay and her husband. They obviously were well acquainted. "Would you show me some of your fabrics?"

Not unaware of who was paying for the gowns, Madame DuBay lifted her glance to Sinjin's greater height for approval.

"You needn't check with the Duke, for he won't be wearing the gown," Chelsea quietly said, her smile still in place although slightly forced, "and green is my favorite color."

An infinitesimal nod from Sinjin solved Madame DuBay's dilemma. "Of course, Madame la Duchesse, whatever you say." Her dark lashes lowered deferentially, and she immediately re-adjusted Chelsea's rank in her internal scheme of things. Spectacular blond beauty did not alone ensure the Duke's interest, she decided; he was up against a very bold spirit this time, no matter her youth. "Please follow me," the dressmaker said with an undertone of the Fens in her speech, for all the frenchified veneer had been added over the years to the young widow from Norfolk. "And we'll show you all our noteworthy greens, Your Grace."

In short order, several male assistants began bringing in the heavy bolts of glorious fabrics: Lyon silks in a veritable forest of greens; Persian Charmeuses threaded with gold or plaided with subtle shades of lavender, peach, nectarine, violet; regal brocades from the looms of Istanbul, woven from sensuous Egyptian cotton for the heat of summer, the underlay always a rich gleaming contrast as that of flowers to foliage. Lute-strings and georgettes were brought out next, then the ubiquitous muslin in summer stripes and patterns, unendingly verdant.

"I think we've seen enough," Sinjin brusquely interjected after a lengthy period in which fabric bolts were being paraded before them. "Do you see some you like?" he asked, turning to Chelsea, who was seated beside him on an settee of dove grey satin and bleached ash.

"Did *you* like any?" she sweetly replied, aware that his attention had lapsed several dozen samples ago.

"Would you like Madame *DuBay* to select some for you?" he countered, a certain grimness infusing his tone; he was not about to contest fabrics with his wife after a sleepless night and the tedium of countless yards of green material blurring before his eyes.

Recognizing a man pressed beyond his normal limits of civility, Chelsea wisely chose to temporarily retreat, and with a polite smile for Madame DuBay, who stood quietly to one side taking in the intriguing struggle between the Duke and his young bride, Chelsea decided, "That and that, the Charmeuse with nectarine"—pointing to the fabrics—"and this one and both of those," she added, indicating some handkerchief silks overembroidered with small red berries.

"We're ready then for the fashion plates and French dolls." Familiar with the process, Sinjin expressed in his tone his preference for speedy proceedings.

Ever eager to please a valued customer who was lavish in his generosity to his lovers, Madame DuBay clapped her hands, raised her voice marginally beyond that considered completely ladylike and, calling out orders to her minions, left the room.

"I thought you said she was tyrannical," Chelsea said as the room emptied. In contrast, Madame DuBay's manner had been considerate, even cordial.

"She must like you," Sinjin blandly replied, realizing that circumstances tempered Madame DuBay's normal decisiveness. Chelsea hadn't insisted on fuchsia satin, or red silk with black lace, or pink lute-string with ostrich feathers and seed pearls. His wife was very different from the highflyers or pretentious noblewomen he usually escorted, and Madame DuBay had responded accordingly.

"Am I more likeable than the others?" Honeyed insinuation clung to Chelsea's words.

The smallest pause ensued in which Sinjin considered how best to answer such a dangerous question. Opting for evasion, which was always appropriate when dealing with female queries, he said with an innocence in his eyes that would do justice to a pious choirboy, "Apparently." He dipped his head in acknowledgment. "My compliments . . ."

"Do you know her well?" She shouldn't have asked. She intended not to; she intended to be as cool as her blasé husband, who never took any relationship too seriously. But she wanted to know more than her powers of restraint could suppress.

Would he tell her?

"Who?" he said as though they'd met on the vastness of the Sahara after ten years' absence and he recognized neither the speaker nor the question.

Not to be eluded, Chelsea replied precisely and clearly, "Madame DuBay."

"Madame DuBay?" Sinjin gently repeated, a whisper of an echo.

"Are you evading the question?"

He grinned. "I think so."

"Tell me."

"Must I?"

"Yes."

His grin touched his eyes with laughter. "No, then, if you must know. Madame DuBay never mixes business with pleasure."

"You asked her."

"I didn't say that."

At which point Madame DuBay returned, interrupting the interrogation, leaving the rest of Sinjin's answer a mystery. She drifted into the room on a cloud of perfume, followed by several young modistes carrying pattern books, all of whom cast admiring glances or smiled or giggled at Sinjin as they placed their books on the table in front of the settee.

Madame DuBay might not fraternize with her customers, but apparently the restriction didn't pertain to her employees, for the young women spoke to Sinjin with an easy informality. Casually accepting the female adulation, comfortable, relaxed, familiar with flirtatious ladies, he exchanged brief comments with several of them.

How democratic of him, Chelsea resentfully considered, observing the smiling repartee. But then she supposed his interest in women of all classes was well documented. And these pretty apprentices preening for his favor probably knew him better than she.

Unaware of Chelsea's rising temper, for he conversed in the most general way with the modistes, Sinjin picked up one of the bound portfolios and handed it to Chelsea. "Select any of the gowns you wish"—he grinned—"in as wild a manner as you please."

"I intend to," Chelsea acerbically replied, annoyed that he could smile with his usual teasing insouciance as though a throng of admirers weren't gazing at him, doubly annoyed that a probable host of past and future paramours were witness to her discomfort. "Do you mind?" Chelsea said in the only consciously imperious utterance of her life, indicating the young modistes with a wave of her hand.

"Thank you all for your help," Sinjin immediately said in the direction of the attentive women, his voice perfectly balanced between dismissal and appreciation, the small bow of his head courtly toward women who were rarely treated as social equals. And as Madame DuBay immediately began shepherding her charges out of the room, he turned back to Chelsea and said very low, "Is that better?"

"No . . . yes . . . I don't know . . . oh hell, give me a damn pattern book and I'll see that those pretty young things are kept busy for a month so they won't have time to flirt with you." Ordinarily she would have been less blunt, but she'd never seen a score of avidly enthusiastic women eager to please her husband, and her resentment gave vent to incautious declaration.

"Are you jealous?"

His query, touched with amusement, further rankled her. "I hardly think that a useful sentiment with you. Would it matter if I were?"

Normally wary of the concept after years of side-stepping serious relationships, Sinjin found himself curiously pleased that his fractious, independent wife might be so inclined. There was no explanation for the feeling, only an oddly elusive elation invading his consciousness. "Everything about you matters," he gallantly replied, taking refuge in a pleasant comment rather than plumb the true depths of his feelings. Too many years of sportive distraction were a convenient barrier to introspection.

In her current state of high dudgeon, Chelsea considered kicking him for his masterful evasion, but since Madame DuBay was about to turn back from shutting the door, she contented herself with quickly sticking out her tongue at him. The childish gesture served as a small measure of retaliation until Sinjin grinned.

Further annoyed by his reaction, she decided he was in need of a much overdue set-down; he'd been too long the unopposed darling of all the London ladies. Would it be possible to discover a means of eliciting a corresponding jealousy in him? Certainly the opportunity existed, with so many noble families still in town. Or would he casually accept her flirtations? Would he consider such behavior the norm in his fashionable world? Would he even notice?

In order to detect *if* he were vulnerable, she would need a radiant wardrobe. And from that moment Chelsea took new interest in the fashion plates, selecting those most likely to garner male interest. She'd always previously considered clothes simply as serviceable, like her brown serge habit, functional rather than beautiful. She intended now to become a bird of paradise, and to that end, everything in the portfolios with diamonté, feathers or sparkle caught her eye.

At the same time that Chelsea was selecting a wardrobe of splendor and magnificence, Sinjin too was sifting through a stack of fashion plates, setting many aside for purchase.

"For you?" Chelsea dryly inquired, wondering instead if some paramour of his was about to increase her wardrobe.

"Humor me," he said, ignoring her irony. "Some of these would do you justice," he added, flipping through the watercolor depictions of fashionable ensembles, "and if you ever choose to please me," he added with a sardonic tilt of one dark brow, "you can wear one."

"Now why would I want to do that?" For a man who spends more time away from home than a sailor, she almost added, wondering how often he casually riffled through these pattern cards and purchased gowns with such largesse?

Because I own you, he wished to say in masculine rebuke that didn't take into consideration the subtle progress of male-female relationships since medieval times. "As a diversion from your unreserved emancipation?" he murmured instead, the nonchalance in his tone mocking her fundamental lack of freedom.

"Forgive my bluntness," she murmured, "but I think the phrase 'when hell freezes over' seems appropriate here."

He laughed, amused and charmed by his wife's sense of self, his own autonomy immune to feminine threats. Turning to Madame DuBay, he handed her a pattern card and said, "White for this one. And we need a minimum of gowns, the birthday dress included, this week."

Familiar with Sinjin's impatience and his stewards' promptness in paying, Madame DuBay replied without demur, "As you wish, of course, Your Grace."

"We also need a new riding habit for summer, immediately. Have you decided on which green fabrics you want?" he asked of Chelsea, leaning back comfortably on Madame DuBay's elegant settee, his selections concluded.

She had no idea, Chelsea realized; dressmaking was so removed from horse training that she might as well close her eyes and point.

At Chelsea's hesitation, Madame DuBay kindly came to her rescue, understanding how someone as young as the Duke's wife might not yet have the necessary skills. With a polished tact, she made suggestions from fabrics to hats to shoes until every bolt selected had been suitably utilized. "Might I suggest, Madame la Duchesse," she said at the last, "your very unusual eyes would be splendidly complemented with a gown in a deep lilac."

At Sinjin's instant frown, she hastened to add, "Not precisely a pastel hue, Your Grace, but one shading delicately into violet."

"Show us the color first. Pastels gag me, as do matronly purples."

At least they agreed on something, Chelsea facetiously thought, but was it enough on which to build a marriage? Her smile at the few elements of concord in their otherwise fractious union brought a searching expression to Sinjin's face.

"Do you agree or disagree?" he mildly said.

"What do you want me to say?" Chelsea murmured, suddenly amused rather than annoyed. How ridiculous to battle over gowns when she was being lavishly supplied with a wardrobe beyond even her most indulgent dreams, when she knew nothing and cared less about what she wore. Surely, if she intended to stand firm on some issue, it could be more relevant than the shade of purple.

"I want you to say whatever you want to say," he quietly replied.

"Well then," she said very softly, "I'd like to say I enjoyed your company at Oakham immensely."

He went so still for a moment that Madame DuBay wondered what his wife had said to him, but then he took a small breath and smiled.

"It's one of my more pleasant memories as well." He spoke very low.

"One of them?" Chelsea softly pursued, her voice half-sardonic, half-teasing.

"*The* most pleasant, if you must know," he said with charming gallantry and a searing honesty.

"In that case, you may select the shade of purple you like best," she facetiously replied, knowing how he hated solemn disclosure.

He laughed out loud, and when his laughter faded, he said with a *small* degree of solemnity, "What am I to do with you?"

She couldn't tell him the truth, of course, for he obviously didn't want to hear it, but she could at least express a partial truth. "Take me riding each day so I don't lose my memories of the country." And those remembrances of their good times together, she wished to add.

"Done," he instantly agreed, her request something he could grant without making any difficult decisions.

But a short time later, when Madame DuBay had Chelsea disrobe to her chemise in order to take the necessary measurements for her new gowns, Sinjin found all the vexing issues flooding back with a vengeance. Tense and restless as Madame DuBay moved the measuring tape from Chelsea's hips to her narrow waist, he stood anticipating the next move. Chelsea's full breasts thrust against the sheer voile of her chemise, and in only seconds Madame DuBay would lift the tape and encircle the soft swelling roundness he'd caressed, held in his hands, felt pressed against him . . .

Standing utterly still, he unconsciously flexed his fingers, as if his urge to touch her manifested itself physically, and he wondered for a transient moment how Madame DuBay would respond to being ordered out of the room. He knew he couldn't continue looking with any equanimity at his wife in a sheer chemise. Either he'd have to leave or she would, and he seriously debated sending her home to Ayrshire. Some excuse could be concocted to allay the gossip, to protect her name from the rumor mongers. As for himself—he'd lived too long in the full glare of notoriety to be overly concerned for his reputation. Plagued by an almost overwhelming desire, he fought for control over his libido. With a single step she'd be close enough to touch; he could smell her perfume, sense the heat of her body, almost feel the remembered silk of her skin beneath his fingers. Could he actually bring himself to send her away? Could he *not* and maintain his distance? Could he continue resisting his carnal urges another second with his wife in luscious undress before his eyes?

"Darling, what do you think of plumes in my hair with the birthday gown?" Chelsea said, lifting her arms above her head in a leisurely, seductive gesture that forced the swell of her breasts above the lace-trimmed neckline of her chemise. Aware of her husband's restless unease, his impatience visible in his posture, his suppressed desire almost palpable, she gazed at him with that elusive promise he'd seen so many times before.

"I dislike plumes," he said, his voice harsh, his brilliant blue-eyed glance drifting over his wife's body with unmistakable carnal hunger. A muscle twitched at the sharp angle of his jaw, his nostrils flaring for a moment before his gaze went suddenly blank. "No plumes," he curtly murmured. "Jed will take you home. I have an appointment at Brookes. Good day, Madame DuBay, la Duchesse . . ." And with a practiced bow he strode from the room.

He should have sent her home, he thought, forcing his way with a purposeful stride and an occasional ill-humored shouldering through the bustle of morning promenaders, shoppers and businessmen crowding the sidewalks on St. James Street. His beautiful young wife plagued him, enticed him, wreaked havoc on his contentment, disrupted the familiar pattern of his life. No one would be surprised if he sent her home, considering their unorthodox marriage; everyone expected the marriage to fail. Brookes' and Whites' betting books gave odds on the duration with cold-blooded practicality. He should send her home and regain his former life.

But he didn't.

And Madame DuBay, despite the discretion essential to her business, having seen in Sinjin's graphic lust for his wife a shocking change in his normal careless regard for women, may have let slip an indiscreet word or two regarding the new Duchess's powerful attraction.

Such combustible gossip passed like wildfire through the exclusive small circles of the Ton, and perhaps the odds began to shift that day in the betting books at the fine gentlemen's clubs in Pall Mall.

Their rides each morning became for Chelsea the glory of her day, without friction or discord, a time of harmony and agreeable companionship, Beau and the boys always a part of the retinue.

When the gowns were delivered, Sinjin escorted her out each night, staying by her side for a minimum time before drifting off to the card rooms. Her birthday ball was the most prominent crush of the season; even the Prince of Wales stayed half the night, dancing with his host's beautiful wife. But Sinjin's entertainments continued apace, once he saw Chelsea home, in a restless perambulation from club to club. If he slept at Seth House, he could hear her breathing next door, or he imagined he could hear her breathing . . . and he wished to avoid the proximity of their adjacent bedchambers with his current reckless need. He hadn't yet decided whether he could submit to an eternity of marriage, and he was cynical or practical enough not to rely on the erratic security of Mrs. Phillips' sheepskins.[11]

As the days progressed, he found no answer. Had he been prone to introspection, that might have been answer enough. But he kept a more watchful eye on his wife at the evening soirees and balls, routs and card parties, heedful of her easy assimilation into the artificial glittering world of the Ton, taking note with a jaundiced, surly scrutiny of the swarms of men vying for her favor.

"He's in a temper," his friend Bucky Leeds said to another guest at the Duchess of Manchester's ball one night as they observed Sinjin moodily holding up a pillar on the perimeter of the dance floor, his gaze on his wife, who was dancing with a young colonel in the Life Guards.

"And damned touchy lately," the heir to the Cordel fortune said.

"He's not sleeping much."

"Which isn't so unusual." Sinjin's progress through the boudoirs of London had always kept him short on sleep.

"I detect a new taut edge to him—the consequence of being shackled, no doubt."

"But he's playing the dutiful husband."

"Or the jealous husband."

"Are you sure about that? He doesn't go home at night. He's been winning the tables at Brookes."

"Knowing Sinjin, he's not taking to marriage with any complacence."

"Knowing Sinjin, he's not taking to marriage at all. Look at his scowl."

"Gossip has it he was nearly killed by the Fergussons."

"Which *could* jeopardize the tender bloom of love."

"Sinjin doesn't know what love is."

"Hmmm," said the older of the two men. "But perhaps he's learning. I'd say he has the look of a jealous man. A rude revelation for The Saint."

"And the beautiful Duchess doesn't seem to notice."

Geoffrey Cordel's gaze narrowed as he followed Chelsea's dancing progress on the arm of the young cub colonel. "And then again," he thoughtfully said, "maybe she knows precisely. Don't you think Sinjin's drinking more than usual?"

Bucky Leeds, who had spent a great deal of time in Sinjin's company, looked momentarily nonplussed. "How the hell can you tell? He can drink anyone under the table, still drive his phaeton to Brighton in record time, take up with the Prince's dissipated crowd and keep 'em company for another day and night. Not to mention the time he emptied that punch bowl at Harriet's and still outperformed every rake there that night. You're jesting, right?"

"All I know," said the older man, having seen Sinjin participate in numerous duels in infinitely better humor than his current sullen temper, "is, I'd stay out of his way tonight if you don't want to be standing in Hyde Park tomorrow at dawn facing the business end of his Manton pistol."

The Bishop of Hatfield, not privy to that advice, strolled into the card room some time later and approached the table where Sinjin was playing.

"Is there room for another player?" he inquired, his monocle idly twirling from one limp-wristed hand.

Sinjin's gaze flashed up at the sound of Hatfield's languid voice. He stared at him for one insolent moment before his eyes flicked over to the single empty chair at the table. "If you feel lucky tonight, Rutledge," he curtly said. "The stakes are high."

"But then your luck is bound to run out sometime, St. John," the Bishop softly murmured, pulling out the chair and taking his place at the green baize table.

"It's not luck, George, in case you want to save your money. My Irish cousins taught me to play when I was four."

"Ah, the dissolute Irish connection . . . but then your mother's beauty overcame even those bloodlines."

Everyone at the table held his breath as Sinjin's glittering blue eyes—much shaded by drink—swung up from his cards. Sinjin adored his mother, everyone knew, as much as he'd abhorred his father.

"I beg your pardon?" Sinjin's voice was barely a whisper.

"I was complimenting your mother's splendid beauty." Either Hatfield was more in his cups than he looked or he was gambling with his life, for a faint impudence continued in his tone.

For the space of two heartbeats Sinjin's piercing gaze drilled into Hatfield, and then, some apparent decision reached, he smiled. "I'll relay your compliments to *Maman*. We're playing five hundred a point, no limits."

And the breath everyone at the table had been unconsciously holding was expelled.

The play went on much as it had before Hatfield's arrival, with Sinjin winning, markers piling up before him in untidy stacks.

"I'm out, dammit, or the old man will have my head in the morning." A younger son of the house of Denfield, only recently bailed out from the money-lenders by his irate papa, had lost his quarterly stipend for the next two years.

"Cash these in, cub," Sinjin said, pushing a large heap of markers toward the apple of the Duke of Paxton's eye, "but don't come back tonight. Your papa would prefer a few hours' reflection, I think, before you venture into the paths of the wicked again." Sinjin's self-deprecating grin took the onus of loss from the youngster.

"Sirrah, I couldn't," the boy just down from Cambridge protested, aware of gentlemen's rules of honor. And he stayed Sinjin's hand.

"Give me one of your grey mare's foals when it pleases you and we're even," Sinjin casually retorted, discharging the boy's debt for a much lesser exchange. "Now take the damn markers, cub, and don't come back until you can remember the last dozen hands played in a game. Then I'll take you and the Denfield money on with pleasure." Pushing the small mountain of markers closer to the boy, Sinjin looked to his friend for support. "Tell him, Bucky, how green young bucks are allowed a mistake or two. How we all bloodied ourselves at one time or another."

"It's true, Denfield, and we've all the scars to prove it. Hell, one time I bet my younger sister and lost. Thought I might as well cut my throat and be done with it, but Baron Verres from Bath relinquished his claim on her and even left me enough money to post home to Kent. My old Pa damn near horsewhipped me to death when he found out, but my sister thought it romantical. Baron Verres was quite the stud in those days. So take the markers and tell your pa you took his advice and didn't gamble this term."

"I'm done too, Sinjin, though you didn't take much of my money. I must be getting better." The Earl of Lester leaned back in his chair and stripped off the leather cuffs he wore to protect the lace at his wrists.

"For a man who's cost me a small fortune over the years, I defer to your modesty," Sinjin replied with an affable nod. "I'll see you later at Brookes." The two best players in England happened to be good friends as well.

"Your wife might prefer your company." No one but Simon would have dared such plain speaking.

"I'll ask her when I see her next," Sinjin smoothly replied. "Who's left here? Should we raise the point stakes to make it more interesting?" And if Simon Castlemane had expected some disclosure, he was disappointed.

"I'll drink then till you're ready to walk to Brookes," the Earl carelessly murmured, signaling for a footman. "Do you think old lady Manchester has a brandy worthy of my palate?"

"I've seen you drinking blue ruin in a Covent Garden stew, Simon, and your palate was noticeably accepting. Get me a bottle too."

"Are you sure?" Simon recognized the glitter in Sinjin's eyes; he'd seen it often enough before some explosion of temper.

"Are you my mother?" Sinjin's drawl held a touch of amusement as well as a hint of menace.

Simon shrugged and smiled a benevolent smile. "Would it help if I was?"

"No," Sinjin said so sharply that a sudden stillness fell over the table.

"Since it's common knowledge you're seldom home, St. John, is your wife fair game now that she's married?"

The Bishop of Hatfield's question, softly uttered, fell into the small silence with a deafening clarity.

Sinjin's hands on the cards he was shuffling instantly quieted, and he glanced over at the Bishop, his eyes cold beneath the black slash of his brows. "You know the rules as well as I do," he curtly said.

They both understood that no wife was fair game until she'd produced an heir.

"And in my case, Hatfield," Sinjin pronounced the name with a lethal softness, "the Duchess is forever 'protected' by my honor."

"She seems extremely well adjusted to the fashionable world," Hatfield said, a strange quiet in his voice. "I thought perhaps she was available for outside friendships." He wasn't quite normal, everyone understood, but until now, no one had considered him stupid. But if he continued to bait Sinjin, he must have lost his senses at last.

Sinjin slid the cards he'd been shuffling into a stack, his slender fingers neatly evening the edges before he set the cards aside. After straightening the lace on his cuffs with an unnecessary meticulousness, he leaned forward, clasped his hands together on the green baize tabletop, looked around the table at all the players as if to say, "Are you listening?" and finally, resting his eyes on Hatfield's enigmatic face, said so softly the sound didn't travel beyond the verges of the green baize, "You're welcome to try and initiate a friendship, George, although I'd recommend you put your estate in order first."

"Is that a challenge, St. John?"

"I certainly intended it to be. Did I understate my purpose?"

"You could die, and then think how your Duchess would feel, left alone."

"You have a sense of humor, George, and if I weren't so drunk, I might appreciate it."

"How arrogant, St. John; you can't always count on your luck."

"How stupid, Rutledge, to call an acquired skill arrogance. I can shoot out your eye at a hundred paces—no luck involved."

"Your wife might not pine . . . have you thought of that?"

"She won't have need to. *You* consider that."

"Perhaps God will be on my side."

"Don't count on it. Rutledge influence might acquire a bishopric for you, but not with God's blessing, I assure you."

"You're hardly one to profess a close association with God."

"I agree, so I understand the difference. Name your weapons, Rutledge, or stay away from my wife. She's not available to you or anyone but myself. That message should be plain enough even for your warped mind." No wife of his, no matter how sham their marriage, was available to anyone but himself. "Touch her, talk to her, even approach her and you die." Sinjin showed his teeth in a smile, although the brief grim upturning of his lips wouldn't be misconstrued as a benevolent expression.

The Duchess of Seth, it was crystal clear, was out of bounds—or at least beyond the reach of those men not willing to put their lives at risk on the dueling field. Every man at the table gazed intently at the two protagonists, wondering if Rutledge's irrational mind might finally bring him to ruin.

Hatfield smiled too, but his faint grin had a wild, lunatic dimension, as though it were disassociated from reason. "I'll pray over my decision," he declared, no more feeling in his voice than if he had been offered two disparate styles of headgear instead of a life-and-death decision.

"I recommend it," Sinjin said. "Now, if you'll excuse me . . ." Leaving his winnings on the table, he rose and walked away. Making his way swiftly to the ballroom, he moved across the crowded dance floor like an irresistible force, a pathway opening up before him.

Hatfield's infuriating comments culminated a fortnight of chafing restraint in which he'd watched his wife play the belle and flirt with every man in the Ton. She dazzled the eye with her golden beauty, Madame DuBay's ball gowns displaying her numerous charms to advantage. Tonight, in silver tissue decorated with silk violets and green ribbons, she fairly took one's breath away. But from now on, that beauty would be his alone, he irrationally thought, goaded by Hatfield's insinuating slurs and two rankling weeks of observation.

Chelsea's dance partner noticed him stalking toward them, and when he caught a glimpse of Sinjin's eyes, he immediately came to a stop. The musicians, anticipating a brawl at the sight of Sinjin's forceful progress through the crowd, ceased playing and moved back toward the protection of the wall should objects begin flying. Sinjin in temper defied normal measures of control.

Chelsea had only a few moments' bewilderment at the abrupt dying away of the music before Sinjin stood before her, towering above her partner with decided menace.

"I find myself suddenly weary," her husband said, although his clenched teeth did much to contradict the softness of his speech. "We're going home."

"You're making a scene." The large diamond pendants swinging from her ears caught the light as if supplementing her words with illuminating emphasis.

"Nothing like the one I anticipate if you don't immediately take my arm and leave," Sinjin snapped, subtle nuances beyond his capacity at the moment.

"Do I have a choice?"

"I don't see one." Immune to the entire ballroom stilled by his action, the hush of hundreds of held breaths palpable in the air, he impatiently waited, a half smile on his face.

Recognizing his restless stance, his hotspur expression, the glittering challenge in his smile, Chelsea understood that no purpose would be served in further argument. Turning to the young man standing at attention beside her, she said, "Thank you, Allen, for your company . . ." She'd never fully realized the galvanic power and authority Sinjin had at his command; her dance partner was clearly in fear of her husband. She smiled in apology. "Tell your sister I'll see her at Jeffrey's tomorrow."

Taking Chelsea's hand in his, the gesture tantamount to a tossed gauntlet, Sinjin softly said, "Thank you, Bosford, for entertaining my wife." But somehow in those few quiet words lay an implicit threat that, should the young man ever contemplate entertaining her again, his life would be at stake. And Sinjin's bow in response to Bosford's stammered response was rudimentary.

"I find this very childish," Chelsea whispered as they left the floor, every guest's gaze avidly attentive, the buzz of titillated comment rising behind them like the hum of summer cicadas as they passed.

"But better than having George Prine's blood on your hands," Sinjin tightly noted.

"What's going on?" An edge of fear touched her voice.

"Hatfield was wondering if you were available. I told him no, nor are you to anyone." In just such a terse forbidding voice the demands of unconditional surrender would be decreed. "He decided," Sinjin went on, his heels marking a brisk tattoo on the parquet floor as a complement to the curtness of his utterance, "not to contest the issue tonight." They'd reached the crest of the staircase, and plunging down the marble steps, he pulled her along without notice of the impediment of her full skirts.

Stumbling after him, Chelsea frantically jerked the tangle of petticoats and voluminous silk out of her way before she lost her footing entirely. Taking note of her distress as her muttered imprecation ended in a muffled squeal when she began falling, Sinjin swiveled around to catch her and swept her up into his arms without checking his swift descent.

"You're drunk!" Chelsea exclaimed, alarmed as he descended the stairs three at a time, his eyes at close range half-lidded, strangely brilliant.

"Not *too* drunk, darling," he murmured. "Not good manners."

"You're going to fall!" They were halfway down the polished marble flight of stairs; the bottom still seemed dangerously remote, and Sinjin's speed excessive.

"Don't worry." His mild voice disregarded her fear; he had accomplished much more difficult athletic feats than running down stairs while in his cups. Strong and sure-footed, he brought them down the formidable descent in short order, then set Chelsea down with a sweeping, sardonic bow, as if to say, "You see, Madame, drinking doesn't unduly affect my coordination." Then, taking her hand once more in his harsh grip, he snapped his fingers at a footman and ordered his carriage.

"My cape . . ." Chelsea protested as he began striding through the doors held open by two nervous-looking servants.

"Leave it."

They were halfway to the mews when their carriage came around the side of the stable block. Before it had completely rolled to a halt, Sinjin issued their direction to the driver, then pulled open the door, lifted her inside and jumped in. Slamming the door shut, he sank onto the seat and, after a great exhaling sigh of exasperation, said, "Damn you to hell, my sweet darling wife, you've bloody well fucked up my life."

"And I love you too," Chelsea retorted, taking exception to his hot-headed imbroglio on the dance floor, to his volatile handling of her, to his churlish words.

"Well, at least we agree on something." And even in the dim light of the carriage lamp, his teeth gleamed white in a wide smile. "I almost killed Rutledge over you. I must be losing my mind."

It was not exactly a declaration of love, rose-garlanded and ornamented with cooing doves, but his words struck her heart with enormous impact. But even to discover he cared in some small measure, she preferred no one die for the insight. "Please don't kill anybody over me," she instantly protested. "It's too archaic."

"Or lunatic. I never fight over women."

Not precisely protestations of undying love, but a start, her youthful heart fondly noted, and as a tidal wave washes away all in its path, his words transformed her resentment. Sliding into the corner, she made herself comfortable on the padded velvet seat, her speculative gaze on her impetuous husband, while small intoxicating possibilities spun through her mind at his ambiguous allusions to love.

In the glow of the carriage lamp, he looked dark as Lucifer, his handsome features starkly modeled in light and shadow, his eyes in contrast romantically dissolved in shade beneath his heavy lashes. The black brocade of his coat, richly textured like the dark silk of his hair, somehow flaunted his powerful masculinity in its showy opulence. The lace at his throat, held in place with a twinkling diamond stickpin, gleamed white in the lamplight. The wide expanse of his shoulders extended from the doorway to the midpoint of the forward paneled wall; his long legs stretched the width of the carriage, so his diamond-buckled shoes rested against the opposite door. And he idly tapped the window, as though all thoughts of challenges and duels and bloodshed were forgotten.

"Did you frighten Hatfield?" She was curious how men handled their affairs; even with three brothers, she'd never been privy to a duel, and she certainly had never before been the reason for one.

"Prine's mind's too demented—as though he were looking at you from another dimension. But I would have killed the bastard, no mistake." A low murmur, no more, gave explanation, but he spoke offhand, his gaze on the street outside.

"I don't understand how you can kill someone over a social slight."

His eyes reluctantly relinquished their focus on London's cityscape, and his gaze swung slowly back to her. "And I don't understand," he casually said, "how women can giggle over a new hairdo." Clearly he didn't take the issue of duels as seriously as she.

"Is it a game?"

He sighed, as though he wished she wouldn't continue asking him questions. "Not precisely."

"What precisely is it?"

"I've been drinking too long for precision, darling," he evasively answered. "Ask me in the morning." The issue was possession, a difficult emotion to explain with chivalric courtesy, and one he preferred not discussing at all.

"Will you be sober then?"

He smiled. "Hard to say."

He often wasn't entirely sober when he met her for their morning rides, but he was always amiable and charming.

He seemed to doze then, and whether by intent or because of inebriation, he no longer answered her questions other than with unintelligible murmurs. But he came awake when the carriage rolled to a stop at Seth House, and he escorted her to the door with obliging good manners. "Good night, darling," he said as though he were seeing her home on a normal night, "I'll see you at eight for our ride."

And without waiting for a reply, he bounded back down the steps and re-entered the carriage.

She heard him say, "Brookes." And while perhaps she should have been angry for being cavalierly hauled off the dance floor at Manchester House, she recalled instead how he'd challenged the despicable Bishop because of her . . . because of his feelings for her . . . however he wished to avoid them.

And she stood for a contemplative moment on the steps of Seth House, her silver gown shimmering in the moonlight, watching his carriage pass through the gate into the street. Her soft goodnight followed him too late on the warm summer air.

Chapter 37

"May I come in?" Sinjin's mother said a short time later, appearing at Chelsea's door soon after she'd been undressed by her maid and readied for bed. Still in her ball gown, Maria St. John apologized for the intrusion. "But I heard of Sinjin's mischief at Hetty Montclair's rout," she explained, "and I came directly home. Are you all right?"

Chelsea's eyebrows rose at the speed with which gossip traveled and at Sinjin's mother's indulgent euphemism for her son's audacious behavior. "I'm fine. Sinjin's gone off to Brookes. Please come in, but you needn't have worried. Sinjin's anger was directed at Hatfield, not me."

Dressed in a froth of dusty rose silk muslin, her hair delicately powdered and ornamented with flowers in the style of her generation, a king's ransom in pearls twined around her slender neck, Sinjin's mother was capable of putting women half her age to shame. She entered the room with a dramatic elegance, as though she were familiar with admiration and homage. Like her son, Chelsea thought; they both could silence a room with their beauty. But like her son too, Maria St. John exuded an enormous charm, and her smile now radiated warm concern. "I suspected as much, but then again," she said with a small pause and one raised brow, "Sinjin does have a bit of a rash temper—although rumor always magnifies, I've discovered . . . but still, I was worried about you."

Sinking into a tapestry chair in an ethereal mist of silk and lace, she waved a dainty hand toward Chelsea's maid. "We won't need you, Eveline, unless you'd like some lemonade or sherry?" she inquired, looking at Chelsea, who stood near her bed in one of Madame DuBay's luxurious peignoirs of white taffeta ruched and ribboned in peach satin.

"Thank you, no. I ate and drank more than I should have at Manchester House. Men are forever asking you what they can bring you, and I always feel guilty saying no."

"You're much too kind, my dear," Maria said with a smile, setting her painted fan on a small table. "Although I'm sure that's one of the reasons Sinjin finds himself enamored of you."

"Do you think so?" Chelsea moved closer, as though the Dowager Duchess of Seth's words had to be felt as well as heard, the hopefulness in her voice conspicuous.

"He may not know yet—but I'm certain."

Sitting down across from Sinjin's mother on a matching chair, Chelsea clasped her hands around her knees, crushing the crisp white taffeta. Leaning forward, she said, "For the first time tonight . . . I find it possible to . . . begin to hope. Tell me I'm not being foolish. You know him so much better than I."

"My darling boy's been fighting his feelings for a fortnight now . . . or perhaps longer, but visibly to me since you arrived. I think your ignoring him"—the Dowager Duchess smiled a small, knowing smile—"has made him consider his emotional involvement. Something awkwardly novel for him, I suspect." Contemplating her next words, Sinjin's mother aligned her delicate fan with the table edge in a brief moment of indecision before quietly continuing. "You don't know, of course, but . . . having Beau has made a tremendous difference in Sinjin's life—although he never would have qualified for sainthood either before or after that event," she added with a smile. "It *has,* however, tempered his feelings on marriage."

"While the circumstances of our marriage would have repelled even the kindliest of souls, I'm afraid. And in honesty, I wished no marriage either; until recently, we were both in accord. Until Hatton," Chelsea added in a suddenly changed voice. "I lost our child at Hatton," she said in a whisper, the words catching in her throat. "I don't know if Sinjin told you . . . but this London visit is his attempt to distract me from that unhappiness."

Maria leaned forward to gently stroke Chelsea's hand, her sympathy mirrored in her eyes. "I'm so sorry . . . I didn't know; Sinjin's rarely open about his life. How terrible for you. As if any of this"—

she gestured with a small sweeping movement of her hand—"can replace a child . . ." And that's why Sinjin wasn't sleeping in his rooms, his mother immediately understood, the natural progression of her thoughts bringing Catherine to mind. Sinjin had been forced into marriage, and now—with the reason for that marriage gone—he considered regaining his freedom. How to diplomatically explain to his new bride, who clearly loved him, the circumstances prompting his behavior?

"There's something you should know," Maria quietly declared, "to better understand Sinjin's restraint. And while he may not realize it fully yet, he does care for you. Although, considering his rather dramatic actions tonight, he may have come to that realization himself. Now, where to begin . . ."

Her small ringed hands fluttered over the sheer muslin of her skirt for a moment in transient anxiety. Only she and Sinjin and his father had known of Catherine, and Sinjin had always guarded that information. But his young wife should know if for no other reason than to ease her feelings of heartache.

"Sinjin never intended to marry after Catherine," Maria St. John bluntly stated, as if the plain words, once out, would force her to go on. "If you understand what happened to Sinjin years ago," she went on in a rush of words, "it might help explain his resistance now and a portion perhaps of his internal struggle."

"Catherine was Beau's mother?"

Maria nodded. "Sinjin was almost eighteen, Catherine a year younger, when she became pregnant. Sinjin, very much in love, wished to marry her immediately, but his father refused because Catherine Canning was only an honorable's daughter and William wanted a more suitable match for his heir. So he had Catherine sent away; her pious family, outraged with her disgrace to their name and extremely well paid for their agreement, concurred with William's wishes. Because Sinjin hadn't yet reached his majority, he was power-less against his father, and when he tried to run away to find Catherine, William had him confined at Kingsway. Shortly after that, he had Sinjin carried aboard a troop ship bound for the colonies, where he was forced into Lord Burghley's regiment. Had he left his regiment in time of war without his superior's consent, Sinjin would have been court-martialed. He had no choice; Burghley wouldn't release him because of William's instructions."

Maria looked down for a moment before speaking again, the memories painful even after all the years, and her blue eyes—so much like her son's—were shaded with sorrow when her gaze lifted. "Catherine killed herself shortly after her son was born by taking an overdose of laudanum. William sent word to Sinjin in America that the child had died as well. I feel an extreme guilt even after all these years," she said with a sigh, wringing a wisp of lace handkerchief between her fingers, "and there's no excuse save that of cowardice." Looking at Chelsea in the candlelight, she added in a soft murmur, "You may have heard of my sister and myself, the Bourke sisters from Waterford. Although our family was titled, we had little money. When Elizabeth and I were brought to London, we understood we were to marry for title and fortune. I'm not excusing myself, only explaining what was expected of me as a seventeen-year-old girl whose only asset was her beauty. I envy you your independence, your racing, your ability to meet Sinjin with a degree of equality. I never felt strong enough to challenge William's control. And he was generous in his own way with my family. I had two younger sisters and a brother in need of funds to make their way in the world, as well as my aging parents to consider, and William always saw that my family was well cared for. But he was a cold, prideful man who wanted a beautiful wife, not a companion; we lived quite separate lives. And if both my accouchements hadn't been life-threatening, he never would have allowed me to give my sons Bourke family names." She seemed to withdraw into herself for a moment, as if recalling those long-ago memories; then, refocusing on the present, she sat up a bit straighter and said with another small sigh, "Forgive me for digressing, but for you to understand Sinjin perhaps some of that matters. Now where was I?"

"Sinjin was told of Catherine's and Beau's deaths." How terrible for him to lose the young girl he loved, Chelsea thought, her heart going out to the young boy, trapped halfway across the world when he heard of his loved ones' deaths. But she felt a hideous guilt too for wanting him for herself, for being able to listen to an infinitely poignant story and feel an awful relief that Sinjin was hers . . . or marginally hers.

"Let me see . . ." Maria said, searching her memory for the correct sequence of events. "William died that winter of a sudden apoplexy, and Sinjin was able to return home. But before formally accepting any of his titles or even talking to the barristers, he went to search out Catherine's grave. A week later, after threatening Catherine's father in order to gain information about her death, he discovered his son hadn't died.

"Seneca had come back to England with Sinjin, and they rode without stopping in the dead of winter north to Manchester, to the doctor's house where Beau had been sent. The doctor, previously warned against Sinjin by Catherine's father, held him at bay with a musket. Blaming Sinjin for Catherine's disgrace, Mr. Canning refused Sinjin rights to his child, although in his piety he wouldn't accept Catherine's illegitimate child into his home either.

"Sinjin finally broke down the doctor's front door, brushed the armed man aside, Seneca said, as though he didn't exist and, after ransacking the house, smashed through another door upstairs where Beau had been locked away. Beau was eight months old and dreadfully ill when Sinjin found him. Sinjin beat the doctor mercilessly when he found his son so cruelly treated, and I'm afraid he later attacked Mr. Canning also, although," she quietly said, "I don't blame him. His poor little son was nearly dead when I first saw him, and so shockingly thin. Beau wouldn't have survived many more days if Sinjin hadn't arrived." Her eyes welled with tears at the remembrance of the emaciated baby Sinjin had carried in to her, tears streaming down his cheeks.

"It was a nightmare he'll never forget," Sinjin's mother whispered, "so you see how important Beau is to him and how strongly he might feel about other children. And despite his reputation for dalliance, he's careful to limit his liaisons to sophisticated women uninterested in having children. You must have quite turned his head, my dear." Maria's smile reminded Chelsea of Sinjin's sweetest young-boy smiles. "He's never allowed himself to disregard his principles before."

"He tried to use . . . well . . . some precautions," Chelsea stammered in embarrassment, "although—"

"Not apparently with any consistency," his mother lightly noted. "And for that he's now faced with a dilemma he'd never anticipated. Beau's been the obsessive love of his life for almost ten years, and forgive me the discourtesy, but Catherine's memory has faded very little, I'm afraid. In a way, she's the embodiment of his idealistic youth, enshrined in death—perfect and inviolable, their love preserved in crystalline purity."

Chelsea would have preferred not hearing those words. She would have preferred a less daunting rival. How did one compete with perfect memory—with the halcyon beauty of youthful love?

"Sinjin fled England," Maria went on, continuing her narrative, drawing Chelsea's thoughts away from a faceless young girl whom

Sinjin perhaps still adored, "once Beau's health permitted, in an effort to escape his memories; he took Beau to Florence for a year, but Catherine's loss followed him. Beau became his life and salvation. Sinjin was twenty-one when he decided to come home." Maria's voice held evidence of the sadness her son had suffered. "He returned a very different man from the young boy who'd fallen in love —more cynical, of course, inestimably practical in his relationships, always maintaining a certain reserve in his amours, as if the game were played within circumscribed boundaries of emotion.

"After Catherine he had no intention of marrying—not for a long time, at least, if ever. Occasionally he'd consider the necessity of an heir to the dukedom, but he also felt comfortable letting the title pass to Damien's sons. So you see," she finished, the sheer lace of the handkerchief in her hands shredded, "he's been shadowed by Catherine's memory all these years."

Chelsea felt distraught at the unutterable pain Sinjin, Catherine and their child had suffered, and yet suddenly, she was curiously elated when she recalled Sinjin's words tonight. Even while she felt a profound pity for Sinjin's unhappy past, an unalloyed joy at her discovery gave her hope. At least she understood now the tempestuous emotions influencing Sinjin's conduct.

"Beau likes me," Chelsea quietly said in a revelation of singular importance.

"He adores you—a fact Sinjin recognizes with what I suspect might occasionally be alarm. He's extremely attached to his son, and now he must consider the possibility of sharing him." She smiled. "You've entered his life with a dynamic force he's not quite sure how to contain."

"Nor am I completely capable of securing his volatile spirit, I suspect," Chelsea replied with a faint grin, "but thank you," she said, heartfelt in her gratitude, "for telling me of Beau's mother. Does Sinjin talk of her to the boy?"

"No, only that she died soon after he was born. At Beau's age, he's not inquisitive yet. Our household is relatively busy, so he doesn't have many lonely moments. Sinjin too, despite his bachelor ways, is with his son a great deal of the time."

"Do you think Sinjin would prefer not having an heir displace Beau?"

"I don't know. I don't think he knows. And avoidance to this point has solved the problem nicely."

"Until my father decided to strong-arm him to the altar."

"Yes." Maria grinned. "But first you turned his head, don't forget, or your father wouldn't have had to intervene. So the responsibility is very much Sinjin's—another truth he has to come to terms with. Although, had other fathers had the Fergusson nerve, perhaps Sinjin would have been married long ago."

"Sassenach power has always been of little consequence to Father."

"Apparently. My father thought differently. And here I am."

"For which I'm very grateful," Chelsea cheerfully countered, her spirits optimistically buoyant. "You gave me Sinjin. And now I think I'll try to keep him. Do you mind?"

"Not in the least. He deserves the happiness you've brought to him. My blessings on your efforts. Can I help?"

Chelsea grinned, a warm, contented assurance spreading through her senses. "Thank you, but no . . . I can manage myself . . ."

Chapter 38

Chelsea intended to go to Sinjin with a proposition, a sensible, open offer he couldn't refuse.

If he didn't want children, she understood. All she asked was that he give her two weeks of his time. If after that interval he still preferred dissolving the marriage, she would leave.

How could he refuse her two short weeks?

He had nothing to lose.

She was the one gambling her happiness, but living with him in the detached manner he now chose offered her more pain than joy. In the weeks Chelsea had been in London, Sinjin had escorted her everywhere, appearing with her at the Opera and plays, at balls and routs, once even at a breakfast party hosted by the Duchess of Devonshire—a demonstration of husbandly devotion so remarkable for Sinjin St. John as to cause comment in the broadsheets—but he'd never crossed the line beyond that of a friendly courtesy. They could have been brother and sister, so casual and familiar was his manner toward her.

She couldn't maintain an asexual distance; she couldn't pretend any longer. And she was willing to risk all on the chance she'd win.

She'd offer her proposition as a wager. A consummate gambler, Sinjin would be intrigued.

But she never had the opportunity to present her case. That

morning, while they rode in Hyde Park, Sinjin told her and Beau he was leaving for Tunis the next day.

He'd reached the decision that morning while watching the sun rise as he sat at Brookes, a bottle of brandy empty at his side, his head aching not just from liquor but from discontent, an irrational need for his wife overwhelming all reason.

If he left for Tunis, the distance would give him opportunity to decide whether lust for a woman was reason enough to be shackled for life. It would also give him a peaceful interval to restore, he hoped, his former view of the world. His factor had intrigued him with news of some exceptional horses being bred by the desert tribes south of Tozeur. Why not appease his unsettled conscience at the same time he pleased himself and gained some new bloodstock?

His yacht was always at the ready. He'd sail tomorrow.

Unable to speak in front of Beau, Chelsea replied to Sinjin's news with the commonplaces of politesse, while she felt as though the smile on her face would shatter any minute and display all her pain.

"You're welcome to stay on at Seth House," Sinjin said, Thune and Mameluke walking side by side down the graveled path, "and enjoy the remainder of the season . . . or go to Kingsway, Oakham or any of my estates. Whatever you wish."

He was all his normal courtesy, but left unsaid were the words indicating she could go wherever she wished and he wouldn't stop her.

"Take me to the yacht, Papa," Beau interjected, his face alight with excitement, "when you go to provision it today." Familiar with Sinjin's travels to Tunis, he usually participated in the departure process. "And you promised me a black Barb this time, Papa, don't forget."[12]

"You'll have your Barb if one exists in the desert, Beau, my word on it. And if you help me lay in supplies today, I'll get you out of your lessons with Dr. Beckett."

"Yowie! I'll work like a dog, Papa. It's loads more fun helping you than conjugating Latin verbs."

And the remainder of their ride revolved around a discussion of the necessary supplies required for the journey to Tunis. Sinjin helped Chelsea dismount when they arrived back at Seth House, but he excused himself from their normal breakfast, giving the shortness of time before his departure as reason.

"My steward is available for anything you require," he said to

Chelsea as he remounted, Beau waiting for him in the courtyard. "Feel free to rely on him for your needs . . ." And with a wave he was gone.

She didn't think Mr. Buckthorn would be available for the particular needs she required, Chelsea morosely thought, a wave of self-pity assailing her. How close she'd come to perhaps reconciling their troubled marriage. But she'd lost . . . and as tears welled into her eyes, she rushed into the house and up the grand staircase, managing to reach the security of her room before she burst into tears.

Sinjin had said, in effect, "Do what you want, go where you want, live as you wish." He wasn't interested, and his detachment was no longer an inconclusive state. He was leaving.

And his message was eminently clear.

Chelsea found herself unable to muster the necessary energy to smile that evening, so she made her excuses to Damien and Maria, both of whom wished her to join them at the opera. Pleading a headache, she stayed in her rooms all day; her heart was breaking, and she didn't wish the gossip tomorrow to make note of her despair. Fashionable ladies never showed their feelings; they laughed even when their hearts were in pieces at their feet. In an effort to make Sinjin notice her, she'd played the brittle role of recognized beauty, she'd laughed and flirted and tossed off bon mots, she'd danced with men who held no interest, she'd conversed in trivialities until she'd wondered if a sensible thought remained in her head.

But after countless dinners, dances and parties, Chelsea found herself restless and bored, the people inconsequential, the conversation predictable. She found she didn't care who was making love to whom, particularly with the ever present danger that her husband's name might figure in these scandals. Equally uninteresting were the shrewish comments on dress, the petty comparisons of coiffures, the uninformed political discussions. And if courtesy required that she eat one more fresh strawberry or green pea or lemon creme meringue, she felt sure she'd be instantly transformed into a true lady of the Ton, insipid, prone to favor the word "vastly," obsessed with her dressing schedule and Vauxhall's ham slices.

Despite her attempt, all her efforts had been in vain, for her husband was leaving her anyway. And right now she only wished to cry for an eternity.

But by evening she'd cried herself dry, her inherent good sense also taking issue with her melodrama. Perhaps Sinjin *had* to go, she noted in a more reasonable frame of mind. Perhaps his decision to leave wasn't prompted by repulsion for her. Perhaps she might actually live to smile another day, she decided with a hiccuping sigh, and view another sunrise with pleasure, even ride Thune again, she more cheerfully concluded, her spirits rising.

While Sinjin hadn't been home all day, his valet had been busy in his chamber next door packing his trunks, the commotion only quieting as she ate a solitary dinner in her room. She was hoping Sinjin would return sometime tonight so she could at least say goodbye to him like a mature adult—she smiled—as a fashionable wife would graciously bid farewell. Or *if* he didn't come back to Seth House tonight, she intended to sleep in her husband's bed so she could at least *imagine* his presence. It was all well and good to pragmatically accept his leaving, to come to terms with the fact that their marriage hadn't prospered. But it was another matter altogether to simply stop loving him. Reason lost at that point to a terrible bleak longing.

It couldn't hurt if she slept in his bed; her action itself wouldn't alter his decision. At the worst, her husband would eventually return and order her out—and she'd be no less alone than presently. If he *didn't* return, she'd spend one last night imagining him beside her, with the familiar scent of his cologne on his pillows and the objects of his life—his boots, quirts, paintings of his horses, portraits of Beau, the disarray of books and spirits, all the clutter of his life—surrounding her.

For after Sinjin sailed, she had no intention of staying in London. Without firm plans in the chaos of her unsettled emotions, she assumed she'd go home to Ayrshire and take up her old life.

She wasn't being devious or manipulative as she considered sleeping in Sinjin's bed; she had no inventive plan, and even if she had, what good would it do when Sinjin left in the morning?

She wished only a modicum of solace after a fortnight of having him hold her at arm's length.

Understanding that loving one's spouse was perceived as awkwardly gauche, Chelsea had attempted to order her feelings into the impassivity prescribed by the beau monde. But unfortunately her love wouldn't conveniently be put aside, despite a brutal, cold-hearted assessment of her place in Sinjin's life.

She couldn't abruptly stop loving him because he wished her to, because it was convenient for him now to disregard their relationship. And if a great sadness hadn't trembled just beneath her self-control, she might have been furious at his nervy arrogance.

But heartache mitigated her resentment, as did her practical assessment of who had entered whose life under what conditions. She smiled as she remembered that first day at Newmarket when Sinjin had opened his carriage door. Even refusing her, he'd seemed to offer something of himself—his unconscious sensuality not easily repressed.

As twilight turned into evening, she sat before the window overlooking the garden, her thoughts centered on her husband's disreputable splendor: his beautiful smile that curved upward slowly as if in remembered pleasure; his teasing eyes that shone, even in half light, so radiantly blue they seemed indeed the shining doorway to his impetuous soul; the galvanic excitement he offered with a lazy look; the feel of his lean muscled body, his strong arms holding her close . . . the sheer pleasure he offered making love, as if he could personally open the vistas of nirvana . . .

It was impossible to docilely walk away, she realized as sweet memory flooded her senses; she wanted Sinjin to make love to her before he left, as poignant closure to their encumbered union. For less credible reasons too—because she was bereaved and desolate and still wistfully in love. He needn't love her or say he loved her; he needn't pledge eternal devotion nor any of the formal phrases of *amour;* she wished only that he hold her close . . . for she was very young, very much in love, and he was leaving her—perhaps forever.

Travel anywhere in an era of brigands and privateers was not without its risks. North Africa under military dynasties presented added dangers. Nor was Sinjin's horse-buying mission looked on with favor by Tunisian authorities. In fact, the Regency prohibited the sale of horses to foreign infidels.

In the moments that elapsed while night fell over the city, coloring the garden below in shades of grey and filling her high-ceilinged room with shadow, Chelsea's previous elusive longing for Sinjin subtly altered to something more determined, and she experienced a flurry of excitement as her new design took form. Her scheme meant taking a wild chance, like the last throw of the dice, or the need to call on one's final shred of inner strength in a mortal contest. But, an inveterate competitor, she anticipated the possibility of success with the same irrepressible confidence she experienced when racing, and her mind was infused with a flaring energy.

Now, how exactly to orchestrate the details on the chance Sinjin might return? How best to make a bid for his attention? She smiled then, pushed her tray aside and walked toward her dressing room.

Surely a man renowned for his love of women shouldn't be too difficult to seduce.

Bringing into play all the feminine procedures for adornment that she'd recently learned in the temple of London fashion, Chelsea began by turning on the bath water.[13] She bathed in rose water, washed her hair with scented French soap, powdered her body with fragrant talc so her skin felt like satin to the touch, drenched herself in costly perfume. Shortly her silken flesh and sinuous curves resembled an aromatic bouquet of rose and lily, sweet as love poetry.

And in the event that the normal feminine enticements failed to seduce, she thought some lengthy time later—walking powdered, perfumed and splendidly nude like a costly courtesan into Sinjin's room—she'd take the less seductive but more practical precaution of dissolving a small dose of cantharides in his cognac decanter.

Having previously noted the small bottle on Sinjin's curio shelf, she held the brown glass container in her hand, debating the ethics of concealing an aphrodisiac. After a brief second or so, her moral dilemma satisfactorily concluded as the phrase "All's fair in love and war" came pithily to mind, she broke the wax seal on the bottle. Apparently, she noted, scrutinizing the intact contents, her husband's sexual urges functioned sufficiently without the help of cantharides. Which thought gave her added resentful impetus as she poured a measure into the cognac.

Further considering that this might be her last opportunity to seduce Sinjin, with his trip imminent and his use for a wife extinguished, Chelsea held the decanter up to the light, paused for a short contemplative moment more and shook in another portion.

Setting the decanter on a convenient table, she placed a glass beside it, added his new copy of the bloodstock book so it was near at hand, stood back to scrutinize the effect, smiled, nodded in appreciation of the added subtlety and walked back into her own room to find the perfect garment to lure a husband. Many in the Ton would say such a gown didn't exist, but youthful hope conspired to overlook more cynical views as she browsed through her wardrobe.

Selecting a negligee Sinjin had purchased for her when they made their wholesale selections at Madame DuBay's, she slipped a filmy lace gown over her head and took momentary pleasure in the sensual drift of white silk sliding down her body. You couldn't fault Madame DuBay's skills in constructing female intimate attire, she decided, gazing at herself in the cheval glass, the sumptuous handmade lace sheer but elegant, the bodice closures two silver bows, easily opened, the narrow shoulder straps tying in ribbon bows as well. Perhaps Sinjin's considerable practice over the years had refined the design.

Garments of such artful seduction had been wasted on her, however, since Sinjin had never ventured into her bedchamber. He must have mistakenly said, "The usual" to Madame DuBay, and London's modish dressmaker had included these unnecessary negligees in his wife's wardrobe.

Should she wear her hair up or down? Standing before the tall mirror, its candle stands lending a soft glow to her image in the glass, she lifted her cloud of golden hair atop her head. Tilting her head one way, then the other, she decided upswept hair would show her earrings off to advantage—her Titian earrings, replicas of the unmatched black and white tear-drop pearls Venus wore in the Venetian portrait.

Perhaps the earrings would bring her Venus's powers tonight. With her husband's cool detachment, she'd need every artful stratagem. Glancing over the variety of jewel boxes that she'd brought into Sinjin's room from her adjacent bedchamber, she considered whether a light necklace or pendant would be appropriate.

The glittering array before her was only a small part of the Seth family jewels, all casually offered to her when she'd come to London.

"Here," Sinjin had said the first morning after her arrival, handing her a key to the strong-room. "Help yourself. You'll need jewelry if you're going out."

So she tried on several pieces from the assortment in the velvet boxes spread over Sinjin's bureau, considering herself light-heartedly like an actress readying herself for a performance. But in the end she wore Venus's pearls in hopes that the goddess's spirit would bring her good fortune.

And arranging herself in a comfortable pose against the pillows on Sinjin's bed, dressed and perfumed and ornamented, she waited against the remote hope her husband would come.

Meanwhile Sinjin had made a last round of his clubs, bade leave of his friends and was now seated in Harriet's boudoir, moodily contemplating the bottom of his brandy glass.

"You haven't looked at another female, Sinjin, since coming back to London. She must mean something to you." Lounging elegantly across from him on a chaise, a glass of champagne in her hand, Harriet raised the stemmed glass marginally in salute. "So why don't you go home and kiss your wife goodbye?"

Sinjin's blue eyes rose, and he looked at the glorious redhead who had been a friend and lover for many years. "How long have I been coming here?" he softly queried, answering her question with another.

"Since you were sixteen, darling. I remember distinctly the day your papa introduced you to me. You were the most beautiful young man I'd ever seen." She smiled. "And considerably more accomplished than your papa thought, as I recall." The seventh Duke of Seth had brought his young heir into Harriet's exclusive brothel to have him taught the intricacies of *amour*. And Harriet had decided to school the boy personally, fascinated then as now with his sensual beauty. At twenty-three, she'd been a successful businesswoman for almost six years, ever since the old Marquess of Hoddington had died and left her enough to open her own establishment, but few men had piqued her interest until Sinjin. They'd instantly become fast friends.

"Have I changed my life much in all those years . . . except for Catherine?" he added, a muscle twitching high over his cheekbone at his addition.

"No, darling," Harriet murmured, having been party to Sinjin's misery at the time, "but maybe this pretty young wife of yours is beginning to change it," she quietly pointed out.

"Maybe I don't want it changed."

"And maybe you don't have any choice." Her voice was soft as the marabou ornament on her creme silk dressing gown, her green eyes compassionate. She'd been observing Sinjin for a fortnight now as he'd avoided the usual array of females in full pursuit. Unfamiliar with The Saint's forswearing boudoir pleasures, many had exerted considerable pressure on him to change his mind, but Sinjin hadn't graced a woman's bed anywhere in town since his return. He wasn't the same man who'd gone north in March to run his horses at Newmarket.

"One always has a choice." His voice was as blunt as his remark.

"But at what price? You're obviously not in the most pleasant spirits—nor have you been anytime this past fortnight."

"I don't wish to be married," he muttered, sliding down in the chair, resting his head against the costly needleworked fabric with a small discontented sigh.

"Surely it needn't be a deterrent . . . as any of your friends will attest." Her amiable smile reminded him of the realities of married life in the Ton.

He gazed at her for a speculative moment from under the dark fringe of his lashes, the bright blue of his eyes strangely muted. "I find my marriage infinitely harder to overlook than others do their conjugal bonds."

"You care for her . . . or you could overlook those bonds with impunity," Harriet quietly prompted. And while she might lose a lover, as his friend she wished Sinjin happiness. Since Catherine, no woman had captured his heart.

He poured himself another drink before answering. Harriet's words struck too close to his own disordered feelings. "Hell and damnation," he softly swore, drinking a large measure of the brandy and sliding fractionally lower down in the comfortable chair Harriet kept for him. He smiled at her. "You've been mother confessor for—"

"Two weeks now," Harriet interjected. "There's some significance in that time period, my *darling* Sinjin." Her smile, compassionate and genial, reflected her affection for the boy who had grown into a wild young man . . . and an intimate friend. "Go home before you run away to Tunis."

"Do you disapprove of my running?" He smiled then as he had at sixteen, with a disarming openness.

She shrugged. "Maybe I disapprove of the reasons you're running—your parents' marriage, men's clubism that instills such selfishness, your fear of sharing Beau, your guilt over relegating Catherine to memory . . . Instead you should *stay* for a more important reason . . . because you love your wife."

Sinjin's smile had widened at her recital. "Have I burdened you with all that these past weeks?" he murmured, his blue eyes suddenly glittering with mischief. "You must send me a bill for curate duty."

He obviously wasn't in the mood for introspection, and perhaps she'd said too much, but he was sailing on the morning tide. She wished him to consider at least the truth of his feelings. "You've paid me enough over the years to make me a rich woman, darling," Harriet replied with a warm smile. "So, unless for other reasons," she suggestively insinuated, "you wish me in my mother superior nun's habit, consider my duties at an end."

"Ummm," Sinjin smiled, recalling Harriet's sensational dramatic abilities. "Perhaps you'll keep yourself in celibacy until I return." He grinned. "And by that time I should have exorcised my demons."

"Willingly, my pet," she replied, not entirely facetiously. Sinjin was one of the few men who interested her, and she chose her lovers with infrequency and care. "Do me a favor, though. Say goodbye to your wife. I remember when Shaw left me without a word; she's very young." Her first lover, Shaw Penthurst, had simply vanished one day without a note or farewell, too embarrassed to tell her his family had found an heiress he must marry. She'd loved him as only a sixteen-year-old girl can love the beautiful young man who first seduced her, and the pain of his unhappy leave-taking had never completely faded.

"Must I?" Sinjin was teasing still, although he knew of Harriet's lifelong fondness for Shaw, who had a rich pinch-nosed wife, eight children, a sprawling pile of Cotswold stone he called home and a tendency to over-drink in compensation for his unhappiness.

"How difficult can it be? Just say goodbye; don't leave her without a word."

He knew that courtesy required he bid his adieus, and he'd been steeling himself to the task. He was simply avoiding the necessary evil as long as possible. "In which case," he said, glancing at the Meissen clock on Harriet's mantel and taking note of the very late hour, "I should see my way home."

"Give her a kiss for me," Harriet said with a grin.

"Who said anything about a kiss? She's a wife, after all," Sinjin lightly replied, heaving himself out of the soft down cushioned chair. "Whoever heard of kissing one's wife?"

Chapter 39

It was almost four when the porter opened the door for him at Seth House. They exchanged murmured greetings as Sinjin crossed the marble floor. Climbing the dimly lit staircase, the frieze and barrel-vaulted ceiling ghostly white, Sinjin suddenly felt the fatigue of too many sleepless nights.

An ending and new beginning faced him in the morning. Despite what Harriet said, he intended to hie himself away to Tunis. He needed respite . . . Lord, he needed rest, he wearily thought; he'd sleep the first several days at sea.

But now to change from his evening clothes . . .

Entering his room, he stopped, disconcerted, on the threshold, his hand still on the door latch. He'd erroneously assumed that four in the morning would be a safe enough time to arrive home. Instead he found his wife asleep on his bed, Madame DuBay's white lace negligee twisted in fascinating disarray over her thighs, her hair like spun gold in the candlelight, her flesh glowing rosy pink, one small hand tucked under her cheek as though she were a child in sleep.

Unlike a child, however, she'd dressed for him in sheer white lace, the Venus earrings and nothing more . . . like a pretty erotic package wrapped up for his pleasure.

The candles, burned low, cast the large bedchamber into a singular sheltering dusk; the gilding on the fantastical palm columns and the frieze from the temple of Antoninus and Faustina seemed suspended in the shrouded interior. He stood for some time looking at his wife, golden and pink beneath the bedside candelabra. With his departure only hours away, he stood arrested, her image burning into his retinas, his feelings restless, ill timed and unruly.

Chelsea's tousled hair, golden, gleaming, lay across his pillows, more ornamental than their rich lace embellishment. Her slender form took on a tactile sensuous volume in the veiled lighting. Her breasts, spilling out of the lacy transparent bodice as she lay on her side, reminded him of plump ripe fruit, the silver bows flimsy security to the pressure of their luscious weight.

He wished overwhelmingly to release the small bows, lift the lace covering her thighs and feel the warmth between her legs. She smelled of sweet rose and the lilies of the field, and she lay in his bed like temptation, Eve in his Garden of Eden. How long had he been without a woman—without her?

He stood in the half light not knowing if he could resist. Would it matter so much? One time more, he wondered, until his small voice of reason reminded him that Chelsea's tantalizing enticement carried a price he might not care to pay.

He could go back to Brookes, he thought with an inward sigh, or any number of other clubs, but Beau would be in very early on this his last morning home . . . What time was it now? When would Beau wake? How long would it take him to make another round trip to Brookes?

Dammit, his brain wasn't easily assimilating his choices . . . or non-choices. He stood, indecisive, in his doorway, thinking how the scent of roses changed the masculine atmosphere of his room. Just as a wife forever altered a man's life . . .

His gaze swept the room as if some answer might lie in the capricious light and shadow, and the decanter of cognac struck his line of vision as a beacon would beckon a man lost at sea.

Softly shutting the door, he crossed the room to the set piece artfully arranged by his wife. Dropping into the gilded chair upholstered in a green damask patterned with the Seth coat of arms, he reached for the decanter and glass. A drink would pass the time while he waited for Beau to come in, bringing security with his presence. Only a short time remained until the summer morning dawned, and the thought of returning to Brookes held no appeal; he'd spent too many nights there lately.

What he failed to acknowledge, what he forcibly repressed, were the more cogent reasons for his staying—desire, need, an urgent longing to hold his wife in his arms again.

A short time later, as Sinjin was pouring his second cognac, his arm accidently brushed against the blown glass decanter top on the table. The stopper spun off the highly polished surface, sailed through the air, crashed into the fireplace grate with a shattering impact. The ringing tone of crystal on metal broke the silence of the room like a small temple bell, followed instantly by the tinkle of exploding glass. Sinjin muttered, "Damn" as Chelsea stirred and came awake.

"Go back to sleep," he said. "I'm leaving in a few minutes."

With a docile wife, perhaps his temperate command would have been obeyed. But Chelsea pushed herself up on the pillows, brushed her hair away from her face and murmured, "How long have you been here?"

Sinjin shrugged. "Twenty minutes . . . Madame DuBay's negligee suits you." His voice held its familiar dispassion.

She smiled a tentative half smile, pleased he'd noticed, although he spoke as he did in London—as if they were strangers. "Thank you . . . and I hope you don't mind me sleeping in your bed . . . but you were leaving in the morning and . . . well . . . Tunis suddenly seemed very far away . . ." Her voice trailed off uncomfortably under Sinjin's cool gaze.

"I don't mind," he replied abruptly, the words too curt for dispassion. And finishing his glass of cognac in one swift draught, he rose from the chair and began walking toward his dressing room. "Excuse me," he said, his head beginning to feel the effects of his drinking. He'd take a headache powder, change quickly and wait in the nursery for Beau to wake. He was finding it increasingly impossible to look at his wife without imagining the small silver bows untied. "I'm going to change," he muttered, his gaze somewhere safely above Chelsea's head, a familiar heat uncomfortably warming his body.

He couldn't stay.

Impromptu adjustments to a scheme only casually planned raced through Chelsea's mind as Sinjin disappeared into his dressing room.

At the soft click of the door closing, Chelsea scrambled off the bed, sprinted to the hall door and locked it, then did the same to the one between their rooms. Tossing the key to her room out the window, she carefully hid the key to the outside door before resuming her position on the bed.

And she waited, her heart thumping so violently against her ribs that the sound echoed in her ears—her normal temerity shaken by her husband's disinterest.

Sinjin came out of his dressing room in very short order, changed into day clothes, his hair newly brushed and twisted into a queue. "If you'd care to join me for breakfast at eight in the morning parlor," he said as he passed the bed, his boots only a whisper on the silk carpet, "we could discuss what money you'll need in my absence." He didn't stop in his progress toward the corridor door, intent on escaping his volatile passions.

Chelsea held her breath as he grasped the door latch.

Spinning around a second later, his spine rigid, his fierce scowl drawing his dark brows together, his feet planted pugnaciously like those of a fighter on the defensive, he snapped, "Don't be childish."

"I miss you," Chelsea quietly said. "I wish I didn't, but I do. I was hoping," she went on, reflecting on the degree of humiliation her next statement entailed, "you might make love to me before you go."

He didn't answer. He went instead to the door between their rooms and tried the latch.

"Give me the key." He held out his hand.

"I threw it out the window."

He sighed. "Give me the other one then."

"You have to come and get it," Chelsea softly replied. She'd stopped him, if only momentarily, and an irreverent sense of power inspired her.

Her tone, or the small faint smile that drifted across her mouth, should have warned him.

"Dammit, I'm not in the mood to play games. Now where is it?"

Lying back against the lace-trimmed pillows as if she were the star in a tableau vivant, Chelsea delicately eased the sheer pale negligee upward, opened her silken thighs leisurely so Sinjin was sure to notice and, moving her right hand downward, pointed to that portion of her anatomy that had consumed her husband's critical attention ever since he'd entered his bedchamber.

He should have known; he shouldn't have so naively walked into that trap. "Very amusing," Sinjin said in short, clipped, angry tones. But his gaze lingered at the site Chelsea so plainly indicated, and burning desire tore through his senses so violently that he clenched his fists against the savage sensation.

"No," he murmured to steady himself. "Bloody fucking no . . ." He hadn't decided yet whether he wanted a wife for life. And the next few hours before his departure weren't time enough to make that decision. "I don't want to take the chance of having a child," he bluntly said. They could use Greek sponges or French letters, but neither was infallible.[14]

However discourteous his rebuff, his statement served to make Chelsea extremely happy, ecstatically joyful, more cheerful than she'd expected on this morning of his departure.

He didn't hate *her*, at least; he was guarding his independence—something she understood very well.

"I'm not trying to trap you," she said with a smile. "Don't you have some Dutch cundums?"

"No . . . not here, this minute. Lord," he exhaled in a great sigh, distractedly running his fingers through his hair. "Why are you doing this?"

"I already told you. No subterfuge. A simple request. And you needn't worry, for I took the precaution of using a Greek sponge. You see how obliging I am."

For a moment he seemed to reconsider, then shook his head. "Look, I'm leaving in a few hours. Let's talk about this when I return."

"No."

His surprise showed. Unfamiliar with intransigent women, he took pause at her refusal. But a second later he turned away without speaking, not in the mood for useless argument. Walking over to the chair he'd previously vacated, he sat down again. "I'll wait till the servants wake," he said, reaching for the cognac. "Surely you won't make a scene before the entire establishment." A complacent security infused his voice, his dilemma reconciled.

Chelsea operated from a security of her own, for she'd seen Sinjin drink the cognac and watched him now re-fill his glass. And she knew his libido.

She wouldn't be denied, she decided. She loved him, as did all the other women in his life. He could give as much to her as he gave them.

She wasn't angry . . . only determined.

With a shuttered gaze, Sinjin watched Chelsea leave the bed and move to the mirror, her bare feet soundless on his carpet, her white lace gown billowing out behind her. Standing before the cheval glass, she paused, her gaze catching his transiently, and she smiled.

He found he needed a steadying drink at that point and emptied his glass. She was too close, too lush, the scent of her pungent in his nostrils, the sight of her too overwhelmingly female.

As she slowly untied the bows at her bodice, her image was reflected in the tall glass, her supple back revealed to him, the extravagant bounty of her form displayed for him in all its delectable dimension. Her breasts, partially unveiled when the ribbons opened, rose in mounded fullness to his eye, the deep shadow of cleavage prominent in the gleam of candlelight. With his breath in abeyance, Sinjin's gaze followed Chelsea's hand as it moved to the shoulder bows.

She opened the silver ribbons slowly, playing to the rapt attention of her audience of one, her gestures languid, letting the silk ties slip away from her shoulders with deliberation. And her breasts were fully exposed as the gown slipped downward, the slither of silk deafening in Sinjin's ears.

"You're wasting your time," he gruffly said, repressing his violent need to rise from his chair and touch her.

"But then I've quite a bit of time until the servants rise," Chelsea replied with a smile, turning toward him so he could see her peaked nipples and her golden-haired sex. Rubbing her palms lazily over the taut crests, she took satisfaction in his apparent interest, his erection prominently visible beneath the buff leather of his breeches. "But the light is so poor in here," she casually murmured, "I can hardly see your erection."

Her comment had the desired effect, as if she'd stroked his arousal with her words, its length increasing, the leather straining to contain it.

"This isn't going to work," Sinjin growled.

"Did I mention I put cantharides in the cognac?"

He went pale beneath his dark skin. "You bitch." Infuriated, he half-rose in his chair until reason drew him back.

"Like Cassandra, you mean."

"No. She does what she's told." A snarl, a soft animal sound, crept through the whisper of his words.

"Sorry," Chelsea replied with a false delicacy, her voice the softest of purrs. She was unintimidated by male fury after years of observing a household of fractious men. "I guess I haven't learned that lesson yet." And if her resolve had been wavering, it instantly steadied at the content of his retort.

She intended to see exactly who wielded the most potent authority. And toward that end, she walked deliberately toward him, turning aside just short of his chair to open a small Chinoiserie cabinet set against the wall.

Having earlier discovered the supply of candles for Sinjin's room, she leaned over slightly to reach some ivory candles on a lower shelf and set about bringing her husband to his knees. Cassandra may do as she's told, Chelsea resentfully reflected, but Scottish lasses did as they pleased—or at least Fergusson lasses did. And if there were lessons to be learned, perhaps her husband could do equally with some schooling.

The curve of her hip and thigh and sweet bottom were mere inches away, her fragrance so overwhelming that Sinjin shifted in unease. He could reach out and stroke her offered delights, her silken thighs framing the shadowed warmth between her legs.

"There," Chelsea commented, standing upright, turning around, a brace of candles held against her breasts. "Don't you think we need more light?" The pressure of the candles bore down on her breasts, their imprint forcing her pliant flesh, making indentations in the softness.

He was aching with need, the pulsing of his blood swelling his erection, a primitive hunger—almost more than he could suppress— eating at his brain. And he was imprisoned in this room with temptation close enough to touch. "I could beat you," he gruffly said, but even his voice failed to impart a genuine threat, for his hushed emphasis on the verb gave it another connotation entirely.

"Perhaps later," Chelsea murmured, understanding more than he wished, and moving past him in a whiff of perfume, she set about to fully illuminate the room.

As she passed from wall sconce to wall sconce, from candelabra to torchiere, setting new candles in all the holders and lighting them with a long taper that she'd ignited from the candles near the bed, she could feel the key inside her. She felt it when she walked, when she bent over, when she stretched upward to reach the gilded sconces. And she mentioned once, on her carefully watched progress about the room, the particular pleasurable sensation induced by the intricately carved key inside her.

"It touches me everywhere when I move," she murmured, bending over to reach a candelabra on his desk top. "I can feel the slippery heat of it," she added in a whisper, turning to glance toward him, "with every small gesture." Her eyes shut for a moment to absorb the tantalizing streak of sensation tingling upward from the intrusive object. "Although," she said on a small caught breath, "it can't"—her voice dropped into a purring resonance—"compare with you . . ."

Sinjin's fingers, clamped around the leopard-head finials of the chair arms, went white at her words as rapacious desire tore through his body, the cantharides in his blood spiking hot and dangerous.

The glittering light from all the abundant candles illuminated Chelsea's voluptuous beauty like the noonday sun, heated the rose-scented interior, added intemperate warmth to Sinjin's arousal, which was peaking now at explosive levels.

The key to his freedom was only a small distance away, he knew, if he dared take it. If he could control his tautly leashed carnal urges . . .

Would he come for the key? Chelsea wondered. Would he come for her? And turning away from the man braced in his chair through sheer force of will, she stood on tiptoe to place her last candle in a torchiere near the bed.

Her slender curved body stretched upward, her heavy breasts lifted high as she reached above her head to set the candle into the feathered, gilded bracket. The perfect beauty of her feet and calves and thighs, poised en pointe, drew his gaze to the silky pale down between her thighs, to the repository of the key to his freedom. But something other than freedom beat at his brain, a barbaric lust so intense his hands were trembling, and as the cantharides in his bloodstream broke through the last vestiges of Sinjin's control, he catapulted out of the chair like a lunging panther.

In three strides he was across the floor, wrenching both the candle and taper from Chelsea's hands, tossing them toward the grate. In the next second he picked her up as though she were weightless and carried her to his bed—the bed reserved for himself alone, the immaculate bed unstained by the prodigality of his passion, his room inviolate male territory . . . until now.

Until a pale golden slip of a girl who called him husband triumphed.

"You knew I couldn't resist you, damn you," he whispered, tossing her on the bed, following her down in the next frenzied moment as he tore at the fastening of his breeches. "Damn you," he whispered, kissing her neck and throat, the words muffled against her sweet-smelling skin, "damn you . . . damn you . . ."

"I didn't know . . . I didn't know . . . but—I wanted you . . . even if it was for the last time," Chelsea breathed, holding his glossy dark head in her hands as his hot kisses trailed over her throat, her eyes closed against the bliss of his body on hers.

And then his fingers slipped inside her and extracted the key, smoothly, deftly, in less than a heartbeat. Flinging it away, he moved over her in the next flashing moment, his blue eyes shut tightly against the critical urgency of his need, knowing only that he would willingly die to feel her around him.

He plunged into her with a low moan, his body on fire from the cantharides, her honeyed sweetness his salvation, his hell, the most exquisite pleasure this side of death. And she clung to him fiercely with a young girl's unconditional passion, with a woman's wild intensity, with love and hope and tears of happiness.

It was over in brief seconds, their celibacy of the past weeks disposing them to impetuous speed and instant gratification, and a sudden quiet descended after their precipitous climaxes, broken only by the harsh rasp of Sinjin's breathing. The powerful beat of his heart thudded above her as he lay braced on his elbows, Chelsea's own erratic pulse echoed in her ears. She thought in post-orgasmic splendor that bliss such as this must surely be beyond the earthly realm . . .

Driven by less rarefied impulses, Sinjin lay quiescent only long enough to gather needed air into his lungs before he withdrew from Chelsea's warmth, rose swiftly from the bed and began stripping off his clothes without care for finesse or costly fabrics. His superfine jacket, meant to be eased on and off, preferably by a valet, rent at the shoulder seams as he tore it off. The fine cambric of his shirt fared no better when he jerked it over his head, and only a muttered imprecation gave notice of its loss. His shoes landed a dozen feet away with a careless kick, and his breeches fell at his feet swiftly, sans buttons and knee buckles for the most part.

"You might be sorry you laced my cognac with beetle dust," he gruffly murmured, moving quickly back to the bed, his clothing scattered, his eyes glittering with arousal, his erection giving no indication of his recent orgasm.

Unfamiliar with the celibacy imposed on her by Sinjin since her arrival in London after months of sharing his bed and volatile passions, Chelsea glowed with a rich, lush desire almost as intemperate as her husband's. "I shan't be sorry, milord, if it brings you back to my bed," she answered with a country girl's honesty and a London lady's flirtatious purr. "Pray allow me to oblige you . . ."

Sinjin's smile was more of a grimace, his wife's affectatious delivery reminding him testily of how far she'd advanced in those ubiquitous vices so rife in the Ton. "Oblige me you will, my lady," he murmured, peevish and moody, "for I've unrestrained need of a ready woman." He pushed her legs apart brusquely, his gestures quick and impatient.

"And you're the only one convenient," he added in a harsh whisper as he climbed between her legs. "Let me know," he went on, guiding himself into her with swift urgency, bereft of his usual seductive charm, his words a hiss from between his clenched teeth, "when you've had enough."

His eyes shut against the exquisite sensation as he plunged into her slick warmth, his mind momentarily distracted from his anger, and he groaned, a low deep pleasure sound. His arms slid around Chelsea of their own accord, and he just held her for a moment while his brain dissolved and his limbs and bones and each small particle of his being worshipped at the shrine of sensual ecstasy.

Chelsea understood his anger but welcomed him in any guise, and when his body claimed hers, she lifted her arms around his neck, melted into him and sighed in exaltation.

She matched him then in the heated rhythms of love, her own need as intense as his; she'd missed the feel of him too long. She'd missed the wonder of him in her arms.

He was frantic in his lovemaking the first few times, powerful, frenzied, uncontrollable. And she welcomed him, irrepressible, passionate beyond his memory.

Beyond her own as well.

But she was eighteen, after all, and too long without the man she loved.

Some hours later, as the sun tinted the horizon with light, they lay sated, twined, content until Sinjin heard her small sniffle. Lifting his head a fraction from the pillow, he noted her tears.

"Don't cry," he whispered, rising on one elbow, and bending his head, he kissed away the wetness on her cheeks. "Lord . . . don't cry."

"I want to," she whispered back, her fingers sliding down his muscled arm, a smile of pure happiness trembling on her lips.

"You're sure?" His voice was hushed, his expression perplexed.

She nodded, hiccuped a little and said, *"Now* I'm sure."

They weren't talking about the same thing, he instantly realized, and with a raised brow and a faint smile, he said, "Something here needs the smallest explanation—although," he abruptly added with great courtesy, "if you'd rather not . . ."

"I needed to know," Chelsea said in a voice still unsteady with emotion. "I *wanted* to know—even if . . . the answer was oppressive . . ." Wiping her eyes awkwardly with a balled fist, as a child does, she went on in the merest whisper, "I couldn't let you just walk away . . ."

Sinjin's sigh rippled through the sudden silence, the sound oddly lucid—as if words of regret had been spoken. "I've been winning so much money lately that none but the reckless will play with me. All I do is sit at Brookes or Boodles or Whites and gamble and drink and want you . . ." His voice was utterly without modulation, as if the plainness of his speech matched the simplicity of his admission.

"Take me with you then! You have to . . . I won't stay . . . I'll make you take me!" Chelsea instantly declared, the glory of his words ringing through her mind. Sitting up abruptly, she took his hand in hers, holding on to him with an impressive strength. "You *have* to," she repeated, intense, determined.

His smile was so beautiful it brought added tears to her eyes, because he'd smiled at her just that way the morning he'd welcomed her to his house at Six-Mile-Bottom. And she'd known even then that she loved him beyond reason.

"I have to?" he said, a teasing undertone to his query.

"Yes, yes . . . you have to," she insisted, breathless, animated. And rising swiftly to her knees, she leaned over and threw her arms around his neck, her mouth sweet inches from his. "You have to . . ." she breathed, her smile more assured now, less apprehensive, his teasing smile the old familiar one she'd known before London.

"I'll use Greek sponges," she said. "I'll bring boxes full . . . You needn't feel trapped . . . I won't make demands, I won't keep you up late, I'll see you're fed, I'll keep your linen clean. You'll find me infinitely useful. Infinitely . . ." she purred in the tone of a lush tigress.

"You sound vastly obliging." A smile touched his words with sweetness.

"You'll see . . . I'll be oceans deep vastly and mountains high vastly and so-o-o-o charmingly obliging you'll think yourself at Harriet's."

Sinjin's eyes widened for an instant.

"It's common gossip, darling," Chelsea said, although her smile was markedly altered, "what good friends you are."

"Were," he said, the single word offering unlimited delight to his wife.

"Then you *must* take me," Chelsea pressed, elated and joyous and so touched by his disclosure that she knew from that moment—if from no other—that he indeed loved her.

A small silence fell between them.

Then it lengthened as Sinjin weighed a lifetime of custom against his staggering need for this pretty young girl kneeling before him, her pansy eyes inches away.

And when Chelsea thought perhaps she'd lost after all, Sinjin said very softly, "Only as far as Naples."

She squealed and tumbled him off his elbow and fell on him with kisses and jubilant thank-yous and exuberant smiles of happiness. "You won't be sorry—you won't—you won't!" Lying soft and warm atop him, she added, with a sensuous, intrinsically female movement of her hips, "Guaranteed . . ."

The rational part of his brain was sorry already, but the rest of his brain and the entirety of his body were enormously pleased.

"We sail midmorning," he cautioned, "which doesn't give you much time to prepare."

"I'll hurry—I'll be ready. Don't move. I'll be right back."

But when she returned a few minutes later, after having rung for her maid and left instructions for packing, she found Sinjin asleep.

He'd slept so little in the past fortnight that his weariness had overcome him, and he lay sprawled on his bed, both arms thrown over his head in the exhausted position of very young children.

He looked thinner, more lean, his cheekbones more prominent, the merest indication of his ribs visible beneath the hard pattern of muscles running down his torso, the shadows beneath his eyes evidence of his dissipated existence since returning to London. And even his strength of will could no longer keep him awake. Pulling the coverlet over him and tucking it around his wide shoulders, Chelsea found she loved him more for his attempts to escape her in an endless round of clubs and nightlife. But she loved him most, she decided with the smallest of smug smiles, for having *lost* his struggle.

Chapter 40

Sinjin rented a villa for Chelsea at Sorrento where the view of the bay was spectacular, the sea bathing superb and the stables adequate for the horses he intended buying in Tunis, and then he spent a week introducing his wife to the odd mix of nationalities making up Neapolitan society.

Britain's ambassador, Sir William Hamilton, showed them every favor, particularly after they invited his paramour Emma Hart to dinner. Thirty-five years his junior and received by many of the nobility, including the King and Queen of the Two Sicilies, the beautiful young Emma proved to be modest, charming and apparently devoted to her patron. Rumor had it Sir William was planning on marrying her if George III would countenance his ambassador's wedding a girl of low birth.

Several English families were in residence. King Ferdinand's Prime Minister—Sir Acton, an Anglo-French adventurer—had connections in England. The Austrian influence, of course, was strong at court with Queen Maria Carolina, the daughter of Maria Theresa. And Germans, Swedes, Italians and Spanish all blended harmoniously in the gay Kingdom of the Two Sicilies.

Sinjin took Chelsea to see Vesuvius light up the night sky with its spectacular fountains of liquid fire; they sailed one day to Capri; they strolled in the Villa Reale in the evening with all the fashionable nobility; he even escorted her to two evening conversaziones before he left for Tunis.

"Ask Lady Chester for advice on any questions of protocol, and stay away from the Neapolitan music masters," Sinjin added with a grin as he prepared to leave one morning, Naples' reputation for easy virtue as well known as its beautiful setting. "See Naples and die" was markedly apt in terms of magnificent prospects, but the lazy, pleasure-loving corrupt capital was also a city of scoundrels and fiddlers, poets and whores.

"Must I?" Chelsea queried with a small teasing smile, sitting on the bed while Sinjin tossed items into his shaving kit. "Stay away from music masters even if they're very old? I've found a wonderful musician who plays the lute, and I've already engaged him for lessons."

"How old is old?" Sinjin asked, looking sidelong at her, possessive in spite of his wish not to be.

"I'm not sure," Chelsea honestly replied, so much of the world falling into the elderly category for an eighteen-year-old.

"Let me see him," Sinjin said more tersely than he found comfortable, jealousy a new emotion for him.

As it turned out, Maestro Minetti was sufficiently old to pass Sinjin's criteria. Having been hastily sent for, he was vetted on the front drive, where Sinjin was issuing orders to his staff concerning his departure. And when Sinjin kissed Chelsea goodbye before entering his carriage, he murmured, "I won't be gone long. Two weeks—three at the most." He'd be forcing the pace, but he found he didn't wish to leave his beautiful wife too long alone in Naples.

"I'll miss you . . . so hurry," Chelsea whispered back, not wanting to relinquish the feel of him in her arms.

Sinjin smiled. "Tribal wars and sandstorms aside, we'll bypass Tunis and travel straight through to Tozeur." Gently grasping her hands, he extricated himself from her embrace. "And I'll expect perfection on that new capriccio by the time I return," he added with a grin.

"Take care," Chelsea whispered, frightened despite Sinjin's casual bearing. The Barbary Coast was a land of violence, unsympathetic to foreigners—where Europeans were routinely held for ransom.

"I'm always careful." He spoke carelessly, his assurance one of politesse. "Don't worry, darling, I'll be back sound and hale before you tire of Lady Chester's gossipy chatter."

And Chelsea smiled then because he wished her to.

"Think of me," he genially murmured, touching the tip of her nose with a light brushing finger.

"Every minute." And while Chelsea tried desperately to fight back her tears, a shining wetness filled her eyes.

"I've done this a dozen times before, sweetheart," Sinjin quietly said, taking her hand in his. "I know the country; you've no cause for alarm. I'll be back very soon, so give me a smile now and bid me bon voyage . . ."

She did to please him, but after his carriage had disappeared down the drive, she went to the small pavilion overlooking the bay and stayed there until the last sight of his yacht dropped beyond the horizon. At the moment the *Aurora* disappeared, she unaccountably shivered in the warm summer air, as if some demons from the netherworld had walked over her soul.

And in the following days—while Chelsea practiced capriccios and medieval airs under Maestro Minetti's competent tutelage, dined with the British colony, explored Pompeii and bathed in the azure sea on the beach below the villa—Sinjin sailed unmolested by corsairs and crossed the Mediterranean in a record thirty hours, journeying west with Sahar and his men from their anchorage at Gabès. Traveling at night to avoid the daytime temperatures reaching 135 degrees, they passed through the gap between the chott and the sea across the alluvium and sand dunes to Kebili. They crossed the Chott Djerid salt flats—where a caravan could sink from sight in the dangerous watery spots should it wander off the narrow path—and reached the oases of the Kriz sill on the fifth day. Tozeur and Nefta, on the very rim of the Sahara, had been trading centers since the fourth millennium of Egypt's dynasties.

Within eight miles of each other, both sites were centers of date-palm cultivation, more than seventy different varieties of dates nurtured in the sumptuous green paradise. As early as 1068, the geographer al-Bekri wrote that almost every day a thousand camels left Tozeur loaded with dates. Other merchandise from the caravan routes of central Africa passed through Tozeur and Nefta as well; Negro slaves sold there for two or three quintals of dates apiece.

The houses, artistically embellished with decorative brickwork facades, boasted cool vaulted chambers and upper stories. Roman ruins gave evidence of earlier conquerors, and Christian churches survived side by side with mosques as late as the fourteenth century; the Byzantine bell tower was now a minaret. Tozeur's 194 water springs and the 152 of Nefta ran in shimmering beauty beneath greenery and blossoms in which kingfishers and turtle-doves flitted and cooed. Peaches, apricots, bananas, plums and almonds grew in the shade of the towering palms, native orchids and flora rioted in opulent festoons. Beholding this, one understood the Arab vision of paradise as a garden.

Of the thirty thousand inhabitants of Tozeur and the thirteen thousand in Nefta, none were Europeans, and had not Sinjin been a previous visitor *and* escorted by Sahar and desert tribesmen, he would have been treated with less hospitality. But the Sultan of Tozeur and the Kaid of Nefta accepted Sinjin's gifts, offered their own lavish hospitality and, after several days of observing the courtesies of sport with their peregrines and sloughis, got down to the business of horses.

And even taking into consideration their more leisurely business practices, all was finalized in under a week, Sinjin richer by two dozen desert coursers.

While the horses were shipped back to his vessel at Gabès under Seneca's charge, Sinjin took a short detour with Sahar and his tribesmen in a sportive raid on one of the Bey's southern arsenals. A recent shipment of arms and ammunition had arrived at the fort near Mareth, and Sahar's tribesmen, in the way of warriors, considered the munitions fair game to anyone reckless enough to take them.

The fort at Mareth, only twenty miles from Gabès and thirty miles from the rim of the Sahara—where Sahar's tribesmen could disappear into the sandy wastes once the munitions were appropriated—stood on an arid sand-hill under the brooding stillness of a summer night, steaming vapor from the cooling sand and the nearby salt flats rising around it.

Rumor had it that no more than a small company of the Bey's army manned the border fort in the summer heat, the greater portion of the normal defense on furlough. Looting the small arsenal of its newest shipment of arms should be a matter of short work.

All went according to plan. These raids were routine for the desert warriors: scouts went over the wall, dispatched the few men on sentry duty and opened the main gateway to the tribesmen, who rode in to hold the soldiers at bay while the new guns were collected. The Bey's soldiers preferred not dying unnecessarily, and once they realized they were outnumbered by Sahar's tribesmen, they surrendered their arms without resistance.

It was a jovial plundering, with much boisterous repartee, and while the Bey's troops were herded into a small guard room, the fort was systematically pillaged.

All the men were heavily burdened when they rode from the fort, but they were cheerful and triumphant. And if the captain of the fort hadn't been returning from Gabès with his bodyguard after spending a pleasant evening with a beautiful Greek courtesan, the raid would have been successfully concluded.

As it was, they rode into a hastily disposed ambush. Scattering at the first sound of gunfire in the manner of desert warfare, Sahar's tribesmen bolted for the safety of the sand dunes. Several were wounded, and two horses went down; the surprise attack was effective at such close range.

The men came back to help the wounded and those unhorsed, Sinjin reaching Sahar first just as he freed himself from the stirrup leather tangled around his left foot. Leaning out of the saddle as he neared Sahar, who waited half-crouched by his downed mount, Sinjin stretched out his arm and, without slowing his horse's full-out gallop, caught Sahar's hand and swept him up behind him.

The newly plundered weapons had been jettisoned to lighten the load, and Sinjin whipped his horse to more speed.

"Make for the shore," Sahar shouted, clinging to the high saddle cantle, knowing their pursuit would be heading south.

"How far?" Sinjin cried, his voice trailing over his shoulder, his eyes straining to see through the vapors of heat rising before them. Carrying double, his mount would be at a disadvantage in speed.

"Two lieues, maybe three . . ."

But the Barb went lame under the heavy load a short distance from the gulf, and stripping off their spurs, the two men made for the coast at a swift pace, aware that a full hue and cry could rouse the authorities in Gabès in a very short time.

The *Aurora* was anchored offshore at Gabès, the harbor such that vessels must lie out a mile or more and unload on lighters. If they could reach the quay before sunrise, there was a good possibility of reaching the *Aurora* undetected.

Following the sandy shore, Sinjin and Sahar skirted the date-palm and olive plantations and made their way to the landing steps near the custom house, where boats might be hired to carry them out into the harbor. Owing to the easterly winds in the summer, the surf at the harbor was against them, but once they were away from shore, speed wasn't a necessity.

They could see the masts of the *Aurora* in the moonlight.

All appeared quiet as they approached the shore near the custom house. With an hour yet before dawn, the city slept, but both Sahar and Sinjin moved with their daggers in hand, alert to danger.

Pointing at a small sailing craft with his weapon, Sinjin motioned Sahar to follow. The two men moved toward the boat through the grey shadows cast by the larger vessels. Sinjin's hand was on the prow, about to push the boat out into the water, when four figures appeared from behind a trawler drawn up alongside. A central figure, still shrouded in shadow—only the insignia of the local kaid catching the light on his fez—stepped forward and said, "We've been waiting for you, *ferenghi*. My lord, the Kaid of Gabès, wishes you welcome."

Spinning on his heel, Sinjin turned to run, but he felt his knees give way first, as though the pistol ball that struck him had injured his legs instead of his temple. Then he felt the pain explode inside his skull as if in delayed reaction, and blood splattered into his eyes before he fell face down onto the wave-washed shore.

How cool the water felt, he thought, as though with his life in jeopardy he had nothing more pressing to consider than the temperature of the Gulf of Gabès. But shock was shutting down his brain in deference to the excruciating pain beginning to gather along his nerve endings. Before he completely lost consciousness, he pleasantly recalled bathing with Chelsea on the beach at Sorrento in equally tepid water. It was a sweet memory on which to drift into the darkness of oblivion.

He didn't even feel the kick to his head when the Kaid's man made sure their prisoner wouldn't be moving any time soon.

And when Sinjin woke two days later, he was being transported by camel caravan, bound to a litter—but gently . . . Although nothing was gentle enough to mitigate the horrendous pounding in his head; even the sunlight, filtered through the cloth tent surrounding him on the baggage camel, hurt his eyes. He shut them against the debilitating glare, but the dancing red lights in his field of vision didn't disappear, nor did the pain, until he lost consciousness again . . .

The Kaid of Gabès was presenting the *ferenghi* lord to the Bey as a personal gift, which meant he'd been sent north with a physician in attendance and servants to care for him. As slave or prisoner held for ransom, Sinjin would profit the Bey, who in turn would remember the service rendered him by his loyal servant at Gabès.

Of less importance to the Kaid with the desert *mekhazeni* a constant scourge in the southern provinces, Sahar was sold the next week at the slave market in Gabès. As it turned out, the agent who purchased him had a very rich client, and Sahar brought a tidy sum to the Kaid's exchequer.

When Sahar was delivered to a small villa in the Kasbah and entered the courtyard, a tall man rose from a chair set under a pepper tree. Walking across the paved courtyard, he thanked the agent in a rough Arabic, although the courtesy phrases were eloquent enough, and brought a further smile to the factotum's face when he handed him an additional bag of gold coins. "For your excellent information," he quietly said.

When the agent left a few moments later—after all the blessings of God and offers of health and happiness had been formally exchanged, and the courtyard door closed on the outside world—Seneca put out his hand in welcome to Sahar.

"Are you well?" he asked.

"I'm well, no broken bones. I can ride."

They both knew what he meant. "Good, we leave this evening. They've taken Sinjin to Tunis—as a gift for the Bey."

Chapter 41

Shortly after Sinjin's capture, Seneca had the horses sent to Naples on a hired ship with a message to Chelsea pertaining to their care. In the note, Seneca made no mention of Sinjin, for his information was as yet incomplete and he had no intention of alarming her.

Instead, Chelsea learned of Sinjin's captivity by accident days later while attending the Queen's conversazione at Caserta. Having escaped the twittering gossip surrounding the Queen's ladies for a moment by slipping out the terrace door, she was resting against the railing overlooking the formal gardens. Hung with twinkling Chinese lanterns, the fairylike panorama reminded her of the gardens at Seth House. And as recollections of Seth House brought thoughts of Sinjin to mind, she heard men's voices nearing, drifting over the azalea border framing the terrace.

They spoke in French, although one man's accent was heavily Andalusian. When she heard the name of the Bey of Tunis, she shamelessly eavesdropped.

"He holds an Inglaise again, my sources in Tunis advise me—and at least for now, without ransom . . ."

"Damn scoundrel!" The Frenchman's voice was peevish, his exasperation obvious. "The tyrant's word means nothing. England pays him tribute to avoid these captures—as do we."

"As does everyone. This time the prisoner is a man of title, my cousin's Moor informant tells him."

"Has the English consul been notified?"

"The Bey denies having the man."

"And no one knows his name?"

"Rumor suggests the young Duke of Seth recently here in Naples. His horses came back without him the other day."

Chelsea had stopped breathing several sentences ago as the awful realization struck her that the man they were so casually discussing could be Sinjin. She stood utterly still, her hands grasping the polished railing for support, her white muslin gown giving her the appearance of an apparition in the summer night—her thoughts as breathless and suspended as her being.

When, after what seemed an endless time, she forcibly wrenched her mind from the horror she'd overheard—as fingers frozen shut from fear have to be released one by one—she drew in a much needed breath and placed her hand over her heart to assure herself she was living still. With the ambassadors' conversation diminishing in sound as they strolled down the garden path, her mind began racing with plans.

She must return to Sorrento immediately. By morning, she could be packed and on her way to Tunis. The city was a thirty-hour run in good weather, Sinjin had said. She'd hire the fastest ship in the bay, but first she needed the British Consul General's name and letters of introduction . . . Lord, what was the name of Sinjin's factor? She couldn't remember.

All the details of leaving tumbled through her mind as she moved away from the railing and began retracing her steps down the terrace. It wasn't enough to simply arrive in Tunis; she'd need a bey's ransom in her portmanteau. So first to speak to Sir William: should she tell him the truth? He must know of the rumors. Or should she speak of her trip in leisure terms? She also needed gold from Sinjin's banker as well as information on a ship and dependable captain. *And* she would need enormous good luck. The Barbary corsairs, despite being paid tribute by most who sailed the Mediterranean, were known to overlook that nicety in their treaties when they were short of ready cash.

But her questions, when she found Sir William in the card room, were general in nature—the kind to arouse no suspicion; she said only that she was considering a short cruise around the isles near Naples. If he were aware of her plans, he'd feel obliged to dissuade her from entering the Bey's domains, for even with treaties, foreign citizens' rights were habitually overlooked by the Bey and his officials.

She left Sir William, after a brief conversation, with the names of the British and Neapolitan consuls, suggestions for sea captains who might oblige her wish for a Mediterranean "cruise" and Sir William's hastily written letter of introduction "to whom it may concern" should she decide to visit some of the adjacent isles.

She didn't mention that her idea of adjacent was thirty-some hours in a fast ship across the Mediterranean.

Very early in the morning—after a sleepless night spent in packing—Chelsea wrote a letter to be sent to her family should she not return in good time. She left detailed instructions for the Italian grooms to care for the new horses in her absence, and then sent for Sinjin's banker.

Signor Vivani's face went pale when she told him the sum she'd require, but immediately rising to the occasion, he promised the money would be dockside in under an hour. As a banker, he kept himself au courant on the latest news; Chelsea had no need to explain her reasons for traveling to Tunis. What the ambassadors knew today, Emilio had known yesterday. He offered to negotiate for the ship she required as well. Would la Duchesse be traveling alone? Impossible! He'd recommend at least a small bodyguard—ten men perhaps? Prestige counted for much in the Bey's domains while a woman alone . . . he shook his head in reproof.

"Even though British women are known for their singular eccentricities," he diplomatically declared, "the Bey recognizes wealth more readily than independence. Independence isn't a characteristic that Tunisian culture values, which explains why the Bedouins who require it live out of reach in the wasteland of the Sahara. Take a small uniformed guard, at least, and a duenna."

"I don't want duennas or bodyguards or anyone to slow me down," Chelsea protested, not wishing any unnecessary companions on a mission requiring speed and possibly stealth.

To which Emilio quietly pointed out that unless she intended to swim ashore in the dead of night, her arrival would be officially noted. The more formal her presentation, and the more consequence alluding to her retinue, the more productive her inquiries at the Dar el Bey.

With a grimace and a sigh, Chelsea deferred to his expertise. "I suppose you've dealt with the Regency before."

"We have a branch of our bank in Tunis—a very old and lovely city, by the way. I wish you time to enjoy the sights . . . perhaps later," he added with consummate sympathy. He chose not to mention that much of the bank's profits were generated by the slave trade, one of the most lucrative industries of the town—and perhaps the oldest. The early Phoenicians who first founded Tunis were famous slave traders; the whole history of Tunis was one of slavery.

Sightseeing in Tunis was so low on her list of priorities at the moment that Chelsea suspected such need would arise shortly after she became Queen of England, but she smiled politely at the man who was giving her a hundred thousand in gold and said, "Perhaps once Sinjin is safe again . . ."

"Of course. Now you intend to sail today?"

"As soon as possible. I'm packed." She said the words in such a way that Signor Vivani understood she meant immediately.

"Very well. I'll meet you in the harbor at our docks in an hour." And rising, he bowed with all the charm of a Neapolitan gentleman and swiftly left the villa.

With an efficiency that had brought his bank ledgers into a remarkable profitability, Emilio was at quayside in an hour with the needed money, a duenna, his promised bodyguard and a fleet sailing ship with a sober respectable captain at its helm.

He wished Chelsea bon voyage with a smile and several letters of introduction to his bank officials—"who will be of more use to you, Madame, than the British consul, who's obliged to consider diplomatic channels. Our bankers operate rather more efficiently.

"And if you need more gold," he added, "they will advise you who to bribe most effectively. The machinery of government in Arab countries is typically run on bribes—openly and without disapproval."

Thus armed with advice, money, official and unofficial letters, Chelsea entered Tunis's harbor, Foum-el-Qued, the next afternoon. As she sailed up the flamingo-haunted El-Bahira, the lake of Tunis, where the fishermen's barques with their ruddy painted sails looked like flamingos themselves, she sensed she was passing through a gate into the Orient.

The temperature was an idyllic seventy-five; the city rose before her on the western hills, glistening white under the golden sun of summer, fifty mosques and five hundred minarets like so many decorative baubles strewn across the cityscape. The scent of roses and jasmine perfumed the air, the former abloom in gardens and courtyards and belvederes, the latter the scent of choice for the natives of the city. The making of perfume was an aristocratic profession, and fragrance not only perfumed the air but scented cigarettes and coffees, sweetmeats and cushions, saddles and tea.

On the quays, all nations and colors met—Arabs, Berbers, Negroes, Europeans, wealthy and poor, businessmen, porters, sailors. Their clothing was as exotic: spotless burnouses in the most delicate light shades of yellow, blue, pale green and salmon, baggy riding breeches, plain haiks of brown camel's hair. And all paused in their business when Chelsea stepped onto the quay. A woman alone, no matter how guarded, was an unusual sight in the Regency of the Bey.

Refusing to be intimidated by the male stares, Chelsea politely acknowledged the European bows but didn't stop, taking her duenna and bodyguard—each cohort plumed and uniformed and bedecked with medals—directly from the Bab-el-Behara, the Sea-gate of the Beys, up the Souk-el Attarin to the Dar el Bey, where the ruler of Tunis held court in the city. She was admitted to the first audience chamber, a spectacular courtyard roofed in glass, the walls and floor embellished with antique mosaics, Kairouan carpets of softest silk piled on the floors in rainbows of gem-rich colors . . . Peep holes for surreptitious viewing of the audience chamber were concealed in the splendid arabesques decorating the throne area.

"But unfortunately," the Bey's chamberlain informed her, "the Bey is currently indisposed."

With unctuous mendacity, he professed grievance at having to respond to her request for an audience in the negative. As to her missing husband, with a shrug and a smile he informed her that no one in the Bey's kingdom would abduct a British citizen. His face a mask of deceit, his eyes cool and distant, he left unsaid the Moslem disregard for females. But an impudent rudeness underlay his words, and with a minimal bow of his crimson fez, he ended the audience and withdrew.

Frustrated, although she'd expected no more, Chelsea went next to the British Consul General, who promised to reiterate her demands for an audience; he would also see if he could gather any information on her husband or his factor's whereabouts. Deferential and sympathetic, he offered condolences. "The Bey is an autocrat to whom civilized rules of conduct mean nothing. But rest assured, Madame Duchess, whatever power we possess is at your service."

Emilio Vivani's uncle and cousins at the Banco di Napoli were in a position to offer more than sympathy. During the short period of time Chelsea had been at the palace and consulate, the ship's captain had delivered a note from Emilio outlining the Duchess of Seth's dilemma, and the Vivanis had compiled a list of likely officials who at least could give them information on whether or not Sinjin was in residence at Tunis—whether he was alive or dead, they privately reflected, although they chose their words more carefully when speaking to his wife.

And while Chelsea took tea with the Vivanis and discussed the style of pressure likely to be useful at the Bey's court, Hamouda, the Bey of Tunis, was smoking his narghile pipe while his chamberlain stood at attention near his silk-cushioned divan. The Bey's private reception room overlooked a courtyard at whose center was an azure pool aplay with numerous fountains, scented by gardens lush with Persian roses.

"Who is the female with golden hair who comes to demand audience?" the Bey languidly inquired, his view of Chelsea from behind the arabesques of the throne dais having intrigued him. Pale women, so rare in Ifrikya, generally found their way into his harem; he was already considering her as a beautiful addition to the seraglio at his Bardo palace.

"Her name escapes me," his personal minister said with a shrug of his shoulder, women being of no consequence in the Moslem world. "An Inglitz."

"She's being followed?" Less embellished than his chamberlain, who was obliged to be recognizably splendid in the crimson and green brocaded djebba of state, the Bey dressed simply in white linen for the summer heat.

"Of course, Your Excellency."

"Will she be here by evening? Golden hair fascinates me . . . ." The Bey inhaled the cooled kif, his eyes shutting for a moment while the poetic pale image of Chelsea filled his mind.

"If possible, my lord. She has bodyguards."

The Bey's eyes opened to narrow slits, not in anger but in lethargy. "Call out the army," he murmured, a man of infinite power in his kingdom.

"Yes, my lord," the minister replied. Contradiction was unknown in the Bey's presence, but he'd prefer a less conspicuous abduction. Although the European powers rarely exerted their political and naval strength to regain a hostage—and, to his knowledge, never for a female, preferring to pay ransom—the minister considered calling out the army to kidnap a woman for the Bey's harem unduly notorious. Tunis was an ancient city of convoluted intricacy. Because of the heavy traffic and narrow streets, even no horses were allowed beyond the gates. All merchandise had to be carried by hand from the port. How easy it would be to separate the lady from her bodyguard in the press of congestion so typical in the Bey's capital city.

Shortly before nine, Chelsea set off for dinner at the British consulate, accompanied by her guard, retainers from the British Consul General and an escort from the Vivanis. No more than ten minutes separated the two residences; the summer moon was full, although seldom visible in the covered passageways, and torchbearers lighted the way through the crowded lanes.

The chamberlain couldn't have planned a more perfect scenario.

Chelsea disappeared between the Café Hamma and the Bab Menara, when a noisy struggle between several men erupted in the doorway of the café, spilled out into the shadowed street and blundered into the formation guarding Chelsea.

In the blink of an eye, she was gone.

A moment later, when the melee quieted, Giacomo Vivani swiftly searched the press of bodyguards for Chelsea, his glance turning frantic after a quick perusal of the street bordering the Kasbah found her missing. He swore in a steady flow of invective directed at the Bey, his fluency in seven languages exhausted before he sighed in thwarted frustration. How expensive if not *impossible* would it be to extricate a woman from the Bey's harem?

At the same time that Chelsea, trussed and gagged, was being carried through the streets of Tunis, Sinjin, tied spread-eagled against the wall of the punishment cell at the Bardo, was being taught compliance by the Bey's torturer.

The crapaudine, in which a man was left in the inhospitable summer heat for two or three days without food or water, was normally effective in teaching obedience.

And if the Bey wanted the Inglitz for stud, stud he would be—if not sooner, then . . . later.

Inshallah—if it please Allah—and he didn't die.

Chapter 42

Which fact—dying—felt like a real possibility at the moment, Sinjin hazily considered. Was this the second night or the third since he'd been tied to this wall? He tried to remember, but his mind floated off into unconsciousness whenever the necessity for clear thinking pressed unduly on his fragile grasp of reality. The soles of his feet were on fire, thanks to a hundred lashes of the bastinado. It was a strange sensation, when he had no intermediate feeling in his legs, as if the excruciating pain flowed directly to his brain.

His tongue was swollen from lack of water so it filled his mouth; his skin so burned that when he last saw his arm and hand, the flesh was flame red. His failing vision had finally shut down—yesterday or was it a month ago? He couldn't say. Nothing but blackness greeted him now when he lifted the swollen lids of his eyes.

Or was his blindness part of the nightmare, and the fragments of sight he'd been slowly losing since his beating at Gabès only part of the delirium? He tried to force his brain into some semblance of deductive reasoning—a concept so far removed from his abilities at the moment that, had his body any moisture left, he would have cried.

Then the dream that sustained him from completely giving up his will to live drifted back into his mind . . . paradise . . . Chelsea riding in a lush green landscape, a pond on the horizon, a bubbling creek running through a grassy meadow . . . her smile beckoning him in its beauty. He spoke her name, although the utterance was no more than a croak of sound from his parched throat.

"He's not dead," the prison guard casually said as Sinjin lay in a heap of sunburned flesh at his feet. He'd thought him beyond even Allah's help when they'd cut him down and he'd made no sound.

"Perhaps the minister will reward us," the Bey's chief torturer remarked, a note of cheer in his voice. He too had considered the prisoner past reviving. "But Mahmoud said three days—"

"The *ferenghis* with white skin never last three days," his companion bluntly noted. "Mahmoud should know better."

"Perhaps he didn't want him to live," the huge Turk, Imir, remarked, clearly in a quandary. All of their lives hung precariously at the whims of the Bey and his ministers.

"You did your duty as directed," the guard who was assisting the torturer pointed out.

The Turk hesitated for a moment. "Take him to the infirmary," he said, "while I check the minister's wishes. The doctor can kill him, if necessary, more easily than I."

But not only did the minister intend Sinjin to live, it became clear as the days progressed, he intended him to live in a great deal of comfort. Sinjin's healing body was ministered to by a staff of minions; his food was fit for the Bey himself, and his apartments—which he investigated without the servants' objection in a slow if sightless perusal—appeared to be lavish and sumptuous.

He chose not to dwell on the fact that his torture had accomplished its mission. On the first day of his hospital stay, when the intensity of his pain allowed him only moments of lucidity, the minister of the household had asked him whether he had changed his mind during the days in the crapaudine.

A diplomat, the minister didn't overtly require Sinjin to agree in detail to the Bey's demands. He simply asked Sinjin for a yes or no answer.

The answer would dictate whether he lived or died, Sinjin knew, and even as he raged at his weakness in not accepting death, he answered yes. He was very young, in love with his wife, and beneath the awful physical helplessness he felt, a singular hope for future freedom dwelled in his heart.

So he said yes . . . thinking his answer conditional in his soul.
So he said yes . . . hoping to live to regain his liberty.
He said yes . . . with the poignant wish to meet his wife again.

The Bey inquired into his prisoner's health often in the following week, his impatience the result of news that his brother Hamet had recently been sighted in Kairouan. The old capital of Tunis, Kairouan was still the religious center of the Regency, and Hamet was there consolidating his position as heir to Hamouda's throne. While the Koran stipulated inheritance through the eldest brother, numerous exceptions to the rule had occurred throughout the Moslem world during the past two centuries, and Hamouda preferred that his son inherit—not his brother who had wished him dead the past decade or more.

And the *ferenghi* lord who had appeared like a gift from Allah— although the Kaid of Gabès had been God's instrument—would become his means of thwarting Hamet. Although the lord was a man of great physical strength, Allah had conspicuously devised a means of making the *ferenghi* blind on the day of his arrival.

What better sign from Allah that Hamouda's plan had the blessings of the Almighty? What more significant mark of His approval could have been presented?

The *ferenghi* lord would be the means of impregnating his harem —a sightless man who wouldn't violate the law against other men viewing the women of his household. The *ferenghi* lord would be the means of securing his throne against his brother. The *ferenghi* lord had been sent by Allah.

Bey Hamouda chose to overlook the fact that Allah's help would not have been needed if he hadn't been unmanned by his excessive use of opium.

No one in the K'sar Said answered Chelsea's questions; no one responded to her anger—neither the women in the harem, who understood the futility of her rage, nor the eunuchs, who in serving the Bey were indifferent to her feelings.

Women existed to service men, a fact that the infidel woman would do well to come to terms with. In the meantime, the eunuchs took measures to drug her food sufficiently to quiet her tantrums. And Chelsea existed for the next fortnight in a lethargy of half sleep, her mind reluctant to do her bidding.

· · ·

The inquiries of the Consul General and the Vivanis at the Dar el Bey met with a stone wall of unconcern. As no officer of the law might violate a harem, when anyone disappeared in a Muhammadan country, the harem system rendered a search impossible. One could be kept a prisoner for life. With frustration and the wisdom of past experience, the Vivanis and the British Consul General began the delicate negotiations for ransom.

Sahar and Seneca, after reconnoitering the environs of the Bardo with the help of Ali Ahmed, discovered that Sinjin still lived, and they sent a messenger south to gather the men necessary to storm the Bey's seraglio. And while they waited, they planned their rescue mission. As warriors, they were disinclined to endure the lengthy period necessary to ransom a hostage. Too many prisoners had languished in the prisons of the Barbary Coast for years while the negotiations proceeded at a snail's pace.[15] Sinjin would expect more haste. He would have done as much for them.

But the day came, while the desert horsemen were still assembling at Djeneien, when Sinjin was sufficiently healed to serve in the capacity for which the Bey had spared his life. And he went in anger and violent emotions, arriving at the first room on the first day of his servitude like some enraged pagan god. And that wildness excited the dissolute Bey like nothing before in his life of ennui and dissipation.

Sinjin St. John—as surrogate for the seed of Hamouda, His Highness the Bey, Possessor of the Kingdom of Tunis—became a nightly diversion of fanatical interest for the impotent ruler.

Chapter 43

Sinjin stood just inside the room, noting the sound of the door quietly closing behind him, knowing that his escort of palace guards remained outside. He was always struck with anger at this point, the heat of resentment coursing through his body at his yoke of servitude. The extent of his subjection stung his pride, and each night as he serviced the Bey's harem, he cursed his captivity.

That anger translated into a high-mettled turbulence, a fevered restlessness the Bey took advantage of. And Pasha Hamouda goaded Sinjin in small sly ways when he had him brought in each afternoon to acquaint him with his night's duties. That repressed violence, kept tractable by Imir's talented whip, was of supreme benefit to the Pasha's concubines, for Sinjin performed his function with a fierce power that brought the man-starved residents of the Bey's seraglio to frenzied climax.

And in terms of breeding, Hamouda understood that a *heurmak*, a fiery stallion, begot strong sons.

Chelsea heard the door opening and closing, and the whisper of a man's footfall. Compelled by threats of death, she had capitulated at last—no other course offered if she chose to live. Now she lay on the Bey's silken divan—an object, an offering, no longer in charge of her soul. She'd been warned against speaking; the Bey tolerated no conversation from the houris who served merely as vessels for his seed. And the murmured stories of labia branded as punishment for those foolish enough to speak served as potent threat. She'd heard other whispers too, of a *ferenghi* milord in the harem, a bull of mythological proportions whose physical prowess was anticipated with delight. But when she'd questioned the odalisques, they'd only smiled or giggled. So she discounted their gossip as typical for women deprived of all male company except their master. As the recognized odalisque tonight, the receptacle for the Bey's seed, she shivered in apprehension. The Bey was determined to get an heir, and to this purpose in the last month, he had systematically made use of his houris, concentrating on the newest and youngest.

The entire day had been devoted to the preparation of the women selected for the Bey's nightly pleasures. Chelsea had been steamed and scrubbed; she'd had *rusma* applied to her skin to remove all the hair from her body. It was considered a sin to have hair on one's private areas, so harem women removed hair, not only from their legs and underarms, but from all body crevices, even nostrils. After being thoroughly washed by slave girls, she'd been moved to the tepidarium, where she'd been massaged, scraped and pumiced. Rinsed one last time with perfumed water, her skin smooth, satiny and aglow, Chelsea had been left to rest while a slave poured cologne on her hair and braided it with pearls and ribbons.

Food was brought to her next: sweetmeats, delicately perfumed sherbet and sliced melon. When she'd finished eating, her hands had been washed in cologne water. Exhausted from the heat of the baths, she fell into a luxurious slumber beneath a coverlet of lilac satin.

And now she was the night's sacrifice, perfumed and pampered, a receptacle to provide the Bey with a male heir. *Woman is a field, a sort of property that a husband may use or abuse as he sees fit,* said the Koran.

Sinjin could feel the warm night air drifting in through the filigreed windows as he walked toward the couch, his senses more acute since his eyesight had failed. And beneath the heavy scent of jasmine and musk and patchouli, he caught a fresh skin fragrance, one he'd never smelled in the harem. He stopped for a moment near the couch—he knew exactly how many steps there were from the door to the bed—lifted his head and stood very still. But the curious odor was gone a moment later as a wave of ambergris incense struck his nostrils.

He dropped his robe on the floor in a soft rustle of fabric and stood patiently waiting for the manipulation that would prepare him to carry out the Bey's orders, no longer fighting his utilitarian function after the Bey's special means of persuasion. His back bore the scars of his occasional resistance, and the Bey's murmured words echoed through his mind whenever he considered rebellion: "I can wait, my fine English lord, and my torturer enjoys his work. When you're ready to do my bidding . . . tell my chamberlain."

He had—after a week of resistance.

Usually the woman that he was to service brought him to readiness with a carnal expertise learned in the harem, but there was no movement on the bed this time. Tonight, in contrast, a woman knelt beside him. He felt her hand on his penis first, and then her mouth. His eyes shut against his body's betrayal as she sucked and massaged, his erection quickly lengthening, pulsing hard and rigid and engorged under her talented skills.

"You are ready, my lord," a soft voice said in Arabic, and a small sound indicated her rising. A gentle hand turned him toward the bed, and feeling the cushioned border of the harem divan against his legs, he knelt on the couch and moved over the woman, waiting to feel her hands welcome him and guide him in. The Bey's houris were always anxious for his services after their lengthy sexual abstinence. The Bey's need for kif, the ultimate fulfillment induced by opium, had enervated his libido. When Sinjin had become the Pasha's surrogate, the protracted wait for his services in a harem of such size induced a certain frenzied impatience.

But this time no welcoming hands came up to guide him. He reached out to determine the exact position of the first odalisque he was to mate with that night. As his hands brushed the woman's shoulder, he realized she was lying tense and unyielding, her arms flung out to either side. Speculating on this restraint when he was generally greeted with impassioned eagerness, Sinjin slid his fingers up the length of one arm.

She was tied, he discovered, astonished. His hand circled the silk cord binding her wrist, and quickly seeking her other hand, he found that wrist similarly secured.

A reluctant houri. Extraordinary. She must be very young and very newly bought. But he dared not speak to calm her fears, for he'd been taught the lesson of silence well with Imir's whip and the crapaudine.

Chelsea scarcely breathed as the man's hand glided over her, her senses taut with dread, the Bey's dispassionate request ringing in her ears. "I have need of you tonight. The eunuchs will come for you at eight." He'd spoken to her as she'd come out of the bath, surrounded by his black eunuchs. His dark eyes assessed her but were untouched by feeling. During the remainder of the day, she'd been readied for his bed. Dressed and ornamented in silk and pearls, she'd been made to drink an elixir that was said to guarantee that the Bey's seed would bear fruit in her body.

A smothered whimper broke the silence, although Chelsea had tried to suppress it, images of the Bey's corpulent body and cold dark eyes striking terror in her soul. How would she endure his touch? How did the others find it possible to smile when they returned from their conjugal unions with the Bey? How humiliating it was to be bound, a slave to the carnal whims of an old man. Suppressing the second cry rising in her throat, the harem warnings too graphic to ignore, she cringed against the cool silk of the coverlet.

Sinjin touched her face gently when she cried out, the pads of his fingers lightly tracing her features. She was blindfolded, like all the women, in order to maintain the fiction of the Bey's presence. His fingers drifted over her eyebrows, passed over her temples—where her pulse beat violently—then glided over the supple smoothness of her cheek. His fingers found her mouth next, her lips slightly parted as her breath came in the shallow rapid respiration of fear.

His gentle touch bewildered her. Chelsea was mystified by the puzzling incongruity. The Bey was not a gentle man; reared in a society in which dominance was sustained by force of arms and military intimidation, Pasha Hamouda seemed incapable of such tenderness. And in the weeks since her capture, she'd seen him dispatch two men to their deaths with striking indifference.

Sinjin caught a flurry of that familiar fragrance again, and he bent his head, as an animal would, to gather the odor more closely into his nostrils.

How could it be?

No . . . of course it wasn't. His wife was hundreds of miles away in Naples. He'd been thinking of her too often lately; his mind was playing tricks on him. Forcibly thrusting aside the impossible notion, he reminded himself cynically that he was there to stand as surrogate for the Bey, and if he didn't, Imir's whip would jog his sense of obligation.

He had a job to do.

The Bey was watching from his usual vantage point behind the carved and gilded *mashrabeyah* screen. Sinjin knew he was, for the Bey commented on various particulars of Sinjin's performance at their daily meeting. So Sinjin salaamed to him—a small insolence, the only one he allowed himself with the Turk always ready to subdue insolence. Then he stepped from the bed to untie the woman's hands.

Once Sinjin had been tamed, he was well cared for; like an expensive stallion at stud, he was attentively fed, his diet rich in eggs, chick-peas, fresh green asparagus buds and camel's milk with honey to promote a prodigious volume of sperm. He was given plenty of rest and pampered with the luxury of his own suite. The skin of his back, arms and legs had healed from the burns and the whip; only the scars bore testimony to his recalcitrance. Now he stood, tall and powerful in the lamplight, his long hair sleek on his shoulders, his erection beautifully formed . . . a perfect specimen in conformation and stamina to impregnate the Pasha's women. Three women lay waiting for him each night, and he never failed to discharge his duty.

Feeling for the terminus of the ropes, he found them fastened to rings on the wall behind the bed, and he swiftly untied the woman's hands. Moving to the bottom of the sofa, he found—as he'd suspected from her stillness—that her feet were tied as well.

A slight flurry of movement indicated the lady's shifting of position once she was freed. When he seated himself on the small divan a moment later, he found her huddled up against the wall.

"The lady is new and must be readied," he'd been told before he'd entered the room, but he hadn't realized *how* new *and* reluctant. Bey Hamouda must be anxious to see her bedded: he hadn't given her harem companions time to educate the young girl in her role.

But he had to entertain her—if such a word could be employed with this terrified woman—no excuses allowed, and with two more women waiting to receive him, time was a consideration. So reaching out to draw her near, his hands closed on her upper arms; exerting pressure, he slid her toward him on the silk coverlet, the slither of sound magnified in the utter silence of the room.

He wanted to comfort her, if that were possible in this monstrously abnormal circumstance, but both understood the injunction against talking. The Bey liked his voyeuristic entertainments undisturbed by sounds other than those of lovemaking, and of course, the command against speaking curtailed the possibility of any friendship developing between his surrogate and odalisques.

To have another man service his harem was unorthodox—but if the Bey didn't have an heir, his hated brother would succeed him. Against that despicable possibility, the Pasha intended to get himself an heir.[16] That Sinjin was sightless mitigated the powerful taboo against another man's gazing upon his women.

Lord, how much time did he have to coax a cowering woman into a degree of incitement necessary for his entry into her? Sinjin wondered. And then, more cynically, he wondered if the Bey had introduced this woman into the nightly repertoire in order to whet his own jaded appetites.

Damnation. This wasn't leisurely lovemaking in some lady's boudoir, where he could take unlimited time to seduce. Did the Bey anticipate instead a ravishment? Was he hoping for a scene of violence? Sinjin allowed himself a small rueful sigh and acknowledged there might indeed be a retributive god. And he was paying atonement for all his previous carnal sins in this bizarre, self-mortifying exercise.

But the terrified lady needn't suffer for his regrettable lapses. His hands lifted to frame her face, and he bent his head to kiss her. He could at least attempt to alleviate her fear with a semblance of tenderness. She tried to draw away, but he held her firmly between his palms, lowering his mouth to hers. He tasted vanilla on her mouth, a sweet lingering suggestion of the elixir she'd been given. He recognized the flavor and wondered briefly whether this reluctant young woman would bear his child.

He hadn't been the Bey's harem stud long enough to have heard whether the Bey's enterprise had proved successful, only two weeks having passed in this nightly game. But he would know shortly, if indeed he would ever be told, and after Hamouda's needed sons were born, he expected, his usefulness would cease.

He'd lain awake many nights in his suite, once he'd decided not to die under Imir's perversity, forced to make merciless decisions. He found that he wanted to live . . . that his impulse for survival was stronger than the Bey's destructive demands, stronger too than conscience or propriety. And a damnably buoyant hope had fortified him —pipe dreams of a reunion with Chelsea. Now that it was ages too late, he'd discovered—with a simplicity at odds with his Byzantine environment and duties—how very deeply he loved his wife.

It was a startling revelation for a man of the beau monde, and an unprosperous one considering his imprisonment and future. But memories of happier times sustained him at his blackest periods of despair, and occasional glimmers of light gave him hope his eyesight might be restored.

If a blow on the head had slowly brought on his affliction, could not the reverse transpire in the same way? He kept that hope alive as a child wished for unlikely things—with faith and trust and determined belief.

She was quivering beneath his touch, her mouth soft, her terror a tangible presence between them. *Hush,* he wanted to say, *I won't hurt you,* but he couldn't, so he tried instead with his kiss to comfort and soothe. His mouth lifted a fraction and his tongue traced the curve of her upper lip, then the fullness of her lush lower one, before he exerted the slightest pressure on her mouth. It was a butterfly kiss, as a young boy might give. His hands swept back into the silkiness of her hair, touched the ornamental pearls braided around her crown, wound through the length of the silken tresses flowing down her back.

He felt the soft skin of her back beneath the filmy volume of her hair and was struck with a subtle sense of recognition. The Circassian women favored in the harems had heavy dark hair, not gossamer angel hair. But he immediately pushed such wild thoughts away and quickly lifted the woman onto his lap, where he could reach her better and more easily arouse her.

She jerked away as her hip brushed his erection, and Sinjin wondered whether she was just a child. If she was, he couldn't despoil her regardless of Imir's punishments. In his need to know what trickery the Bey might have conceived, his hands quickly sought the curve of her shoulder and, moving downward, glided over the fullness of her breasts. Sliding around their flared outside curves, his hands swept downward to cup her breasts in his palms. He lifted their heaviness for a moment as if in consideration, and then his hands released her.

No child here. These were a woman's breasts, voluptuous, firm, smooth as silk to the touch.

Whose hands were these, Chelsea suddenly thought, their gentleness familiar, and whose strong thighs cradled her bottom? The Bey was short and old and debauched by his opium. Were the harem whispers true? Was there a *ferenghi* lord after all? It shouldn't have calmed her so to know she was simply captive to another man, but spontaneous relief flooded through her mind at that knowledge.

Anyone would be preferable to the Bey, she impulsively thought, as if she'd been given reprieve from a death sentence. And while such unnatural consolation should have scandalized her sense of propriety, she decided that in her present circumstances she would take comfort where she could. Propriety wasn't going to save her from submission, nor from her captivity. She was entirely on her own.

Curiosity overcame her unexpectedly, and if she hadn't been thoroughly cowed by the tales of recrimination by the Bey's torturer, she would have ripped off the bindings covering her eyes. Which thought substantiated her conjecture. If this man was truly the Bey, why would he insist on blindfolds? The Lord of Tunis came into the harem often, his person openly visible to all.

Sinjin was startled to feel the lady's fingers on his face. She'd hardly moved, so her touch surprised him, but he allowed her exploration with his blessings. If knowing what he looked like would lessen her fear, he was pleased to accommodate her.

Her fingers gently read each feature, lingering for a moment on his lips, and when she felt him smile, her fingertip delicately traced the upward curve.

As if in speech, he moved his hand to her mouth and found there the most tentative of answering smiles. And a faint pleasure surprised his senses, which were normally immune to any delicacy of feeling during these nightly rituals. His mouth followed to taste her vanilla-scented lips, and when he exerted the pressure necessary to open her mouth to his, she consented.

That small victory pleased him out of all proportion, even knowing they were no more than mating animals for an impotent voyeur. In contrast to the voracious sexual appetites and amorous expertise of the harem houris he'd serviced, she was enchantingly different.

He teased her with his tongue in a lazy arousal until she answered him, until her breathing changed the smallest trifle, and her shoulders under his hands lost their rigidity. He lifted her hands from her lap then and placed them lightly on his shoulders. She allowed them to be moved without resistance, and he felt that acquiescence pulse through his erection.

He could abhor his body's impelling urges, but he had no control over those impulses once he was brought to arousal by the odalisques. And had he turned away with stern self-restraint, the ever watchful Bey would have taken offense.

Sensation was more acute in the quiet of the room, in the closed world he now lived in, and when he gently squeezed the nipple of the lady who now welcomed his caresses, the sound of her small gasp touched a nerve.

She shouldn't be feeling these trembling sensations, Chelsea thought, this warming of her blood, the shudder of arousal, caused by a man she couldn't see and didn't know. Was she becoming as erotically focused as the other women in the harem, who spent their days dreaming of love? But his warm mouth closed on her nipple, and a shocking heat replaced speculation in her mind as he sucked gently at first and then more firmly. A mild cantharis had been placed in her sherbet (although she didn't know of it), heightening sensation, adding an urgency to her sexual response, causing a hot, molten desire to melt through her body. And she felt the warm lubricant of desire where the man's powerful thighs met her flesh.

She tried to move then, appalled at her yielding, but he wouldn't let her go, nor would he release the hardened bud of her nipple from his mouth. His arms imprisoned her, his large palms splayed across her back and she cried out then as a thrill of rapture streaked from the pressure of his mouth to her vulva.

Her cry could have been heard in a chorus and he would have known it, for that same bewitching sound of passion had echoed at Oakham and Hatton and London. Even as his head lifted, his rational mind discounted the outrageous truth. Until a moment later, as his hands ran over her body, unbelieving, he felt his heart stop. He knew each curve and volume and tactile sensation intimately, her image reconstructed by his searching fingers. And he was wretchedly struck at the horrendous extent of her danger.

She had come for him, he knew without a doubt, and if he hadn't known he loved her before, he would have surely then. She was here beside him, he thought for a blinding moment of happiness before the enormity of her peril overwhelmed him.

And a kind of terror he'd never felt before—even in his worst moments under Imir's evil ministrations—inundated his soul at the thought of Chelsea in such capricious captivity. The Bey had been known to have his houris killed if they displeased him in any inconsequential way, and each moment she existed in his seraglio was one of danger.

"I'm impatient." Although the Bey's voice was softly slurred, its autocratic command was unmistakable.

Chelsea went rigid, a terrified shiver chilling her body.

Manner the eleventh, Sinjin thought, his orders for the positions from *The Perfumed Garden* specifically defined each evening.[17] And he hadn't engaged the lady swiftly enough for his jaded master. The fact that the Bey spoke indicated either extreme annoyance or an excess of opium, neither mental state likely to be cordial.

While Sinjin's mind struggled to come to terms with all that had happened, he automatically reached for one of the large cushions propped at the head of the divan. Manner the eleventh could no longer be delayed.

He kissed Chelsea with a fierce passion that spoke for all the tumult of his feelings, even while he understood how dangerous it was to reveal his emotions. Her mouth opened under his and she moaned softly at the hard pressure. He lifted her then so the Bey would be entertained. And her life wouldn't be at risk.

Laying her on the silk coverlet, he lifted her bottom enough to slide the satin cushion beneath her, and he spread her thighs so her pouty vulva was prominently displayed. Moving between her legs, he stroked the mounded fullness of her breasts, slid his hands upward to the slender column of her throat and, leaning forward, kissed her parted lips.

His erection lay hard against her belly, and she rose up into it as he kissed her, the drugs in her bloodstream arousing her, the feel of his rigid manhood rousing her, the penetration of his tongue into her mouth suggesting a consummation she craved.

With her eyes closed against the heated sensations flaming through her body, she reached down to touch him. But when her fingers grazed the crest of his erection, he moved out of her reach. The Bey liked his women to beg—the only words he permitted. He liked subjugation to the authority of the male; he liked prolongation until the woman was completely submissive.

Foreplay didn't interest the Bey, and with the harem women so anxious to be mounted, that style of delayed pleasure was hardly required. But a supplicating woman was necessary to gratify his brutish instincts, so Sinjin had to tease and withhold as a means of discipline—another means of female repression for the Bey's reprobate soul.

What generally happened was the odalisque climaxed before he entered her, so her orgasm was less complete, less satisfying, than had she been impaled on his lance. And then she would beseech and implore Sinjin to give her relief, to drive into her quivering sweetness, her crying words and her pleading entreaties the drama required by her master the Bey.

And did she obey Sinjin's commands, promptly, meekly, in total submission, she would be rewarded. The word wasn't his, but that of the Lord of Tunis.

Long ago, as a very young man, Sinjin had learned *imsak,* the special art of delaying male orgasm; able to control his discharge, he could remain vigorous and hard for as long as the Bey desired each melodrama to last.

But tonight the enactment of the familiar scenario seemed an intolerable burden, and heedless of the strictures on speech, he whispered with a breath of sadness for what he must do, "Forgive me."

"Sinjin!" Chelsea's small sound bespoke exaltation, the glorious end of her quest, all the curiosities of the evening explained in a rush of comprehension.

Her body had known.

Her senses had known.

The lightest touch of the man she loved had been recognized by her flesh, welcomed as no one else would be . . . could be. Her arms laced tightly around his neck and she clung to him mutely, for she understood how even *more* dangerous communication was now.

If the Bey knew they were husband and wife, their lives were forfeit.

Sinjin held heaven in his arms, although the blackest of blackguard abysses stood ready to swallow them. "You must beg me now," Sinjin breathed into her ear, a signal, a cryptic warning, all he dared explain.

And she did . . . as she would have without his cue, for her body was burning with desire, her passion greedy, her need of him unsated.

"Please . . . Lord of my Need, come inside me," she pleaded, reaching for the hard length of him.

But he retreated beyond her reach and kissed her lightly.

"You must be humble," he murmured, setting her hands at her sides, his voice raised enough to reach their small audience.

"Humble me, my lord, I will be in all things agreeable to you. I am ripe fruit for you to eat, if you but taste me . . ." And she reached out again for his shoulders to pull him close.

"If your vulva is not sufficiently sweet and fleshy," Sinjin gently chided, "how can I taste you?" Sitting back on his heels, he ran his fingers over the swollen dampness between her thighs as her sex lay open to him, raised high on the pillow for easy penetration.

She shut her eyes against the shuddering ecstasy his touch induced and whispered in a voice heedless now of everything but her need, "Enter me, my lord . . . and see . . . I'm ready for you . . . I'm aching for want of you . . ."

Sinjin's slender finger glided across her aroused flesh, the fluid of her desire slippery under his touch, and he stretched the opening slightly with a small pressure, as though testing its dimension and compatibility. "You seem to be . . . nearly . . ." He slid two fingers inside her a small distance and watched her hips rise to take them in more deeply. "Ready," he finished, penetrating her heated tightness until his long fingers disappeared inside her.

Feeling her trembling contractions begin as he stroked her slick interior, he pressed down on her mons with his other hand as her orgasmic scream began.

Enormously less submissive than the harem women, Chelsea gave a shattering cry that filled the room, pierced the Bey's opium-hazed mind, exploded through the boredom in his brain like a meteor shower, grabbed his jaded senses with a riveting attention.

Swiftly positioning himself between Chelsea's legs, Sinjin entered her just as her last sighing breath fell away, his enormous arousal forcing her passage. She tried to stop him momentarily, for her body wasn't ready yet to accept the intensity of another arousal.

"No," she said, placing her hands on his chest. "Not yet, please . . ."

"Are you begging me?" Sinjin murmured, continuing inexorably to fill her pulsing cleft, ignoring her words, her importuning hands.

"Yes, I'm begging . . ." Chelsea pleaded, trying to retreat backward on the satin pillow, her nerves still hypersensitive.

"You must yield . . ." His voice, deep and low, compelled her.

"No . . ." she protested still, but a small heat began deep inside her, and her utterance drifted away on a hushed sigh.

She had no choice, nor did he, in this command performance, and with a methodical deliberation, Sinjin reached for her ankles. Twining her legs around his waist, he placed the soles of her feet together, rendering her passage more open to his assault. "A woman must surrender to a man," he said, as a mullah might quote the Koran. And he drove in powerfully, no longer restraining his penetration.

"I surrender," Chelsea breathed as the swollen crest of Sinjin's erection pressed hard against her trembling womb, and intoxicating sensation burned like flame through her body.

He moved then, controlled, proficient at his work. And she followed him, the carnal dance begun, and the rhythm of their desire matched as it had so often in the past, the fit of their bodies perfection, their emotions so feverish and violent that both forgot for transient moments the hideous circumstances of their imprisonment.

Chelsea wept at the end, tears of joy and ecstasy, tears flowing from the fullness of her heart, tears impelled by trembling fear of exposure now that she'd found her love again—alive. The chaos and tumult and dizzy insanity of happiness and fear overflowed, and she cried and sobbed in a great outpouring of emotion.

Her poignant tears broke her husband's heart, and he crushed her to him as though his body and love could surround her, protect her, comfort her. And he seriously considered, for a fleeting moment, trying to find the Bey behind the screen and choking him to death.

But life was too precious now, its precariousness beyond description. If he'd wanted to live even at the very nadir of despair, how could he describe his indescribable need to live now? He held his dear, beloved wife in his arms, if even for a few stolen moments. His wildest dreams had come true.

"Wonderful. Exquisite. Praise be given to God, who has placed man's greatest pleasure in the natural parts of woman," the Bey intoned, moved as never before by a performance. "Tomorrow you will entertain me again." And he rose heavily from his chair, his opium eating causing a sluggish lethargy.

At the unusual sound of his movement, Sinjin quickly withdrew from Chelsea's body and, pulling her into a sitting position, covered her with a silk sheet. Why was the Bey moving from his chair?

"The *ferenghi* woman has glorious hair," the Bey said, walking unsteadily into the room. "Like sunshine in the morning. Does it feel warm?"

At the Bey's indication that he might touch Chelsea, Sinjin came to his feet, putting Chelsea behind him, his stance protective.

The Bey chuckled as he approached, in good spirits after the magnificence of his entertainment. The two slaves mated with a fiery attraction, like a satyr and a nymph. "See the stallion guard his harem mare," the Bey waggishly said. "Look, my golden flower, at this blind stallion."

Blind! Chelsea ripped off the silk covering from her eyes and looked up at Sinjin, who stood between herself and the amused Bey. She thought that the room had been in darkness and he hadn't known her at first, or that he'd feigned ignorance for her protection. But he was blind!

She forced herself to show no emotion.

"Do you like him?" the Bey inquired, his expression still wreathed in smiles.

"If it pleases you, my lord," she sensibly replied, aware of the life-and-death control he held over their lives.

"It pleases me," he gruffly said.

"Then humbly, my lord, he pleases me as well."

"Tomorrow night you can show me how much he pleasures you. As for you, my fine stud," he went on, reaching out to stroke Sinjin on the arm as he might pet one of his stallions, "eat well, for I have need of your sperm. Guard!" he shouted. "Show them away."

In the snatched moment that the Bey looked away toward the door, Chelsea reached for Sinjin's hand and slipped her fingers through his. He squeezed them hard, then gently, like a parting kiss, before he quickly pulled away. Reaching for the robe he'd placed on a hook near the bed, he covered himself.

And gave no further indication he was aware of her.

Chelsea had fresh tears in her eyes when they led her away.

Chapter 44

They became, in the course of the following days, the Bey's indispensable diversion . . . his pleasure, his obsession. The other harem women languished, for Hamouda would have his *ferenghi* lord mate only with the golden-haired woman. What wild delirious drama—what moody tempests—what passion! He must have their child! He would see the pale beauty pregnant within the month, and to that purpose, he watched them make love each night.

As for the participants in the Bey's fanatical tableau vivant, it was a most terrible obsession.

It was heaven.

It was awful.

It was wonderful.

It was madness, agony, intoxication, reckless need; it was an inspiration for living and the harshest goad to an irresponsible urge to escape.

A dozen times a day, Sinjin thought of escape, particularly when his sight began returning—strips of vision on the periphery of his blindness. But even if he were reckless enough to attempt to break free, the passages between his quarters and the seraglio were a well-guarded maze, and he'd never reach Chelsea alive.

He was restless, pacing during the daytime hours as though physical activity would wear away his agitation. He surreptitiously memorized the sentinel towers visible from his courtyard, the multitude of corridors between his rooms and the stage on which he and Chelsea performed each evening; he counted guards and weapons; he noted the Mamelukes in Hamouda's palace—those Christian slaves converted to Islam whom the Bey used for his personal guard. Would some of those reach for freedom if it were offered? How securely were they committed to the Bey?

He planned and estimated and took note of the winds without giving indication of his altered vision. Where was the *Aurora* riding anchor? What progress had Seneca and Sahar made in rescue plans? He knew his friends would be searching for a way to free him. But was it possible to breach the Bey's bastion? Was it possible for them to find him within the complex of five hundred rooms?

And then find Chelsea as well . . .

Frustration overwhelmed him each time at that point in his reflections, for the sheer *size* of the Bardo was the Bey's greatest protection. Even if some of its inhabitants could find the means and courage to break out, they would be defeated by the intricacy and immensity of the palace and grounds.

And of course time was an issue . . . though not immediately pressing. But once the Bey was assured of heirs, Sinjin's usefulness would end.

But he never admitted despair to Chelsea. "We'll get out," he'd whisper when he tasted her tears on his lips. "Be brave." And only sheer willpower kept him from throttling the Bey once his eyesight improved and he could see the shadowy form behind the arabesque. Only a few strides or a powerful leap, he estimated, and his fingers could be curled around the Bey's flabby throat, the fragile arabesque no protection against his rage.

His love for Chelsea stopped him each time. And his dream of them together again in England.

He prayed for the first time in his life—for restraint, for patience, for a stoicism he'd never had to cultivate in a freewheeling life of license. He had the courage and perseverance to prevail and the firmness of purpose; he just wasn't sure he had the caution.

The British Consul General introduced Seneca and Sahar to the Vivanis, although Sinjin's friends had already made the acquaintance of one of the cousins while out reconnoitering the palace environs one evening. And the Bedouins and Neapolitans combined their efforts, both factions liberal with their bribes—the most useful method of entry into the Bardo. Once they were inside, however, their fate depended on their quickness and skill with a blade.

The following Friday, the Sabbath day for Moslems, was agreed on as the day of their attack. Nominally Moslems, the Bedouins regarded religion less seriously than the Arabs, their warrior culture still deeply attached to pagan beliefs. And more important than the sanctity of the Sabbath as a day ripe for surprise was the fact that the moon was just past new on Friday.

Seneca and the Bedouins came in the dead of night, leaving a swift trail of death from the outer gates to the corridor facing Sinjin's rooms, stopping just long enough each time they slit a throat to drag the Tunisian guard out of sight. Within the time allotted, they arrived at Sinjin's room, the door opening only long enough to silently admit the score of warriors.

"They're keeping the western gateway unlocked for five minutes more," Seneca tersely said, dispensing with a salutation, time too precious. The Vivanis waited at the gate, the guards in their pay, but routine patrols circulated throughout the palace on a fifteen-minute schedule. And ten minutes were gone.

"We have to get Chelsea," Sinjin said, throwing a djellaba over his shoulders at the same time he accepted a curved dagger from Sahar. "They'll have to wait longer."

"She's alive then." Relief infused the simple words for a moment before Seneca brusquely added, "How fast can you find her?"

"Running full out, three minutes," Sinjin replied, having timed the distance in his mind a thousand times. "Considering the guards in the way . . ." He shrugged. "And I can't count on my sight . . ." He was already moving toward the door.

"I'll be beside you," Seneca quietly said, falling into step at his side.

"And my knife too," Sahar murmured, taking his place on Sinjin's right, his black robe an extension of the darkness.

And they broke into a run, no further explanations required. The desert men operated on instinct, the methods of warfare instilled into their minds and bodies with their mother's milk. None of the twenty men asked questions; they sprinted down the corridor to the seraglio, their soft boots soundless on the marble.

.   .   .

The seraglio doors burst open. Twenty men poured into the large courtyard around which the individual chambers lay, and Sinjin shouted, "Chelsea!" his voice booming in the absolute silence of the darkened atrium.

No matter her fear, the sound of his voice was a miracle. Throwing the covers aside, she jumped up from her bed, crying, "Here, here . . . I'm coming . . ." In that instant, she thought not of fear of discovery but only of seeing her husband again. He was shouting her name—no whispers, no caution, his potent energy ricocheting from the mosaic walls as the echoes of his powerful voice swept around the arched, colonnaded courtyard.

And in an instant he was before her, the silhouette of his muscular form filling the doorway of her room, his hand outstretched, a galvanic strength emanating from his person as though he could take her from this prison through the power of his will alone. And when her fingers slid through his, she felt the vitality of his spirit give her courage. "Stay by me," he said. "You'll be safe," he added with a natural reassuring firmness, strong-willed and unafraid. "But be ready for bloodshed." He wished his warning unnecessary, that it were possible to guard her from the sights she was about to see, but their escape route was fast closing. And he pulled her close to his side, the protection of his body shield for the gauntlet they must run.

The eunuchs had fled by the time they stepped back into the courtyard. All the terrified harem women huddled in their rooms except for a young Greek girl who had been captured from a merchant ship on her journey home to Alexandria last summer. "I'm going with you," she flatly declared, choosing French as a common language, running up to them as Chelsea and Sinjin crossed the black and white marble floor surrounding the pool.

"Seneca," Sinjin said, the word both an inquiry and an apology, as he nodded his head in the direction of the girl. Selfishly, he could only protect Chelsea. If the young girl wished to accompany them, someone else would have to care for her.

"You'll have to run like the wind," Seneca stated, his French colored with the patois of the Canadian French so long friends of his people. Putting his hand out to her, he added, "And don't cry out, no matter what you see."

"Kill them all," the young girl curtly said. "Starting with the Bey. Give me a knife and I'll help you."

And when he did, she grasped the hilt with the sureness of much practice and said, "Lead the way; I can keep up . . ."

"What's your name?" Seneca queried a moment later, as though they weren't already racing down the corridors toward the west gate, as though they were meeting at an afternoon tea and he was admiring the chaste beauty of her classic features.

"Cressidia," she replied with a dazzling smile, "and I can outrun you."

How strange, Seneca thought, that in ultimate peril of his life, deep in the bowels of a tyrant's palace, racing toward the possibility of a gruesome death, he found himself curiously affected by a woman for the first time since his wife had been killed. The spirits had found him once again years later, leagues from home. "You fascinate me," he said, "and you can't," he added with a grin, thinking how ludicrous it was to be flirting with a harem beauty when he might be dead in the next few moments.

Then no further time for conversation existed, for a trumpet sounded the alarm, and within moments the palace came alive with troops. They fought their way through the courtyard adjacent to the western gate, leaving a trail of carnage behind them, fighting literally for their lives . . . which incentive brought a ferocious, implacable intensity to their sword arms. The Vivani cohorts met them valiantly as they entered the yard, their assistance unflinching and gallant. Cutting their way to the gate, the escapees sprinted toward the horses kept at the ready by a Vivani groom.

The Bedouins, on horseback from infancy, flung themselves into the saddles; the others, as nimble, vaulted onto the horses, the thought of freedom giving wings to their feet. It felt like heaven to be riding again with a swift horse beneath her, Chelsea buoyantly thought, the cool night air rushing by her face, and the smile she turned toward Sinjin, who was racing a black stallion beside her, gave indication of her enormous good spirits. She knew she could outrace any man, and a sense of confidence animated her. "How far to the shore?" she shouted.

"Two miles . . . we'll take the city route. They won't expect us to ride through town."

Chelsea grinned. The route would be like a gymkhana, a sportive challenge for only the best of riders. "And they can't ride, the palace guard . . . not as well as the Bedouins . . ."

None but desert horsemen and the most proficient riders would have survived the narrow thoroughfares, the swift descent on cobblestone, the punishing pace over hurdles: walls, shop stalls, courtyard gardens. And Seneca found further reason to be charmed by the beautiful young Cressidia; she rode like the wind.

Swinging around the quays when they reached the port, the horsemen pounded down the shore, the *Aurora* lying beyond the Foum-el-Qued, offshore past the shoals. The entire north shore of the harbor remained yet between them and freedom. Sinjin whipped his mount; Chelsea followed suit, as did the entire troop. Everyone understood that a slow brutal death awaited them if they were captured.

The sight of the *Aurora,* pale against the dark sky, full-rigged and swift, cheered them.

The longboats were waiting when the mounted group swooped down to the shore, the waves small swells, the water only a whisper of sound on the sand. A sultry peace and darkness enveloped the small peninsula stretching out into the Mediterranean as brief salutations were exchanged, the men's voices low, hurried. The women were to be carried out to the boats first, they'd leave the horses, *hurry!* for the palace barracks would be emptied by now and the guard in hot pursuit.

The women were being lifted into the first boat when the Mamelukes appeared.

"I'd say a mile," Sinjin curtly said, Seneca beside him with Cressidia in his arms.

Seneca cast a glance back, swore and softly replied, "No more than that and coming fast."

Sinjin stood for a moment in the knee-deep water with Chelsea in his arms while their limited options flashed through his mind. A pulse beat passed; his gaze rapidly took in the decreasing distance between themselves and the Pasha's guards—and his decision was made. Bending his head, he touched his mouth to Chelsea's in a soft, gentle kiss.

"You're my life . . . my happiness," he whispered, holding her close for a moment, wishing he had time to say more, wishing the Mamelukes would disappear, wishing he'd discovered how much he loved his wife in more opportune circumstances. "I love you with all my heart," he murmured, placing her away from him on the seat in the bow.

Sinjin's words struck terror in her soul; they were too ominous, too much like those of farewell. "You're coming *too,*" Chelsea fearfully blurted. "Don't *talk* this way . . . get in beside me . . ." But her voice trailed away because she saw his eyes and knew he wasn't coming. "Oh God," she breathed.

"I'll be right behind you," he said, purposely keeping his voice impassive to allay her fear, taking precious moments that he didn't have to kiss her one last time . . . his mouth lingering on hers too long . . .

Seneca touched his arm gently—a reminder of the Mamelukes' speed.

"Au revoir," Sinjin said, brushing a finger over Chelsea's soft bottom lip, finding it almost impossible to leave.

And then he broke away, turning without a backward glance, surveying the shoreline, calculating the time remaining to them.

The moon was too slender to cast much light, but the silver helmets of the palace guard glittered in the night, the tips of their lances like dancing points in the darkness.

"Take the women out to the *Aurora* and set sail," Sinjin ordered the sailors, helping to push the stern of the longboat out to sea. "Don't wait, don't hesitate, weigh anchor immediately. We'll meet you in Naples." Each word was uttered in a blunt staccato, the sound of galloping horses echoing down the quiet seashore.

"There's time, Sinjin . . . to load everyone! Don't go!" Chelsea cried, scrambling over the seats, trying to reach him. "We can get away!"

"Hold her," Sinjin murmured, his voice without inflection, his instruction a clear and certain order no matter how quiet. "Now go!" he commanded, already moving away from the boat.

"Sinjin! . . . No!" Chelsea's tortured cry of pain carried over the water, ending at the last in a whimper as the sailor holding her forcibly kept her from jumping overboard.

"The Mamelukes may not all stand and fight," Cressidia said, her eyes narrowed to make out the advancing shapes of the guard as the sailors strained at the oars and pulled them swiftly away from shore. "They don't fight for love of the Bey . . ."

"There are too many," Chelsea whispered, poignantly aware that she might never see Sinjin again, her gaze on his broad-shouldered form striding toward shore. "And so few to face them . . ." she finished, her voice raw with grief.

Hauling off his djellaba as he splashed through the shallows, Sinjin dropped the robe into the water, automatically checking the knives tucked into his belt, casting a glance around to find Seneca and Sahar in the multitude of men and ponies on shore. Tender thoughts of love were set aside, his mind intent on the immediacy of survival: assessing their assailants' numbers, the effectiveness of their own strike force, the remote possibility of escape from the potent might of Hamouda's rage. Stripped for battle to only loose Turkish trousers and boots, he pulled the rifle from his saddle holster, slipped the sling over his shoulder and leaped onto his desert stallion. Drawing out a long-bladed dagger with a rhinoceros tusk hilt, he smiled faintly at Seneca and Sahar, who were mounted beside him. "Ready?" he said, and at their affirmative nods, he nudged his horse into a canter.

In moments they were racing their combat ponies directly at the serried ranks of the advancing palace guard, the Bedouins' battle cry screaming on the wind, their reckless charge characteristic of desert warfare, where individual courage and boldness marked a warrior.

Rifle shots rang out at fifty yards as each Bedouin sighted in on a lancer, the odds considerably diminished by their second volley. Then, without time to reload, they drew their lethal blades, which were honed to razor sharpness, and a clash of steel signaled the joining of the combatants. Horses squealed and reared; human screams, shrill and harrowing, pierced the summer air as the desert horsemen slammed into the solid ranks of the Mamelukes.

The scene of battle was too distant now to easily discern from the sea, the limited moonlight insufficient for sight. And an utterly helpless rage filled Chelsea's brain as the *Aurora* weighed anchor and the sails filled with wind. She couldn't fight beside Sinjin or make him leave with her; she hadn't the physical competence, nor perhaps the nerve, to face the ruthless Mamelukes. Powerless, she was being sent away when they'd been *so* close to deliverance, and all she could do was grieve and lament or mourn at Sinjin's graveside.

Damn him! Why did he have to play the hero? There would have been time for everybody to reach the boats. There *would* have been time! She hated him for leaving her, for turning back like some resolute chivalrous knight—when any *sensible* person would have hastily loaded everyone on board the longboats and *thumbed* his nose at the Mamelukes!

Allowing himself a fleeting glance out to sea while warding off a saber blow, Sinjin saw with relief that the *Aurora* was taking wind in her sails. Good, Chelsea was safe . . . from the Bey, from physical harm, from the idiosyncrasies of a country that caged women like animals. He'd stayed behind to ensure her safety, to make certain she didn't live out her life in an autocrat's harem thousands of miles from home. Their rear-guard action would gain the *Aurora* valuable minutes to get under way and put to sea.

Swinging his horse around, he eluded the thrust of a scimitar, introspection abruptly curtailed by more pressing matters of survival. He intended, God willing, to make his way home, and urging his mount into a canter, he came up on a Mameluke from behind at full speed, his knife poised for that target area between the ribs that offered passage to the heart.

The soldier's death scream gave him enormous satisfaction. He only wished it were the Bey's soft body in which his knife was buried hilt-deep. But there was no time for impractical reflections of revenge, Sinjin rapidly considered, jerking his blade out from between the ribs of the dying man. The Mamelukes were better armed, more numerous, trained to fight to the death—paradise awaiting those who fell in battle.

Wheeling his horse, Sinjin turned again, raised his knife arm-high and galloped back into the mass of battling men, blood streaming from his wounds, his powerful muscles glistening with sweat, his long black hair windswept, his cry of vengeance unearthly, as if the Devil himself rode into the midst of the carnage.

Chapter 45

Standing at the rail, Chelsea watched the Tunisian shore recede from view through a veil of tears. She wept for the man she loved; she cried in melancholy despair, in frustration and anger, her tears the eternal weeping of women left behind when the brutal affairs of men find resolution only in armed combat.

Although she knew Sinjin would never have stayed behind if not for her. Fresh tears stung her eyes, choked her throat. *"How can I live without you?"* she wretchedly lamented. *"Don't leave me . . ."* And between her anguish and yearning, searching for a fragment of sanity in her crumbling world, needing to *do* something, she began devising means of succor to give her hope.

She'd hire soldiers in Naples. Austrian and Spanish troops, German soldiers from the northern duchies, Italian recruits from the principalities of the peninsula collectively served in the army of the Two Sicilies. Surely there were mercenaries who would sail back with her.

If it wasn't too late, she thought.

And when Cressidia came to stand by her, bringing them woolen cloaks for protection against the cool sea air, Chelsea said in a voice still unsteady but resolute, "I'm going back for them . . . as soon as we reach Naples. Sinjin has money enough to hire the whole of Ferdinand's army."

"My father will help," Cressidia said as coolly as though they were talking of buying apples, poised and tranquil as she'd been from the beginning. "Deopolis Bank has a branch in Naples."

"You're almost home then . . ." She'd have a home again if she found Sinjin; the thought gave her purpose.

Cressidia smiled. "Close enough . . . although Alexandria is home. I owe you an unpayable debt," she quietly declared—her words, more than her expression, indicating the power of her emotions.

"Had you given up?" Chelsea asked, her gaze focused far out to sea, unseeing for a moment as images of the seraglio filled her mind. Everyone did give up at one time or another in the harem, the existence so remote from the world, so isolated from reality.

Cressidia shrugged, understanding Chelsea's query but unwilling to burden Chelsea with a long story when Sinjin's plight was so uncertain. "My name disappeared when I entered the harem," she simply said, "so I knew my father couldn't find me." And something of the universal despair underlying harem life echoed in her voice. But a moment later, brushing her dark wind-tossed hair from her face, she purposely forced away the old dreads and tersely said, her black eyes shining fiercely, "Your husband gave me back my life. My family's wealth is at your disposal. And personally," she went on with a grim smile, "I'd like to watch Hamouda die a slow lingering death on the impaling hooks overlooking the harbor. I'd like to see if he dies as casually as he took my life from me."

Chelsea didn't know if she could watch the cormorants pick Hamouda's eyes out and feast on his entrails with any pleasure. "I just want Sinjin and his friends back," Chelsea softly said, content to leave vengeance for others. "I hope . . . he's alive." Her murmured words drifted away on the night air. Stay alive for me, she silently pleaded . . . stay alive . . . her hope drifting back across the sea to Africa's shores . . . as a talisman to guard him.

She stayed up all night at the stern of the yacht, unable to sleep, gripped with a terrible fear: if she closed her eyes, she irrationally thought, he might die . . . The litany was bereft of reason, but like the senseless rhymes of childhood, it wouldn't dislodge from her mind, and the sing-song incantation intimidated and terrified and kept her awake.

How could it hurt to soothe the spirits or gods or mythical beings? she reflected, forlorn and artless in her need—grasping for any shred of hope. If the jinns would restore Sinjin to her, she would willingly give up sleep forever. She offered preposterous concessions to the spirit world if it would save Sinjin; she promised and prayed and entreated throughout the long sleepless hours. And she understood for the first time how faith had assembled crusading armies and built soaring cathedrals, how it had glorified the Parthenon and raised the Pyramids. *"Bring him back to me,"* she whispered into the dark night, *"and I'll do anything . . ."*

The ship slipped over the horizon into her field of vision just as wispy light separated day from night. The dark sails of the Moslem man-of-war were distinctive against the lemon yellow strip of dawn framing the curvature of the earth.

Immediately warning the man at the wheel, Chelsea stood transfixed, watching the ominous silhouette framed against the rising sun. The captain, wakened by the alarm bell, hurried from his cabin and quickly called for all the sail. Understanding the peril facing them, every hand went aloft, and soon the *Aurora* was racing for Naples, every inch of canvas unfurled. But the Moslem frigate stayed with them like a shadow, despite the weight of its guns and size, for it carried double the sails. And slowly it closed on its quarry. By late morning, when the man-of-war was close enough to open with her bow chasers if she chose, the vessel was made out to be a shallow draft felucca, specially designed as a warship for the reefs and shoals of the Barbary Coast.

She carried no flag.

Until a white pennant was run up her foremast.

"You can't trust a corsair's flag of surrender," Cressidia said, standing beside Chelsea at the rail. "They routinely use it to approach for boarding. And why should they be surrendering? We don't carry more than ten guns to their hundred. I won't go back," she abruptly added, her voice dead calm.

Faced with the same prospect of captivity for all the hours since first sighting the ship, Chelsea had avoided the ghastly choice, although Cressidia's blunt declaration seemed to match some kindred emotion yet unstated in her own mind. Gazing at the fleet warship moving inexorably closer, she gravely said, "We'll need a gun either way. Sinjin had a pair in his cabin." She hesitated for a moment, not wishing to come to terms with death, but realistically understanding that their choices were limited. "You might want to find them," she added.

And when she was left alone, Chelsea scanned the approaching craft, wondering if she could actually kill herself when the time came. At eighteen, death had always seemed impossibly . . . distant.

In her reverie, her unconscious took note of the figure first, drawing her eye back to the flash of movement on the foredeck of the felucca. A certain familiarity—of stride, perhaps, or form— caught her attention, and she strained her eyes to define that moment of recognition. But the man had disappeared behind the standing jib sail when she inspected the vessel more closely.

A small agitation, disordered yet acute, gripped her, and she found herself moving her position to improve her view of the forward deck. The man's hair had been of a certain length . . . and black. Reminding herself in the next moment that every other Moslem had black hair as well, she forced her emotions into a semblance of sanity. Get a grip on yourself, she harshly chastised.

She should be considering a swift method of dying instead of dwelling on elusive shadows. And for a full five minutes, she turned from the ship in pursuit and centered her interest on the sailors in the riggings of the *Aurora,* who were coaxing more speed from her sails.

Centered her *attention,* to be precise—not her interest. Her interest perversely continued to digest the minutiae of detail pertaining to the dark-haired man sighted on the Moslem felucca. It was his stride, his swinging gait, she decided, that looked so familiar—or was it the shining length of his hair . . .

But then Cressidia returned, her expression somber. "The captain's ordered us below. They may be engaging soon, and he doesn't want us on deck."

"Did you find the pistols?" In the second just past, Chelsea had suddenly reached a firm decision, as if some inner voice spoke without argument. If Sinjin was dead—and that possibility was very real, considering the Bey's savagery—there was no point in her living incarcerated again in some corsair's seraglio. A harem was a prison for life, or a living death. Why prolong one's agony?

But after twenty minutes below in Sinjin's cabin, Chelsea found waiting for the unknown more terrible than facing death squarely, and she said, "Stay if you wish, but I'm going back on deck. I want to see what I'm dying for."

Cressidia grinned. "It's rather like chickens in a coop waiting for the hatchet to fall. I consider myself more a bird of prey. Perhaps I can take a corsair or two with me to hell."

"Don't turn religious now when I'm complacently considering the golden spires of paradise or the green Elysian fields as my next venue." Chelsea found herself in remarkably good humor, and she wondered if those about to die attained some philosophical bliss. "Although my resentment at the Barbary corsairs, Hamouda included," she went on in her newfound good spirits, "for ruining my life might induce me to slightly even the score before I die. Is this gun loaded properly?"

"The first mate loaded them both. We can but hope he's competent." Cressidia held the mate to Chelsea's dueling pistol, double-barreled Mantons that Sinjin had had specially made for him. Her smile reflected a new sense of purpose. "After you," she said with a small bow.

Chelsea opened the cabin door, stepped out into the companion-way and cautiously made her way to the stairway leading above decks. In the commotion generated by defense of the *Aurora,* the women slipped aft unnoticed and hid themselves behind the water barrels.

In the twenty minutes that had passed, the Moslem ship had gained two hundred yards, and several white flags fluttered from the foreshrouds. Knowing they were too common a subterfuge in the Mediterranean, the Aurora's captain ignored the pennants. He was making for the Tyrrhenian Sea, hoping to reach the safety of Trapani before the felucca overtook him.

And then the dark-haired man who had plagued her subconscious, his tanned body covered only in Turkish trousers, scrambled up the bow rigging with two hastily constructed signal flags, the dripping paint coloring his arms as he climbed the swinging ropes.

It was enough. She recognized the familiar athletic configuration of perfectly coordinated muscle and sinew and bone as he nimbly ascended the rigging—his dark silken hair tossed and windblown, the powerful arms and long muscled legs, the broad shoulders that had blocked out the light on more than one occasion, the graceful dip of his spine where it slid beneath the waistband of his trousers—the body she knew better than her own . . . And racing to the stern rail despite the captain's warning shout, she knew, she *knew* without seeing his face, and she screamed so she could have been heard across to the African shores, *"Sinjin!"*

He spun around at the sound of her voice, dropping the flags, almost falling himself, hanging from the rigging by one hand until he found a foothold, floating for an instant in the blue empty space of sea and sky, untrammeled grace, glorious, god-like—even with one shoulder bandaged. Then he flashed his free arm in a sweeping wave of hail and welcome, flashed a smile that dazzled even across that infinite distance and dropped to the deck twenty feet below bellowing orders, the radiant god transformed into her rash, splendid Sinjin.

The captain of the *Aurora* immediately cut sail and threw out drags to slow the yacht while the felucca continued full out on course. When it closed ten minutes later, Chelsea was at the rail, ecstatic, transported, too happy to stand still, smiling, crying as she kept pace with the felucca coming alongside. While grappling hooks secured and steadied the hulls of the two ships, she ran forward to meet Sinjin. When he swung aboard, she threw herself into his arms with such force that he stumbled back to keep his balance and sucked in his breath at the stabbing pain of his wounds.

But his arms didn't release their grasp, his grip vise-like, and they clung to each other like lovers who'd returned alive from the black abyss, unutterably grateful, hysterical with elation, their memories of loss still too explicit, too terrible, to take any chances with separation.

After endless moments in which blessed sensation compensated for the grave they'd so recently survived and the blissful solid feel of each other calmed the worst of their fears, Chelsea gazed up, her chin resting on the warmth of Sinjin's chest, and said those words she'd prayed for during the long lonely night: "You're alive . . ." Her face was wreathed in smiles, her words breathless declaration but tentative too, her need for reassurance trembling beneath her smile.

"Yes, alive," Sinjin softly agreed—a very questionable state short hours ago, he thought. The lightly guarded felucca had been a veritable gift from God. "I must live right," he murmured with the faintest smile, a whisper of his old sardonic teasing evident in his tone. Although he'd wondered, in his blackest moments during his captivity, if somehow he *hadn't* lived right and an angry god was exacting punishment.

"You can't *ever* go back." She would keep him safe always in her arms.

Sinjin grinned down at his wife, heaven regained—or more appropriately, considering his previous life, newly found—the most lurid and graphic of his demons fading from the forefront of his consciousness. "Perhaps more aptly, *you* should never go back. Or at least not until you can handle a dagger with more dispatch."

"You *have* to promise me." Less bold perhaps than Sinjin, or more touched by the supernatural, Chelsea experienced inexplicable terror that their happiness might be probationary, easily revoked by some petty warlord in Tunis or Algeria or anywhere else fine horses were bred. And clinging tightly to him, she challenged, "You must promise . . ."

"I promise," he casually replied, in no mood for contention, gratified to bask in the happiness enveloping his soul. "I'm completely at your beck and call." His smile offered her anything, everything . . . all. He rarely argued with women, and particularly now—he couldn't imagine disagreeing. Not when he had been given back his life; not when he had a future again. Not after their badly outnumbered skirmish with the Mamelukes, when they'd almost *not* fought their way through.

"Now tell me you love me," he murmured, "and after paying our respects to the captain . . ." He grinned, feeling less punished by fiends from hell, feeling more normal. "I think I need a rest." He looked around as though the vastness of the sea held significant signposts. "We're roughly twenty hours from Naples. That should be time enough."

"To sleep?" Chelsea's amused question came in response to a familiar message in his voice.

"Not exactly . . ." Sinjin's dark lashes lowered over the insinuation in his eyes.

Sinjin was back . . .

She held his strength and warmth and power beneath her hands, against her heart, and she felt as though she owed someone somewhere an eternal debt. But selfishly she'd consider debts tomorrow. And now— "I *should* say something to Cressidia," she murmured.

"Seneca will amuse her." Glancing over Chelsea's head at the two people deep in conversation, Sinjin corrected with a knowing smile, "*Is* amusing her."

"You really *should rest,* darling," Chelsea said, very much aware of Sinjin's wounds, the knife slashes swollen and red, some in need of stitching, his bandaged shoulder giving him some discomfort despite his reticence.

"I didn't know if I'd ever see you again," he quietly said, the slim margin of their escape sure to cause a future nightmare or two. "So rest isn't high on my list of priorities," he added. "Talk to me of that in a month or two."

He wished instead to be reminded of life and living, to forget how close he'd come to dying. And true to his word, the Duke and his Duchess stayed in his cabin until Naples came into view.

Several mornings later, Sinjin and Chelsea stood at the pasture fence of the villa at Sorrento, surveying the new Barb horses Seneca had sent home from Gabès. Chelsea leaned against Sinjin, his arm curved around her shoulder, the world bathed in sweet sunshine, the discussion centering on the best route home for the horses. They'd tentatively decided on Naples to Genoa by boat, then overland to Montpellier and north to Paris. Neither cared to risk the corsairs twice in one season; the horses would go by land to England.

"Why don't we leave in, say, two weeks?" Sinjin said. "That will get us home in good weather even if we linger on the way."

"I might stay here for a while," Chelsea quietly said. "If you don't mind?"

Sinjin looked down at her swiftly, his brows drawn together in mild disapproval. "I do mind. We have to get our horses home for the fall meets." And he wouldn't find pleasure in living anywhere without her.

"A problem's arisen . . ." Uncertainty had changed to certainty in the past week.

"What kind of a problem?" His arm dropped from her shoulder, and he turned her to face him, his eyes taking on a flinty hardness. "Is your family interfering—"

"No . . . my family's safely in Scotland—or at least," Chelsea added with a small smile, *"in* Scotland. Neil still has a penchant for Englander beeves."

"He's going to be strung up someday from a Cumberland tree," Sinjin grumbled, but his eyes held a sparkle of mischief. He'd gone out more than once himself under a reiving moon. Raiding was a game, an excitement, a challenge. He envied Neil his convenient location in Dumfries.

"Papa will pay to see that he doesn't hang, should it come to that," Chelsea replied, "but I'd still like to stay in Naples for the winter."

"The winter! Good God . . . that's months. No, that's too long."

"I have to."

"Of course you don't. You're my wife. You don't *have* to do anything."

"You probably would wish me to if you knew," she cryptically said.

"What the hell are you talking about?" He leaned closer, as if his understanding would improve with less distance. "Speak plainly. I'm not going to eat you alive."

"You might." Her voice was almost inaudible.

"Word of God, I won't," he declared, astonished at her apprehension; his wife wasn't timid. "Now tell me what this unintelligible conversation is about."

"There weren't any Greek sponges in the harem." She hadn't the nerve to say the words directly, her fear of losing him a constant in her mind the past few days.

"And?"

"And . . . so . . . I couldn't use any."

It struck him then. "Is it mine?" He shouldn't have been so selfish, considering the extent of their imprisonment. He contemplated for a moment whether he could accept the Bey's child as the next Duke of Seth.

"You can't ask," she said, a critical earnestness in her voice despite its quiet tone. "I won't go through that again. And that's why I wish to stay here." The Bey had never touched her, but she, too, had her demons. After the myriad problems with her last pregnancy, she'd vowed never again to compromise herself for a man's sense of affront. Here in Naples, nothing seemed a problem, but England could be different. The Ton could be vicious if Sinjin expressed doubts about the paternity of his child; the Ton could be vicious, even without Sinjin's doubts, when news of her captivity in a harem circulated—as surely it would, with the British consul involved.

"If I said it didn't matter, would you come home with me?"

"If I come back with you, this child—if a boy—will be the next Duke of Seth." She wanted him to understand completely the terms under which she went back to England. Returning to England meant their old problems resurfacing: her family; his family; his friends; the great discrepancies in their lives; Sinjin's unwillingness to have children. She could stay comfortably in Naples; many expatriates spent their lives away from England.

"If you don't miscarry."

It wasn't an answer but evasion still—or as always. "I'll not gallop days cross-country this time," she said firmly. "You must decide." She loved him with all her heart, but she loved her honor too, and going back to their former life filled her with foreboding. In the pause that ensued, she prayed for divine intervention, asking as she had as a child for impossible things . . . for the love of a man who had never known what love meant, for an answer any man would balk at.

Sinjin was silent for a time. Then he softly said, "I want you back."

He hadn't answered completely. "I need to know about the child."

"The child is mine, then," he simply said.

"You're sure?"

He smiled. "I'll take Gengis Khan's child to have you with me."

"The Bey never touched me, not even in passing."

His brows rose the merest distance. "This was a test then."

"I wanted you to be sure this time."

"Last time only the musket bore was sure."

His words were without inflection, quietly uncertain in mood. "Something like that," Chelsea carefully replied, not sure all was reconciled after all.

"And now I have a test for you." Sinjin's grin was familiarly wolfish, the sparkle in his eyes blatant mischief.

There. She knew. And her answering smile shone without reservation. "For some reason I'm not alarmed."

"Perhaps you should be. I can be very difficult."

He could also be the source of all her happiness and joy. "Ask me and I'll answer."

"Do you love me more than anything—more than your horses?"

"Thune, too?" she said, teasing him for a moment.

"Thune most of all."

"I do," she said. "And do you love me?" She asked very, very softly. He'd never said the words to her until so very recently, and she often wondered how much captivity had to do with his feelings. Now that he was free again and society clamoring for his favors, perhaps he would reconsider on worldly matters of love. She was unwise, she knew, to press him when life held such sweet promise— even without the words . . . but she wished to hear them.

"I've said I do."

"I need to be told again."

"This is not something I do with ease," he qualified.

And she wondered whether he was trying to avoid her frank inquiry. "Tell me," she said, as impertinent as he.

"I love you, Chelsea Amity Fergusson St. John," he said, the words sweet on his tongue. He grinned. "Did I do well?"

"Fair." Her own grin matched his in mischievous insolence.

"I know other more effective ways to demonstrate my love, although," he went on, "if you prefer *words* . . ."

"How effective?" Her voice was a soft purring resonance.

"I think you might forget what day it is . . ."

"Or what week?"

"That depends on your stamina," he murmured.

"Two weeks?"

"You're pressing the wrong man."

"Have you?"

"Of course not," he lied.

"Will you show me?"

"With pleasure."

And he did.

Epilogue

As it turned out, Sinjin's demonstrations of love took more than two weeks, which put their journey home into October. Even with a leisurely progress in consideration of Chelsea's enceinte condition, the Duke and Duchess of Seth arrived in England in time for the late fall race meets at Newmarket.

"Was it just early spring that we met?" Chelsea remarked on their first day at the fall meet, struck by the familiar circumstances as they prepared to leave Six-Mile-Bottom for the race track.

"Yes, and two pregnancies later," Sinjin mentioned with a grin, holding the carriage door open for her. "I think we should consider building a larger racing box for your healthy state of conception."

"I thought you didn't want more children."

"I didn't," he bluntly said. His dark brows rose wolfishly. "Until I met you."

"You'll have to stay home then and give up your carousing, for I won't raise a family myself."

"Must I?"

They were settled in the same carriage in which they'd first met the previous spring, Jed up on the box, the only difference the colors of an autumn landscape visible through the windows.

"I'll contrive to amuse you," she said, no longer insecure on issues of her husband's love. Sinjin's conduct since their return had been so sharply different from his previous life that the clubs were taking bets now on the birth dates of his children rather than on the brevity of his love affairs. And settling back against the soft cushioned seat, Chelsea softly murmured, "I like this carriage."

"You look as luscious as you did the first day I met you," Sinjin murmured, his restful pose on the opposite seat a tantalizing sprawl of long lean muscled body. "Although deliciously riper, my darling . . ." His blue eyes were affectionate beneath his teasing. "Are you giving me a girl or a boy?"

"I'll tell you if you promise not to go back to Tunisia."

Intrigued at her certainty, he agreed, thinking there was time enough to change her mind later if he did choose to return. Which, at present, wasn't prominent in his plans. "How *do* you know?" he went on, shifting his posture, leaning forward in interest, fascinated by her assurance.

"Mrs. Hobbs informs me you can tell from the heartbeat, and my old Nanny says you can leave a meal for the fairies at midnight, and depending on what they eat, the sex of the child will be revealed."

"And Steeley says it's going to be a boy because she's knitting a boy's sweater," Sinjin added with a grin. "Since we're dealing with such reasonable data . . ."

"I want a girl."

"Then you must have one." And if it were in his power, he would give her one . . . for her happiness was his, a fact so simple he wondered he'd never known it before.

Most of their horses won at the fall meet at Newmarket—as usual, the competition muttered. But at least the Duchess wasn't riding, or the Seth stable would have taken all the firsts. And if Sinjin continued diligent in his husbandly duties, at least they'd be assured she'd not be up riding any time soon . . . leaving them a prize purse or two in consolation.

When the fall race season came to a close, Sinjin and Chelsea retired to the hermitage they liked best at Oakham for Christmas and to await the birth of their child. Beau was in residence as well. When the baby was born in the spring, Steeley was wrong this time—for which Sinjin rewarded her generously.

Chelsea had the daughter she wanted: "There'll be time later for a son," she said, "if you wish." She understood his love for Beau.

And in the course of the next ten years, two more children were born, a boy and a girl. And the Duke of Seth, contented, in love, enormously happy, became the paragon of fatherhood, just as he'd once been the licentious prototype for London's wild set. But his stark good looks still drew amorous sighs from the ladies, and while his intemperate life had ended, he charmed as effortlessly as in the past. Which left the ladies eternally hopeful.

And in only a few brief years, Beau claimed the position his father had previously held as the most fascinating rake in the Ton. Just down from Cambridge with plenty of money, an earldom, dark sensual beauty and, perhaps most important, enormous stamina, he was blazing a wide and profligate path through the boudoirs of London.

"Blood tells," those aristocrats who knew both father and son ironically remarked as the rash and reckless Beau St. Jules set new records.

Another Seth was back at stud in the marketplace, every woman of beauty cheerfully noted—and each found means of making herself known to the engaging young rogue.

Beau was given a mark of his celebrity that spring to add to his lengthy list of family names. The ladies called him Glory in a particularly purring way.

And it wasn't for his smile.

It had instead to do with the measure of his physical splendor.

Notes

1. The Iroquois Confederation (Oneida, Mohawk, Onondaga, Cayuga, Seneca) at one time spread from New York State to the Ohio. The tribes were courted as allies by both the French and English; Jesuit and Anglican missionaries were active in Iroquois country from the early seventeenth century.

Although many of the Indians cared little for the whiteman's marriage ceremony and preferred their own funeral rites, they often wished their children to be christened. Like all good parents, they wanted their children to have advantages.

By the mid-eighteenth century, when Sinjin's friend Seneca was born, over a hundred years of European influences had permeated the Eastern tribes, and many Indians were further Anglicized or Frenchified with surnames as well as Christian names.

2. Eclipse lived—and lived gloriously—from 1764 to 1789. He wasn't raced until he was five years old, and then only for two seasons. He was never beaten, and his brilliance both on the turf and at stud has been praised by turf writers for over two hundred years.

He became virtually the father of the modern thoroughbred.

When he went into serious training in April 1769, he had a secret trial on Banstead Downs. The touts came. "They were a little late; but they found an old woman who gave them all the information they wanted. On inquiring whether she had seen a race, she replied she could not tell whether it was a race or not, but she had just seen a horse with a white leg running away at a monstrous rate, and another horse a great way behind, trying to run after him; but she was sure he never would catch the white-legged horse if he ran to the world's end."

Eclipse first ran before the public in a race of four-mile heats for fifty pounds at Epsom on May 3, 1769. Rumors circulating after the trial had made his price 4-1 on. He won the first heat easily, at which point an Irish gambler named Dennis O'Kelly stepped forward. Disliking the odds for the second heat, he offered for any sum to name the *placings* of the runners. His prediction is the most famous five-word phrase in racing history: "Eclipse first, the rest nowhere."

3. Society was very small.

At the accession of George III in 1760, there were only 174 British peers. Up until the premiership of the Younger Pitt in 1784–85, there was no purchase of titles and no expansion of the peerage, so the number of peers held fairly stable—although some English holders of Irish peerages had been added. By the end of the eighteenth century, following Pitt's liberal grants of titles, the number had risen to nearly 300: if Irish titles were included, to about 500.

Many of the newly ennobled were successful admirals or generals, with a sprinkling of politicians, while the majority of new peers were younger sons of old landed families. The population of the entire urban complex which made up London was about 1 million, but society—those families who socially and politically controlled the refined existence of the other face of London—consisted of about 300.

Henry Fielding sardonically defined "nobody" as "all the people in Great Britain except about 1200."

4. The nobles were not early risers—at least not in London. In 1782, breakfast was rarely served before ten o'clock, and often not earlier than eleven. The Duchess of Devonshire writes of her French hairdresser arriving at eleven in the morning to ready her for the day and of the grand breakfast given by the Prince of Wales which lasted from noon to six o'clock in the evening.

In an age when all fashionable people kept late hours, it was hardly surprising they weren't out of bed until afternoon.

And then three to six in the afternoon was devoted to shopping and visiting. Dinner was served anytime from six to eight. After dinner, men and women of the haut ton sought the real interest of the day . . .

Many went to the theatre, where the performances began about seven and ended between eleven and twelve. After the drama and opera came balls, masquerades, parties, receptions and social pleasure.

At an assembly, no one dared to arrive until eleven. The fashionable hour at Vauxhall began at eleven or eleven-thirty. The House of Commons didn't sit until the end of the afternoon and regularly worked all night.

5. "Bedouin" is a corruption of the Arab word *badwi,* which is derived from the substantive *badu*—"open country." Therefore, "Bedouin" means one who lives in the open country.

6. Walled townhouses were a necessity until the beginning of the nineteenth century, when an organized police force was first developed.

In the eighteenth century, thieves and housebreakers in London were daring. No door, even in the humblest dwelling, was safe unironed, no window free from night attack when unprotected by a grill. Every yard was fortified by high walls and stout gates. And robberies took place every night on the roads and streets of town. When Dr. Johnson wrote his poem entitled "London," he observed:

Prepare for death if here at night you roam,
And sign your will before you sup from home.

Highwaymen stopped and searched coaches traveling to and from town with the regularity of ticket collectors, and servants took to the road between their engagements.

In addition to robbery as a reason for walled houses in town, the political system in the eighteenth century, one historian has written, was that of "aristocracy tempered by rioting."

The license demanded by the mob, and the good humor with which that license was conceded in England, allowed the classless to let off steam without the explosive violence of a French Revolution. Throughout the letters of Horace Walpole is an under-current of rioting, borne by the sufferers without the least panic: riots about weaving, in which the indignant Duke of Bedford received a stone weighing six pounds; riots about Wilkes, in which the Austrian Ambassador was taken out of his coach by the mob, turned upside down and the number "45" chalked on the soles of his shoes; riots about an address to the King, in which a hearse was driven into St. James's Palace with an executioner and an axe on top, and during which the pugilist Lord Talbot managed to bag a rioter; riots about printing libels, in which George Selwyn and Charles James Fox were rolled in the gutter and King George was pelted with an apple; riots about admirals, in which Pitt, Fox and the Duke of Ancaster, drunk, joined the demonstrators and chose the best windows to smash; riots about Popery, in which it was rumored that the lions had been loosed from the Tower menagerie; and riots about Peace, in which, according to Lord Onslow, "the insulting abuse offered to His Majesty was what I can never think of but with horror, nor ever forget what I felt when they proceeded to throw stones in the coach, several of which hit the King."

In the "No Popery" riots of 1780, Lord Mansfield's house was burned to the ground with its priceless library, and so were those of Sir John Fielding and many others.

7. "Vastly" was one of the favorite pet words of the era. According to correspondence of the Duchess of Devonshire, Giardini's music was "vastly pretty"; Rockingham's stables were "vastly well designed." In the eighteenth century, "vastly" was the "awfully" of a later generation.

8. The married life of Elizabeth Stanley was an open scandal almost from the beginning.

Edward Stanley, twelfth Earl of Derby and the richest man in England, led to the altar a reluctant beauty of nineteen who was sacrificed to his arms, a contemporary author states, by the vanity of her mother, the Duchess of Argyll. "Such a union promised but little happiness and the sighs of the fair were heard frequently amidst the shades of the Oaks [Derby's country estate]."

Lady Derby, however, found resources in town, he goes on, and Lord Derby had other interests as well. And when Lord Derby met Elizabeth Farren, a Covent Garden actress, four years later, he tried to divorce his wife.

Mrs. Boscawen writes to Mrs. Delany of the scandal: "Since I wrote the enclosed I have heard that Lord Derby announced to his lady on Friday last that their divorce was begun in the Commons, which news threw her into fits. She went as soon as she was able to her brother, then the Duke of Dorset waited on Lady Derby and Duke Hamilton and declared to both his intentions to marry her as soon as possible."

(The Duchess of Devonshire told her mother that she had always considered the Duke of Dorset the most dangerous of men. "For with that beauty of his he is so unaffected, and has a simplicity and a persuasion in his manner that makes one account very easily for the number of women he has had in love with him.")

When the divorce case was heard, the mutual infidelities of the Earl and Countess Derby were soon the general theme of the town, and those of the lady were made public in a Court of Justice. But as she had full proof of her recrimination against her husband, a separation was all he could obtain, and he was forced to leave her in possession of the title of Derby.

Lady Derby, later deserted by the fickle Duke of Dorset, received much sympathy from her friends, but the Queen would no longer receive her.

Lord Derby was left to wait impatiently for his wife's death so he could marry the fashionable young actress Elizabeth Farren. Lady Derby didn't die until 1797, and not until then did Elizabeth Farren marry Edward Stanley, the little man who was supposed to be the ugliest as well as the richest peer of the realm.

9. The Arabs of the Sahara sum up a horse's perfection in this way: He must be able to carry a man, his weapons, a change of clothing, provisions for both of them and a banner, even on a windy day, drag a corpse if need be and gallop all day without thinking of eating or drinking.

On the subject of the great distances covered by desert-bred horses, the following story—one among thousands, this one from a desert warrior—recounts the endurance of the desert Barbs.

I had arrived in the Tell with my father and members of our tribe to buy grain. It was under the Pasha Aly. The Arbaa had had some terrible encounters with the Turks, and as their interest at the moment made them feign a complete submission in order to obtain the forgetfulness of what had happened, they agreed that they would win over with silver the entourage of the pasha and they would send to the pasha himself, not a mediocre horse, as was usual, but a beast of the greatest distinction. It was a misfortune; but it was God's will and there was nothing else to do but be resigned. The choice fell on a mare, the gray of pebbles in a river, known throughout the Sahara. She belonged to my father. He was told to hold himself in readiness to leave the following day to take her to the pasha. After the evening prayer my father, who took great care not to make any comments, sought me out and said: "Ben-Zyan, do you feel like yourself today? Are you going to leave your father in this strait; are you going to be the cause of reddening his face?"

"Only your will is in me, sire," I answered. "Speak and if your orders are not carried out it will be because I am dead."

"Listen. Those sons of sin want to appropriate my mare in order to ingratiate themselves with the sultan. You know—my gray mare that has always brought good luck to our camp, to my children, to my camels; my gray mare, she who was foaled the same day that your youngest brother was born. Speak! Are you going to allow them to thus disgrace my white beard? The jubilation and happiness of our family are in your hands. Mordjana [Arabic for "Coral," the mare's name] has eaten her barley; if you are truly my son, sup, take your arms and as soon as night falls, flee far into the desert with the treasure that we all love."

Without saying a word, I kissed my father's hand, ate my supper, and departed from Berouaguia, happy to be able to prove my filial affection and laughing to think of the discomfiture of our sheiks in the morning.

I traveled far, afraid of being pursued, but Mordjana was well up on the bit and it was more a question of holding her back than of urging her on. The night was about two-thirds over and I began to get sleepy and halted. I dismounted, took the reins and wound them around my wrist. I placed my rifle under my head and went to sleep, lying comfortably under one of those dwarf palms which are common in our land. At the end of an hour I awoke and saw that Mordjana had eaten all the palm fronds. We went on. Dawn found us in Souagui; the mare had lathered and dried three times and I applied the spur. She drank at Sidi-bou-Zid, in the Ouad-Ettouyl, and I made my evening prayers in Leghrouat after I had given her a bit of hay in order to make her wait patiently for the large nose bag of barley which was coming to her.

The man had traveled eighty leagues in twenty-four hours; his mare had eaten nothing but the fronds of the dwarf palm under which he had slept; she had drunk but once, halfway on the journey, and he swore to General Eugene Daumas, to whom he was relating the story, that by the head of the Prophet he could have gone on the following day to spend the night in Ghardaia—forty-five leagues farther on—had his life been in danger.

10. *Bled* is one of the many Arabic words which admit of no clear translation. As opposed to a town, it means a village or encampment; as opposed to that, it refers to the open land, a plain or a particular district. Oftentimes, the word denotes the barren desert or, more technically, the soil.

11. The Mrs. Phillips referred to was the daughter of Captain Thomas Phillips of the 5th Dragoon Guards. Under the patronage of the Duchess of Bolton, Constantia Theresa Phillips went to a prestigious finishing school in Westminster, but by 1721, at the young age of thirteen, she was already mistress to the Earl of Chesterfield.

This was the start of a series of amours which she documented in several editions of her life, entitled *Apology.* Many courtesans used such memoirs as means to blackmail former lovers, but the Earl of Chesterfield, for one, adopted the attitude of "publish and be damned."

An enterprising young lady, Mrs. Phillips established a business in 1738 called the Green Canister in Half-Moon Alley (now Bedford Street), although it's more probable she let her name be used as a front. Considering her well-known liaisons with the Earl of Chesterfield and other scions of the nobility, her name guaranteed publicity.

The secret of the success of Mrs. Phillips' shop was that her "engines" (condoms) were made in the original manner—using sheep gut, which ensured elasticity and imperviousness. They were more expensive than cheaper ones made of treated linen.

A 1786 James Gillray cartoon sustains Mrs. Phillips' reputation as an exporter of her wares. In the drawing "A Sale of English Beauties in Madras," near the auctioneer's rostrum on the dock is a bale of goods from "Mrs. Phillips, original inventor, in Leicester Field, London."

Gillray depicts the sale of Covent Garden prostitutes, transported as minor criminals, the ladies being auctioned off like cattle on their arrival in India. They were bought by the personnel of the East India Company.

12. Observations of the Emir Abd-el-Kader on horse colors: The most highly regarded horse is the black with a star on his forehead and white markings on his feet.

The most spirited is the black.

The black brings good luck.

The black *(el kahal, el deheum)*. "He should be black as a night without moon or stars."

13. Waterwheels were pumping Thames water to parts of the City from 1581, and up ninety-three feet to other parts of London from the 1650s; the latter supply was the work of an ingenious gentleman virtuoso, Sir Edward Ford.

At the end of the seventeenth century, the use of steam for power, first predicted in the 1650s by the Marquess of Worcester, was made effective by Thomas Savery. Savery supplied what he called "fire-engines" (soon to be radically improved by Thomas Newcomen) to a number of houses in the early eighteenth century. In 1712, for example, a pump worked by a Savery engine was installed at Campden House in Kensington. It could raise three thousand gallons an hour up fifty-eight feet to a cistern at the top of the house.

The York Water Company pumped water by means of a Newcomen steam engine from the Thames up to the new Cavendish-Harley estate in North London. By the time Celia Fiennes was touring England in the late seventeenth and early eighteenth century, water was being supplied for indoor fountains, baths and water closets, but it was still novel enough for her to describe.

14. The original inventor of the condom—called a "machine" or "engine" in the eighteenth century—was the Italian Gabriele Fallopio, who about 1550 (using part of a sheep's intestine) manufactured a sheath to be worn as a protection against the epidemic of syphilis then sweeping over Europe. He also recommended it as a contraceptive against pregnancy.

The earliest contraceptives in England were imported from France, and the best "engines," known for their superior quality, continued to be imported from either France or Holland. John Wilmot, the rakish Earl of Rochester, extolled them in his 1674 *Panegyrick upon Cundums.*

They were usually sold in packets of eight in three sizes tastefully bound in a silken sachet with silk ribbons, hence the term "French letters." In *The Potent Ally* (1741) are the lines:

Happy is the Man who in his Pocket keeps
Whether with Green or Scarlet ribbons bound
A well-made cundum . . .

15. The Barbary States regularly captured vessels in the Mediterranean, selling those on board in the slave markets of North Africa. And unless a nation or individuals met ransom demands, prisoners could contemplate perpetual confinement or an early death from hard labor, torture and disease.

Once the United States was no longer a part of Britain and under the protection of England's treaties with the Barbary States, U.S. vessels were fair game for the corsairs. And as a young poor nation, the United States often couldn't afford to meet the ransoms demanded by the Barbary pirates. The larger nations of Europe all paid tribute to the Barbary States to protect their vessels—a practice of long standing—and they weren't necessarily eager for the new United States to continue trading under its own flag in the lucrative Mediterranean market.

The story of 119 Americans held captive in Algiers was told by John Foss in a book he wrote about his imprisonment. Under often brutal conditions, the Barbary prisoners called out to their families and friends, politicians and preachers to come to their aid. Their captors willingly forwarded the petitions in hopes of the ransom they might bring. In 1792, a group of American prisoners in Algiers sent a plaintive message to Congress, pleading for the legislators to "consider what our sufferings must have been for nearly seven years in captivity."

16. According to Moslem law, the eldest living male, not the eldest son, was always heir, so fratricide was often practiced to eliminate future threats by other brothers.

In an attempt to avoid the perils of disputed succession, Mahomet the Conqueror (reigned 1451–81) passed the Zanan-nameh. It read, "The majority of legists have declared that those of my illustrious children and grandchildren who shall ascend the throne shall have the right to execute their brothers, in order to insure the peace of the world."

In 1603, when Sultan Ahmed I ascended the throne, he founded the Kafes, or Cages, because he rebelled against the barbaric custom of fratricide. And for the next two centuries, rather than being murdered when a new sultan ascended the throne, possible claimants were incarcerated, with deaf-mutes for servants and barren odalisques for companionship.

There are, however, countless exceptions to the rule of succession: brothers who escaped and came back for the throne at the head of an army; princes whose mothers, often strong political powers in their own right, placed them on the throne regardless of their position in the line of succession; powerful generals who displaced sultans and pashas by force of arms.

17. Sometime prior to the year 1850, a French army officer stationed in Algeria came across an Arabic manuscript copy of *The Perfumed Garden*. The officer, whose name is hidden under the designation Monsieur le Baron R, set to work translating the book into French—although publication was delayed until 1876.

The first edition, known as the autograph edition, consisted of only thirty-five copies.

The original lithograph edition was counterfeited by Liseux in Paris during 1885, and the Kama Shastra Society edition, translated from French into English by Sir Richard Burton, was published in 1886.

In 1888, Burton began a new translation of *The Perfumed Garden,* this time direct from an Arabic manuscript—including those portions originally left out because of the modesty of the original French translator. Burton died in 1890, leaving the new manuscript of Nefzawi's *Garden* not quite complete. As is well known, his wife burned all his work, and his newly annotated version was lost.

The Perfumed Garden was first written at the beginning of the sixteenth century by Sheikh Nefzawi for the Bey of Tunis. It's based in part on previous works by Arabian and Indian writers, and it was commissioned to analyze "the source of our greatest pleasure."

The Perfumed Garden is a carefully compiled, systematized and detailed manual of Arabian sex practice; it is also a collection of sensual delights, joyous sexual expression, wry humor and homilies, expressed as both a panegyric to love and a glorification of desire.

Dear Reader,

Sinful began with two names. I'd always loved the name Sinjin, and when a friend of mine who knows Gaelic lore told me Sinjin means St. John, I knew Sinjin's last name had to be St. John. Don't ask me why—reason never enters these decisions, only a fait accompli revelatory inspiration.

My heroine's name appeared to me years ago and, finding it visually beautiful and slightly odd for a Scottish girl, I wrote it down along with a short page of family background that entered my consciousness along with the name. Then in a rare fit of straightening up my office shelves, I found the sheet of paper with Chelsea's name. And I knew instantly I'd found the perfect match for Sinjin.

I liked the juxtaposition of a feminine, almost prim name and my heroine's unconventional view of life. I liked the thought of this unsophisticated young girl discomposing a worldly, self-indulgent man like Sinjin.

I knew they'd have fun together.

I hope you enjoyed your brief trip into the eighteenth century as much as I enjoyed researching the era. Talleyrand once remarked with an air of regret, "They who did not live before 1789 knew not the sweetness of life." For the wealthy and privileged, indeed it was true; it was a time of intellectual and fashionable brilliance never equaled since.

By the way, there really is a Six-Mile Bottom near Newmarket, and my husband and I stayed in a country house there. It happened to be the house where Lord Byron courted his half sister and where their child Medora was born. And while Sinjin's home is placed on that site it's architecturally different—but that's the great joy of writing fiction. I can make up my own world.

Best wishes,

Susan Johnson

P.S. I enjoy hearing from readers. If you have any questions or comments I'd be delighted to answer them.

13499—400th Street
North Branch, MN 55056